SISTERS IN CRIME 2

Edited by
Marilyn Wallace

BERKLEY BOOKS, NEW YORK

W9-BZP-670

SISTERS IN CRIME 2

A Berkley Book/published by arrangement with
the editor

PRINTING HISTORY
Berkley edition/February 1990

ISBN: 0-425-11966-1

A BERKLEY BOOK® TM 757,375
Berkley Books are published by The Berkley Publishing Group,
200 Madison Avenue, New York, New York 10016.
The name ''BERKLEY'' and the ''B'' logo
are trademarks belonging to Berkley Publishing Corporation.

PRINTED IN THE UNITED STATES OF AMERICA

10 9 8 7 6 5 4 3 2 1

For my sons, Mark and Jeremy, with love.

You make me smile.
You make me think.
You make me proud.

Contents

Foreword

How exciting to follow the success of the first volume of the *Sisters in Crime* anthology series with this collection! All the stories in this volume were written especially for this anthology and appear here for the first time. As in the first volume, all the stories were written by American women, some of whom are members of the organization called Sisters in Crime, while others are not. Collectively, these writers are responsible for a steady flow of lively, engrossing, and entertaining novels and short stories; they are all part of what critics are calling the Second Golden Age of American mystery fiction.

As in Volume I, some authors have written stories featuring their series characters, to the satisfaction of their fans. Others have taken the opportunity to try something unexpected, to the delight of their fans. The stories encompass a wide range of subjects and styles. Some poke not-such-gentle fun at the often bewildering diversity of human experience. Others force us to examine what moves us, what frightens us, what we are trying to hide from ourselves.

Still, for all that variety, these stories can all be called mysteries. According to several studies, the mystery is one of the most popular forms of contemporary fiction. For years, critics, writers, and readers have attempted to explain this phenomenon.

Some propose that in a world where disorder seems the rule, neat resolutions satisfy a deep hunger for closure. For others, the vicarious ability to get away with murder, at least for a while, is a safe vent for those uncivilized impulses we've learned to inhibit. It's my theory that one of the reasons the mystery is so popular is because it is a literature of participation—the writer engages the reader in a conspiracy to work along with a sleuth in unraveling layers to get to the bottom of things. The balance between fair play and surprise—delicate, shifting first in one direction and then in the other—is a hallmark of the modern mystery. The reader's active involvement is required to make things come out right.

While theories are fun and probably all contain a kernel of

truth and a glimmer of insight, they are, after all, only attempts to explain a phenomenon. When the hypothetical discussions are done, one essential fact remains: Mysteries are superb entertainment—and this anthology provides proof of that!

The stories are arranged in alphabetical order, according to the author's last name. As you'll see in the introductions, many of the contributors are award recipients. For those of you not familiar with the awards, Edgars are the Edgar Allan Poe awards, given each May by Mystery Writers of America, Inc.; Anthonys, named for writer/critic Anthony Boucher, are awarded each October at Bouchercon, the annual mystery convention; Shamus awards are also given at Bouchercon, by Private Eye Writers of America; Macavitys are awarded each spring by Mystery Readers International; and Agathas are given at Malice Domestic, a convention celebrating traditional mysteries.

I hope that you'll meet at least one new author in these pages, and that you'll find some old favorites here. For me, I continue to be proud and pleased to have the opportunity to work with so many exciting and talented writers.

—Marilyn Wallace
San Anselmo, CA
May 1989

P. M. Carlson's background in linguistics and psychology is used to wonderful advantage by her amateur sleuth Maggie Ryan. A bright, lively, and sometimes outrageous statistician, Maggie is featured in Audition For Murder, *1986 Anthony nominee* Murder Is Academic, Murder Is Pathological, *1988 Macavity nominee* Murder Unrenovated, *and* Rehearsal For Murder. *Actress Bridget Mooney was introduced in the short story* "Father of the Bride; or, A Fate Worse Than Death!," *a 1988 Agatha award nominee.*

In "Death Scene; or, The Moor of Venice," Bridget discovers that the quality of her patience, if not her mercy, is strained during an 1880 theatre company tour.

DEATH SCENE; or, The Moor of Venice

by P. M. Carlson

NOTE: This story is based on the actual tour of America by the great Italian actor Tommaso Salvini in 1880–81.

I KNOW, I know, a proper young lady is not supposed to smoke. But hang it, there'd been so much bother that day, what with Zeb disappearing and the Pinkerton men asking about those burglaries back in St. Louis. When sorrows come, they come not single spies, but in battalions. So don't you think a girl's entitled to a few puffs as a tonic for her nerves?

Besides, I've noticed that in these times it's very difficult to be a proper young lady.

I was standing alone on the back platform of our speeding Pullman car watching the still-leafless Mississippi Valley hills roll by. I blew a last smoke ring into the wind and reckoned it was time to rejoin my colleagues inside. Gathering up the velvet train of my favorite traveling skirt, a lovely emerald green to set off my Titian-red hair, I tossed my cigar onto the tracks and reentered the car. Instantly, I smelled trouble.

1

I heard it too. A glorious, resonant Italian voice filled the car, just as it had filled countless theatres on three continents. But this time the words were not Shakespeare's. I stood amazed while the ringing tones listed every Italian curse I had learned over the last four months and added a passel of new ones. The great Salvini was vexed, yes indeed. *"Ladro sudicio!"* he hollered. *"Dannato!"* He was standing in the aisle at the front end of the car, flinging his arms about expressively, almost felling the Italian translator who fluttered about him like a lost chicken, unable to get in a word.

The only person near me was the colored Pullman porter, hovering bright-eyed and mystified by his linen closet, one dark hand tugging nervously at the bill of his cap. So I rustled on into the car and leaned toward the nearest ear. Letitia's pink shell-like ear, as it turned out. "What's wrong?" I asked.

"Ooh! Bridget!" squeaked Letitia. Offstage she worked hard at being a darling little thing and therefore took every opportunity to squeak. "Bridget Mooney, how you startled me!"

"I do apologize, Letty. But tell me what's wrong!"

"Why, I'm sure I don't know! Mr. Salvini just began to, well, to roar!"

Hopeless. How a little goose like Letitia could ever remember Desdemona's lines, I couldn't guess. Keeping my eye on the raging Salvini, I moved up to the next seat where Charlie Lloyd sat. He played Roderigo. A proper swell indeed with his shining smile, except that offstage he used so much Macassar oil on his hair that he had the look and smell of a gambler. Some said he was one. I asked, "Charlie, what's the matter?"

" 'I understand a fury in his words,/But not the words,' " he quoted. "Perhaps he just heard his wife was unfaithful. Perhaps he sat on a tack." Charlie was a great one for inventing stories. But hang it, he was as useless as the dim-witted Letitia. I wished again that young Zeb hadn't disappeared. Zeb was inexperienced, only eighteen, but always willing to give a civil answer.

Across the aisle from the well-oiled Charlie sat old Jack

Bowles. Jack was a cheerful codger who tippled too much and couldn't seem to save a penny of his salary. But his white beard and noble demeanor had won him the part of a Venetian senator. He was serious now, his flask capped beside him as he squinted at Salvini. Timing himself carefully, he waited till the Italian tragedian reached the end of a string of colorful words and was drawing breath again. Then, deftly, Jack inserted a shout. "Mr. Salvini, sir! What's the matter?"

The great Italian eyes flashed at us and Salvini burst again into excited, useless syllables. But this time his eloquent hands shaped a distinctive crescent in the air. I exclaimed, "Your scimitar?"

"*Sì*, Breedgeetta!" He always had trouble saying Bridget. "*La mia spada!* Teef! Dirty teef!"

"Dirty thief!" echoed the translator, holding up the bag that normally contained Othello's great curved sword. Scuffed and stained, it gaped empty now. My heart sank.

Now, I reckon you must be thinking we'd all taken leave of our senses to attempt such a tour in the first place. Mr. Salvini spoke only Italian. The rest of us onstage with him spoke only English. Pure madness, we all muttered as we signed our contracts, fully expecting our tour to collapse and leave us stranded somewhere like Memphis or Cincinnati. An actor's life is filled with adventure, yes indeed. But for once fortune smiled upon Bridget Mooney, because it turned out that in this case language didn't matter. Mr. Salvini somehow transmitted Shakespeare's passionate hero straight from his heart into ours. Critic after critic proclaimed him the greatest Othello ever seen.

But that scimitar was crucial. Salvini played Othello as a North African, darkening himself to a coppery brown rather than black, and wearing a splendid authentic costume of scarlet tarboosh, white turban, and white burnoose. The first time we saw him in costume Letitia and I tittered to each other that if Moorish men all looked so dashing, it was time to quit the stage and become Moorish ladies. We were accustomed to seeing cool British Othellos reciting in blackface and committing the climactic suicide with a decorous thrust of a dagger into a cool British breast. Not Salvini. His heroic Moor of Venice was transformed before our very eyes into a roaring vengeful beast. I reckon I've never seen such a thrilling death scene! Salvini seized the scimitar, one hand on the hilt and the other grasping the tip of the shining blade, and held the great crescent aloft. Then he slashed his own throat, brutally sawing the blade back and forth with both hands and collapsing at last amidst spasms and hideous gurgles. What a moment! Audiences gasped, and so did I.

Oh, I know, I know, as Iago's wife I wasn't supposed to gasp, I was supposed to be stone-dead already. But it was such a bore to lie there like some old possum while the greatest death scene in the world took place just inches from my nose. So don't you think a girl might take a little peek? Besides, I reckon that just then there wasn't a soul in the house looking at me.

So now, at the news of Mr. Salvini's loss, a groan of unhappiness ran through the company. That authentic, jewel-hilted scimitar was too important to be replaced by mere pasteboard. I asked, "Was it stolen in St. Louis? Or just now?"

Mr. Salvini and his translator chattered together in Italian for a moment. Then the assistant said, "Signor Salvini looked in the bag when we first took our seats, to see if it had been dented when we boarded. He saw it then. Then he placed the bag on top of the other baggage while we got out some drinks." He indicated a heap of Gladstone bags near the front of the car.

"So that means it disappeared in the last hour or so," Jack Bowles said slowly. He uncorked his flask and took a swig.

"But no one has left the car," Charlie pointed out.

"Well, then it must be here somewhere!" Letty exclaimed with surprising logic. We all joined in the search of the car and all its closets. We owed it to Salvini to find the precious blade. Hang it, we owed it to Shakespeare too.

But nothing turned up. "Perhaps it's in someone's bag," suggested Charlie. "Perhaps out the window. Perhaps one of us is a sword swallower." I returned his smile but couldn't help pondering our chain of misfortunes.

This was the third calamity. The first had occurred after

our final St. Louis performance, a matinee. We had only a few minutes before the departure of the train to New Orleans, so we were particularly vexed when the Pinkerton detectives stopped us on the platform as we waited to board our Pullman. They explained that during our performance, the homes of three audience members had been burgled.

"But why are you stopping us?" asked our company manager indignantly. "Our train leaves in eighteen minutes!"

"We must search your things, sir."

"Confound it, this is outrageous!"

Well, of course it was outrageous, but sometimes there's no explaining to gentlemen who aren't show people. Ignoring our protests, whether in English or Italian, they hunted through our trunks while the big station clock ticked ever nearer our doom. I watched them search Charlie and Jack as I waited where our Pullman car would stop, with Letitia and Zeb Adams. Zeb was our all-purpose understudy, a slim, dark-eyed Southerner who had conned every part—yes, even Letitia's and mine, though he made a very rugged-looking sort of female. He was eagerly ready to play any role if illness struck the company, but we were in excellent health. He helped with our trunks and kits cheerfully enough. But he was worried now, too, watching that clock. "Will we miss our train?" he fretted.

I shrugged. " 'Like as the waves make towards the pebbled shore, so do our minutes hasten to their end.' "

"Beautiful, Bridget," said Zeb, "but not at all reassuring."

Our desperation increased as the train, rumbling and hissing clouds of smoke and steam, rolled into the station. Ten minutes.

Still, they were efficient, those detectives, sifting quickly through the costumes and personal items we had packed so carefully, and it began to look as though we might be able to board in time after all. Jack Bowles had even capped his flask. Then two of the Pinkerton men approached us. There was no problem until Letitia said, "Bridget is from St. Louis, you know."

Well, have you ever heard of such a goose as Letty? Minutes away from departure and she tries a blame-fool stunt like that! I cast a glare in her direction but she was too busy simpering at Zeb and Charlie.

I gave up trying to shame Letitia. Much as I hated to discuss my family in front of her, I realized that I had to concentrate on satisfying the Pinkerton men. Contradicting Letty would make them suspicious, and the tour might be delayed so long, our salaries would all be docked for missing our New Orleans performance. I admitted, "Yes, sir, but this is the first time I've been back here in seven years."

"Do you have family here?"

I smiled the special mournful smile that I used onstage listening to Desdemona's willow song. "Not a real family," I said. "Papa lives here, Ty Mooney. And my Uncle Mike O'Rourke."

From the expression on their faces I could see they knew those two reprobates. Now that Aunt Mollie was no longer watching their accounts, Papa and Uncle Mike were wasting away their lives in barrooms. My short visit with them had been full of mawkish talk about dear departed Aunt Mollie and dear departed Mama, punctuated with requests for a loan. " 'Neither a borrower nor a lender be,' " I advised them at last, and went flouncing back to the theatre.

The Pinkerton men didn't seem any more enthusiastic about my relatives than I was. They changed the subject.

"Are you acquainted with Mr. Silas Moore?"

"I've heard of him, of course, sir," I answered cautiously. "Owns a steamboat company, doesn't he?"

"Yes. And Mr. Phineas McCoy?"

"He's also well known in St. Louis. A railroad fortune."

"But you wouldn't have gone calling in their houses, now would you?"

Was this a trick? I doubted that those rich and proper citizens had even noticed a skinny red-haired little girl ten years ago delivering Aunt Mollie's work to the back door. They certainly wouldn't believe that she'd become a Shakespearean actress. But just in case one of them had remembered, I said, "My aunt did copy work for businesses. I sometimes delivered it. Tradesman's entrance."

The second Pinkerton man leered and said, "That old drunkard Mooney wouldn't be invited in through the front door."

They both had a good chuckle at the thought of Papa in those rich and proper mansions, and I joined in dutifully, then asked, "Are those the houses that were burgled, sir?"

"Yes. And Mr. Healey's too. Mrs. Healey's tiara was taken."

"Oh, gracious!" I exclaimed. Banker Healey would not have recognized me either. I'd been very young. But I remembered that tiara's icy fire. "I heard about that tiara when I was a girl."

"Well, we've all heard about it now," said the detective morosely.

The clock ticked on. "Sir," I said boldly, "we were onstage during the matinee. Not stealing jewels."

They nodded, impressed by my reasoning. "True enough, my girl. But we have to ask. The thief was quite brazen, marching right into the kitchens, his face muffled. Tied up the servants and went straight to the hiding places. One of the kitchen maids said he acted like a stage outlaw. So we had to ask."

Two minutes till the train left. "But we were onstage, sirs," I repeated desperately. "I imagine that the culprit is still right here in St. Louis."

They agreed, and one of them called out to the impatient company that since they'd found nothing in our trunks, we could depart. There was a great scramble and heaving of bags and trunks as we fell over each other getting into the Pullman. But at last we were aboard, panting but safely on our way to New Orleans.

Then we realized that in the hubbub about the burglaries we somehow had left young Zeb behind.

He must have run into the station restaurant for a moment, I told myself. He must have thought we'd never make this train. I half expected him to rejoin us in New Orleans, abashed at having missed it. But if he didn't—well, I worried about those burglaries.

You see, there were several things I hadn't mentioned to

the Pinkerton men. One was a conversation I'd had on the long trip from Chicago to St. Louis a week or two ago. The five of us who usually sat in the back seats had talked about St. Louis families—and the three who were burgled had been among them. It had started when Jack Bowles had cocked a bushy white eyebrow at me and asked, "So you're a St. Louis girl, Bridget!"

"Yes. But I haven't been back there for a long time. Aunt Mollie brought me East, and she passed away there." I avoided mentioning Papa and Uncle Mike whenever possible.

Charlie Lloyd shifted on his seat. His glossy black hair left a smear on the plush upholstery. "Was your Aunt Mollie an actress too?"

"No. But she wanted me to become an actress. She brought me East so I could have proper voice lessons."

"Why, however did she manage that, Bridget?" asked Letitia. I knew what she was hinting. Her family had prospered in the lumber business, and she had many options besides the itinerant life of an actor, yes indeed. She never let us forget, always giving herself airs.

I said, "My aunt was a copyist with a flair for accounts. She helped some of the best St. Louis businesses."

"Rich men?" asked Jack Bowles between swallows.

"Rich for St. Louis," I admitted. "They live in mansions. Their wives wear the latest fashions. And jewels! Mrs. Healey has an emerald tiara that would dazzle your eyes."

"Goodness, Bridget, how did you come to know all these things? Did you read about them in the newspapers?" Letitia was after me again, trying to show that I was a mere guttersnipe.

I put on my most cultivated attitude. Strut about as she might, Letitia knew that I had studied with the great Shakespearean actress Mrs. Fanny Kemble, a far more illustrious tutor than hers. I spoke in my most Kemble-like tones as I told her, "You mustn't think that all copyists are spurned by the prosperous element of society, Letty. Of course we were not invited to grand balls, but we were certainly received into their homes on occasion. Even I, as a child, was received."

Zeb, his dark eyes sparkling, asked eagerly, "Tell us about

their mansions, Bridget.'' He was the fifth son of a Louisiana plantation family, impoverished by the war but fascinated by the gracious things in life. Charlie claimed that he gambled, and Charlie should know. But Zeb was so young and kind-hearted and fond of Shakespeare that he'd become our pet.

"Well, take Mr. Moore, the steamboat man,'' I said, humoring him. "His mansion is Greek style, with four enormous columns in front and a grand staircase in the hall. He has Sèvres porcelain, and a library full of portraits.''

Letty was looking at me with narrowed eyes. I wasn't about to admit that my knowledge of the Moore mansion had been gleaned from glimpses through the windows as I went around to the tradesmen's entrance where I sometimes delivered Aunt Mollie's copy work. After all, I had been inside the house, even if only in the kitchen. In those days I was a skinny chit of a girl, and the jolly cook had taken one look at me and thrust a piece of peach pie into my thin hands. My wide-eyed childish questions about the dazzling mansion had served me well. The servants had bragged about their positions in this grand house, about the porcelain, and more. So now I could say to Letitia, "Behind one of the portraits in the library there's a locked cabinet. That's where Mrs. Moore keeps her jewels.''

"Fascinating!'' said old Jack Bowles.

"And then there's the McCoys,'' I said. "Railroad money. A great brick mansion, very modern, built after the war.''

"Are the wives beautiful?'' asked Charlie, with a wriggle of his dark eyebrows. "Should I go a-wooing?''

"You'd be tarred and feathered, Charlie. Besides, they're not young,'' I explained, "and they're more than plump, most of them. But they do have stylish dresses and jewelry.''

"Oh, Bridget, go call on them, do!'' exclaimed Zeb, adding with a twinkle, "Then I can play Iago's wife at last!''

" 'Vaulting ambition,' '' sniffed Charlie, and we all laughed.

Except Letitia. She asked innocently, "And where does Mrs. McCoy keep her jewels?'' She was trying to prove that I'd never visited the mansion. But I had spent a profitable time gossiping in the McCoy kitchen too. Yes indeed. I smiled kindly at Letty and said, "She's much more original than Mrs. Moore. She has a mantel clock with a false base."

Jack Bowles chuckled. "Well, you're certainly on intimate terms with the cream of society in St. Louis!" he said jovially. Letitia tried to hide a pout by looking out the window.

"Do you know other great families in St. Louis?" asked Zeb.

"And do you know where they keep their jewels?" Charlie put in, with a grin to show that he was joking. Charlie had a fine white set of teeth and I always enjoyed seeing him smile. Letitia still sulked, her gaze on the landscape.

I smiled back at Charlie. "Well, there's the banker. Mr. Healey. A section of baseboard in his bedroom opens out to reveal a small compartment. Mrs. Healey's jewels and her emerald tiara are hidden there."

Letitia's head snapped around and triumph sparkled in her eyes. "Ooh, Bridget, I'm shocked!" she squeaked. "In Mr. Healey's bedroom?"

I withered her with a Lady Macbeth glare. Banker Healey was the richest and most proper of them all, yes indeed. "That's what Mrs. Healey told me," I said icily.

Jack Bowles had another question. "And who else is of interest in St. Louis?"

"Well, those people all live in the center of town," I said. "There were also some famous farms nearby. President Grant's, for example." I continued telling them about the town, a little more cautiously after my slip about the Healey house. In fact, Mrs. Healey hadn't mentioned the baseboard compartment to me. I'd discovered it myself one afternoon when I was a scrawny fourteen-year-old who looked younger but already hankered after a life on the stage. Mrs. Healey was away visiting her sister, and I was prowling quietly about the room because Mr. Healey had dropped off to sleep after—well, suffice it to say that Aunt Mollie was a very enterprising woman. When she noticed that Banker Healey's eye often roved from his rotund wife toward more youthful females—extremely youthful, one might say—she made a little business arrangement with him that required my presence.

I know, I know, but how do you expect a poor untutored

girl to pay for elocution lessons? By cashing in dividends? My Aunt Mollie struck a good bargain with the rich and proper Mr. Healey, and put the money out at six percent so that a few years later it paid for both our tickets East.

But that's by the by.

When the Pinkerton men told us about the burglaries, I of course didn't wish to add to our delay by mentioning the conversation on the train. But now I settled into my seat across from Letitia and pondered. Here was a puzzle worthy of Hawkshaw himself. Unfortunately there wasn't a Hawkshaw to be seen. It was up to me.

Could one of us possibly have taken those jewels? The St. Louis theatre manager had come beaming to us earlier in the week, telling us the names of the local luminaries who would be attending Salvini's great performances. I had thought I was the only one taking any notice of him. But if someone else had listened, had noted that three of the families attending our last matinee kept jewels in hiding places I'd mentioned, he—or she—would have had time to locate the houses, even study the habits of the servants. Why, I'd taken a constitutional or two myself along the grand avenue where those three pillars of St. Louis society lived. But was it truly possible that one of my colleagues had stolen the jewels?

I settled back into my seat, as far as one can with a bustle, and gazed at the passing hills. The Illinois Central route to New Orleans allows occasional glimpses of the great Mississippi, and I watched the setting sun glint on the majestic waters as I considered Letitia. She could be a greedy little creature, yes indeed. She doubtless coveted the jewels. And there was another point that strongly favored her. The Pinkerton men had been very thorough in their search of our trunks and bags and cloaks. They had even politely inspected the men's pockets. But of course they had not been so brazen as to look closely at the ladies' clothing. I myself have found it very convenient, since bustles first became fashionable, to tuck a few items into a special pocket sewn into the skirt drapery. My jewelry, my most treasured letters, my special Civil War souvenir, my cigars—all can be kept there in snug security, although I'm bound to admit it's not so comfortable

to sit down. Letitia easily could have hidden the stolen items,
even the tiara, from the Pinkerton men.

I stole a look at her across from me, dozing to the rocking
motion of the train. Unfortunately, there was a flaw in my
case against Letitia. As Desdemona, she was onstage fre-
quently from the beginning to the end of the play. She didn't
have time to go burgle three houses. Besides, she was such a
silly ninny, I couldn't believe she could even think of a sensible enough plan, much less execute it.

I turned to look across the aisle. Charlie Lloyd, perhaps?
He was intelligent enough, and often complained about how
difficult it was to make ends meet on an actor's wages. Gambling is not a cheap recreation, and the price of Macassar oil
goes up every day. Also, Charlie's character, Roderigo, was
not onstage very often in Salvini's version of the play. He
might have been able to slip away for two hours or so.

Or consider Jack Bowles. He had need of a secure old age,
and even greater need of a bottle. And his opportunity was
ample. His venerable Venetian senator was onstage only at
the very beginning and very end of the play. And the same
was true of young Zeb Adams, whose help was needed chiefly
before and after performances.

But the jewels were still in St. Louis, I was sure, because
the detectives had searched all three men quite thoroughly. I
remembered Zeb, standing next to Letitia and me, rolling his
dark eyes at us in mock exasperation as the Pinkerton men
pulled his watch and handkerchief and cigars from his pockets. So I was convinced that none of us had done it.

Until Zeb had missed the train.

The train that would take him into his home state of Louisiana.

I wanted to believe that he had innocently gone back into
the station, inadvertently missing the departure. But there
were other possibilities, and—well, my imaginations were as
foul as Vulcan's stithy.

Surely Zeb was not a thief! But he'd listened to my indis-
creet conversation on the train. He'd had time to slip away
during the matinee while the families—and their burly coach-
men—were at the theatre. He could act a stage outlaw as well

as Jack or Charlie. He could have stolen the jewels, hidden them someplace so that they were not among his things while the Pinkerton men searched.

And then, unable to recover them in time to board, he'd missed the train.

I leaned forward and touched Letitia's arm, waited for her to jump and squeak, and then asked, "Letty, where did Zeb go when he left us?"

"Dear me, Bridget, I don't know. He was there, and then he wasn't."

"He was there while the Pinkerton men talked to him, and to you."

"And to you. At least"—she put on her prettiest thoughtful look—"at least at the beginning. But I wasn't taking note of him."

She was taking note of what I was telling them about my wretched family, I thought grimly. But I pursued the question. "What about during the announcement, when the detective was telling us we could leave?"

"Well, my skirt caught on something, and I had to adjust it," she said, flipping the pretty rose-pink train to illustrate, "and I thought he was climbing into the Pullman because he was nearest the steps. I thought he would help us board. But he didn't."

"He certainly didn't," I agreed. That was unlike the gallant, charming Zeb. Another horrible possibility was nibbling at my consciousness. Suppose Zeb had hastened into the Pullman prematurely, as Letitia thought, preparing to help us, and instead had stumbled across a clue? In the crush and noisy confusion while we all struggled to board the car at once, it would have been possible for the malefactor to—

My thoughts recoiled. But there was no escaping my own logic.

The scimitar had been stolen after the train was on its way. Therefore the thief was on board.

Zeb was not on board.

Maybe he'd gone into the station restaurant. Or maybe he'd burgled the St. Louis houses, stayed in St. Louis to collect his swag, and a completely different thief on board just happened to choose this moment to take the scimitar. Or maybe—

I was beginning to sound as outlandish as Charlie. I faced it: Poor Zeb was probably not a thief, but a victim. He was probably dead, pushed from the train, his body lying beside the tracks somewhere.

And we were traveling with his killer.

Which of my companions was guilty?

Mind, now, I'm not foolish. Aunt Mollie explained to me many a time that in this wicked world it's best to keep your own counsel until the truth is clear. So I did not pose this interesting question to my companions. I merely watched the darkening valley and pondered. And when a glimmer of the solution occurred to me, I did not leap up shouting "Eureka!" but waited patiently for a distraction.

It came at last in the form of bedtime. The Pullman porter, his eyes sparkling kindly in his dark face, emerged from his closet bearing stacks of bed linens. He went to the front of the car, Mr. Salvini's end, and began to lower the upper bunks to make up the beds. All eyes followed him in this interesting task. I stood up and wandered toward the back platform, glancing into the porter's closet on my way. There was a padded bench bearing his large carpetbag and the stacks of linens he had readied. They were none too clean. Mr. Pullman ought to be ashamed. I picked up the porter's carpetbag and slipped out onto the back platform.

Cold air swirled about me, and ragged wisps of cinder-laden smoke from the speeding train. The great iron wheels clattered against the rails. A half-moon grudgingly oozed gray light.

I opened the carpetbag. Inside I glimpsed clothing, yes; but also a great jeweled scimitar, and a smaller drawstring bag. When I untied it, I saw a glint of emeralds.

Suddenly a bar of yellow light fell across the platform as the door opened. He'd come sooner than I expected. I whirled, thrusting the carpetbag behind me, and faced him.

The Pullman porter.

"Zeb!" I exclaimed.

"Clever Bridget. However did you guess?" He closed the

door and we were alone in the feeble moonlight on the clattering, rocking platform.

"I knew you were not a real porter, Zeb."

"Cruel maid, you cut me to the quick! You insult my abilities as an actor!"

"Not at all, Zeb," I hastened to assure him. "Your acting was excellent. But when I passed by, you smelled of greasepaint. Most porters don't."

"I see."

"And most porters don't dirty the bed linens, because their hands aren't smeared with makeup."

He laughed merrily, like the old Zeb. "Mr. Salvini was right! I am a dirty teef!"

I smiled and continued. "Jack and Charlie also had time during the matinee to steal the jewels. But later, you were the only one standing close enough to Letty to kick your bag of jewels under her skirts when the Pinkerton men came to search you."

"You saw that?" He stepped closer.

"No." I tried to step back but felt the protective rail at the edge of the platform. "But she said her skirts had caught on something, and the platform was bare. It was you, wasn't it, snatching back the jewels and rushing onto the train to hide them anew? But tell me, why did you have to impersonate the porter? Did he see you hide the jewels?"

"Foolish old darkie!" complained Zeb. "I thought I had escaped notice. But as I leapt up the steps, I saw him staring at me. There was no choice. My gambling debts are urgent. So I pushed him into the closet, closed the door behind us, and, well, silenced him."

That got my dander up. This damn Rebel was talking about silencing darkies for the sake of a gambling debt, as though we'd never fought that bloody war. "You made up your skin and put on his uniform," I accused. "And threw him from the train."

"Yes, dear clever Bridget. Just as you must be thrown."

He lunged. I dodged but tripped against the carpetbag. My flailing hand closed over something.

The hilt of the scimitar.

I brandished it before me. Even in the feeble moonlight the great blade shone and the jewels glinted. "Hold, sir!" I exclaimed in my most ringing Kemble tones.

But, hang it, he didn't hold. He lunged at me again and wrenched the hilt from my hand. I saw the gleaming crescent rising high to smite me down.

So I reached into my bustle pocket, drew out my Civil War souvenir Colt, and shot him in the throat.

He slumped to the platform with a gurgle worthy of the great Salvini.

I know, I know, but it's so difficult these days to be a proper young lady. Besides, he hadn't been very sporting either, had he?

I tucked away my revolver, slid the scimitar carefully into his ragged wound because I dislike questions about my Colt, and staggered back into the Pullman. "Help!" I gasped in the tones I use for my own death scene. "Help! Suicide!"

Mr. Salvini was coming down the aisle, perhaps to ask why the porter had not finished making up the beds. He peered out the door onto the back platform, exclaimed, *"Santo cielo! La mia spada!"* and regaled us with another medley of rare Italian words.

Eventually Charlie's fertile imagination supplied a story that satisfied everyone. Young Zeb Adams, Charlie's account went, hoped to save the family plantation from foreclosure, so he'd stolen the jewels. But then, overcome with remorse, he had made himself up as the Moor of Venice and cut his own throat in a death scene as dramatic as Salvini's own. A lovely story, yes indeed. No mention of unhappy details like Pullman porters or gambling debts or attempts to smite innocent young ladies.

Our tour continued to wild acclaim, in city after city. Othello's death scene was even more moving than before.

Of course the jewels were returned to their St. Louis owners, most of them, and we actors shared in the rewards that had been offered. Unfortunately Zeb had already disposed of the emerald tiara, perhaps pawned in St. Louis, as Charlie suggested. But I'm bound to admit that a few years later a very similar piece served as a crown for the much-praised

Lady Macbeth I played. The costume was dazzling. Emeralds look absolutely splendid against my red hair.

Oh, I know, I know, Aunt Mollie would scold too. But don't you agree that a rich and proper man like Banker Healey still owed me a trifle or two?

Perhaps he always will.

Ever since the publication of Where Are the Children? *Mary Higgins Clark has been a premier purveyor of psychological suspense. President of Mystery Writers of America, Inc., in 1988, Mary's best-selling novels (*Weep No More My Lady; The Cradle Will Fall; A Stranger Is Watching; While My Pretty One Sleeps, *etc.) are avidly devoured by her faithful readers—and for good reason. Hers is the supreme story-teller's gift, for which her legions of fans are grateful.*

In "Voices in the Coalbin," a young husband tries to still the ominous chorus that haunts his wife.

VOICES IN THE COALBIN

by Mary Higgins Clark

IT WAS DARK when they arrived. Mike steered the car off the dirt road down the long driveway and stopped in front of the cottage. The real estate agent had promised to have the heat turned up and the lights on. She obviously didn't believe in wasting electricity.

An insect-repellent bulb over the door emitted a bleak yellowish beam that trembled in the steady drizzle. The small-paned windows were barely outlined by a faint flicker of light that seeped through a partially open blind.

Mike stretched. Fourteen hours a day of driving for the past three days had cramped his long, muscular body. He brushed back his dark brown hair from his forehead wishing he'd taken time to get a haircut before they left New York. Laurie teased him when his hair started to grow. "You look like a thirty-year-old Roman Emperor, Curlytop," she would comment. "All you need is a toga and a laurel wreath to complete the effect."

She had fallen asleep about an hour ago. Her head was resting on his lap. He glanced down at her, hating to wake her up. Even though he could barely make out her profile, he knew that in sleep the tense lines vanished from around her mouth and the panic-stricken expression disappeared from her face.

Four months ago the recurring nightmare had begun, the nightmare that made her shriek, *"No, I won't go with you. I won't sing with you."*

He'd shake her awake. "It's all right, sweetheart. It's all right."

Her screams would fade into terrified sobs. "I don't know who they are but they want me, Mike. I can't see their faces but they're all huddled together beckoning to me."

He had taken her to a psychiatrist, who put her on medication and began intensive therapy. But the nightmares continued, unabated. They had turned a gifted twenty-four-year-old singer who had just completed a run as a soloist in her first Broadway musical to a trembling wraith who could not be alone after dark.

The psychiatrist had suggested a vacation. Mike told him about the summers he'd spent at his grandmother's house on Oshbee Lake forty miles from Milwaukee. "My grandmother died last September," he'd explained. "The house is up for sale. Laurie's never been there and she loves the water."

The doctor had approved. "But be careful of her," he warned. "She's severely depressed. I'm sure these nightmares are a reaction to her childhood experiences, but they're overwhelming her."

Laurie had eagerly endorsed the chance to go away. Mike was a junior partner in his father's law firm. "Anything that will help Laurie," his father told him. "Take whatever time you need."

I remember brightness here, Mike thought as he studied the shadow-filled cottage with increasing dismay. I remember the feel of the water when I dove in, the warmth of the sun on my face, the way the breeze filled the sails and the boat skimmed across the lake.

It was the end of June but it might have been early March. According to the radio, the cold spell had been gripping Wis-

consin for three days. There'd better be enough coal to get
the furnace going, Mike thought, or else that real estate agent
will lose the listing.

He had to wake up Laurie. It would be worse to leave her
alone in the car, even for a minute. "We're here, love," he
said, his voice falsely cheerful.

Laurie stirred. He felt her stiffen, then relax as he tightened
his arms around her. "It's so dark," she whispered.

"We'll get inside and turn some lights on."

He remembered how the lock had always been tricky. You
had to pull the door to you before the key could fit into the
cylinder. There was a night-light plugged into an outlet in
the small foyer. The house was not warm but neither was it
the bone-chilling cold he had feared.

Quickly Mike switched on the hall light. The wallpaper
with its climbing ivy pattern seemed faded and soiled. The
house had been rented for the five summers his grandmother
was in the nursing home. Mike remembered how clean and
warm and welcoming it had been when she was living here.

Laurie's silence was ominous. His arm around her, he
brought her into the living room. The overstuffed velour furniture that used to welcome his body when he settled in with
a book was still in place but, like the wallpaper, seemed
soiled and shabby.

Mike's forehead furrowed into a troubled frown. "Honey,
I'm sorry. Coming here was a lousy idea. Do you want to go
to a motel? We passed a couple that looked pretty decent."

Laurie smiled up at him. "Mike, I want to stay here. I
want you to share with me all those wonderful summers you
spent in this place. I want to pretend your grandmother was
mine. Then maybe I'll get over whatever is happening to
me."

Laurie's grandmother had raised her. A fear-ridden neu-
rotic, she had tried to instill in Laurie fear of the dark, fear
of strangers, fear of planes and cars, fear of animals. When
Laurie and Mike met two years ago, she'd shocked and
amused him by reciting some of the litany of hair-raising
stories that her grandmother had fed her on a daily basis.

"How did you turn out so normal, so much fun?" Mike used to ask her.

"I was damned if I'd let her turn me into a certified nut." But the last four months had proved that Laurie had not escaped after all, that there was psychological damage that needed repairing.

Now Mike smiled down at her, loving the vivid sea-green eyes, the thick dark lashes that threw shadows on her porcelain skin, the way tendrils of chestnut hair framed her oval face. "You're so darn pretty," he said, "and sure I'll tell you all about Grandma. You only know her when she was an invalid. I'll tell you about fishing with her in a storm, about jogging around the lake and her yelling for me to keep up the pace, about finally managing to outswim her when she was sixty."

Laurie took his face in her hands. "Help me to be like her."

Together they brought in their suitcases and the groceries they had purchased along the way. Mike went down to the basement. He grimaced when he glanced into the coalbin. It was fairly large, a four-feet-wide by six-feet-long plankboard enclosure situated next to the furnace and directly under the window that served as an opening for the chute from the delivery truck. Mike remembered how when he was eight he'd helped his grandmother replace some of the boards on the bin. Now they all looked rotted.

"Nights get cold even in the summer but we'll always be plenty warm, Mike," his grandmother would say cheerily as she let him help shovel coal into the old blackened furnace.

Mike remembered the bin as always heaped with shiny black nuggets. Now it was nearly empty. There was barely enough coal for two or three days. He reached for the shovel.

The furnace was still serviceable. Its rumbling sound quickly echoed throughout the house. The ducts thumped and rattled as hot air wheezed through them.

In the kitchen Laurie had unpacked the groceries and begun to make a salad. Mike grilled a steak. They opened a bottle of Bordeaux and ate side by side at the old enamel table, their shoulders companionably touching.

They were on their way up the staircase to bed when Mike spotted the note from the real estate agent on the foyer table:

"Hope you find everything in order. Sorry about the weather. Coal delivery on Friday."

They decided to use his grandmother's room. "She loved that metal-frame bed," Mike said. "Always claimed that there wasn't a night she didn't sleep like a baby in it."

"Let's hope it works that way for me." Laurie sighed. There were clean sheets in the linen closet but they felt damp and clammy. The boxspring and mattress smelled musty. "Warm me up," Laurie whispered, shivering as they pulled the covers over them.

"My pleasure."

They fell asleep in each other's arms. At three o'clock Laurie began to shriek, a piercing, wailing scream that filled the house. "Go away. Go away. I won't. I won't."

It was dawn before she stopped sobbing. "They're getting closer," she told Mike. "They're getting closer."

The rain persisted throughout the day. The outside thermometer registered thirty-eight degrees. They read all morning curled up on the velour couches. Mike watched as Laurie began to unwind. When she fell into a deep sleep after lunch, he went into the kitchen and called the psychiatrist.

"Her sense that they're getting closer may be a good sign," the doctor told him. "Possibly she's on the verge of a breakthrough. I'm convinced the root of these nightmares is in all the old wives' tales her grandmother told Laurie. If we can isolate exactly which one has caused this fear, we'll be able to exorcise it and all the others. Watch her carefully, but remember. She's a strong girl and she wants to get well. That's half the battle."

When Laurie woke up, they decided to inventory the house. "Dad said we can have anything we want," Mike reminded her. "A couple of the tables are antiques and that clock on the mantel is a gem." There was a storage closet in the foyer. They began dragging its contents into the living room. Laurie, looking about eighteen in jeans and a sweater, her hair tied loosely in a chignon, became animated as she went through them. "The local artists were pretty lousy," she laughed, "but the frames are great. Can't you just see them on our walls?"

Last year as a wedding present, Mike's family had bought them a loft in Greenwich Village. Until four months ago, they'd spent their spare time going to garage sales and auctions looking for bargains. Since the nightmares began, Laurie had lost interest in furnishing the apartment. Mike crossed his fingers. Maybe she *was* starting to get better.

On the top shelf buried behind patchwork quilts he discovered a Victrola. "Oh, my God, I'd forgotten about that," he said, "What a find. Look. Here are a bunch of old records."

He did not notice Laurie's sudden silence as he brushed the layers of dust from the Victrola and lifted the lid. The Edison trademark, a dog listening to a tube and the caption *His Master's Voice* was on the inside of the lid. "It even has a needle in it," Mike said. Quickly he placed a record on the turntable, cranked the handle, slid the starter to ON, and watched as the disk began to revolve. Carefully he placed the arm with its thin, delicate needle in the first groove.

The record was scratched. The singers' voices were male but high-pitched, almost to the point of falsetto. The effect was out of synch, music being played too rapidly. "I can't make out the words," Mike said. "Do you recognize it?"

"It's 'Chinatown,' " Laurie said. "Listen." She began to sing with the record, her lovely soprano voice leading the chorus. *Hearts that know no other world, drifting to and fro.* Her voice broke. Gasping, she screamed, *"Turn it off, Mike. Turn it off now!"* She covered her ears with her hands and sank onto her knees, her face deathly white.

Mike yanked the needle away from the record. "Honey, what is it?"

"I don't know. I just don't know."

That night the nightmare took a different form. This time the approaching figures were singing "Chinatown" and in falsetto voices demanding Laurie come sing with them.

At dawn they sat in the kitchen sipping coffee. "Mike, it's coming back to me," Laurie told him. "When I was little.

My grandmother had one of those Victrolas. She had that same record. I asked her where the people were who were singing. I thought they had to be hiding in the house somewhere. She took me down to the basement and pointed to the coalbin. She said the voices were coming from there. She swore to me that the people who were singing were in the coalbin.''

Mike put down his coffee cup. "Good God!"

"I never went down to the basement after that. I was afraid. Then we moved to an apartment and she gave the Victrola away. I guess that's why I forgot.'' Laurie's eyes began to blaze with hope. "Mike, maybe that old fear caught up with me for some reason. I was so exhausted by the time the show closed. Right after that the nightmares started. Mike, that record was made years and years ago. The singers are all probably dead by now. And I certainly have learned how sound is reproduced. Maybe it's going to be all right.''

"You bet it's going to be all right.'' Mike stood up and reached for her hand. "You game for something? There's a coalbin downstairs. I want you to come down with me and look at it.''

Laurie's eyes filled with panic, then she bit her lip. "Let's go,'' she said.

Mike studied Laurie's face as her eyes darted around the basement. Through her eyes he realized how dingy it was. The single light bulb dangling from the ceiling. The cinderblock walls glistening with dampness. The cement dust from the floor that clung to their bedroom slippers. The concrete steps that led to the set of metal doors that opened to the backyard. The rusty bolt that secured them looked as though it had not been opened in years.

The coalbin was adjacent to the furnace at the front end of the house. Mike felt Laurie's nails dig into his palm as they walked over to it.

"We're practically out of coal,'' he told her. "It's a good thing they're supposed to deliver today. Tell me, honey, what do you see here?''

"A bin. About ten shovelfuls of coal at best. A window. I remember when the delivery truck came how they put the chute through the window and the coal roared down. I used to wonder if it hurt the singers when it fell on them.'' Laurie tried to laugh. "No visible sign of anyone in residence here. Nightmares at rest, please God.''

Hand in hand they went back upstairs. Laurie yawned. "I'm so tired, Mike. And you, poor guy, haven't had a decent night's rest in months because of me. Why don't we just go back to bed and sleep the day away. I bet anything that I won't wake up with a dream.''

They drifted off to sleep, her head on his chest, his arms encircling her. "Sweet dreams, love,'' he whispered.

"I promise they will be. I love you, Mike. Thank you for everything.''

The sound of coal rushing down the chute awakened Mike. He blinked. Behind the shades, light was streaming in. Automatically he glanced at his watch. Nearly three o'clock. God, he really must have been bushed. Laurie was already up. He pulled khaki slacks on, stuffed his feet into sneakers, listened for sounds from the bathroom. There were none. Laurie's robe and slippers were on the chair. She must be already dressed. With sudden unreasoning dread, Mike yanked a sweatshirt over his head.

The living room. The dining room. The kitchen. Their coffee cups were still on the table, the chairs pushed back as they left them. Mike's throat closed. The hurtling sound of the coal was lessening. *The coal.* Maybe. He took the cellar stairs two at a time. Coal dust was billowing through the basement. Shiny black nuggets of coal were heaped high in the bin. He heard the snap of the window being closed. He stared down at the footsteps on the floor. The imprints of his sneakers. The side-by-side impressions left when he and Laurie had come down this morning in their slippers.

And then he saw the step-by-step imprint of Laurie's bare feet, the lovely high arched impressions of her slender, fine-boned feet. The impressions stopped at the coalbin. There was no sign of them returning to the stairs.

The bell rang, the shrill, high-pitched, insistent gonglike

sound that had always annoyed him and amused his grandmother. Mike raced up the stairs. Laurie. Let it be Laurie.

The truck driver had a bill in his hand. "Sign for the delivery, sir."

The delivery. Mike grabbed the man's arm. "When you
started the coal down the chute, did you look into the bin?"

Puzzled faded blue eyes in a pleasant weather-beaten face
looked squarely at him. "Yeah, sure, I glanced in to make
sure how much you needed. You were just about out. You
didn't have enough for the day. The rain's over but it's gonna
stay real cold."

Mike tried to sound calm. "Would you have seen if someone was in the coalbin? I mean, it's dark in the basement.
Would you have noticed if a slim young woman had maybe
fainted in there?" He could read the deliveryman's mind. He
thinks I'm drunk or on drugs. "God damn it," Mike shouted.
"My wife is missing. My wife is missing."

For days they searched for Laurie. Feverishly, Mike
searched with them. He walked every inch of the heavily
wooded areas around the cottage. He sat, hunched and shivering on the deck as they dragged the lake. He stood unbelieving as the newly delivered coal was shoveled from the bin
and heaped onto the basement floor.

Surrounded by policemen, all of whose names and faces
made no impression on him, he spoke with Laurie's doctor.
In a flat, disbelieving tone he told the doctor about Laurie's
fear of the voices in the coalbin. When he was finished, the
police chief spoke to the doctor. When he hung up, he gripped
Mike's shoulder. "We'll keep looking."

Four days later a diver found Laurie's body tangled in weeds
in the lake. Death by drowning. She was wearing her nightgown. Bits of coal dust were still clinging to her skin and
hair. The police chief tried and could not soften the stark
tragedy of her death. "That was why her footsteps stopped
at the bin. She must have gotten into it and climbed out the
window. It's pretty wide, you know, and she was a slender
girl. I've talked again to her doctor. She probably would have
committed suicide before this if you hadn't been there for

her. Terrible the way people screw up their children. Her doctor said that grandmother petrified her with crazy superstitions before the poor kid was old enough to toddle.''

"She talked to me. She was getting there." Mike heard his protests, heard himself making arrangements for Laurie's body to be cremated.

The next morning as he was packing, the real estate agent came over, a sensibly dressed, white-haired, thin-faced woman whose brisk air did not conceal the sympathy in her eyes. "We have a buyer for the house," she said. "I'll arrange to have anything you want to keep shipped."

The clock. The antique tables. The pictures that Laurie had laughed over in their beautiful frames. Mike tried to picture going into their Greenwich Village loft alone and could not.

"How about the Victrola?" the real estate agent asked. "It's a real treasure."

Mike had placed it back in the storage closet. Now he took it out, seeing again Laurie's terror, hearing her begin to sing "Chinatown," her voice blending with the falsetto voices on the old record. "I don't know if I want it," he said.

The real estate agent looked disapproving. "It's a collector's item. I have to be off. Just let me know about it."

Mike watched as her car disappeared around the winding driveway. *Laurie, I want you.* He lifted the lid of the Victrola as he had five days ago, an eon ago. He cranked the handle, found the "Chinatown" record, placed it on the turntable, turned the switch to the ON position. He watched as the record picked up speed, then released the arm and placed the needle in the starting groove.

"Chinatown, my chinatown . . ."

Mike felt his body go cold. *No! No!* Unable to move, unable to breathe, he stared at the spinning record.

". . . hearts that know no other world drifting to and fro . . ."

Over the scratchy, falsetto voices of the long-ago singers, Laurie's exquisite soprano was filling the room with its heart-stopping, plaintive beauty.

Susan Dunlap's Pious Deception *introduced private investigator Kiernan O'Shaugnessy, a former forensic pathologist. While she enjoys her material comforts—her San Diego beach house is maintained by ex–offensive lineman Brad Tchernak—more than Berkeley detective Jill Smith (*Too Close to the Edge, A Dinner to Die For, *etc.) or utility meter reader Vejay Haskell (*The Last Annual Slugfest, Diamond in the Buff*), Kiernan shares with them keen wit, compassion, and integrity.*

In "The Celestial Buffet," offerings of unearthly delight continue to entice the narrator, who doesn't intend to be limited to just desserts.

THE CELESTIAL BUFFET

by Susan Dunlap

I HADN'T STEPPED onto the celestial escalator with the escort of two white-suited angels like I had seen in the 1940s movies, but I did have the sense that I had risen up. I was very aware of the whole process, which is rather surprising considering what a shock my death was. I hadn't been sick, or taken foolish chances. I certainly didn't plan on dying—not ever, really—but in any case not so soon.

I looked down from somewhere near the ceiling and saw my body lying on the floor. I should have been horrified, overwhelmed by grief, more grief than I'd felt at the sight of any other body, but I really felt only a mild curiosity. My forty-year-old body was still clad in a turquoise running suit. It was, as it had been for most of its adult life, just a bit pear-shaped around the derriere. It could have stood to lose five pounds (well, too late now). It was lying on the living room floor, its head about six inches from the coffee table, the stool overturned by its feet. How many times had Raymond told me not to stand on that stool to change the light bulb? If he had seen me holding the last, luscious bite of a Hershey bar in my left hand he would have said, "One of these days, you'll fall and kill yourself." And, of course, he would have been right. Now, I recalled wavering on that rickety stool, knowing I should reach up and grab onto the light fixture, hesitating, unwilling to drop the chocolate. It was still there, in my hand, clutched in a cadaverous spasm. How humiliating! I could almost hear Raymond's knowing cackle. At least that infuriating cackle was not the last sound I'd heard in life. If I had felt anything at all for that body on the floor I would have hoped Raymond wouldn't tell anyone how it died.

But the body and the possibility of its being ridiculed didn't hold my attention for long. I left it there on the floor and rose up. Exactly how I rose is unclear. I didn't take a white escalator, or a shimmering elevator, or any more sophisticated conveyance; I just had the sense of ascending till I reached a sort of landing.

I can no more describe the landing than I can the means of reaching it. There were no clear walls or floor, no drapes, no sliding gossamer doors, no pearly gates or streets paved with gold. Nothing so obvious. Just a sense, a knowing that this was the antechamber, the place of judgment. I stood, holding my breath (so to speak). Somewhere in the Bible it speaks of the moment of judgment when the words each of us has whispered in private will be broadcast aloud. A distinctly uncomfortable thought. I had rather hoped that if that had to happen it would be at a mass event with a lot of babble and confusion, and everyone else as embarrassed at his own unmasking as I was. But here I was, alone, surrounded by silence. I waited (what choice had I?) but no public-address system came on. So the celestial loudspeaker, at least, was a myth.

But even with that out of the way, I still knew (knew, rather than was told, for it was apparent to me now that communication in this place was not verbal or written—things simply were known) that there was a heaven and, God forbid, a hell, and this was the last neutral ground between the two. In a short time I would know which I was to reside in. Forever.

But I had led a decent life. There was no reason to worry.

I had worked hard . . . well, hard enough. I'd voted, even in off-year elections. I'd spent Christmas every other year with my parents when they were alive. (Weren't my parents supposed to be here to meet me? Surely their absence wasn't because they were not in heaven? No. More likely, the greetings by all those who had gone on before was another myth.) I realized that my conception of this place was as ephemeral as the room itself. I hadn't given it more than the most cursory of thoughts, being sure that, at worst, I had years to form an idea of it. So what expectations I did have came mostly from Sunday school, and of course, forties movies.

The waiting was making me uneasy. Couldn't I move on to eternal bliss now? Why the delay? I had been a good person. I had followed the Ten Commandments, as much as was reasonable for someone living in San Francisco. I had honored my mother and father on those Christmases and long distance after five and on Saturdays. I had kept the Sabbath when I was a child, before they televised the football games, which is all that could be legitimately expected. I had even gone to a series of Krishnamurti lectures on Sundays a year or two ago.

But my parents and the Sabbath were only two commandments. What of the other eight? What *were* the other eight? That was a question I had considered only in connection with the Seven Dwarfs or the eight reindeer. Commandments? Ah, taking the name of the Lord in vain. Oh, God! Whoops! Admittedly, I'd been less than pure here, but who hadn't? If that commandment had been pivotal there would be no need for this room at all. The escalator would only go down.

Regardless, I felt distinctly uncomfortable. I looked around, searching for walls, for a bench, for something solid, but nothing was more substantial than a suggestion, a fuzzy conception way in the back of my mind.

Then, suddenly, there were double doors before me. With considerable relief, I pushed them open and walked into a large room, a banquet hall. To my right were the other guests. I couldn't make out individuals, but I knew they were seated at festively decorated tables, with full plates before them and glasses of Dom Perignon waiting to be lifted. No words were distinct, but the sounds of gaiety and laughter were unmistakable. Maybe the welcoming of those who had gone on before was *not* a myth. A welcoming dinner!

To my left was a buffet table.

It had been a long time since that fatal chocolate bar. The whole process of dying had taken a while, and the Hershey's had been a preprandial chocolate. Now that I was no longer distracted by apprehension, I realized I was famished. And I couldn't have been in a better place. I was delighted that this was not to be a formal dinner with choice limited to underdone chicken breast or tasteless white fish and a slab of Neapolitan ice cream for dessert. For me a buffet was the perfect welcome.

The buffet table was very long and wonderfully full. Before me were bowls of fruit. Not just oranges or canned fruit cocktail, but slices of fresh guavas and peaches, of mangoes and kiwi fruit, hunks of ripe pineapple without one brown spot, and maraschino cherries that I could gorge on without fear of carcinogens. As I stood pleasantly salivating, I knew that here at the celestial buffet I could eat pineapple and ice cream without getting indigestion, mountains of coleslaw or hills of beans without gas. And as much of them as I wanted. Never again the Scarsdale Diet. No more eight glasses of water and dry meat. Never another day of nine hundred or fewer calories. I could consume a bunch of bananas, thirty Santa Rosa plums, enough seedless grapes to undermine the wine industry, and remain thin enough for my neighbor's husband to covet me.

But that was a topic I did not want to consider in depth. Surely, in business, in the twentieth century, in California, a bit of extramarital coveting was taken for granted. I hadn't, after all, coveted my neighbor's husband (he was sixty, and *he* only coveted a weed-free lawn). I hadn't really coveted Amory as much as I did his ability to make me district manager. After the promotion I hadn't coveted him at all. And his wife never knew, and Raymond only half suspected, so that could hardly be considered Mortal Coveting. Besides, there wouldn't be guavas in hell.

A plate, really more of a platter than a mere one-serving

plate, hovered beside me as if held up on the essence of a cart. Balancing the plate and the cup and holding the silver and napkins was always such a nuisance at buffets (and balancing, as I had so recently been reminded, was not my best skill). So this floating platter was a heavenly innovation. I was pleased that things were so well organized here. I scooped up some guava, just a few pieces, not wanting to appear piggish at my welcoming dinner. I added a few more, and then a whole guava, realizing with sudden sureness that at this banquet greed was not an issue. I heaped on cherries, berries, and peeled orange sections soaked in Grand Marnier. Had this been an office brunch, I would have been ashamed. But all the fruit fit surprisingly well on the platter and, in truth, hardly took up much of the space at all. It must have been an excellent platter design. Each fruit remained separate, none of the juices ran together, and I knew instinctively that the juices would never run into any of the entrées to come.

I moved along and found myself facing lox, a veritable school of fresh pink lox, accompanied by a tray of tiny, bite-size bagels, crisp yet soft, and a mound of cream cheese that was creamy enough to spread easily but thick enough to sink my teeth into. And there was salmon mousse made with fresh dill weed, and giant prawns in black bean sauce, and a heaping platter of lobster tails, and Maryland soft-shell crab, and New Jersey bluefish that you can't get on the West Coast, and those wonderful huge Oregon clams. I could have made a meal of any of them. But meal-sized portions of each fitted easily onto the platter. More than I ever coveted.

Coveting again. I may have coveted my neighbor's goods, but I had certainly not broken into his house and taken them. Oh, there had been the notepads and pens from the office, a few forays into fiction on my tax returns, but no one fears eternal condemnation for that. And there was the money from Consolidated Orbital to alter the environmental survey, but that was a gift, not stolen, regardless of what the environmentalists might have said. No, I could rest assured on the issue of coveting my neighbor's goods.

I adore quiche, and for the last three years it has given me indigestion. But there is no need for plop-plop fizz-fizz amongst the heavenly host. And the choice of quiche here was outstanding. Nearest me was Italian Fontina with chanterelle mushrooms, New Zealand spinach, and—ah!—Walla Walla onions that were in and out of season so fast that a week's negligence meant another year's wait. Beside it, bacon. Bacon throughout the quiche and crisp curls decorating the top! The smell made me salivate. I could almost taste it. Bacon loaded with fat and sodium and preservatives and red dyes of every number. I had forced myself to forgo it for years. And crab quiche, and one with beluga caviar sprinkled—no, ladled—over the top. I couldn't decide. I didn't have to. It was truly amazing how much fit onto the platter. I was certainly glad I didn't have to hold it up. Had I even contemplated eating this much on earth, I would have gained five pounds. Ah, heaven! On earth, I would have killed for this.

I smiled (subtly speaking, for my spiritual face didn't move but my essence shifted into the outward show of happiness). *Thou shalt not kill.* Well, I wasn't a murderer either. And that was a biggie. The closest I had come to a dead body was my own. I moved on to the meats—rare roast beef with the outside cuts ready for my taking, and crispy duck with no grease at all. Admittedly, Milton Prendergast, my predecessor as district manager, had killed himself, but that was hardly my fault. I didn't murder him. He was merely overly attached to his job. I added some spareribs to my platter. I could sympathize with Prendergast's attachment to the job. I had aimed for it myself, and there was a lot of money to be had through it. But still, suicide was hardly murder, even if he did tell me he would kill himself if I exposed him. And I had to do that, or even with Amory's help I couldn't have gotten the job. Well, knowing the shenanigans Prendergast had been involved in, at least I knew I wouldn't be running into him up here.

The roast turkey smelled wonderful, a lifetime of Thanksgivings in one inhalation. With that sausage stuffing my Mom used to make. And fresh cranberries. My whole body quivered with hunger at the smell. I took a serving, then another.

There was still room for the muffins and breads—steaming

popovers, orange nut loaf, Mexican corn bread with cheese and chiles—and for the grand assortment of desserts beyond.

But I was too hungry to wait. The juices in my empty stomach swirled; and I found myself chomping on my tongue in juicy anticipation. I needed to eat *now*. And this was, after all, a buffet. I could come back—eternally.

I reached for my platter.

It slipped beyond my grasp.

I grabbed.

Missed!

I heard laughter. Those diners at the tables—they were laughing at me.

My stomach whirled, now in fear. Surely this couldn't mean that I was in . . . I lunged. But the platter that had been right beside me was suddenly, inexplicably, three feet away. Too far to reach, but near enough for the sweet smell of pineapple to reach me. Despite my fear, my taste buds seemed to be jumping up and down at the back of my tongue. The laughter from the tables was louder.

I didn't dare turn toward the diners. Judgment Day separated the sheep from the goats. And even I, a city person, knew that sheep don't laugh. And there was a definite billy-goat quality to that cackle.

I stood still, smelling the salty aroma of the caviar, the full flavor of that freshest of salmon, the smell of the bacon, of the turkey dressing. The platter stayed still, too, still out of reach. The smell of the cranberries mixed with tangy aroma of the oranges. I inhaled it, willing it to take substance in my throbbing stomach. It didn't.

If I couldn't capture that platter . . . but I didn't want to think about the hellish judgment that would signify. But there was no point making another grab. The laughter was louder; it sounded strangely familiar.

Slowly I turned away from the platter, careful not to glance out at the diners, afraid of what I might see. Head down, shoulders hunched over, I took a shuffling step away from the food. I could sense the platter following me. I took another step. From behind me, the oranges smelled stronger, sweeter. I could almost taste them. Almost. I lifted my foot as if to take another step, then I whirled around and with both hands lunged for the food. The hell with the platter.

The laughter pounded at my ears.

Let them laugh. I'd come up with one hand full of cranberries and the other grasping a piece of caviar quiche. I had my food. Triumphantly, and with heavenly relief, I jammed half the quiche in my mouth. No eternal damnation for me. The laughter grew even louder. I knew that laugh; it came from a multitude of mouths, but it was all the same cackling sound. I swallowed quickly and poured the whole handful of cranberries into my mouth.

That cackle—Raymond's laugh!

I swallowed and pushed the rest of the quiche into my mouth. Then the oranges from the now near platter, and the salmon, and the pineapple, the prawns in black bean sauce, the turkey, and the Oregon clams, and the Walla Walla sweet onions.

But there was no silencing Raymond's knowing cackle. And there was no denying where I was—eternally. I'd got my food all right, but it all tasted exactly the same. It tasted of nothing but ashes—like it had been burned in the fires of hell.

Jean Fiedler's first published story appeared in the Pittsburgh (PA) Post Gazette *when she was eleven—and she hasn't stopped writing since. Author of twenty-one books for young people; numerous short stories; a suspense novel,* Atone for Evil; *and* Isaac Asimov, *a critical analysis of that writer's science fiction, Jean's abiding interest in the eccentricities and obsessions that drive people to extreme measures is fertile ground for her fiction.*

In "The Snake Plant," a woman struggling to survive has a critical insight into the heart of her troubles.

THE SNAKE PLANT

by Jean Fiedler

S HE GLANCED AT it lovingly. It stood on the dresser, tall, strong, flourishing, surrounded by get-well cards and vases of flowers. And tomorrow she would be taking it home.

From the beginning Diane and the plant were, in a way she could not apply reason to, bound up with each other—as though the fate of one depended on the fate of the other. Her colleagues at the publishing house had sent it to her two weeks ago, a week after the infarction.

Diane had been talking to Margy, who lay in the next bed, recovering from a coronary bypass, when the plant was delivered, swathed in green florist paper with a card attached to it that read, "Our love and best wishes for a speedy recovery. All of us at BCK, Inc."

Finally unveiled, it had stood green and aloof, a rubberlike plant, the green-and-gray leaves edged in butter yellow, its name on the small card attached to it, *Sansevieria*.

"*Sansevieria*," Diane said slowly.

36

"Snake plant," Margy said. "That's what it's called in America. I think the British call it 'Mother-in-law's tongue.' It's a tough plant. Who's it from?"

"My staff at the publishing house." Diane had laughed, and Margy smiled. Diane knew that it still hurt her to laugh. "We're all very close—not just the editors but the secretaries and the receptionist. I suspect they wanted to get me a hardy plant." She didn't add, "One that would survive," but she thought it. Was this the beginning of the bond between her and the plant?

That her staff had chosen a strong plant was confirmed by her associate editor, Rachel Marx, who had visited her that same evening. "We didn't want to get you a fragile little plant that would die in a few weeks. When we found out it was called a snake plant, we hoped you'd think it was funny. Imagine sending your boss something called a snake plant!"

"I figured if you wanted to give me a dig, you'd have been more subtle," Diane said lightly.

Rachel had walked over to the dresser and examined the plant. "There's a brown leaf." With a pocket scissors, she snipped it off. "There, it looks fine now. Be sure not to overwater it. Once a week is plenty."

"Good," Diane said. "My plants at home thrive on neglect. I never overwater. It's only guilt that reminds me to water at all."

Now, two weeks later, the scenes replayed themselves. The lights were out, but she lay awake—she had refused the sleeping pill because she hated the groggy feeling that lasted into the next day—and she saw again Rachel snipping off the brown leaf. An involuntary shudder passed through her body. Had Rachel left the brown leaf, would its decay have spread and harmed the healthy leaves? Would *her* traumatized heart weaken the rest of *her* body? Or would she, as Dr. Soames had promised, regain her strength and resume the rest of her life? She knew that many things can happen in those first post-infarction weeks, but as each day passed, his assurances had become more convincing.

Eight years ago when Robert had died so suddenly of a stroke at the age of forty, she had thought there was no life left for her. She had been completely bereft—he had been her husband, lover, friend, companion. There were no children to share the ache of her loss. But strangely, her own life force had been strong, and she had survived.

And then, two years ago, her marriage to Brian had seemed an idyllic stroke of fortune. They had met at a party for one of her authors. Odd, she had thought at first, that a stockbroker would be interested in such a literary gathering. But when they began to talk, she had learned that he was a writer manqué—he said this ironically—who had written several novels that resided in his desk drawer. Now, though, he was working on a current one that he would show her sometime if she was interested.

"Why did you go into the stock market?" she had asked, her curiosity aroused. When he didn't reply immediately, a flush appearing on his face, she had said hastily, "I'm sorry. That may not be a question you care to answer."

"It's not that. There are all kinds of memories attached to that, most of them unpleasant."

"Forget it, please," she said, but he shook his head.

"No, there's no reason not to talk about it. I wanted to write but my father thought that was stupid, that the logical place for me was on Wall Street in his business. So we made a bargain. I can still remember the way he put it. 'I'll give you a year to do nothing but write. If something happens within that year, something accepted for publication or even something that leads me to believe that you will be published one day, I'll agree to let you do whatever you want.' I took him up on that, worked my tail off for one solid year, and nothing happened. Not one goddamn thing. So . . . I kept my end of the bargain."

"And you're there now . . . in your father's firm?"

"No!" He laughed without apparent amusement. "My father lost his shirt and got out of the business six months before he died. I've been a one-man company for years now."

He had asked her to dinner the following week, and she learned that he had been married earlier for a brief time. They began to see each other for lunches, dinners, concerts, until she realized that they were spending most of their free time together. When he said, "Let's get married," she could see no reason not to.

The first year had been fine, it seemed in retrospect. There had, however, been that difficult time when he showed her his newly completed novel. As hard as she had tried to appear enthusiastic, her professional integrity had kept her from lying to him.

"You think it's lousy, don't you?" he had accused her.

"Of course it's not lousy, Brian. It's just . . . not good enough."

"Thank you." He paused and added quietly, "For being honest at least." Taking his coat from the closet, he had walked out of the house and come home at dawn, drunk and tired. He had never showed her any of his writing again.

But this had passed, and in some ways she was happier than she had ever expected to be again. It was she who suggested that they have joint bank accounts—both savings and checking—and that they invest in stocks together. This was partially due to guilt that the house and her mother's trust fund were in her name only. Her attorney had been adamant on that score, and because she and Richard had been friends for a long time, she had acquiesced to his insistence that some money remain hers alone. Inwardly, she had rationalized that at some future time she would override Richard's opinion.

When had it begun to change? Now lying in bed awake, she thought back to the second year and the more and more frequent business trips, the skipped dinners, sometimes even without a phone call, the nights when he came home long after she was in bed. The night of her heart attack, she had steeled herself to face him and ask if he wanted a divorce.

He had appeared shaken, she recalled now, but then her own body had taken over and betrayed her with a burning, piercing pain that made her gasp, "Call an ambulance, Brian . . . please!"

The strong memory of the pain made her fear for a terrifying instant that it had returned, and she forced herself to lie quietly and relax her body.

Now, the infarction three weeks behind her, she was ready to go home. Tomorrow Brian would come for her.

He had visited her each day. For the first few days when she was in intensive care, he had hardly left the hospital. Then when she was moved to another wing, he would come in the evening just as visiting hours began. He had brought her flowers and magazines and had even insisted on taking home her nightgowns so that Mary, the woman who cleaned for them three days a week, could launder them. There were no business trips; he phoned her from the office just to ask how her night had been, and she had begun to wonder if she hadn't imagined those ten or eleven months that preceded the heart attack.

The morning of her homecoming, she dressed early and sat on a chair, her plant still on the dresser. It looked strong, healthy—a good omen, she told herself. Brian came up for her, took her small suitcase, and waited for her to step through the doorway. But she held back. "My plant . . . I want to take my plant home."

He frowned. "Diane, must we? The house is full of plants. Do we really need this . . . this one? It's hardly a beauty. In fact, it's downright ugly."

Fiercely she rushed to its defense. "It's beautiful to me! It's . . . strong." And then she blurted it out. "My friends sent it—you know that, and when it came I was still sick, but then I began to feel better. Each day the plant grew greener and stronger. There are even new leaves . . . and each day I felt better."

He stared at her with incredulity. "Do you see this plant as some kind of symbol of your survival? If it survives, so will you?"

Heat rose to her face. "It sounds stupid when you put it like that. Call it a fancy, a foolish fancy if you prefer"—her tone grew firmer now—"but okay, that's the way I feel. I want to take it home."

"Whatever you say," he said quietly. Picking up the plant with care, he carried it downstairs to the car.

They were both silent on the trip home. He opened the door for her and went back to get the plant and her suitcase.

A strong lemony smell greeted her nostrils. "What's that?" she said, sniffing. "Is Mary using a new deodorizer?"

He shook his head. "Mary outdid herself. The smell of the ammonia was so strong, I thought I'd better try to mask it—a bit, at least."

"Oh," she said, wondering why he seemed strained, why his sensitive skin was flushed. And then she realized that he was lying. Mary hardly ever used ammonia. It made her cough. The lemon deodorizer was to cover another smell. Perfume? she asked herself.

But now the task at hand was to place the plant where it would get some sun but was out of drafts. The bookshelf adjacent to the window seemed the perfect spot. "Next to the bowl of seashells," she directed him, observing the odd expression on his face as he set the plant down and surveyed it.

"Ugly, isn't it?" he commented. "But you're right. It does look strong. You know, *you* have unusual strength, Diane."

"How do you mean? I feel weak as a kitten."

"Dr. Soames said it was your strength that pulled you through. It was a massive heart attack . . . you know that."

Aware that a pulse had begun to beat at the side of her temple, she said, "Dr. Soames said that about my unusual strength?"

"Not in so many words, darling. He said it was lucky you were a strong, healthy woman . . . that everything else was in good working order."

"I sound like a machine," she said, vaguely uneasy. *Massive heart attack* sounded so . . . awful. Yes, she had survived, but she was just three weeks away from it all, and she had read enough to know that she was still very vulnerable.

"What's the matter, Di?" Brian asked solicitously.

"Nothing. I don't like the subject."

"I'm sorry, darling. It's just that talking about the plant reminded me of how lucky we are that your own strength was so great."

A niggling pain had started in her shoulder. "Brian, get my bag, please. I need a nitro."

"What's the matter, Diane? Pain?"

She nodded—the pain was in her chest now. "Please, Brian."

The nitro did what it was supposed to do, and in a few seconds her pain was gone. But she felt—no, she was convinced in spite of the rational part of her that stood apart in dismay—that he had caused this sudden pain just as her mention of a divorce had precipitated her heart attack in the first place.

The next morning when Mary arrived to clean, Diane made sure to tell her not to water the new plant. "I'll do it myself," she said somewhat apologetically.

"That's a good-looking plant," Mary said with admiration. "It looks real healthy."

Thank you, Diane said silently.

And so it began that each morning on awakening, she would go down to see her plant. If it survived, so would she—at least for that day.

Her brain protested that this was idiocy, sheer idiocy, superstitious nonsense. Yes, she admitted, linking her destiny to a plant was insanity, but all the same, she watered it only once a week, and she secretly exulted in its vigor.

Brian had never been so solicitous. Those first weeks, he insisted that she not overdo, that her meals be brought up to her. He had arranged that Mary come in each day so that Diane wouldn't run the risk of getting tired.

"I'm supposed to get up, Brian," she would protest. "Dr. Soames said so."

"Of course he said so. He didn't want to upset you. You were badgering the poor man to death."

"What are you talking about?" Her voice had risen. "When did I badger him?"

"You've forgotten, darling. But never mind. You can be up for half an hour at a time, and then back to bed."

Protesting meant an argument, and the resultant pain that led to her taking the nitros—too many of which gave her a headache.

Each evening now, Brian retired to his study directly after dinner—making sure to load the dishwasher first—to work. He was writing, he said.

After he had been following this routine for two weeks, she called after him, "Is it another novel?" He had not discussed his writing with her since the evening when he had demanded the truth about his novel. And yet, she thought, it seemed boorish to refrain from expressing any interest in something that obviously absorbed him.

He turned and gave her a strange, enigmatic look, as if he were staring at something beyond her. After a long pause, as if what she had asked required reflection, he said, "I'm not sure yet."

She felt impelled to say, "You do your first draft in longhand?"

He nodded and continued upstairs.

The exchange left her feeling uneasy and restless. Trying to distract herself, she went up to their bedroom and turned on a sitcom. She gave up after half an hour, showered, and went to bed with one of the new books sent to her by the office. About to drift off, she thought she heard Brian's voice.

After a long time, when he finally came to bed, she said, "Were you talking on the phone?"

He gave a short laugh. "When I do dialogue, I talk it."

"Oh," she said, and turned on her right side, feeling as if she had been rebuffed and not quite knowing why.

Diane had begun to spend more and more time out of bed, saving her resting time for when Brian was home. On her first visit to the doctor after the hospital—Brian made sure he was home to take her—she was relieved to hear Dr. Soames say, "You're doing fine, young lady. Now, Diane, I want you up and around. Rest when you're tired, but start doing things normally."

On her way to the bathroom, she passed Brian, who was sitting and reading a magazine in the reception area. She was startled not to see him when she came out.

"Where is my husband?" she asked the nurse.

"In with the doctor, Mrs. Kane. I'm sure he'll be right out."

In with the doctor. But why? What was Dr. Soames saying to him that he could not say directly to her? Anxiety settled over her, and when Brian came out a few minutes later, she said sharply, "Why did you want to speak to the doctor, Brian? What did he say to you?"

Brian held up a hand. "In a minute, darling, as soon as we're in the car. This is a tiring trip for you. I want to get you home."

Helping her on with her coat, he took her arm and carefully steered her out of the office. "You're treating me as if I were a hundred years old," she protested.

His hold on her arm remained firm. "I'm sorry, Di. I almost lost you. Let me coddle you a bit."

This last warmed her so that she forgot to ask about the doctor until they were home, having dinner. Then she remembered and asked again. "Why did you want to talk to Dr. Soames?"

His eyes shifted away from her face, and he appeared uncomfortable.

"Brian"—her voice was shrill—"tell me!"

"I didn't ask to see him," he said gently.

"Then . . . he asked to see you?"

He nodded with obvious reluctance.

"But why? What's wrong with me?"

"Nothing, Di, nothing. He wants you to rest more. He wants you to remember that you were a very sick girl."

"But he said . . . he said to rest only when I'm tired!"

"You hear what you want to hear, Diane. He knows you're a stoic. That's why he called me in."

She felt weak suddenly, and very tired. With difficulty she said, "I'm not very hungry. I'd better go to bed."

"Good," he said approvingly.

Later, as she heard him climb the stairs to his study, she called out, "I'm going to phone Dr. Soames and ask why he wanted to see you."

Brian stopped at the door to the bedroom. A shade of annoyance may have passed over his face. Too gently he said, "Diane, he's the last person in the world to want to upset you. He'll say I wanted to see him."

"Then I can't trust him," she said, hearing the hopelessness in her own voice.

"Of course, you can, Di. He saved your life, and he wants it to stay saved. So do I."

That night Diane took a sleeping pill and tried to forget the incident. But the following day when she went down to look at her plant, she saw to her horror that it had been freshly watered—a day after she had watered it herself.

Fury with Mary made the heat rise to her cheeks. Realizing that anger was an emotion she could ill afford, she forced herself to breathe deeply as she willed herself to relax, and when Mary came down from vacuuming the upstairs, she said quietly, "Mary, please don't ever water this plant again."

"What plant, Mrs. Kane?"

"My plant! I asked you specifically not to water it, and then you did when you watered the other plants."

Mary stood there, a blank expression on her ruddy face. "I don't know what you're talking about. I never watered your hospital plant. You told me not to."

She sounded so sincere that Diane believed her. But if Mary had not watered it, who had? The answer was obvious. She decided not to mention this to Brian.

The next morning Diane saw that the plant had been given even more water, and now the tip of one leaf was brown-edged. My God, she thought in a panic. Running for the scissors, she took the leaf and carefully snipped off the edge as Rachel had done. But the plant was too wet. She knew it.

All that day she felt tired and listless, and the angina of which she had been free for some time reappeared. As the pellet of nitroglycerin began to dissolve under her tongue, she thought, *This is madness. I'm identifying with a plant! Maybe I should get rid of it.* But the thought brought another twinge, and she tried to empty her mind of all thoughts.

Walking over to the shelf, she touched the snipped leaf tenderly. "We'll be all right," she said softly. "Don't worry."

When she viewed the situation objectively, of course, it was ludicrous, talking to a plant like this, reassuring it. But maybe her closeness to death had increased her sensitivity, her awareness of all living things. She was sure she had read about this kind of empathy at some time, and the thought gave her comfort. She began to feel better.

Over cocktails that evening—she was allowed a small glass

of white wine—she broached the subject carefully. "My plant has been overwatered."

Brian frowned, annoyance evident in the set of his mouth. "Tell Mary not to do it again."

On the verge of saying "Mary isn't watering it," she stopped and with deliberate nonchalance said, "Yes, of course."

If he was doing this, he had a reason. It was not his custom to water the plants at all. His initial comment about the plant had been that it was ugly—but was that enough for him to destroy it?

It was easier to return to Mary. Mary was hardly above what she probably thought of as "a little white lie." She recalled questions she had forced herself to ask in the past: "Mary, did you have a chance to vacuum the couch today?" And the answer: "Oh yes, it was so dusty, one vacuuming didn't even get rid of it all." Quick thinking—a lie or the truth. Diane had never felt sure.

Somehow recalling this, she felt relieved. It didn't hurt to suspect Mary as it did Brian. As she climbed the stairs, she remembered to walk slowly. Stopping outside the half-closed door of his study, she heard his voice and smiled. He was rehearsing lines of dialogue.

His voice was low, and through the opening she saw that he was cradling the phone in his hands, his back to her. He was talking into the phone very softly, but Diane could hear the strain in his voice. "I can't! Not now! I'm in over my head. Be patient, for God's sake."

A spurt of apprehension made her turn and walk quietly back down the stairs. To whom had he been talking? Certainly someone he knew very well—judging from what he was communicating. Why hadn't he said anything to her?

The easy resolution to blame Mary seemed cheap and childish now, and yet what had she really overheard that was making her feel so troubled and anxious?

When Brian came down for their customary cup of cocoa before bedtime, she said, "Are you worried about anything, Brian?"

His eyes refused to meet hers. "Why . . . what gives you that idea?"

Unwilling to confront him when he was so obviously lying, she murmured something evasive and drank her cocoa.

The next morning he left earlier than usual, not even stopping for breakfast. Since she was awake, she decided to get up too. The ringing of the telephone coincided with the whistle of the teakettle. It rang a number of times before she answered it somewhat breathlessly. But there was no answer to her hello, and when finally the line went dead, she hung up, aware of a vague disquiet that bordered an elusive memory.

Two or three times in the early morning when she was half dozing and Brian was getting ready for work, the phone had rung. When it happened, she would ask sleepily, "Who was that?"

"Some idiot with a wrong number."

She had accepted this explanation without thought—until now. If the phone call had been for Brian and the caller wanted to avoid speaking to her, certainly he—or she—would have hung up. He or . . . she? A man would probably have left a message. A woman would not have if the call was personal rather than business. Business at seven A.M.? Not likely. Had those other calls—the ones she just vaguely recalled—not been wrong numbers at all?

Diane's thoughts returned to the one-sided conversation she had eavesdropped on the previous night. Instinctively she sensed that the caller was the same as the one who made the morning calls.

A twinge of angina made Diane recall that she had not taken her morning medication. She took the two small pills and within minutes was free of pain. But the angina reminded her of something she had been shielding herself from during the period of the infarction, and later, her convalescence.

That night—the night it happened—she had asked a question: "Do you want a divorce?" He had never really answered it. And she, shielded by tranquilizers and medication, had succeeded in pushing the incident away from conscious thought.

If Brian had been having an affair before the heart attack, would it have ceased? A woman who was getting impatient might have been urged to "Be patient, for God's sake!" The words rang in her head.

Strangely, though, she felt no sense of devastation, not even of betrayal, and to her surprise, there was no sharp painful physical reminder that she must not upset herself. Physically, she realized, she felt fine.

She prepared her juice, cereal, and even brewed herself a cup of decaffeinated coffee. It smelled like real coffee, and although at the beginning she had missed the quick jolt of adrenaline that caffeine provided, she no longer did.

Calmly she decided to confront Brian with the same question she had asked six weeks earlier. Now she had an advantage, but to confront him without being positive, herself, seemed unfair. The task now was to make sure.

It was easy to act drowsy in the mornings and note the occasional call that came somewhere between seven and seven-fifteen. Once she asked sleepily, "Who was it?" His reply was abrupt. "Nobody on the line."

In the evenings when he was home—he had begun again to have meetings and dinner engagements with "clients"—she would tiptoe up the stairs and listen to his phone calls, his part of them. And one night she heard him say, "Oh, darling, be patient, please!"

Amazed that she felt so calm, she was aware that her uncertainty was over. All she felt was enormous relief. Abruptly she realized that she had been so busy watching Brian, she had not looked at the plant that morning. She hurried down to the living room where it sat on the shelf. The soil was sopping wet, and now there were many brown leaves.

It's dying, she thought sadly, as distressed over the fact that someone she had loved was trying to kill it as that it was dying. But there was no answering reaction in her own body. The relief was dizzying.

Now she knew that it was Brian, but she still did not know why. She was completely recovered now—she would be returning to work in another week. If he wanted a divorce, he had only to ask for it.

At dinner the next evening, she decided to give him an opening and mentioned a friend who was being divorced. Instead of following her lead, he merely looked uncomfortable and changed the subject.

Five more days passed. Diane was aware that the plant was being watered each day now. At breakfast on Sunday morning with no preamble, she said, "Brian, before I . . . got sick, I asked you if you wanted a divorce. My heart attack shelved that, but now I want to bring it up again." She was about to say "I want a divorce" when he held up his hand in protest.

"Diane, don't! I know I've been a bit abstracted lately but there are problems at work I haven't wanted to burden you with. I don't want a divorce. . . . I love you."

She listened, detached, hardly hearing the words, wondering why he was saying them.

That night he tried to initiate lovemaking. "You're fine now. The doctor said so."

But she shook her head, forcing a smile. "I'm tired tonight, Brian. Give me a rain check."

Did a shade of relief flit over his face? She couldn't be sure, but even the thought of his hands on her body revolted her.

She was sleepless all night, but she avoided taking the Valium that would knock her out. She wanted to think, undistracted. He had unequivocally refused a divorce, but she knew now that there was a woman whom he called darling. If he did not want a divorce, what did he want?

Finally she took refuge in the Valium and dreamed. She dreamed that she found an earring in his jacket pocket.

The dream was so vivid that when she awakened—Brian was already gone—she went directly to his closet and rifled the pockets of his suit jackets. She found little—a book of matches, some small change. No lipsticks, no handkerchiefs with lipstick on them, no earrings, no letters.

All the clichés she had ever read about returned, and when she had gone through his closet, disgusted with herself, she found she couldn't stop. On she went to his chest of drawers and finally into his study. The desk revealed nothing. And then she moved on to his files. Neatly alphabetized, the Pendaflex folders stretched in front of her.

As she was about to close the drawer, her eyes fell on her own name. She reached in and lifted out the folder, but it contained an envelope that seemed to be sagging. Her fingers touched something that felt like straw. Slowly she brought it out, her bewildered eyes hardly able to recognize what it was.

Then she saw it, a straw doll with a few strands of auburn hair pasted to its head—her own hair, she realized at once— a needle pierced through its chest, a needle holding a note.

A sharp jab of angina made her gasp; her nitroglycerin was in the bedroom. Instinctively she reached out and gently removed the needle from the doll's chest. Then slowly she walked into the next room and put a pellet of nitro under her tongue.

The pain subsided quickly, and she went back to the study. She picked up the note, its corner torn by the needle, and began to read it. "I'm waiting! But how long must I wait!"

She opened the folder again and at first thought she must be hallucinating. The neatly typed heading read, "The Diane File." She could hardly believe the words she was reading. He had actually kept a record of her illness from the onset to the present, the most recent insert dated a day earlier. And then she came upon a fresh sheet of paper. The title brought chills to her entire body. "Eulogy for Diane." The date was this year's—space was left for the month and day. The rest of the page was blank.

She steadied herself by holding on to the file cabinet, surprised by her lack of emotion as the pieces of the puzzle began to form a whole.

That first meeting—he had approached her at the party after he had learned she was a senior editor at a large publishing house. How naïve she had been. After she had read his novel and given him an honest appraisal, he had never showed her anything again. He had hated his father for discouraging him, had seemed elated that his father had lost his fortune and died shortly afterward. She could still hear his short laugh when he spoke about it.

Remembering the hatred, she shivered, knowing that she had become the recipient of it.

With fingers that hardly trembled, she replaced the note on the doll, fastening it with the needle, and put the file back in his drawer.

And finally it was all clear. Now she knew why Brian did not want a divorce. A divorce would divide their assets, but the house was not to be shared, nor her trust fund. The infarction had been a fortunate accident, one that had given him hope of having it all. The plot was a stupid cliché, but she had provided him with an unusual angle. By revealing her empathy with the plant, she had given Brian what he would have deemed a safe, psychological weapon.

Diane glanced at her watch. It was only nine A.M., but there were many things to do. First she checked on the plant. It seemed fitting that it should be dead. She put a plastic bag next to her purse. After a shower and breakfast, she dressed to go out.

The first stop was the bank. Meticulously, she had worked out all the steps. She withdrew all the money in their joint accounts, closed them, started two new accounts for herself with half the money, and got a bank check made out to Brian for the other half.

Then she proceeded to the florist's, showed the clerk her dead snake plant, and was able to buy a duplicate. When the clerk said, "Too bad. Would you like me to dispose of it for you?" she said, "No thank you," hoping that her refusal hadn't sounded horrified. It would have seemed a sacrilege to throw her plant into a trash can.

This accomplished, she put her packages in the car and took herself out to lunch. Then she proceeded to shop successfully for a beige pantsuit, a tweed jacket and skirt, and tan leather boots. She had never enjoyed spending money so much.

When she got home, she went out to the backyard and dug a shallow hole. Carefully, tenderly, she placed the dead snake plant in it and covered it with earth. Placing a stone on the barely perceptible mound, she smiled at her own sentimentality. Then she put the new snake plant on the shelf next to the bowl of shells. The phone call to her broker took five minutes.

When Brian came home for dinner, she acted normally. She wondered how long it would take him to notice the new plant and observed him covertly, making sure that she was in the living room when he was. He looked at the plant for a long time, finally turning away with a puzzled expression that she caught.

It was then that she said, "It's rejuvenated! For some wonderful reason it's come back to life, Brian. And now I know I'm going to make it too."

"You really believe there's some magical link between you and the plant," he said with the mild sarcasm she had always hated.

A strange joy filled her now, a kind of exultation. "Brian, I have something to give you."

Her purse was on the coffee table. Taking out the bank check, she handed it to him.

He stared at it, obviously troubled, not taking it from her hand. "What is this? Why are you giving me a bank check?"

She could feel pity for him because he would never know for certain what had precipitated this. "I'm divorcing you, Brian," she said quietly. "This is my house, and I'd like you to pack and get out."

Her heart continued its steady, normal beat. And the new snake plant, in its place of honor, assured her that all was well and would continue to be.

With the publication of Magic Mirror, *Mickey Friedman (herself a former reporter for the* San Francisco Examiner*) introduced Georgia Lee Maxwell, a free-lance writer starting a new life in Paris. Georgia Lee's second adventure,* A Temporary Ghost, *took her to the south of France. Mickey's novels (*Hurricane Season, The Fault Tree, Paper Phoenix, Venetian Mask*) are filled with memorable characters and intriguing situations and feature such finely drawn renderings of Venice, India, Paris, Provence, and Florida, that readers may close the pages and wonder why they don't have jet lag.*

In "Lucky Numbers," Beth Carson counts on the New York lottery to turn the odds in her favor.

LUCKY NUMBERS

by Mickey Friedman

7

*T*ERRY'S AGE. THE *first number has to be for Terry.*

At eight A.M. in a coffee shop on Hudson Street, Beth Carson fills out a bet slip for the Saturday night Lotto drawing. Her name isn't really Beth Carson, but that's the name she's using. If Beth's prim, small-featured face looks drawn and pallid, if she seems distracted by an intense inner dialogue, so do several others slumped over steaming cups at the counter.

Although it's late September and the morning is chilly, Beth has no coat or sweater. She's wearing her best outfit, a gauzy cream-colored blouse with frills at the neck and wrists and a black velvet skirt, but the blouse is wrinkled and the hem of the skirt is hanging down on one side, as if it had snagged on something. A bad scuff mars the toe of one of her dressy black pumps.

This week's jackpot is only seven million dollars. Although

collecting it will be a risk, Beth thinks her identity will hold up. There won't be much interest in such a small sum, and Beth won't allow the newspapers to publish her picture when she wins. Beth has to win.

"Use only blue or black ball point pen or pencil for marking," the instructions say. Beth found a pencil in her purse, a stub with Terry's teethmarks on it. No eraser. Beth has to make the right decision the first time. She marks over and over the seven in the top row.

The drawing is tonight at 10:55. "Play Lotto. Now Bigger than Ever," the brochure says, above a picture of happy people, trees, purple-and-gold mountains. The picture is nothing like New York City. Nothing like the place Beth and Terry came from, either. Terry would love those purple-and-gold mountains, although when Beth asks her Terry always says she doesn't mind the city, doesn't mind the crummy illegally sublet apartment, doesn't mind walking past people sleeping in doorways. She didn't even mind the man in the park with his head split open and the blood dripping down in a puddle.

Beth heard Terry talking about the man in the park with Rasheena from downstairs, Rasheena's dark head and Terry's blond one close together. "I won't say what he said, but I'll spell it," Terry told Rasheena. "He said, 'F-u-c-k you, leave me alone.' "

Terry said she didn't mind. Terry wanted to be with Beth. Magda hated Terry, Terry said, no matter how sweet she'd acted in front of the judge. Beth couldn't stand the thought of Magda being hateful to Terry.

They'd leave New York now. Had to.

Beth hasn't seen Terry since yesterday morning. She hopes to God Terry is all right. She bears down with her pencil, blackening the white space around the seven.

23

My birthday. June 23. My birthday.

Beth puts the pencil down. The counter waitress asks, "More coffee?" but Beth doesn't hear or respond. The waitress moves on. She sees a lot of strange behavior, day in and day out.

Beth's birthday, June 23, was three months ago. That night she and Dan made love for the first time, two fugitives from what their lives had been.

Beth had seen Dan at the mailboxes: tall, gray-bearded, with a domed forehead and a fringe of thinning curls, he was scholarly-looking and vaguely elegant in the smelly, littered hallway. A man like that living in a tenement walk-up? Of course there was a story behind it. The snatches he'd eventually revealed added up to a life ruined by booze. She could fill in for herself the embittered wife in a suburban house, estranged children, lost jobs, family occasions missed or spoiled, hospitalization. Now he was sober and alone. He'd done terrible things in his life, she supposed, but she wasn't in a position to pass judgment.

Beth picks up the pencil. She begins to blacken 23.

They'd occasionally smiled at each other at the mailboxes. Even in New York, that much was possible. Then the heat went out, the last big storm of the winter. She and Terry were practically turning blue that night, and nobody answered the landlord's phone. Rasheena and her family were in Queens for a wedding. Beth didn't know anybody else in the building. She walked upstairs and knocked on his door. She waited a long time before he said, "Who's there?"

The delay, the sound of his voice, made her feel flustered. She directed a quavery explanation at the closed door. Downstairs neighbor. Heat. Then he said, "Just a minute," and she waited a long time again before he opened the door.

He was wearing an Irish fisherman's sweater buttoned up to the neck. His eyes were blue and slightly bulbous. When he said, "Yes, it's off up here too," a teakettle started to whistle.

"I see," she said, and that seemed to be that.

She was turning back to the stairs when he raised his voice over the shrill noise and said, "I'm about to make tea. Would you like a cup? Maybe we can figure out who to call."

"My little girl—"

"Bring her up."

It had been warmer in his place. Seemed warmer. Terry, wrapped in blankets, drooped with sleep, and Beth and Dan drank tea and discussed whether they had the landlord's home number or knew the names of his relatives. Dan's apartment was almost unfurnished—an old couch, a drop-leaf table under the window, two mismatched dining chairs. Through the bedroom door Beth glimpsed a mattress on the floor, tangled bedding. This man was a restless sleeper. He had a few ratty paperbacks, a small television set. Nothing on the walls. In a Coke bottle on the table were two pink chrysanthemums. They were so beautiful, Beth couldn't stop looking at them.

Then the whole building seemed to knock, clank, and shudder, and the heat was on again. They never knew what had happened. Beth felt as giddy as if it were New Year's as they laughed and shook hands and she gathered Terry for the trip downstairs.

But they didn't make love until Beth's birthday. They barely spoke again until then. Beth met him by chance as she struggled into the building after work with bulging plastic bags of groceries. Terry would be home already, playing at Rasheena's.

Dan helped her with the bags. They climbed the stairs, Beth flexing her fingers to get the circulation going where the plastic had cut in, and Scotch-taped on her door was a surprise. Terry had drawn a picture: a house, tree, sun, blond Terry, brown-haired Beth, and Pepper, the dog Terry had had to leave behind at Raymond and Magda's. In red crayon, in shaky letters, Terry had written, "Happy Birthday, Mom, from Teresa."

Beth had told her a million times not to call herself Teresa anymore.

Beth started to cry. Dan said, "Don't cry. It's your birthday." And when she didn't stop, "Let's go to dinner. Celebrate."

Would Dan call 23 a lucky number now?

"Hey, don't poke a hole in the card," the counter waitress says to Beth. "The machine won't take it. You'll have to start over."

29

Terry's birthday. I'll tell her, "Our birthdays did it, Terry. That's why we won."

On March 29, seven years ago, Beth and Raymond drove to the hospital past dark brown fields scattered with receding patches of snow. The sky was milky pale. Beth clutched the door handle and stared at the road ahead, listening to the rush of the wheels. Perspiration stood on her upper lip. She didn't look over at Raymond. She already knew this baby wasn't going to make any difference.

But she'd been wrong.

What had life been like without Terry? Beth remembered incidents with no focus or center. High school, marriage to Raymond, taking the business course—she'd drifted through these steps on a path someone else had marked. Getting pregnant had been the next step, and she'd taken it even though by that time she didn't like Raymond very much. Raymond sat at the kitchen table and watched Beth put the dishes in the dishwasher, as if every move she made were stupid and wrong. He left the house hours early for his shift, and Beth was glad to see him go. Then Terry changed everything.

Beth had stayed home for a while. When she'd gotten the bookkeeping job at J&M Enterprises, putting Terry in day care was anguish. Raymond was right, though. They needed the money. The mill was up and down, Raymond's job was diccy. "We can't afford for you to sit home on your butt all day" was Raymond's way of putting it. So she'd gone to work for J&M.

She and Raymond finally split when Magda came along. After that, Beth's job was even more important. Raymond would look for any excuse to get Terry away, and Beth knew it. How could Beth have quit? She'd checked around, but there was nothing where she could make nearly as much as J&M was paying her. She was stuck.

When she first uncovered the discrepancies, she thought there had been a mistake. She took the books in and showed them to Mr. Morrison. She explained how the error had been made. Mr. Morrison was a big man, florid and full of good cheer. He was on the phone constantly to customers and suppliers, telling them jokes. When he laughed, you could hear him through the closed door of his office.

He didn't laugh at Beth. As she talked, he leaned back in his chair, smoothing his tie. Something was burning somewhere, and yellow smoke drifted past the window. Mr. Morrison had a benevolent look on his face as he nodded at Beth. When she finished, the look on his face didn't change. At last he said, "I see."

He swiveled his chair around and gazed out at the smoke. He said, "I think you've miscalculated, dear."

Beth started to shake her head, but he wasn't looking at her. "It's the way we do things here," he said. "Take another look. You'll see what I mean."

She gathered the books and left. A week later she got a big raise. She was really stuck.

40

West Fortieth Street. China Art Imports and Mr. Chan.

Mr. Chan is not at all like Mr. Morrison. Mr. Chan never laughs. He never calls Beth "dear." Mr. Chan has jug ears and wears shiny gray cardboard-stiff suits. Mr. Chan gave Beth a job, asked no questions, saved her life you might almost say. Beth won't be showing up for work on Monday. She wonders what Mr. Chan will think.

"More coffee?"

Beth hears the waitress this time. "I guess so." Her voice is uninflected.

Hot liquid swirls into Beth's cup. The waitress taps the bet slip with a red fingernail. "When I win, I'm outa here," she says. "Next flight to L.A."

Beth has stopped listening. She is blackening 40, thinking about Mr. Chan.

He must have known Beth wasn't on the up-and-up. She answered his ad, appeared in his tiny, cluttered office not only without references but without a permanent address. Beth didn't know why she'd picked his ad from the others. What did she know about looking for a job in New York? She left

Terry locked in the hotel room watching television. Terry was tired from the trip. She lay listlessly on the bed, her eyes expressionless and heavy-lidded, watching cartoons. She had wanted to come. She didn't like Magda. She'd wanted to even when Beth said they couldn't bring Pepper.

Beth made her way to West Fortieth Street, overwhelmed by the traffic, the noise, the bustle on the streets. She had thought they could get lost in New York. Among those millions of people, what were two more? But with the adrenaline rush dissipated, she felt raw, terrified, exposed. The windows, thousands of them, glared down at her, saying: You thought you could run? You thought you could hide?

She wouldn't have done it if Raymond and Magda hadn't taken Terry away. The judge agreed: Terry shouldn't stay with a mother who might have to go to jail. Giving her up had been bad, but Beth had done it. Then Terry said Magda hated her. Terry wanted to be with Beth.

After the investigation started at J&M, Beth began getting phone calls. She'd answer, and nobody was on the line. Excrement was smeared on the windshield of her car. This wasn't surprising. The J&M people knew she'd try to work out a deal with the feds. At the same time, they were accusing her of pulling the whole scam on her own, filling Swiss bank accounts with the money. Beth sometimes wished she'd done it. If she had, she wouldn't be sitting here filling out a Lotto slip.

Mr. Morrison had a nephew named Wally, a gangly young man with a big wart beside his nose so it looked like he had three nostrils. Wally the Wart, she'd called him to herself even before everything blew up, when he spent afternoons lounging in the office at J&M chewing gum and waiting for his uncle to get off the phone. During the investigation, Beth saw Wally hanging around her apartment. If she went to the supermarket Wally might be there, standing in front studying the advertised specials posted in the window. He never spoke. He only made sure she saw him.

Between Wally the Wart and the feds, the situation was very tense for Beth. She couldn't sleep nights. As she saw it, she was going to lose either way. She could've toughed it out, though, if she hadn't been afraid they'd do something to Terry. One day she couldn't stand it anymore, and she and Terry took off.

In New York, Beth looked at the want ads and answered Mr. Chan's.

Mr. Chan wanted somebody to do his books, and he wanted that person right away, and he didn't want to pay a lot. To offset the low wages, he was willing to pay in cash. Beth thought maybe he hired her because he knew how it was to be alone and in need. Since he never spoke about himself, she didn't know if that was true. Getting the job with Mr. Chan on West Fortieth Street had been very, very lucky.

11

The number of months we lived in New York.

Beth is running out of lucky numbers. She sips her coffee and blots her forehead with the scratchy paper napkin. All her trouble started with numbers, so why is she doing this?

She's doing it because she has to get away, and she can't see any other hope.

They made it in New York eleven months. Long enough to create a few ties. Long enough for Beth to let down her guard and stop looking behind her at every step.

Dan was the mistake. Beth can see it now, when it's too late. Dan was like the handkerchief a magician flourishes to draw attention while preparing the trick with the other hand.

Terry was in school, Beth had a job. Every day Beth Carson grew stronger, and the other woman, the one who'd gotten into deep trouble far away, faded and blurred. Until one day Beth Carson believed she was real and could have things real people have. She let herself get distracted.

Beth shivers in the cold draft when the door opens. A tall, gangly man wearing sunglasses has come into the coffee shop. The wart beside his nose looks like a third nostril. He sits at a table by the window and takes the menu from its place between the sugar dispenser and the salt and pepper shakers. Bent over her bet slip, Beth doesn't turn around.

14

The number of stairs between my apartment and Dan's.

She had counted them, like a teenager with a crush. Only fourteen stairs between them. She could walk up fourteen stairs and knock on his door, and he would open it and be happy to see her.

Dan was quiet. Often he seemed vacant and preoccupied, and she knew he was thinking about the turns his life had taken. Dan had a job selling computers in an electronics store in midtown. He worked, went to AA, did crossword puzzles, watched baseball on television. Many essential things were left unsaid between them. The relationship slid over the surface of their lives, rarely encountering friction from what lay hidden below.

Terry was a little fearful of Dan, and he was shy with her. Beth told herself Terry hadn't known a man with a beard before, but she knew it wasn't that. She knew Terry was afraid Dan would take Beth away and Terry would be alone.

Some days, though, were almost all right. Dan had an air conditioner and Beth didn't, so on meltingly hot summer Saturdays the three of them would stay at his place, drinking lemonade and watching the game. Terry brought crayons and a coloring book and sat on her skinny haunches working on a winged pig. She finished it and waved the picture around, saying, "Mommy! Daddy! See what—" Then she realized what she'd said. She gave Dan a shocked look.

He didn't answer for a minute. Then he took the picture from her hand and said, "Hey, that's great, Terry." Terry quailed and turned away.

Terry came first with Beth. But Terry had asked to go to Queens with Rasheena, to visit Rasheena's cousins for the weekend. Beth had let her go. She admitted to herself she wanted some uninterrupted time with Dan.

Fourteen steps. That was the distance between them. Beth bears down hard, obliterating fourteen.

They were going out to dinner. Dan had courtly manners, and he liked to go to nice places. Beth was dressed in her best outfit. With her coat over her arm, she climbed up to Dan's place.

Wally the Wart was waiting on the staircase above Dan's floor. The building had no particular security, but Beth hadn't counted on heavy security. She'd counted on not being found.

He came down toward her, the gun in his hand. He looked scared, his Adam's apple bobbing.

Dan was expecting her. They were about to leave, and his door was ajar. Beth gasped when she saw Wally, a strangled gurgle, and Dan heard her and rushed out. Beth was close enough to see Dan's face close down with fear.

Wally's arm jerked. Something thumped the wall beside Beth. Beth heard another loud report, and Dan curled over beside her and fell without a sound. Wally, still on the stairs, said, "Aw—*shit*!"

Beth dropped her coat on top of Dan. She ran into his apartment and slammed the door. The kitchen window, leading to the fire escape, was half open. She pushed it up and scrambled through.

Once she made it to the ground, she seemed to float through the night. She was never cold. She was in a bookstore, but it closed at one A.M. She sat in a bar. The woman next to her muttered over and over, "Where is he? Where is he?" She hadn't seen Wally again.

She has to get back with Terry, and she and Terry have to get away. When Beth wins the seven million, they can get away.

Beth wishes she could tell Dan how sorry she is. She is sorry, but she has things to do. The drawing is tonight at 10:55. Beth has to turn in her numbers and buy her ticket. She puts her pencil down and fumbles in her purse for money to pay for the coffee. The man with the wart watches her over the top of his menu.

Elizabeth George's A Great Deliverance, *nominated for an Edgar and a Macavity and winner of an Agatha for Best First Novel of 1988, introduced Detective Inspector Thomas Lynley and Detective Sergeant Barbara Havers, British sleuths who return in* Payment in Blood *and* Well-Schooled in Murder *to solve cases in which love, betrayal, and the often-unrecognized burdens of the past are key elements. British sites and sounds abound, providing palpable settings for Elizabeth's astute observations of human nature.*

In "The Evidence Exposed," hidden motivations are brought to light after a member of a class in British architecture dies on an excursion.

THE EVIDENCE EXPOSED

by Elizabeth George

ADELE MANNERS GAVE her room one last look. The bed was made. The clothes were picked up. Nothing betrayed her.

She shut the door and descended the stairs to join her fellow students for breakfast. The dining hall rang with the clatter of their dishes and silverware, with the clamor of their talk. As always, one voice managed to soar above the rest, shrill and determined to fix attention upon the speaker. Hearing it, Adele winced.

"Hypoglycemia. Hy-po-gly-*ce*-mia. You know what that is, don't you?"

Adele wondered that anyone could avoid knowing since, in their two weeks at St. Stephen's College, Noreen Tucker hadn't missed an opportunity to expatiate upon hypoglycemia or anything else. Seeing that she was doing so once again, Adele decided to take her plate of scrambled eggs and sausage to another location, but as she turned, Howard Breen came to her side, smiled, said, "Coming?" and carried his

own plate to where Noreen Tucker reigned, outfitted by Laura
Ashley in an ensemble more suited to a teenager than a romance writer at the distant end of her fifth decade.

Adele felt trapped. She liked Howard Breen. From the first
moment they had bumped into each other and discovered they
were neighbors on the second floor of L staircase, he had
been very kind to her, preternaturally capable of reading past
her facade of calm yet at the same time willing to allow her
to keep personal miseries to herself. That was a rare quality
in a friend. Adele valued it. She valued Howard Breen. So
she followed him.

"I'm just a martyr to hypoglycemia," Noreen was assert-
ing vigorously. "It renders me useless. If I'm not careful . . ."

Adele blocked out the woman's babbling by scanning the
room and engaging in a mental recitation of the details she
had learned in her two weeks as a student in the Great Houses
of Britain class. *Gilded capitals on the pilasters,* she thought,
a segmented pediment above them. She smiled wryly at the
fact that she'd become a virtual encyclopedia of architectural
trivia while at Cambridge. Cram the mind full of facts that
one would never use and perhaps they might crowd out the
big fact that one could never face.

No, she thought. *No, I won't. Not now.* But the thought of
him came to her anyway. Even though it was finished between
them, even though it had been her choice, not Bob's, she
couldn't be rid of him. Nor could she bury him as he deserved
to be buried. She had made the decision to end their affair,
putting a period to five years of anguish by coming to this
summer session at St. Stephen's College in the hope that an
exposure to fine minds would somehow allow her to forget
the humiliation of having lived her life for half a decade in
the fruitless expectation that a married man would leave his
wife for her. Yet nothing was working to eradicate Bob from
memory, and Noreen Tucker was certainly not the incarna-
tion of razor intellect that Adele had hoped to find at Cambridge.

She gritted her teeth as Noreen went on. "I don't know
what would have happened to me if Ralph here hadn't insisted

that I go to the doctor. Always weak at the knees. Always feeling faint. Blacking out on the freeway that time. On the freeway! If Ralph here hadn't grabbed the wheel . . .'' When Noreen shuddered, the ribbon on her straw hat quivered in sympathy. "So I keep my nuts and chews with me all the time. Well, Ralph here keeps them for me. Ten, three, and eight P.M. If I don't eat them right on the dot, I go positively limp. Don't I, Ralph?"

It was no surprise to Adele when Ralph Tucker said nothing. She couldn't remember a time when he had managed to make a satisfactory response to some remark of his wife's. At the moment his head was lowered; his eyes were fixed on his bowl of cornflakes.

"You *do* have my trail mix, don't you, Ralph?" Noreen Tucker asked. "We've got the trip to Abinger Manor this morning, and from what I could tell from looking at that brochure, it's going to be lots of walking. I'll need my nuts and chews. You haven't forgotten?"

Ralph shook his head.

"Because you did forget last week, sweetie, and the bus driver wasn't very pleased with us, was he, when we had to stop to get me a bit of something at three o'clock?"

Ralph shook his head.

"So you *will* remember this time?"

"It's up in the room, hon. But I won't forget it."

"That's good. Because . . ."

It was hard to believe that Noreen actually intended to go on, harder to believe that she could not see how tiresome she was. But she nattered happily for several more minutes until the arrival of Dolly Ragusa created a diversion.

Silently, Adele blessed the girl for having mercy upon them. She wouldn't have blamed Dolly for taking a place at another table. More than anyone, Dolly had a right to avoid the Tuckers, for she lived across the hall from them on the first floor of M staircase, so there could be no doubt that Dolly was well versed in the vicissitudes of Noreen Tucker's health. The words *my poor blood* were still ringing in the air when Dolly joined them, a black fedora pulled over her long blond hair. She wrinkled her nose, rolled her eyes, then grinned.

Adele smiled. It was impossible not to find Dolly a pleasure. She was the youngest student in the Great Houses class—a twenty-three-year-old art history graduate from the University of Chicago—but she moved among the older students as an equal, with an easy confidence that Adele admired, a spirit she envied. Dolly's youth was fresh, unblemished by regret. This was not a girl who would be so stupid as to give her love to a man who would never return it. This was not a weak girl. Adele had seen that from the first.

Dolly reached for the pitcher of orange juice. "The Cleareys had a real knockdown drag-out this morning," she said. "About six-thirty. I thought Frances was going to put Sam through the window. Did you guys hear them?"

The question was directed to both the Tuckers, but it was Noreen who answered, looking up from straightening the sailor collar on her dress. "A fight?"

The question was spoken casually enough, but Adele saw how the information had piqued Noreen's interest. She had made no secret of her fascination with Sam Clearey, a U.C. Berkeley botanist.

"It was a doozy," Dolly said. "Apparently, Sam was just getting in. Just getting in at six-thirty in the morning! Can you believe it? He spent the night in someone else's room!" She grinned. "I love these Cambridge intrigues, don't you? It's sorta like high school all over again. Where d'you think he was?"

"Not with me, I'm afraid," Adele replied. "You're a better bet than I am to catch his fancy."

Dolly laughed. "*Me?* Adele, he's at least sixty years old! Come on!" She twirled a lock of hair around her finger and looked reflective. "But he *is* pretty great for an older guy, isn't he? All that gray hair. The way he dresses. I wonder who snagged him?"

"I saw him in the bar last night with that blonde from the Austen class," Howard Breen offered. "They seemed friendly enough."

Noreen Tucker's lips pursed. "I hardly think that Sam Clearey would be taken in by a forty-nine-year-old divorcee with three teenagers and dyed hair. He's a college professor, Howard. He has taste. And intelligence. And breeding.''

''Thanks. You *were* talking about me, I assume?'' Cleve Houghton slid into place next to Dolly Ragusa, carrying a plate heavily laden with eggs and sausages, grilled tomatoes and mushrooms.

Adele felt a quick release of tension at Cleve's arrival. Through mentioning the fact that Sam Clearey had shown interest in another woman, Howard Breen had innocently raised Noreen's ire. And Noreen was not the type of woman to let such a slight go by unanswered. Cleve's presence prevented her from doing so for the moment.

''Ran eight miles this morning,'' he was saying. ''Along the backs to Granchester. The rest of you should try it. Hell, it's the best exercise known to man.'' He tossed back his hair and contemplated Adele with a lazy smile. ''The *second* best exercise.''

Heat took Adele's face. She crumpled her napkin in her fist.

''Goodness. In mixed company, Cleve.'' Noreen Tucker's gaze was hungrily taking in the most salient aspect of Cleve Houghton's figure: jeans sculpted to muscular thighs. He was fifty but looked at least a decade younger.

''Damn right in mixed company,'' Cleve Houghton replied, digging into his eggs. ''Wouldn't consider it in any other kind.''

''I certainly hope not,'' Noreen declared. ''There's nothing worse than a man wasting himself on another man, is there? In one of my novels, I deal with just that topic. A woman falls in love with a homo and saves him. And when he realizes what it's like to have a woman and be normal, he melts. Just melts. I called it *Wild Seed of Passion*. *Seed* seemed appropriate. There's something in the Bible about spilling seed, isn't there? And that's exactly what those homos are up to. If you ask me, all they need is a real womanly woman and that would take care of that. Don't you agree, Howard?''

Adele offered a quick prayer that Howard Breen would see

the barb for what it was and would hold his tongue. But Noreen's provocation was too much for him.

"I'd no idea you'd done research in this area," he said.

"I . . . research?" Innocently, Noreen pressed a hand to her chest. "Don't be silly. It's only reasonable to assume that when a man and a woman . . . Heavens, surely I don't have to point out the obvious to *you*? Besides, a creative artist sometimes has to take license with—"

"Reality? The truth? What?" Howard spoke pleasantly enough, but Adele saw the tightening muscles of his hand and she knew very well that Noreen saw the same.

Noreen reached across the table and patted his arm. "Now, confess to us, Howard. Are you one of those San Francisco liberals with half a dozen homosexual friends? Have I offended you? I'm just an old-fashioned girl who loves romance. And romance is all about true love, which as we all know can only exist between a man and a woman. You know that, don't you?" She smiled at him coolly. "If you don't, you can ask Dolly. Or Cleve. Or even Adele."

Howard Breen stood. "I'll forgo that pleasure for now," he said, and left them.

"Gosh. What's the matter with him?" Dolly Ragusa asked, her fork poised in midair.

Cleve Houghton lifted a hand, dropped it to dangle limply from his wrist. "Figure it out for yourself. It shouldn't be tough. Howard's a hell of a lot more likely to chase after me than you."

"Oh, Cleve!" Noreen Tucker chuckled, but Adele did not miss the glint of malicious triumph in her eyes. She excused herself and went in search of Howard.

She didn't find him until eight forty-five, when she went to join the rest of the Great Houses class at their appointed meeting place: the Queen's Gate of St. Stephen's College. He was leaning against the arch of the gateway, stuffing a lunch bag into his tattered rucksack.

"You all right?" Adele tried to sound casual as she took her own lunch from the box in which the kitchen staff had deposited it.

"I took a walk along the river to cool off."

Howard didn't look that composed, no matter his words. A tautness in his features hadn't been there earlier. Even though she knew it was a lie, Adele said, "I don't think she really knew what she was saying, Howard. Obviously, she *doesn't* know about you or she wouldn't have brought the subject up at all."

He gave a sharp, unamused laugh. "Don't kid yourself. She's a viper. She knows what she's doing."

"Hey, you two. Smile. Come on!" Some ten yards away, Dolly Ragusa held a camera poised. She was making adjustments to an overlarge telephoto lens.

"What are you shooting with that thing, our nostrils?" Howard asked, and Adele heard in his voice the quick change of mood that Dolly seemed capable of inspiring in people.

Dolly laughed. "It's a macro-zoom, you dummy. Wide angles. Close-ups. It does everything."

Nearby, Cleve Houghton was pulling on a sweater. "Why are you carting that thing around anyway? It looks like a pain."

Dolly snapped his picture before she answered. "Art historians always have cameras smashed up to their faces. Like extra appendages. That's how you recognize us."

"I thought that's how you recognize Japanese tourists." Sam Clearey spoke as he rounded the yew hedge that separated the main court from the interior of the college. As had been his habit for all their excursions, he was nattily dressed in tweeds, and his gray hair gleamed in the morning sunlight. His wife, a few steps behind him, looked terrible. Her eyes were bloodshot and her nose was puffy.

Seeing Frances Clearey, Adele felt a perfect crescent of pain in her chest. It came from recognizing a fellow sufferer. *Men are such shit,* she thought, and was about to join Frances and offer her the distraction of conversation when Victoria Wilder-Scott steamed down from Q staircase and rushed to join them, clipboard in hand. Her spectacles were perched on the top of her head, and she squinted at her students as if perplexed by the fact that they were out of focus.

"Oh! The specs! Right," she said, lowered them to her

nose, and continued breezily. "You've read your brochures, I trust? And the section in *Great Houses of the Isles*? So you know we've dozens of things to see at Abinger Manor. That marvelous collection of rococo silver you saw in your text-book. The paintings by Gainsborough, Le Brun, Lorrain, Reynolds. That lovely piece by Whistler. The Holbein. Some remarkable furniture. The gardens are exquisite, and the park . . . well, we won't have time to see everything but we'll do our best. You have your notebooks? Your cameras?"

"Dolly seems to be taking pictures for all of us," Howard Breen said as Dolly snapped one of their instructor, whirled and took another of Howard and Adele.

Victoria Wilder-Scott blinked at the girl, then beamed. She made no secret of the fact that Dolly was her favorite student. How could she be otherwise? They shared a similar education in art history and a mutual passion for objets d'art.

"Right. Then, shall we be off?" Victoria said. "We're all here? No. Where are the Tuckers?"

The Tuckers arrived as she asked the question, Ralph shoving a plastic bag of trail mix into the front of his safari jacket while Noreen stooped to pick up their lunches, opened hers, and grimaced at its contents. She followed this with a wink at Sam Clearey, as if they shared a mutual joke.

Her students assembled, Victoria Wilder-Scott lifted an umbrella to point the way and led them out of the college, over the bridge, and down Garret Hostel Lane toward the minibus.

Adele thought that Noreen Tucker intended to use their walk to the minibus as an opportunity to mend her fences with Howard, for the romance writer joined them with an alacrity that suggested some positive underlying intent. In a moment, however, her purpose became clear as she gave her attention to Sam Clearey, who apparently had decided that a walk with Howard and Adele was preferable to his wife's accusing silence. Noreen slipped her hand into the crook of his arm. She smiled knowingly at Howard and Adele, an invitation to become her fellow conspirators in whatever was to follow.

Adele shrank from the idea, feeling torn between walking

more quickly in an attempt to leave Noreen behind and remaining where she was in the hope that somehow she might protect Sam, as she had been unable to protect Howard earlier. The nobler motive was ascendant. She remained with the little group, hating herself for being such a sop but unable to abandon Sam to Noreen, no matter how much he might deserve five minutes of her barbed conversation. She was, Adele noted, even now winding up the watch of her wit.

"I understand you were a naughty little boy last night," Noreen said. "The walls have ears, you know."

Sam seemed to be in no mood to be teased. "They don't need to have ears. Frances makes sure of that."

"Are we to know the lady who was favored with your charms? No, don't tell us. Let me guess." Noreen played her fingers along the length of her hair. It was cut in a shoulder-length pageboy with a fringe of bangs, its color several shades too dark for her skin.

"Have you read the brochure on Abinger Manor?" Adele asked.

The attempt to thwart Noreen was a poor one, and she countered without a glance in Adele's direction. "I doubt our Sam's had much time to read, Adele. Affairs of the heart always take precedence, don't they?" She gave a soft, studied laugh. "Just ask our Dolly."

Ahead of them, Dolly's laughter caught the air. She was walking with Cleve Houghton, her gait like a bounce. She gestured to the spires of Trinity College to their right and bobbed her head emphatically to underscore a comment she was making.

With Sam within her grasp, Noreen's suddenly dropping the subject of his assignation on the previous night and moving on to target Dolly seemed out of character. It was not quite in keeping with Noreen's penchant for public humiliation, especially since there was no chance that Dolly could hear her words.

"Just look at them," Noreen said. "Dolly's digging for gold and she's found the mother lode."

"Cleve Houghton?" Howard said. "He's probably older than her father."

"What does age matter? He's a doctor. Divorced. Piles of money. I've heard Dolly sighing and drooling over those slides Victoria shows us. You know the ones. Antiques, jewelry, paintings. Cleve's just the one to give her that sort of thing. And he'd be happy to do so, make no mistake of that."

Sam Clearey was examining the shine on his well-buffed shoes. He cleared his throat. "She doesn't seem the type—"

Noreen squeezed his arm. "What a gentleman you are, Sam. But you didn't see them in the bar last night. With Cleve holding forth about seducing women by getting to know their souls and appealing to their minds, and all the time his eyes were just boring into Dolly. Ask Adele. She was sitting right next to him, weren't you, dear? Lapping up every word."

Noreen's teeth glittered in a feral smile, and for the first time Adele felt the bite of the woman's words directed against herself. A chill swept over her at the realization that nothing escaped Noreen's observation. For she *had* listened to Cleve. She had heard it all.

"Little Dolly may like to play virgin in the bush," Noreen concluded placidly, "but if Cleve Houghton's doing eight miles in the morning, I'd bet they're right between Dolly's legs."

Sam Clearey's skin darkened. Whether it was rage or embarrassment, it was difficult to tell, for he was careful to let neither color his remark. "How can you possibly know that?"

Noreen favored him with a tender look. "She's right across the hall from me. And I told you, Sammy. The walls have ears."

Sam disengaged her hand from his arm. "Yes. Well. If you'll excuse me, I'd better see to Frances."

Once he had gone, Noreen Tucker seemed to feel little need to remain with Howard and Adele. She left them to themselves and went to join her husband.

"Still think she doesn't mean any harm?" Howard asked. When Adele didn't reply, he looked her way.

She tried to smile, tried to shrug, failed at both, and hated herself for losing her composure in front of him. As she knew he would, Howard saw past the surface.

"She got to you," he said.

Adele looked from Dolly Ragusa to Cleve Houghton to Sam Clearey. She had received Noreen's message without any difficulty. Nasty though it was, it was loud. It was clear. As had been her message to Howard at breakfast. As, no doubt, had been her message to Sam Clearey. Whatever it was.

"She's a viper," Adele agreed.

The worst part of those brief moments with Noreen was the fact that her cruelty brought everything back in a rush. No matter that there was no direct correlation between Noreen's comment and the past; her veiled declaration of knowledge did more than merely make perilous inroads into Adele's need for privacy. It forced her to remember.

The minibus trundled along the narrow road. Signposts flashed by intermittently: Little Abington, Linton, Horseheath, Haverhill. Around Adele, the noise of conversation broke into Victoria Wilder-Scott's amplified monologue, which was droning endlessly from the front of the bus. Adele stared out the window.

She had been thirty-one and three years divorced when she'd met Bob. He'd been thirty-eight and eleven years married. He had three children and a wife who sewed and swept and ironed and packed lunches. She was loyal, devoted, and supportive. But she didn't have passion, Bob declared. She didn't speak to his soul. Only Adele spoke to his soul.

Adele believed it. She had to. Belief gave dignity to what otherwise would have been just a squalid affair. Elevated to a spiritual plane, their relationship was justified. More, it was sanctified. Having found her soul mate, she grew adept at rationalizing why she couldn't live without him. And how quickly five years had passed in this manner. How easily they decimated her meager self-esteem.

It was two months now since Bob had been gone from her life. She felt like an open wound. "You'll be back," he'd said. "You'll never have with another man what you have with me." It was true. Circumstances had proven him correct.

"You can't get anything inside the bus. There's not enough light."

Adele roused herself to see that Cleve Houghton was laughing at Dolly Ragusa. She was kneeling backward on the seat in front of him, focusing her camera on his swarthy face.

"Sure I can." *Click*. And to make her point. *Click*.

"Okay. Then let me take one of you."

"No way."

"Come on." He reached out.

She dodged him by scampering into the aisle. She moved among the seats, snapping away at one student after another: Ralph Tucker dozing with his head against the window, Howard Breen reading the brochure on Abinger Manor, Sam Clearey turning from the scenery outside as she called his name.

From the front of the minibus, Victoria Wilder-Scott continued her monologue about the manor. ". . . family remained staunchly Royalist to the end. In the north tower, you'll see a priest's hole where Charles I was hidden prior to escaping to the Continent. And in the long gallery, you'll be challenged to find a Gibb door that's completely concealed. It was through this door that King Charles—"

"Doesn't she think we can read the brochure? We know all about the paintings and the furniture and the silver geegaws, for God's sake." Noreen Tucker examined her teeth in the mirror of a compact. She rubbed at a spot of lipstick and got to her feet—intent, it seemed, upon Sam Clearey, who sat apart from his wife.

Restlessly, Adele turned in her seat. Her eyes met Cleve Houghton's. His gaze was frank and direct, the sort of appraisal that peeled off clothing and judged the flesh beneath.

He smiled, eyelids drooping. "Things on your mind?"

Dolly's shout of laughter provided Adele with an excuse not to answer. She was perched on the arm of Ralph Tucker's seat, talking to Frances Clearey. Her face was animated. Her hands made shapes in the air as she spoke.

"I think it's great that you and Sam do things like this together," Dolly said. "This Cambridge course. I tried to get my boyfriend to come with me, but he wouldn't even consider it."

Frances Clearey made an effort to smile, but it was evident

that her concentration was on Noreen Tucker, who had dropped into the vacant seat next to Frances's husband.

"D'you two do this sort of thing every summer?" Dolly asked.

"This is our first time." Frances's eyes flicked to the side as Noreen Tucker laughed and inclined her head in Sam Clearey's direction.

Dolly spoke cheerfully. Adele saw her move so that her body blocked Frances's view of Sam and Noreen. "I'm going to tell David—that's my boyfriend—all about you two. If a marriage is going to work, it seems to me that the husband and wife need to share mutual interests. And still give each other space at the same time. Like you and Sam. David and I . . . he can really be possessive."

"I'm surprised he didn't come with you, then."

"Oh, this is educational. David doesn't worry if I'm involved in art history. It's like him and his monkeys. He's a physical anthropologist. Howlers."

"Howlers?"

Dolly lifted her camera and snapped Frances's picture. "Howler monkeys. That's what he studies." She grinned. "Their poop, if you can believe it. I ask him what he's going to learn from putting monkey poop under a microscope. He says looking at it's not so bad. Collecting it is hell."

Frances Clearey laughed. Dolly did likewise. She took another picture and danced up the aisle.

Adele marveled at how easily the girl had managed to bring Frances out of herself, even for a moment. How wise she was to point out subtly to Frances the strengths of her marriage instead of allowing her to sit in solitude, brooding upon its most evident weakness. Noreen Tucker was nothing, Dolly was saying. Other women are nothing. Sam belongs to you.

Dolly's was a decidedly insouciant attitude toward life. But why should she offer any other perspective? Her future stretched before her, uncomplicated and carefree. She bore no scars. She had no past to haunt her. She was, at the heart of it, so wonderfully young.

"Why so solemn this morning?" Cleve Houghton asked

Adele from across the aisle. "Don't take yourself so seriously. Start enjoying yourself. Life's to be lived."

Adele's throat tightened. She'd had quite enough of living. *Click.*

"Adele!" Dolly was back with her camera.

When they arrived at their destination, the sight of Abinger Manor roused Adele from her blackness of mood. Across a moat that was studded with lily pads, two crenellated towers stood at the sides of the building's front entry. They rose five stories, and on either side of them, crow-stepped gables were surmounted by impossibly tall, impossibly decorated chimneys. Bay windows, a later addition to the house, extended over the moat and gave visual access to an extensive garden. This was edged on one side with a tall yew hedge and on the other with a brick wall against which grew an herbaceous border of lavender, aster, and dianthus. The Great Houses of Britain class wandered toward this garden with a quarter hour to explore it prior to the manor's first tour.

Adele saw that they were not to be the only visitors to the manor that morning. A large group of Germans debouched from a tour coach and joined Dolly Ragusa in extensively photographing the garden and the exterior of the house. Two family groups entered the maze and began shouting at one another as they immediately lost their way. A handsome couple pulled into the car park in a silver Bentley and stood in conversation next to the moat. For a moment, Adele thought that these last visitors were actually the owners of the manor—they were extremely well dressed and the Bentley suggested a wealth unassociated with taking tours of great houses. But they joined the others in the garden, and as they strolled past Adele, she overheard a snatch of conversation pass between them.

"Really, Tommy, darling, I can't recall agreeing to come here at all. When did I do so? Is this one of your tricks?"

"Salmon sandwiches" was the man's unaccountable reply.

"Salmon sandwiches?"

"I bribed you, Helen. Early last week. A picnic. Salmon sandwiches. Stilton cheese. Strawberry tarts. White wine."

"Ah. *Those* salmon sandwiches."

They laughed together quietly. The man dropped his arm around the woman's shoulders. He was tall, very blond, clear-featured, and handsome. She was slender, dark-haired, with an oval face. They walked in perfect rhythm with each other. Lovers, Adele thought bleakly, and forced herself to turn away.

When a bell rang to call them for the tour, Adele went gratefully, hoping for distraction, never realizing how thorough that distraction would be.

Their guide was a determined-looking girl in her mid-twenties with spots on her chin and too much eye makeup. She spoke in staccato. They were in the original screens passage, she told them. The wall to their left was the original screen. They would be able to admire its carving when they got to the other side of it. If they would please stay together and not stray behind the corded-off areas . . . Photographs were permissible without a flash.

As the group moved forward, Adele found herself wedged between two German matrons who needed to bathe. She breathed shallowly and was thankful when the size of the Great Hall allowed the crowd to spread out.

It was a magnificent room, everything that Victoria Wilder-Scott, their textbook, and the Abinger Manor brochure had promised it would be. While the guide cataloged its features for them, Adele dutifully took note of the towering coved ceiling, of the minstrel gallery and its intricate fretwork, of the tapestries, the portraits, the fireplace, the marble floor. Near her, cameras focused and shutters clicked. And then at her ear: "Just what I was looking for. *Just.*"

Adele's heart sank. She had successfully avoided Noreen Tucker in the garden, after having almost stumbled upon her and Ralph in the middle of a Noreenian rhapsody over a stone bench upon which she had determined the lovers in her new romance novel would have their climactic assignation.

"The ball. Right in here!" Noreen went on. "Oh, I *knew* we were clever to take this class, Ralph!"

Adele looked Noreen's way. She was dipping her hand into

the plastic bag that protruded from her husband's safari jacket. Ten o'clock, Adele thought, trail-mix time. Noreen munched away, murmuring, "Charles and Delfinia clasped each other as the music from the gallery floated to caress them. 'This is madness, darling. We must not. We cannot.' He refused to listen. 'We *must*. Tonight.' So they—"

Adele walked away, grateful for the moment when the guide began ushering them out of the Great Hall. They went up a flight of stairs and into a narrow, lengthy gallery.

"This long gallery is one of the most famous in England," their guide informed them as they assembled behind a cord that ran the length of the room. "It contains not only one of the finest collections of rococo silver, which you see arranged to the left of the fireplace on a demi lune table—that's a Sheraton piece, by the way—but also a Le Brun, two Gainsboroughs, a Reynolds, a Holbein, a charming Whistler, and several lesser-known artists. In the case at the end of the room you'll find a hat, gloves, and stockings that belonged to Queen Elizabeth I. And here's one of the most remarkable features of the room."

She walked to the left of the Sheraton table and pushed lightly on a section of the paneling. A door swung open, previously hidden by the structure of the wall.

"It's a Gibb door. Clever, isn't it? Servants could come and go through it and never be seen in the public rooms of the house."

Cameras clicked. Necks craned. Voices murmured.

"And if you'll especially take note of—"

"Ralph!" Noreen Tucker gasped. *"Ralph!"*

Adele was among those who turned at the agitated interruption. Noreen was standing just outside the cord, next to a satinwood table on which sat a china bowl of potpourri. She was quite pale, her eyes wide, her extended hand trembling. Hypoglycemia seemed to be getting the better of her at last.

"Nor? *Hon*? Oh, damn, her blood—" Ralph Tucker had no chance to finish. With an inarticulate cry, Noreen fell across the table, splintering the bowl and scattering potpourri across the Persian carpet. Down the length of the room, the

satin cord ripped from the posts that held it in place as Noreen Tucker crashed through it on her way to the floor.

Adele found herself immobilized, although around her, everyone else seemed to move at once. She felt caught up in a
swell of madness as some people pressed forward toward the
fallen woman and others backed away. Someone screamed.
Someone else called upon the Lord. Three Germans dropped
in shock onto the couches that were made available to them
now that the cord of demarcation was gone. There was a cry
for water, a shout for air.

Ralph Tucker shrieked, "Noreen!" and dropped to his
knees amid the potpourri and china. He pulled at his wife's
shoulder. She had fallen on her face, her straw hat rolling
across the carpet. She did not move again.

Adele called wildly, "Cleve. *Cleve,*" and then he was
pushing through the crowd. He turned Noreen over, took one
look at her face, said, "Jesus Christ," and began adminis-
tering CPR. "Get an ambulance!" he ordered.

Adele swung around to do so. Their tour guide was rooted
to her spot next to the fireplace, her attention fixed upon the
woman on the floor as if she herself had had a part in putting
her there.

"An ambulance!" Adele cried.

Voices came from everywhere.

"Is she . . ."

"God, she *can't* be . . ."

"Noreen! Nor! Hon!"

"Sie ist gerade ohnmächtig geworden, nicht wahr . . ."

"Get an ambulance, goddamn it!" Cleve Houghton raised
his head. His face had begun to perspire. "Move!" he yelled
at the guide.

She flew through the Gibb door and pounded up the stairs.

Cleve paused, took Noreen's pulse. He forced her mouth
open and attempted to resuscitate her.

"Noreen!" Ralph wailed.

"Kann er nicht etwas unternehmen?"

"Doesn't anyone . . ."

"Schauen Sie sich die Gesichtsfarbe an."

"She's gone."

"It's no use."

"Diese dummen Amerikaner!"

Over the swarm, Adele saw the blond man from the Bentley remove his jacket and hand it to his companion. He eased through the crowd, straddled Noreen, and took over CPR as Cleve Houghton continued his efforts to get her to breathe.

"Noreen! Hon!"

"Get him out of the way!"

Adele took Ralph's arm, attempting to ease him to his feet. "Ralph, if you'll let them—"

"She needed to eat!"

Victoria Wilder-Scott joined them. "Please, Mr. Tucker. If you'll give them a chance . . ."

The tour guide crashed back into the room.

"I've phoned . . ." She faltered, then stopped altogether.

Adele looked from the guide to Cleve. He had raised his head. His expression said it all.

Events converged. People reacted. Curiosity, sympathy, panic, aversion. Leadership was called for, and the blond man assumed it, wresting it from the guide with the simple words, "I'm Thomas Lynley. Scotland Yard CID." He showed her a piece of identification she seemed only too happy to acknowledge.

Thomas Lynley organized them quickly, in a manner that encouraged neither protest nor question. They would continue with the tour, he informed them, in order to clear the room for the arrival of the ambulance.

He remained behind with his companion, Ralph Tucker, Cleve Houghton, and the dead woman. Adele saw him bend, saw him open Noreen's clenched hand, saw him examine the trail mix that fell to the floor. Cleve said, "Heart failure. I've seen them go like this before," but although Lynley nodded, he looked not at Cleve but at the group, his brown eyes speculating upon each one of them as they left the room. Ralph Tucker sank onto a delicate chair. Thomas Lynley's companion went to him, murmured a few words, put her hand on his shoulder.

Then the door closed behind them and the group was in the drawing room, being asked to examine the pendant plasterwork of its remarkable ceiling. It was called the King Edward Drawing Room, their much-subdued guide told them, its name taken from the statue of Edward IV that stood over the mantelpiece. It was a three-quarter-size statue, she explained, not life-size, for unlike most men of his time, Edward IV was well over six feet tall. In fact, when he rode into London on February 26, 1460 . . .

Adele did not see how the young woman could go on. There was something indecent about being asked to admire chandeliers, flocked wallpaper, eighteenth-century furniture, Chinese vases, and a French chimneypiece in the face of Noreen Tucker's death. Adele had certainly disliked Noreen, but death was death and it seemed that, out of respect to her passing, they might well have abandoned the rest of the tour and returned to Cambridge. She couldn't understand why Thomas Lynley had not instructed them to do so. Surely it would have been far more humane than to expect them to traipse round the rest of the house as if nothing had happened.

But even Ralph had wanted them to continue. "You go on," he had said to Victoria when she had attempted to remain with him in the long gallery. "People are depending on you." He made it sound as if a tour of Abinger Manor were akin to a battle upon whose outcome the fate of a nation depended. It was just the sort of comment that would appeal to Victoria. So the tour continued.

Not that it would have been allowed to disband. Something in Thomas Lynley's face indicated that.

Everyone was restless. The air was close. Composure seemed brittle. Adele had no doubt that she was not the only person longing to escape from Abinger Manor.

The guide was asking for any questions about the room. Dolly cooperatively inquired if King Edward's statue was bronze. It was. She photographed it. The tour moved on.

There was a murmur when Cleve Houghton rejoined them in the winter dining room.

"They've taken her," he said in a low voice to Adele.

"And that man? The policeman?"

"Still in the gallery when I left. He's put out a call for the local police."

"Why?" Adele asked. "I saw him looking at . . . Cleve, you don't . . . she seemed healthy, didn't she?"

Cleve's eyes narrowed. "I know a heart attack when I see one. Jesus, what are you thinking?"

Adele didn't know what she was thinking. She only knew that she had recognized something on Lynley's face when he had looked up from examining Noreen Tucker's trail mix. Consternation, suspicion, anger, outrage. Something had been there. If that were the case, then it could only mean one thing. Adele felt her stomach churn. She began to evaluate her fellow students in an entirely new way: as potential killers.

Frances Clearey seemed to have been shaken from her morning's fury at her husband. She was close at Sam's side, pressed to his arm. Perhaps Noreen's death had allowed her to see how fleeting life was, how insignificant its quarrels and concerns were once one came to terms with its finitude. Or perhaps she simply had nothing further to worry about now that Noreen was eliminated.

She hadn't been at breakfast, Adele recalled, so she could have slipped into Noreen's room and put something into her trail mix. Especially if she knew that Sam had spent the night with Noreen. Removing a rival to a man's love seemed an adequate motive for murder.

But Sam himself had also not been at breakfast. So he, too, had access to Noreen's supply of food. If Noreen had known with whom he had spent the night—and surely that's what she had been hinting at this morning—perhaps Sam had seen the need to be rid of her. Especially if she had been the woman herself.

It was hard to believe. Yet at the same time, looking at Sam, Adele could see how Noreen's death had affected him. Beneath his tan, his face was worn, his mouth set. His eyes seemed cloudy. In each room, they alighted first upon Dolly, as if her beauty were an anodyne for him, but then they slid away.

Dolly herself had come into breakfast late, so she also had access to Noreen's supply of nuts. But Noreen had not given Dolly an overt reason to harm her, and surely Noreen's gossip about the girl—even if Dolly had heard it, which was doubtful—would only have amused her.

As it would have amused Cleve Houghton. And pleased him. And swelled his ego substantially. Indeed, Cleve had every reason to keep Noreen alive. She had been doing wonders to build repute of his sexual prowess. On the other hand, Cleve had come into breakfast late, so he, too, had access to the Tuckers' room.

Howard Breen seemed to be the only one who hadn't had time to get to Noreen's trail mix. Except, Adele remembered, he had left breakfast early and she hadn't been able to find him.

Everyone, then, had the opportunity to mix something in with the nuts, raisins, and dried fruit. But what had that something been? And how on earth had someone managed to get hold of it? Surely one didn't walk into a Cambridge chemist's shop and ask for a quick-acting poison. So whoever tampered with the mix had to have experience with poisons, had to know what to expect.

They were in the library when Thomas Lynley and his lady rejoined them. He ran his eyes over everyone in the room. His companion did the same. He said something to her quietly, and the two of them separated, taking positions in different parts of the crowd. Neither of them paid the slightest attention to anything other than to the people. But they gave their full attention to them.

From the library they went into the chapel, accompanied only by the sounds of their own footsteps, the echoing voice of the guide, the snapping of cameras. Lynley moved through the group, saying nothing to anyone save to his companion, with whom he spoke a few words at the door. Again they separated.

From the chapel they went into the armory. From there into the billiard room. From there to the music room. From there down two flights of stairs and into the kitchen. The buttery beyond it had been turned into a gift shop. The Germans made for this. The Americans began to do likewise.

Adele could not believe that Lynley intended to allow them to escape so easily. She was not surprised when he spoke.

"If I might see everyone, please," he said as they began to scatter. "If you'll just stay here in the kitchen for a moment."

Protests rose from the German group. The Americans said nothing.

"We've a problem to consider," Lynley told them, "regarding Noreen Tucker's death."

"Problem?" Behind Adele, Cleve Houghton spoke. Others chimed in.

"What do you want with us anyway?"

"What's going on?"

"It was heart failure," Cleve asserted. "I've seen enough of that to tell you—"

"As have I," a heavily accented voice said. The speaker was a member of the German party, and he looked none too pleased that their tour was once again being disrupted. "I am a doctor. I, too, have seen heart failure. I know what I see."

Lynley extended his hand. In his palm lay a half dozen seeds. "It looked like heart failure. That's what an alkaloid does. It paralyzes the heart in a manner of minutes. These are yew, by the way."

"Yew?"

"What was yew—"

"But she wouldn't—"

Adele kept her eyes on Lynley's palm. Seeds. Plants. The connection was horrible. She avoided looking at the one person in the kitchen who would know beyond a doubt the potential for harm contained in a bit of yew.

"Surely those came from the potpourri," Victoria Wilder-Scott said. "It spilled all over the carpet when Mrs. Tucker fell."

Lynley shook his head. "They were mixed in with the nuts in her hand. And the bag her husband carried was filled with them. She was murdered."

The Germans protested heartily at this. The doctor led

them. "You have no business with us. This woman was a stranger. I insist that we be allowed to leave."

"Of course," Lynley answered. "As soon as we solve the problem of the silver."

"What on earth are you talking about?"

"It appears that one of you took the opportunity of the chaos in the long gallery to remove two pieces of rococo silver from the table by the fireplace. They're salt cellars. Very small. And definitely missing. This isn't my jurisdiction, of course, but until the local police arrive to start their inquiries into Mrs. Tucker's death, I'd like to take care of this small detail of the silver myself."

"What are you going to do?" Frances Clearey asked.

"Do you plan to keep us here until one of us admits to something?" the German doctor scoffed. "You cannot search us without some authority."

"That's correct," Lynley said. "I can't search you. Unless you agree to be searched."

Feet shuffled. A throat cleared. Urgent conversation was conducted in German. Someone rustled papers in a notebook.

Cleve Houghton was the first to speak. He looked over the group. "Hell, I have no objection."

"But the women . . ." Victoria pointed out.

Lynley nodded to his companion, who was standing by a display of copper kettles at the edge of the group. "This is Lady Helen Clyde," he told them. "She'll search the women."

As one body, they turned to Lynley's companion. Resting upon them, her dark eyes were friendly. Her expression was gentle. What an absurdity it would be to resist cooperating with such a lovely creature.

The search was carried out in two rooms: the women in the scullery and the men in a warming room across the hall. In the scullery, Lady Helen made a thorough job of it. She watched each woman undress, redress. She emptied pockets, handbags, canvas totes. She checked the lining of raincoats. She opened umbrellas. All the time she chatted in a manner designed to put them at ease. She asked the Americans about their class, about Cambridge, about great houses they had seen and where they were from. She confided in the Germans about spending two weeks in the Black Forest one summer and confessed to an embarrassed dislike of the out-of-doors. She never mentioned the word *murder*. Aside from the operation in which they were engaged, they might have been new acquaintances talking over tea. Yet Adele saw for herself that Lady Helen was quite efficient at her job, for all her friendliness and good breeding. If she didn't work for the police herself—and her relationship with Lynley certainly did not suggest that she was employed by Scotland Yard—she certainly had knowledge of their procedures.

Nonetheless, she found nothing. Nor, apparently, did Lynley. When the two groups were gathered once again in the kitchen, Adele saw him shake his head at Lady Helen. If the silver had been taken, it was not being carried by anyone. Even Victoria Wilder-Scott and the tour guide had been searched.

Lynley told them to wait in the tearoom. He turned back to the stairway at the far end of the kitchen.

"Where's he going now?" Frances Clearey asked.

"He'll have to look for the silver in the rest of the house," Adele said.

"But that could take forever!" Dolly wailed.

"It doesn't matter, does it? We're going to have to wait to talk to the local police anyway."

"It was heart failure," Cleve said. "There's no silver missing. It's probably being cleaned somewhere."

Adele fell to the back of the crowd as they walked across the pebbled courtyard. A sense of unease plucked at her mind. It had been with her much of the morning, hidden like a secondary message between the lines of Noreen Tucker's words, trying to fight its way to the surface of her consciousness in the minibus, lying just beyond the range of her vision ever since they had arrived at the manor. Like the children's game of What's Wrong With This Picture, there was a distortion somewhere. She could feel it distinctly. She simply couldn't see it.

Her thoughts tumbled upon one another without connection

or reason, like images produced by a kaleidoscope. There were yew hedges in the courtyard of St. Stephen's College. Sam and Frances Clearey had had a fight. The walls have ears. The silver was available. It was pictured in their text. It was in the brochures. They'd seen both in advance. Dolly wanted Cleve. She loved antiques. Sam Clearey liked women, liked the blonde from the Dickens class, liked . . .

Once again Adele saw Lady Helen go through their belongings. She saw her empty, probe, touch, leave nothing unexamined. She saw her shake her head at Lynley. She saw Lynley frown.

The two groups entered the tearoom and segregated themselves from each other. The Americans took positions at a refectory table at the far end. The Germans lined up for coffee and cakes.

"Victoria, can we go back to Cambridge?" Frances asked. "I mean, when this is over? We've another house to see today, but we can drop it, can't we?"

Victoria was hesitant. "Ralph did specifically want us to—"

"Screw Ralph Tucker!" Sam said. "Come on, Victoria, we've had it."

"There's the minibus to consider, the driver's salary . . ."

"Couldn't we just chip in some money and tip him or something?" Dolly set her camera on the table in front of her. She folded her hands around it, her shoulders slumped. "I mean . . . oh, I guess that's dumb. Forget it."

And there it was in an instant. Right before her. Adele saw it at last. She knew what Noreen Tucker had been saying during their walk to the bus. She knew the source of her own disquiet on the journey to Abinger Manor. She acknowledged what she had seen without seeing from the moment they had arrived at the manor. Thirty-six was the key, but it had been exceeded long ago. The knowledge brought to Adele an attendant rush of wrenching illness. Thomas Lynley had made an assumption from the facts at hand.

But Lynley was wrong.

She pushed herself to her feet and left the group. Someone called after her, but she continued on her way. She found

Lynley in the drawing room, directing three workmen who were crawling across the floor.

How can I do this? she asked herself. And then, *Why? With the future a blank slate upon which nothing but hope and success were written. Why?*

Lynley looked up. Lady Helen Clyde did likewise. Adele did not even have to speak to them. They joined her at once and followed her to the tearoom.

"What's going on?" Cleve asked.

Adele didn't look at him. "Dolly, give the inspector your camera."

Dolly's blue eyes widened. "I don't understand."

"Give him the camera, Dolly. Let him look at the lens."

"But you—"

Lynley lifted the camera from the girl's shoulder. Lined along its strap were containers for film. All of them were empty. Adele had seen that earlier, had seen it and had thought no more about it than she had thought about the fact that there had been no film in Dolly's shoulder bag. Nor had there been any in her pockets. She'd been shooting pictures all morning with no film in her camera at all, in order to conceal her real reason for carrying the camera with her to the manor in the first place.

Lynley twisted off the macro-zoom lens. It was useless, hollowed. Two pieces of rococo silver tumbled out.

Howard dropped into the seat next to Adele. "You okay?"

"Okay." She didn't want to talk about it. She felt like a Judas. She wanted to go home. She tried to keep from thinking about Dolly being led off by the police.

"How did you figure Dolly?"

"She took too many pictures. She would have had to change film, but she never did that. Because there was no film."

"But Noreen. Why did Dolly . . ."

Adele's limbs felt numb. "She didn't care one way or the other about Noreen. Probably intended the seeds to make Noreen good and sick, not kill her. She just needed a diversion to get to the silver."

"I don't get it. How could she possibly have known what yew seeds do?"

"Sam. He probably didn't know what he was telling her or why she was asking. He probably didn't think of anything except what it felt like to be his age and to be in bed with someone like Dolly." Even that was hard to bear. Knowing that Dolly's solicitous conversation with Frances Clearey about her marriage had been nothing more than part of the game. Just another diversion, just another lie.

"*Sam* and Dolly?" Howard looked across the aisle to where Cleve Houghton lounged in his seat, eyes half closed. "I thought Cleve . . . when Noreen was telling us that Cleve was talking last night about seducing women . . ."

"She was talking to me. About me. Cleve wasn't with Dolly last night, Howard." Adele looked out the window, said nothing more. After a moment, she felt Howard leave the seat and move away.

I will bury you, Bob, she had thought with Cleve Houghton. *I will end it between us this way.* So she had drunk in the college bar with him, she had walked on the backs and listened to him talk, she had pretended to find him intriguing and delightful, a man of passion, a soul mate, a replacement for Bob. And when he wanted her, she had obliged. Hurried grappling, urgent coupling, a body in her bed. To feel alive, to feel wanted, to feel a creature of worth. But not to bury Bob. It hadn't worked that way.

"Hey." Adele pretended not to hear him, but Cleve crossed the aisle and dropped into the seat. He carried a flask in his hand. "You look like you need a drink. Hell, I need one." He drank, spoke again in a lower voice. "Tonight?"

Adele raised her eyes to his face, trying and failing to force his features into the shape of another man's.

"Well?" he said.

Of course, she thought. Why not? What difference did it make when life was so fleeting and youth without meaning?

"Sure," she said. "Tonight."

Sue Grafton's energetic private eye Kinsey Millhone plies her trade from the coastal town of Santa Teresa, which clever Californians might think is very like Santa Barbara. Kinsey's combination of wit and grit have endeared her to a multitude of readers as her exploits take her through the alphabet in "A" is for Alibi, "B" is for Burglar (winner of a Shamus award), "C" is for Corpse (A, B, and C are all winners of Anthonys), "D" is for Deadbeat, "E" is for Evidence, and "F" is for Fugitive.

In "A Poison That Leaves No Trace," Kinsey advises a client there is no such thing—until she discovers the toxic nature of certain bitter pills.

A POISON THAT LEAVES NO TRACE

by Sue Grafton

THE WOMAN WAS waiting outside my office when I arrived that morning. She was short and quite plump, wearing jeans in a size I've never seen on the rack. Her blouse was tunic-length, ostensibly to disguise her considerable rear end. Someone must have told her never to wear horizontal stripes, so the bold red-and-blue bands ran diagonally across her torso with a dizzying effect. Big red canvas tote, matching canvas wedgies. Her face was round, seamless, and smooth, her hair a uniformly dark shade that suggested a rinse. She might have been any age between forty and sixty. "You're not Kinsey Millhone," she said as I approached.

"Actually, I am. Would you like to come in?" I unlocked the door and stepped back so she could pass in front of me. She was giving me the once-over, as if my appearance was as remarkable to her as hers was to me.

She took a seat, keeping her tote squarely on her lap. I went around to my side of the desk, pausing to open the French doors before I sat down. "What can I help you with?"

She stared at me openly. "Well, I don't know. I thought you'd be a man. What kind of name is Kinsey? I never heard such a thing."

"My mother's maiden name. I take it you're in the market for a private investigator."

"I guess you could say that. I'm Shirese Dunaway, but everybody calls me Sis. Exactly how long have you been doing this?" Her tone was a perfect mating of skepticism and distrust.

"Six years in May. I was with the police department for two years before that. If my being a woman bothers you, I can recommend another agency. It won't offend me in the least."

"Well, I might as well talk to you as long as I'm here. I drove all the way up from Orange County. You don't charge for a consultation, I hope."

"Not at all. My regular fee is thirty dollars an hour plus expenses, but only if I believe I can be of help. What sort of problem are you dealing with?"

"Thirty dollars an hour! My stars. I had no idea it would cost so *much*."

"Lawyers charge a hundred and twenty," I said with a shrug.

"I know, but that's in case of a lawsuit. Contingency, or whatever they call that. Thirty dollars an *hour* . . ."

I closed my mouth and let her work it out for herself. I didn't want to get into an argument with the woman in the first five minutes of our relationship. I tuned her out, watching her lips move while she decided what to do.

"The problem is my sister," she said at long last. "Here, look at this." She handed me a little clipping from the Santa Teresa newspaper. The death notice read: "Crispin, Margery, beloved mother of Justine, passed away on December 10. Private arrangements. Wynington-Blake Mortuary."

"Nearly two months ago," I remarked.

"Nobody even told me she was sick! That's the point," Sis Dunaway snapped. "I wouldn't know to this day if a former neighbor hadn't spotted this and cut it out." She tended to speak in an indignant tone regardless of the subject.

"You just received this?"

"Well, no. It come back in January, but of course I couldn't drop everything and rush right up. This is the first chance I've had. You can probably appreciate that, upset as I was."

"Absolutely," I said. "When did you last talk to Margery?"

"I don't remember the exact date. It had to be eight or ten years back. You can imagine my shock! To get something like this out of a clear blue sky."

I shook my head. "Terrible," I murmured. "Have you talked to your niece?"

She gestured dismissively. "That Justine's a mess. Marge had her hands full with that one," she said. "I stopped over to her place and you should have seen the look I got. I said, 'Justine, whatever in the world did Margery die of?' And you know what she said? Said, 'Aunt Sis, her heart give out.' Well, I knew that was bull the minute she said it. We have never had heart trouble in our family. . . ."

She went on for a while about what everybody'd died of; Mom, Dad, Uncle Buster, Rita Sue. We're talking cancer, lung disorders, an aneurysm or two. Sure enough, no heart trouble. I was making sympathetic noises, just to keep the tale afloat until she got to the point. I jotted down a few notes, though I never did quite understand how Rita Sue was related. Finally, I said, "Is it your feeling there was something unusual in your sister's death?"

She pursed her lips and lowered her gaze. "Let's put it this way. I can smell a rat. I'd be willing to *bet* Justine had a hand in it."

"Why would she do that?"

"Well, Marge had that big insurance policy. The one Harley took out in 1966. If that's not a motive for murder, I don't know what is." She sat back in her chair, content that she'd made her case.

"Harley?"

"Her husband . . . until he passed on, of course. They took out policies on each other and after he went, she kept up the premiums on hers. Justine was made the beneficiary. Marge never remarried and with Justine on the policy, I guess she'll get all the money and do I don't know what. It just doesn't seem right. She's been a sneak all her natural life. A regular con artist. She's been in jail four times! My sister talked till she was blue in the face, but she never could get Justine to straighten up her act.''

"How much money are we talking about?"

"A hundred thousand dollars," she said. "Furthermore, them two never did get along. Fought like cats and dogs since the day Justine was born. Competitive? My God. Always trying to get the better of each other. Justine as good as told me they had a falling-out not two months before her mother died! The two had not exchanged a word since the day Marge got mad and stomped off.''

"They lived together?"

"Well, yes, until this big fight. Next thing you know, Marge is dead. You tell me there's not something funny going on.''

"Have you talked to the police?"

"How can I do that? I don't have any *proof*."

"What about the insurance company? Surely, if there were something irregular about Marge's death, the claims investigator would have picked up on it.''

"Oh, honey, you'd think so, but you know how it is. Once a claim's been paid, the insurance company doesn't want to hear. Admit they made a mistake? Uh-uh, no thanks. Too much trouble going back through all the paperwork. Besides, Justine would probably turn around and sue 'em within an inch of their life. They'd rather turn a deaf ear and write the money off.''

"When was the claim paid?"

"A week ago, they said."

I stared at her for a moment, considering. "I don't know what to tell you, Ms. Dunaway. . . .''

"Call me Sis. I don't go for that Ms. bull."

"All right, Sis. If you're really convinced Justine's implicated in her mother's death, of course I'll try to help. I just don't want to waste your time.''

"I can appreciate that," she said.

I stirred in my seat. "Look, I'll tell you what let's do. Why don't you pay me for two hours of my time. If I don't come up with anything concrete in that period, we can have another conversation and you can decide then if you want me to proceed.''

''Sixty dollars,'' she said.

''That's right. Two hours.''

''Well, all right. I guess I can do that.'' She opened her tote and peeled six tens off a roll of bills she'd secured with a rubber band. I wrote out an abbreviated version of a standard contract. She said she'd be staying in town overnight and gave me the telephone number at the motel where she'd checked in. She handed me the death notice. I made sure I had her sister's full name and the exact date of her death and told her I'd be in touch.

My first stop was the Hall of Records at the Santa Teresa County Courthouse two and a half blocks away. I filled out a copy order, supplying the necessary information, and paid seven bucks in cash. An hour later, I returned to pick up the certified copy of Margery Crispin's death certificate. Cause of death was listed as a ''myocardial infarction.'' The certificate was signed by Dr. Yee, one of the contract pathologists out at the county morgue. If Marge Crispin had been the victim of foul play, it was hard to believe Dr. Yee wouldn't have spotted it.

I swung back by the office and picked up my car, driving over to Wynington-Blake, the mortuary listed in the newspaper clipping. I asked for Mr. Sharonson, whom I'd met when I was working on another case. He was wearing a somber charcoal-gray suit, his tone of voice carefully modulated to reflect the solemnity of his work. When I mentioned Marge Crispin, a shadow crossed his face.

''You remember the woman?''

''Oh, yes,'' he said. He closed his mouth then, but the look he gave me was eloquent.

I wondered if funeral home employees took a loyalty oath, vowing never to divulge a single fact about the dead. I thought I'd prime the pump a bit. Men are worse gossips than women once you get 'em going. ''Mrs. Crispin's sister was in my office a little while ago and she seems to think there was something . . . uh, irregular about the woman's death.''

I could see Mr. Sharonson formulate his response. "I wouldn't say there was anything *irregular* about the woman's death, but there was certainly something sordid about the circumstances."

"Oh?" said I.

He lowered his voice, glancing around to make certain we couldn't be overheard. "The two were estranged. Hadn't spoken for months as I understand it. The woman died alone in a seedy hotel on lower State Street. She drank."

"Nooo," I said, conveying disapproval and disbelief.

"Oh, yes," he said. "The police picked up the body, but she wasn't identified for weeks. If it hadn't been for the article in the paper, her daughter might not have ever known."

"What article?"

"Oh, you know the one. There's that columnist for the local paper who does all those articles about the homeless. He did a write-up about the poor woman. 'Alone in Death' I think it was called. He talked about how pathetic this woman was. Apparently, when Ms. Crispin read the article, she began to suspect it might be her mother. That's when she went out there to take a look."

"Must have been a shock," I said. "The woman did die of natural causes?"

"Oh, yes."

"No evidence of trauma, foul play, anything like that?"

"No, no, no. I tended her myself and I know they ran toxicology tests. I guess at first they thought it might be acute alcohol poisoning, but it turned out to be her heart."

I quizzed him on a number of possibilities, but I couldn't come up with anything out of the ordinary. I thanked him for his time, got back in my car, and drove over to the trailer park where Justine Crispin lived.

The trailer itself had seen better days. It was moored in a dirt patch with a wooden crate for an outside step. I knocked on the door, which opened about an inch to show a short strip of round face peering out at me. "Yes?"

"Are you Justine Crispin?"

"Yes."

"I hope I'm not bothering you. My name is Kinsey Millhone. I'm an old friend of your mother's and I just heard she passed away.''

The silence was cautious. ''Who'd you hear that from?''

I showed her the clipping. ''Someone sent me this. I couldn't believe my eyes. I didn't even know she was sick.''

Justine's eyes darkened with suspicion. ''When did you see her last?''

I did my best to imitate Sis Dunaway's folksy tone. ''Oh, gee. Must have been last summer. I moved away in June and it was probably some time around then because I remember giving her my address. It was awfully sudden, wasn't it?''

''Her heart give out.''

''Well, the poor thing, and she was such a love.'' I wondered if I'd laid it on too thick. Justine was staring at me like I'd come to the wrong place. ''Would you happen to know if she got my last note?'' I asked.

''I wouldn't know anything about that.''

''Because I wasn't sure what to do about the money.''

''She owed you money?''

''No, no. I owed *her* . . . which is why I wrote.''

Justine hesitated. ''How much?''

''Well, it wasn't much,'' I said, with embarrassment. ''Six hundred dollars, but she was such a doll to lend it to me and then I felt so bad when I couldn't pay her back right away. I asked her if I could wait and pay her this month, but then I never heard. Now I don't know what to do.''

I could sense the shift in her attitude. Greed seems to do that in record time. ''You could pay it to me and I could see it went into her estate,'' she said helpfully.

''Oh, I don't want to put you to any trouble.''

''I don't mind,'' she said. ''You want to come in?''

''I shouldn't. You're probably busy and you've already been so nice. _ . .''

''I can take a few minutes.''

''Well. If you're sure,'' I said.

Justine held the door open and I stepped into the trailer, where I got my first clear look at her. This girl was probably thirty pounds overweight with listless brown hair pulled into an oily ponytail. Like Sis, she was decked out in a pair of jeans, with an oversize T-shirt hanging almost to her knees. It was clear big butts ran in the family. She shoved some junk aside so I could sit down on the banquette, a fancy word for the ripped plastic seat that extended along one wall in the kitchenette.

"Did she suffer much?" I asked.

"Doctor said not. He said it was quick, as far as he could tell. Her heart probably seized up and she fell down dead before she could draw a breath."

"It must have been just terrible for you."

Her cheeks flushed with guilt. "You know, her and me had a falling out."

"Really? Well, I'm sorry to hear that. Of course, she always said you two had your differences. I hope it wasn't anything serious."

"She drank. I begged her and begged her to give it up, but she wouldn't pay me no mind," Justine said.

"Did she 'go' here at home?"

She shook her head. "In a welfare hotel. Down on her luck. Drink had done her in. If only I'd known . . . if only she'd reached out."

I thought she was going to weep, but she couldn't quite manage it. I clutched her hand. "She was too proud," I said.

"I guess that's what it was. I've been thinking to make some kind of contribution to AA, or something like that. You know, in her name."

"A Marge Crispin Memorial Fund," I suggested.

"Like that, yes. I was thinking this money you're talking about might be a start."

"That's a beautiful thought. I'm going right out to the car for my checkbook so I can write you a check."

It was a relief to get out into the fresh air again. I'd never heard so much horsepuckey in all my life. Still, it hardly constituted proof she was a murderess.

I hopped in my car and headed for a pay phone, spotting one in a gas station half a block away. I pulled change out of the bottom of my handbag and dialed Sis Dunaway's motel room. She was not very happy to hear my report.

"You didn't find anything?" she said. "Are you positive?"

"Well, of course I'm not positive. All I'm saying is that so far, there's no evidence that anything's amiss. If Justine contributed to her mother's death, she was damned clever about it. I gather the autopsy didn't show a thing."

"Maybe it was some kind of poison that leaves no trace."

"Uh, Sis? I hate to tell you this, but there really isn't such a poison that I ever heard of. I know it's a common fantasy, but there's just no such thing."

Her tone turned stubborn. "But it's possible. You have to admit that. There could be such a thing. It might be from South America . . . darkest Africa, someplace like that."

Oh, boy. We were really tripping out on this one. I squinted at the receiver. "How would Justine acquire the stuff?"

"How do I know? I'm not going to set here and solve the whole case for you! You're the one gets paid thirty dollars an hour, not me."

"Do you want me to pursue it?"

"Not if you mean to charge me an arm and a leg!" she said. "Listen here, I'll pay sixty dollars more, but you better come up with something or I want my money back."

She hung up before I could protest. How could she get her money back when she hadn't paid this portion? I stood in the phone booth and thought about things. In spite of myself, I'll admit I was hooked. Sis Dunaway might harbor a lot of foolish ideas, but her conviction was unshakable. Add to that the fact that Justine was lying about *something* and you have the kind of situation I can't walk away from.

I drove back to the trailer park and eased my car into a shady spot just across the street. Within moments, Justine appeared in a banged-up white Pinto, trailing smoke out of the tail pipe. Following her wasn't hard. I just hung my nose out the window and kept an eye on the haze. She drove over to Milagro Street to the branch office of a savings and loan. I pulled into a parking spot a few doors down and followed her in, keeping well out of sight. She was dealing with the branch manager, who eventually walked her over to a teller and authorized the cashing of a quite large check, judging from the number of bills the teller counted out.

Justine departed moments later, clutching her handbag protectively. I would have been willing to bet she'd been cashing that insurance check. She drove back to the trailer where she made a brief stop, probably to drop the money off.

She got back in her car and drove out of the trailer park. I followed discreetly as she headed into town. She pulled into a public parking lot and I eased in after her, finding an empty slot far enough away to disguise my purposes. So far, she didn't seem to have any idea she was being tailed. I kept my distance as she cut through to State Street and walked up a block to Santa Teresa Travel. I pretended to peruse the posters in the window while I watched her chat with the travel agent sitting at a desk just inside the front door. The two transacted business, the agent handing over what apparently were prearranged tickets. Justine wrote out a check. I busied myself at a newspaper rack, extracting a paper as she came out again. She walked down State Street half a block to a hobby shop where she purchased one of life's ugliest plastic floral wreaths. Busy little lady, this one, I thought.

She emerged from the hobby shop and headed down a side street, moving into the front entrance of a beauty salon. A surreptitious glance through the window showed her, moments later, in a green plastic cape, having a long conversation with the stylist about a cut. I checked my watch. It was almost twelve-thirty. I scooted back to the travel agency and waited until I saw Justine's travel agent leave the premises for lunch. As soon as she was out of sight, I went in, glancing at the nameplate on the edge of her desk.

The blond agent across the aisle caught my eye and smiled.

"What happened to Kathleen?" I asked.

"She went out to lunch. You just missed her. Is there something I can help you with?"

"Gee, I hope so. I picked up some tickets a little while ago and now I can't find the itinerary she tucked in the envelope. Is there any way you could run me a copy real quick? I'm in a hurry and I really can't afford to wait until she gets back."

"Sure, no problem. What's the name?"

"Justine Crispin," I said.

I found the nearest public phone and dialed Sis's motel

room again. "Catch this," I said. "At four o'clock, Justine takes off for Los Angeles. From there, she flies to Mexico City."

"Well, that little shit."

"It gets worse. It's one-way."

"I knew it! I just knew she was up to no good. Where is she now?"

"Getting her hair done. She went to the bank first and cashed a big check—"

"I bet it was the insurance."

"That'd be my guess."

"She's got all that money *on* her?"

"Well, no. She stopped by the trailer first and then went and picked up her plane ticket. I think she intends to stop by the cemetery and put a wreath on Marge's grave. . . ."

"I can't stand this. I just can't stand it. She's going to take all that money and make a mockery of Marge's death."

"Hey, Sis, come on. If Justine's listed as the beneficiary, there's nothing you can do."

"That's what you think. I'll make her pay for this, I swear to God I will!" Sis slammed the phone down.

I could feel my heart sink. Uh-oh. I tried to think whether I'd mentioned the name of the beauty salon. I had visions of Sis descending on Justine with a tommy gun. I loitered uneasily outside the shop, watching traffic in both directions. There was no sign of Sis. Maybe she was going to wait until Justine went out to the gravesite before she mowed her down.

At two-fifteen, Justine came out of the beauty shop and passed me on the street. She was nearly unrecognizable. Her hair had been cut and permed and it fell in soft curls around her freshly made-up face. The beautician had found ways to bring out her eyes, subtly heightening her coloring with a touch of blusher on her cheeks. She looked like a million bucks—or a hundred thousand, at any rate. She was in a jaunty mood, paying more attention to her own reflection in the passing store windows than she was to me, hovering half a block behind.

She returned to the parking lot and retrieved her Pinto, easing into the flow of traffic as it moved up State. I tucked in a few cars back, all the while scanning for some sign of Sis. I couldn't imagine what she'd try to do, but as mad as she was, I had to guess she had some scheme in the works.

Fifteen minutes later, we were turning into the trailer park, Justine leading while I lollygagged along behind. I had already used up the money Sis had authorized, but by this time I had my own stake in the outcome. For all I knew, I was going to end up protecting Justine from an assassination attempt. She stopped by the trailer just long enough to load her bags in the car and then she drove out to the Santa Teresa Memorial Park, which was out by the airport.

The cemetery was deserted, a sunny field of gravestones among flowering shrubs. When the road forked, I watched Justine wind up the lane to the right while I headed left, keeping an eye on her car, which I could see across a wide patch of grass. She parked and got out, carrying the wreath to an oblong depression in the ground where a temporary marker had been set, awaiting the permanent monument. She rested the wreath against the marker and stood there looking down. She seemed awfully exposed and I couldn't help but wish she'd duck down some to grieve. Sis was probably crouched somewhere with a knife between her teeth, ready to leap out and stab Justine in the neck.

Respects paid, Justine got back into her car and drove to the airport where she checked in for her flight. By now, I was feeling baffled. She had less than an hour before her plane was scheduled to depart and there was still no sign of Sis. If there was going to be a showdown, it was bound to happen soon. I ambled into the gift shop and inserted myself between the wall and a book rack, watching Justine through windows nearly obscured by a display of Santa Teresa T-shirts. She sat on a bench and calmly read a paperback.

What was going on here?

Sis Dunaway had seemed hell-bent on avenging Marge's death, but where was she? Had she gone to the cops? I kept one eye on the clock and one eye on Justine. Whatever Sis was up to, she had better do it quick. Finally, mere minutes before the flight was due to be called, I left the newsstand, crossed the gate area, and took a seat beside Justine. "Hi," I said, "Nice permanent. Looks good."

She glanced at me and then did a classic double take. "What are you doing here?"

"Keeping an eye on you."

"What for?"

"I thought someone should see you off. I suspect your Aunt Sis is en route, so I decided to keep you company until she gets here."

"Aunt *Sis*?" she said, incredulously.

"I gotta warn you, she's not convinced your mother had a heart attack."

"What are you talking about? Aunt Sis is dead."

I could feel myself smirk. "Yeah, sure. Since when?"

"Five years ago."

"Bullshit."

"It's not bullshit. An aneurysm burst and she dropped in her tracks."

"Come on," I scoffed.

"It's the truth," she said emphatically. By that time, she'd recovered her composure and she went on the offensive. "Where's my money? You said you'd write a check for six hundred bucks."

"Completely dead?" I asked.

The loudspeaker came on. "May I have your attention, please. United Flight 3440 for Los Angeles is now ready for boarding at Gate Five. Please have your boarding pass available and prepare for security check."

Justine began to gather up her belongings. I'd been wondering how she was going to get all that cash through the security checkpoint, but one look at her lumpy waistline and it was obvious she'd strapped on a money belt. She picked up her carry-on, her shoulder bag, her jacket, and her paperback and clopped, in spike heels, over to the line of waiting passengers.

I followed, befuddled, reviewing the entire sequence of events. It had all happened today. Within hours. It wasn't like I was suffering brain damage or memory loss. And I hadn't seen a ghost. Sis had come to my office and laid out the whole tale about Marge and Justine. She'd told me all about their relationship, Justine's history as a con, the way the two women tried to outdo each other, the insurance, Marge's death. How could a murder have gotten past Dr. Yee? Unless the woman wasn't murdered, I thought suddenly.

Oh.

Once I saw it in *that* light, it was obvious.

Justine got in line between a young man with a duffel bag and a woman toting a cranky baby. There was some delay up ahead while the ticket agent got set. The line started to move and Justine advanced a step with me right beside her.

"I understand you and your mother had quite a competitive relationship."

"What's it to you," she said. She kept her eyes averted, facing dead ahead, willing the line to move so she could get away from me.

"I understand you were always trying to get the better of each other."

"What's your point?" she said, annoyed.

I shrugged. "I figure you read the article about the unidentified dead woman in the welfare hotel. You went out to the morgue and claimed the body as your mom's. The two of you agreed to split the insurance money, but your mother got worried about a double cross, which is exactly what this is."

"You don't know what you're talking about."

The line moved up again and I stayed right next to her. "She hired me to keep an eye on you, so when I realized you were leaving town, I called her and told her what was going on. She really hit the roof and I thought she'd charge right out, but so far there's been no sign of her. . . ."

Justine showed her ticket to the agent and he motioned her on. She moved through the metal detector without setting it off.

I gave the agent a smile. "Saying good-bye to a friend," I said, and passed through the wooden arch right after she did. She was picking up the pace, anxious to reach the plane.

I was still talking, nearly jogging to keep up with her. "I couldn't figure out why she wasn't trying to stop you and then I realized what she must have done—"

"Get away from me. I don't want to talk to you."

"She took the money, Justine. There's probably nothing in the belt but old papers. She had plenty of time to make the switch while you were getting your hair done."

"Ha, ha," she said sarcastically. "Tell me another one."

I stopped in my tracks. "All right. That's all I'm gonna say. I just didn't want you to reach Mexico City and find yourself flat broke."

"Blow it out your buns," she hissed. She showed her boarding pass to the woman at the gate and passed on through. I could hear her spike heels tip-tapping out of ear range.

I reversed myself, walked back through the gate area and out to the walled exterior courtyard, where I could see the planes through a windbreak of protective glass. Justine crossed the tarmac to the waiting plane, her shoulders set. I didn't think she'd heard me, but then I saw her hand stray to her waist. She walked a few more steps and then halted, dumping her belongings in a pile at her feet. She pulled her shirt up and checked the money belt. At that distance, I saw her mouth open, but it took a second for the shrieks of outrage to reach me.

Ah, well, I thought. Sometimes a mother's love is like a poison that leaves no trace. You bop along through life, thinking you've got it made, and next thing you know, you're dead.

ANDREW, MY SON

by Joyce Harrington

"**D**O YOU HEAR the cats?" Andrew asks me. He is standing by the window, peering out into the deep winter darkness.

I have heard no cats, but I listen carefully. If I could make my ears twitch, I would. It's always best, with Andrew, to put on a good show.

I make a noncommittal sound, "Um-hum," which could mean yes. Or no. A mistake. Andrew can't abide inattention or ambivalence.

"Listen, will you!" he shouts. "They're out there yowling. I'll put poison out. I swear I will." He paces in front of the fireplace. The flickering logs light his narrow face from below. His eyes are fierce, feral. This is my son.

"Alley cats," I murmur. "A female in heat. They're fighting over her. It's what they do." I still haven't heard them.

"Disgusting." He bends over me to spit the words into my face. "You're disgusting. To even think such a thing." He flings himself away and into the tall armchair opposite mine.

Then he simply sprawls and stares at me. I wonder what he's thinking.

Andrew was a pretty child—fine golden curls, an angelic smile, huge eyes of a deep indigo verging on purple. Now he is a handsome young man. The golden curls have thickened and burnished; the eyes have narrowed with intelligence and temperament.

The smile is still angelic, but wasn't Lucifer once an angel? I do not like my son.

I rise from my chair. My neglected book falls to the floor, face down, its pages crumpled. "Good night, Andrew," I say. "Sleep well."

"Pleasant dreams, Mother," he says. His tone conveys unmistakably that he wishes me nothing of the kind. It was a mistake telling him of the nightmares that have begun to plague me. I am always making mistakes with Andrew. Do all mothers make mistakes with their sons?

I stoop to pick up my book. His foot extends to kick it out of my reach. I straighten to gaze sorrowfully down at him, lolling and smirking in his chair.

"You shouldn't read such trash," he says.

"It's harmless. It helps me sleep." Once again, I bend and reach for it.

He swoops to pick it up and tosses it into the fire.

It's only a paperback, a romance of other times and of people engaged in passion and adventure. It can be replaced. I stand and watch the flames flirt with its pages. When it is fully ablaze, I turn and stride from the room. My shoulders are straight and my head erect.

Andrew's merry laughter follows me.

In the morning, the house is cold and Andrew is gone. He hasn't slept in his bed. He's turned the thermostat down. Another of his tricks. I turn it up and get back into bed to wait for the heat to rise. It would be nice to have a cup of hot tea, but I lack the energy to go down to the kitchen to make it. Or am I afraid?

Alone in the darkened bedroom, waiting for heat and daylight, I argue the point with myself. What is there to be afraid of? That he has left surprises for me? Constructed booby traps? In many ways, Andrew is still a child, dependent on me for what little love there is in his life. And like a child, reaching for independence, he resents me. I try to make allowances for that.

Often, I wish that he would marry. I dream of a lovely young woman for him and sons of his own. The little family would live nearby, but not too near. They would visit occasionally, but not too often. Christmas, Thanksgiving, the Fourth of July. We would have laughter and feasting. I would make the peach cobbler that Andrew's father loved so well.

There are tears on my cheeks and I wipe them away with the back of my hand. The radiator clanks and pale gray daylight shows outside my window. Bare branches gleam with a frosting of ice.

It's silly to be afraid of the kitchen. I get up and wrap my fleecy robe over my flannel nightgown. My slippers are lined with lambswool. I will drink my cup of tea and go about my business until Andrew returns. Today will be a good day to work on the sweater I am secretly knitting for his birthday.

And then there is my appointment this afternoon.

The doctor sits as usual in his wheelchair, his fat legs and little feet hanging motionless down. I wonder, as I always do, why his legs are so fat if they are paralyzed. But I don't know what disease confines him to the chair, and I would never dream of asking. He probably wouldn't tell me. We are here to talk about me, not about him.

He waits, with infinite patience, for me to begin.

I tell him about Andrew burning my book.

"Was it a good book?" he asks.

"It was just a book." I know I am being evasive.

"Were you enjoying it?"

"Ummm. Yes."

"Is that why Andrew burned it?"

"I suppose so. We hadn't talked about it. He couldn't know whether I was enjoying it or not."

There is a long pause.

Then I tell him about Andrew turning the thermostat down.

"I think he's trying to freeze me to death." I laugh a little to show I don't mean it literally.

But the doctor doesn't laugh. "Do you think Andrew would kill you?" he asks.

"No!" I exclaim. "What would he do without me?"

"Exactly," says the doctor.

There is another long pause. Long enough for the doctor to start the next round.

"Tell me about the accident," he says.

"I've told you about that. Many times."

"Yes. But each time, we learn something new. Isn't it so?"

I nod. And then I begin. "It was winter. This time of year. The anniversary is in a few weeks. Twenty years ago. Andrew was eight years old. Carl had sprained his ankle, so I was driving him to the station. He was taking a later train that morning. Andrew was in the back seat. I was going to drop him off at school. The roads were icy." My voice tapers off. This part is always so difficult.

"Go on," the doctor prompts.

"The roads were icy. I was supposed to have had the snow tires put on, but I hadn't got around to it yet. I was in the early months of pregnancy and not very energetic. Lazy, I suppose. Andrew was leaning over the back seat with his arms around my neck. I had told him to sit down, but he wouldn't. Carl started scolding him. I couldn't bear for anyone to scold Andrew, not even his father. We began to argue. Carl said I was pampering the boy, making a sissy out of him. Andrew was crying. His arms tightened around my neck. I couldn't breathe. I took my hands off the steering wheel to loosen his grip. We were cresting a hill. The car swerved into the other lane just as another car came up from the other side. We crashed. That's all."

I had been speaking rapidly, repeating the facts as I had repeated them so many times in this heavy room. I am out of breath and sitting bolt upright in my chair, reliving the moment. This doctor does not use a couch. I think he likes to watch the faces of his patients. Sometimes, I think he lives their lives in these tormented moments. In that wheelchair, he can't have much of a life of his own.

"Relax now," he says softly. "There is more."

"More," I murmur. "Yes. Of course there's more. The aftermath. Carl died. I lost the baby."

"And Andrew?"

"Andrew was . . . seriously injured. He flew over my shoulder and went through the windshield. His head . . ."

"Yes?"

"He has scars to this day. Fortunately, his hair is thick and they can't be seen."

The doctor sighs. I don't blame him. It's a sad story.

"Do you blame yourself?" he asks.

"I guess I do. I was driving."

"Do you blame Andrew?"

"No. How could I? He was only a child."

"His arms around your neck, choking you?"

"He was frightened. His father was angry with him."

"Do you blame Carl?"

"How can you blame a dead man?"

The doctor sighs again. "It's hard work," he says. "It goes slowly. But you must try to be honest. For your own sake. So Andrew . . . he was seriously hurt?"

"I thought he would die."

"And . . . ?"

"He didn't."

"He didn't," the doctor repeats. "He got well and went back to school?"

I have to think about that. "He got well and . . . and I had a teacher come to the house."

"What was her name?"

"It wasn't a woman. It was a man."

"What was his name?"

"I can't remember. It was so long ago."

The doctor rolls his wheelchair behind his desk, a sign that our time is up. "Will you try to remember for next time? Perhaps there are some records you could look up."

"Yes," I promise earnestly. "I'll try. I'll look."

His attention is on his desk calendar and I know I am dismissed. Somehow, I feel that he is disappointed with me. I leave the dark cave of his office, wondering if I will return next week. What began as something to cure my nightmares has suddenly turned threatening.

Andrew doesn't like his dinner. He sits at the table, moodily pushing his food around on his plate. "Why don't we ever have fish?" he whines. "Don't you know that red meat is bad for you?"

"You don't like fish," I tell him. "You've always liked rare roast beef, just like your father."

"You killed my father. If you hadn't killed him in the car, you would have killed him with roast beef." He picked up his plate and dumps his dinner into my lap.

I sit there with gravy soaking through the skirt of my green wool jersey dress. It brings a heat and a wetness to my thighs, a mockery of the ancient act of love. Carefully, I gather the mess into my napkin and carry it into the kitchen. The dress may not be ruined. I sponge it off as best I can, and then go upstairs to change. There is no point in being angry with Andrew. He will not listen. I think it's better not to provoke him. Tomorrow, I'll get some nice fillet of sole.

Instead of going downstairs to sit with Andrew in the living room, I climb on a chair to reach into the top of the closet. There, in an old suitcase, I know are papers, old photographs. I had promised the doctor to look. The suitcase is dusty. I wipe it off before putting it on the bed. I have not looked into this suitcase for many years. My hands fumble reluctantly with the latches. Before I can open them, Andrew appears in the doorway.

"Having a nostalgia trip?" he sneers.

"I thought I'd look," I mumble.

"Want to twine my innocent baby curls around your finger? I'll bet you saved each tooth I put under my pillow. Go ahead and open it. I'd like to see too."

"You've seen already." I know I am accusing him, but suddenly, I don't care. "You've been snooping into this. How dare you?"

"Snooping, Mother?" He is sly, self-righteous. "But it's my life too. Isn't it? Isn't that what you've got stored away in there? My brief life?"

"What are you talking about?" I realize I am shrieking like a madwoman. I say it again, softly and reasonably. "What are you talking about, Andrew?"

"You don't really want me to say it. Come downstairs and have some coffee. I've made it. It's all ready and waiting for you."

I am overcome by his sudden kindness. Perhaps we can have a pleasant evening together. We'll talk about the future. He'll tell me of his fiancée, his *secret* fiancée, whom I've never met. He'll ask me if she may come to dinner, and we'll plan together for a wedding in the summer.

He has gotten out the silver coffee service and my best china cups and saucers. "Andrew! How nice!" I exclaim. I can smell the fragrant fresh-brewed coffee.

Andrew, solicitous, takes my arm and ushers me to my chair. He pours a cup of coffee and brings it to me. He smiles benignly as I lift the cup to my lips. I sip. And the cup flies out of my hand, my lips sting, my tongue is seared. "Water!" I gasp.

Andrew laughs. His bitter laughter rings in my ears as I run to the kitchen and rinse my mouth directly under the faucet. When the awful burning in my mouth recedes to a prickling, stinging pain, I raise my head and turn the water off. There on the counter is an open can of Drāno.

"What's wrong, Mother? Don't you like my coffee?" He is hovering nearby, his face a mask of solicitude.

I cannot speak. My lips will crack. I walk past him and go back upstairs to my room. I lock the door. In the mirror, I see that my mouth and tongue are blistered. I also see the reflection of the old suitcase, just where I left it on the bed. I turn and stare at it. Is it time to open it? Now? After all these years?

I sit on the bed and remember a trip when the suitcase was new. Yes, it was our honeymoon. Carl's and mine. We had no knowledge then of Andrew. We were only and selfishly together, the two of us. We went to San Francisco, a city neither of us had seen and we both had dreamed of. We thought of living there, if Carl could arrange a transfer. But he couldn't and so that part of our dream faded. San Francisco does not have icy roads. I have often thought that Andrew was conceived in a room at the Palace Hotel. The timing was right. We should never have left that room. Or, perhaps, never have found it.

I open the suitcase. It's not so difficult after all to release the latches and raise the lid. Inside, I find old rags, shreds of yellowed newspapers, broken toys. No documents. No photographs. Ah, Andrew.

For a week, I have been left in peace. Andrew does this from time to time. Usually after one of his more outrageous pranks. I don't know where he goes, nor do I ever ask. Some things, it's better not to know. He will return filthy and repentant. He will say, "Mother, I'm sorry."

And I will forgive him. What else can I do?

The blisters on my mouth are almost healed, but the doctor notices immediately. I tell him about Andrew's coffee. I tell him I could find no papers.

"Would you like to take a rest?" he says. "I can get you a room."

"A rest? You mean in a hospital?" I am shocked that he would suggest such a thing. And yet, I am tempted. Yes, very tempted.

"It's not a hospital. It's a private facility. For people who just need a little time out from their worries. I would like you to consider it." His voice is so soothing. It seems like such a good idea.

"Oh, no," I hear myself saying. "I couldn't do that. Andrew needs me. He'll be coming home soon. I've bought him new clothes. I've almost finished his sweater. His birthday will be soon. He'll be home for that."

The doctor is silent. Waiting.

I try to wait him out, in silence. But I can't do it. I've become too accustomed to the luxury of talking. I haven't told Andrew of my visits to the doctor. In the beginning, the doctor wanted to speak to Andrew, but I told him that would be dangerous. He believed me.

At last, I am forced to ask the question that has troubled me for years. "Why does he do these things? I've been so good to him. I've tried so hard to make up to him for all that he's lost.''

"What has he lost?'' the doctor asks in that quiet, insistent voice of his.

"Why, you know. I've told you.''

"Tell me again.''

It's not possible that he doesn't remember. He just wants to torture me by going over and over it. I shake my head. I simply cannot do it again.

"What has Andrew lost?'' He is implacable. Cruel.

"His father,'' I mutter.

"What else?''

"I don't know.'' I seldom perspire, but now my hands, my face, my entire body, even my feet are slick and damp. My whispered words reverberate in the hazy room.

"You know,'' the doctor insists.

I try to get out of the chair. I don't have to stay and submit to this. I can get into my car and drive home. I have a feeling that Andrew will come home tonight. I can't get up. Something keeps me nailed to the chair.

"Try to say it. I know it's difficult for you. But you'll feel so much better. What has Andrew lost?''

I remain mute. The words will not come. And yet, the thought is there. Oh, yes. The thought. It's always been there. Hasn't it? Yes.

The doctor is giving up. I can see it in his eyes. He's losing interest. A patient who will not speak is useless. I hate to feel useless. I begin to chatter. I intend to use up my hour. After all, I'm paying for it.

He listens, not interrupting, until I've exhausted my store of trifles. Then he says, "Will you come in tomorrow? I think it's important. We've reached a crucial point.''

"Tomorrow? I don't know. It depends.'' But I am flattered by this attention. I make a show of consulting my date book. There is nothing written on tomorrow's page, yet I frown over it as if I had appointments of great moment. "Yes, all right,'' I allow. "I can make it. Same time?''

As I am driving away from the medical center where the doctor has his office, I see Andrew walking toward me along the street. This is an unpleasant part of town, old and seedy, inhabited by riffraff. He is walking with a woman. She is not young. She wears too much makeup to compensate for her loss of youth. She teeters along on extravagantly high heels, and she is wrapped in an imitation fur coat. I drive on past them, hoping that Andrew has not seen me or recognized the car. He has given no sign, but Andrew wouldn't. Why is he here? What has Andrew lost?

"Hello, Mother."

He has caught me by surprise, my knitting in my lap. I try to hide it under a magazine. Even from across the room, I can smell the liquor on him and the cheap perfume. "Would you like some shrimp salad?" I ask. I'll never risk roast beef again.

Andrew makes a rude, gagging noise like a child rejecting a dish he does not like. Then he asks, "What were you doing in town today, Mother? Spying on me?"

"No, of course not. I had an appointment."

"Oh, an appointment. Not with a doctor, by any chance?"

"No. I . . . I went to see a decorator. Don't you think it's time I redid this room?"

He strolls around the living room, examining the wallpaper, kicking at the chairs. "Don't change it," he says. "I like it this way. Just the way it was twenty years ago." Then he swings on me, his face contorted with fury. "And don't lie to me! Don't ever lie to me. You went to see a psychiatrist. A nut doctor. Are you crazy, Mother?"

I remain outwardly calm, but my hands clutching my knitting are clammy. "I am not crazy, Andrew. And *you* have been spying on *me.*"

He laughs at that. "Don't you know by now that you have no secrets from me? That thing in your lap, for instance. It's a sweater, isn't it? To keep your little boy warm and cozy. Too bad he'll never wear it. I wouldn't be caught dead in that ugly piece of trash."

It's so hard to keep from crying, but I've learned that that's the biggest mistake of all. To let Andrew see my weakness. "Go take a bath," I tell him. "You smell."

"Ah, but I smell of life, Mother. Something you know nothing about." Nevertheless, he disappears up the stairs and I am left alone.

I pick up my knitting and try to concentrate, but it's useless. I might as well rip it all out and make pot holders out of the yarn.

The next day, Andrew is repentant. He brings me breakfast in bed. Two soft-boiled eggs, buttered toast, fresh orange juice, a pot of tea. The white wicker bed tray is one I used during Andrew's long recuperation after the accident.

"How lovely!" I exclaim. "Andrew, you can be so thoughtful."

He sits at the foot of the bed and smiles at me. "You're the only mother I have." Angelic. "I don't know why I do the things I do."

"Let's forget all that," I tell him. "We'll go on from here, this moment. You have your whole life ahead of you."

"Yes," he broods. "And yours is almost over. I haven't given you much joy."

"Oh, yes, you have. Why, I remember . . ."

"Please, Mother. Don't remember. It makes me sad." But then he grins impishly and says, "Let's do something special today. Let's start redoing the living room. You were right about that. It's old and gloomy. I'd like to tear that old wallpaper right off the walls. It's peeling off anyway. Come on, Mom. Put on your working clothes and let's get busy." He leaps off the bed and dashes out the door.

"Wait!" I call after him. "We can't do it all ourselves."

"Yes, we can!" he shouts back as he goes thundering down the stairs.

By the time I am dressed, he has already torn long strips of wallpaper off the wall. He has taken the draperies off the windows, and the room, in the cold winter daylight, looks shabbier than I realized it was.

"You'd better make a list," he tells me. "New draperies, new furniture; the piano can stay but only if you play it for me."

"I haven't played for years," I tell him. "I don't know if I remember how. You always said it made you nervous."

"Sit down and play," he commands, "while I get on with the wallpaper. It's all got to go. Every scrap of it."

I sit on the bench and open the lid covering the keys. "It's probably out of tune," I murmur. But I tentatively finger the keys and begin with something simple. Carl always liked me to play "Smoke Gets in Your Eyes."

"That's right, Mom." Andrew is on top of the ladder, scraping away at the wallpaper near the ceiling. "Sing for me. I want to hear you sing."

"Oh, no," I protest. "I never could sing. Even your father had to admit that."

Andrew turns and stares down at me. "Sing," he says softly.

And I do. I can't remember all the words and my voice creaks and cracks, but it seems to please Andrew. He hums along and works steadily. Soon one entire wall of the living room is bare, down to the plaster, except for some places where the paper refuses to peel away.

"I'll have to get a blowtorch," he says. "That's the only way. And I can use it to strip the old paint off the woodwork. Oh, we're going to have fun. This room is going to look wonderful! And then we can start in on the rest of the house."

"I don't know," I whisper weakly. "Isn't a blowtorch dangerous?"

"Not if you know how to use it."

And then he is gone.

Maybe he won't come back. I have spent the past two hours waiting for him. I have missed my appointment with the doctor, but I can't leave with the house in such a mess and Andrew not back yet. I know I should be doing something, but I don't know what to do. I haven't even washed my breakfast dishes. I want to be happy that Andrew is finally taking an interest in the house and I am, really, but all this sudden change is making me uneasy. I prowl the disheveled living room, fingering the dusty old draperies, crackling the torn wallpaper under foot, remembering when it was all new and gleaming and I was young and proud.

The phone rings, but I can't bring myself to answer it. It might be the doctor, wanting to know why I didn't show up. How can I tell him that I don't need him anymore? That Andrew has changed and we are going to be all right now, a family. I won't have any more nightmares. The phone stops ringing.

He's back, carrying a blowtorch and a big greasy can of some kind of fuel.

"Don't put it on the rug," I warn him.

"It doesn't matter," he says. "The rug has got to go. We'll have a new one. Pale green, I think. Like the grass in springtime." And he smiles.

"What took you so long?" I ask.

"You weren't supposed to ask," he says, "but since you did, I might as well tell you. I was getting a surprise for you." He reaches into his pocket and pulls out a small white box. "This is for you," he says. "Because I've been such a bad boy." He hands me the box.

I am thunderstruck. It is the first time Andrew has ever given me a gift.

"Open it," he urges.

I open it and there on a bed of soft blue velvet lies a gold heart-shaped locket on a thin gold chain. "Andrew!" I exclaim. "How pretty!"

"Open the locket," he says.

My hands can hardly manage the delicate latch, but at last the locket springs open. On one side, there is a picture of me as I was twenty years ago. On the other, Andrew's baby face beams up at me, golden curls, huge eyes, sweet innocent smile. "Oh, Andrew!" is all I can say before the tears gush forth.

"Now, Mom," he says. "It's nothing to cry about. Here, let me put it on for you."

While he fastens the golden chain around my neck, I wipe my eyes and try to compose myself. When he finishes, he is all business once again. "Back to work for me," he says, "and back to the piano for you. Music makes the time fly."

I am in an ecstasy of delight and I try to play the old songs as best I can. I am dimly aware of Andrew doing something with the blowtorch and the can of fuel. I play on, one song after another. Andrew goes quietly about his work. For the first time in years, we are happy with each other. What more could a mother ask?

The doorbell rings, but I can't stop to answer it. I don't want anyone to interrupt this precious time. There is a pounding at the door and I hear voices calling my name. "Go away!" I shout, before starting another song.

The flames are licking at the torn wallpaper now. And Andrew is smiling. Somehow he seems younger, as if the years are rolling back and he is becoming a boy again. The rug is smoldering. Andrew was never a gawky adolescent. He was a handsome teenager, never a spot of acne, never an awkward moment. The smoke brings tears to my eyes, but after so many years of not crying, I don't mind. Andrew looks about twelve years old, but that could be an illusion caused by the smoke. It's very warm in the room. The old sofa is burning now. The piano is near the picture window and hasn't caught fire yet.

Andrew stands in the flames and smiles at me. He beckons to me, this ten-year-old boy. "Mommy, Mommy," he calls. "Isn't this fun?"

On the other side of the picture window, I can see agitated faces. The doctor is there, in his wheelchair. And the woman from his office. I am astonished and secretly pleased that he's come all this way just for me. Sirens wail in the distance, coming closer.

Andrew's eyes are closing. Blood gushes from his head and cascades down his pale face. He crumples and falls to the floor. I have seen him this way before. It is the way he was after the accident. I rise from the piano bench. This time I am determined I will save him.

But before I can reach him, there is a tremendous crash of glass behind me. Two tall men leap through the broken window and pick me up. "My son! My son! Andrew, my son! Save him first."

But they pay no attention. It is all so undignified. They

bundle me into an ambulance, but not before I notice the great hoses they are aiming into my house. I can hear my doctor talking to the ambulance attendants. "Suicidal," he says. "But I never thought she'd do something like this."

How little he understands. Andrew will be back. Andrew *always* comes back. The fire is a good thing. It has burned away the past. Now we'll really fix up the house, make it better than new, with no memories. Andrew and I will be happy together. Forever.

Carolyn G. Hart is a former journalist, the author of nineteen novels, and the recipient of the Oklahoma Writers Award for 1983. Carolyn introduced Annie Laurance, owner of a mystery bookstore, in Death on Demand, *a 1987 Anthony award nominee. Annie and Max Darling (". . . rich, good humored and totally convinced that love is a good deal more important than work . . .") continue their charming adventures in* Design for Murder, Something Wicked *(winner of an Agatha award for Best Novel of 1988),* Honeymoon with Murder, *and* A Little Class on Murder.*

In "Upstaging Murder," Annie's mother-in-law, Laurel, discovers that all the world's become a stage—and one of the players isn't sticking to the rules.

UPSTAGING MURDER

by Carolyn G. Hart

LAUREL DARLING ROETHKE was a latecomer to mysteries, but, as with all her enthusiasms, she gave her new interest her all. She subscribed to both *Ellery Queen Mystery Magazine* and *Alfred Hitchcock Mystery Magazine,* belonged to the Mystery Guild, and was on the mailing list of a half dozen mystery bookstores, from Grounds for Murder in San Diego, California, to The Hideaway in Bar Harbor, Maine. Her heart, of course, belonged to Death on Demand, the mystery bookstore so ably directed by her dear daughter-in-law, Annie Laurance Darling. She adored Annie, though it was a bit of a puzzle that Max had chosen such a serious young woman to be his wife. Oh, well, one could never quite understand the squish of another's moccasins.

Still, it was Max's love for Annie that had led Laurel to the mystery. A true thrill was discovering the delights and pleasures of mystery weekends, from the Catskills to the Sierras, from the Louisiana bayous to the Alaskan tundra.

Annie encouraged her, of course. Dear Annie. So thoughtful to send a brochure on that Tibetan weekend, Murder at the Monastery. But she was already committed to Death Stalks the Smokies at this gorgeous inn in southeastern North Carolina, and it would only make sense to visit Annie and Max on her way home. She was so near.

So far, this weekend had been such a wonderful experience, a welcoming dinner devoted to one of Laurel's favorite authors, Leslie Ford, with choice tidbits about three of Ford's most famous characters, Grace Latham and Colonel Primrose and *dear* Sergeant Buck.

Laurel hummed vigorously as she inspected her image in the mirror. What was it that lovely police chief, the guest of honor, had murmured as they danced last night? That she had a Grecian profile and hair that shimmered like moonlight on water? How sweet! Men were so often obtuse, but they added such spice to life. She brushed a soupçon of pale pink gloss to her lips, nodded in satisfaction, and turned toward the door. Not that she expected to encounter anyone else abroad at this hour, but a woman owed it to herself always to look her best.

She slipped quietly down the hall. After all, you couldn't be too careful at mystery weekends. Everyone was so determined to win. Very American, of course, the spirit of competition. Some people (her mind skittered to Henny Brawley, one of the most avid mystery readers to frequent Annie's store) would do almost anything to win. So Laurel felt it was quite fair to scout out the territory in advance.

The Big Ben–like tone of the grandfather clock on the landing tolled the hour. Boom. Boom. So *quiet* at two A.M. Then she paused, one hand lightly resting on the heavy mahogany newel post at the foot of the stairs. Switching off her pencil flash, she cocked her head to listen.

A footstep.

No doubt about it.

How odd.

Perhaps another mystery competitor. She felt a quiver of disappointment. She'd so often triumphed because most people, face it, were slugabeds. She, of course, scarcely needed any sleep to function quite successfully. Darting into the cav-

ernous library, which also served as the inn's lobby and as
an auditorium, she found shelter behind heavy red velvet
drapes as another stealthy footstep sounded.

Her heart raced in anticipation. Perhaps this weekend would
be decidedly special. There were many reports of ghosts in
these backwoods. Could it be that she would soon witness a
spectral apparition? Laurel considered herself something of
an authority on unearthly visitants. She was quite familiar
with the works of the Society for Psychical Research, having
read the ambitious, two-volume, 1,400-page work, *Phan-
tasms of the Living*, published in 1886, and certainly she was
cognizant of the apparitional research of that modern giant in
the field, Dr. Karlis Osis.

Eagerly, she peered from behind the drapes. When a gray-
robed figure glided into view, she was at once disappointed,
yet intrigued. This was no ghost. After all, apparitions have
no need of flashlights. But this was decidedly curious! Something was afoot here, no doubt about it. The dimly seen gray
figure in the long, sweeping, hooded robe aimed a pencil
flash, a twin to the one Laurel carried, down the center of
the huge room. Laurel followed the bobbing progress of the
light to the small stage where the mystery play would be
presented tomorrow night. Such a clever idea, as touted in
the brochure. As is customary at mystery weekends, a murder would be discovered shortly after breakfast, teams formed,
and an investigation begun. The young actors hired to play
suspects' roles would provide grist for the weekend detectives' mills. But, in addition, this weekend would feature a
suspense play to be presented after dinner and before the
announcement of the winning detective team at, of course,
the stroke of midnight.

The hooded figure ran lightly up the steps and the pencil
flash illuminated a narrow portion of the stage. The set included a yellow pine nightstand beside a rickety wooden bed
with a pieced quilt cover. The figure placed the flash on the
bed, the sliver of light aimed at the nightstand.

A gloved hand pulled open the drawer and lifted out a
pistol.

Laurel strained to see the robed figure, dimly visible in the backwash of the flash, the sharply illuminated gloved hand, the gun. A crisp click, the gun opened. Another click, it shut. The gun was replaced in the drawer, the drawer closed, and the pencil flash lifted.

The hooded figure passed very near, but there was no visible face, just folds of cloth. There was an instant when Laurel could have reached out, yanked at the robe, and glimpsed the face of the intruder. She almost moved. To unmask the villain now—and the click of the pistol signaled unmistakable intent to Laurel—would perhaps protect the victim in this instance. But what of the future? Laurel remained still and listened to the fading footsteps, and then the figure was gone.

The police chief, such a handsome man and, understandably, a bit confused as to the purpose of her visit, welcomed her eagerly to his room. She soon put things clear, however. Then it took a bit of persuasion, but finally the chief agreed to her plan.

"Damned clever," he pronounced. "And, now, my dear, perhaps, after all your exertions, you might enjoy a glass of wine?"

Laurel hesitated for a moment but, after all, nothing more could be accomplished in her quest for justice until the morrow. She nodded in acquiescence, bestowing a serene smile upon her coconspirator. She couldn't help but appreciate the enthusiastic gleam in the chief's dark eyes.

Over a breakfast of piping hot camomile tea and oat bran sprinkled with alfalfa sprouts, Laurel studied the program of *Trial*, described as "a drama of life and death, of murder and judgment, of passion and power. An abused wife, Maria, is on trial for her life in the shooting death of her husband. A vindictive prosecutor demands a death for a death. Her fate will lie in the hands of the judge." Laurel thoughtfully chewed another sprig of alfalfa and committed to memory the five young faces of the cast.

Kelly Winston, the abused wife, had sharply planed, dramatic features and soulful eyes. She was a drama graduate of a Midwestern college. Beside her studio picture was a single quote: "I want it all."

"Hmm," Laurel murmured as she admired the really very handsome features of Bill Morgan, the abusive husband slain by Maria. Such an attractive young man, though, of course, handsome is as handsome does. His quote: "George M. Cohan has nothing on me!"

Handsome was not the word for Carl Jenkins, who portrayed the prosecutor. His dark face glowered up from the program, thin-lipped and beak-nosed. "I'll see you on Broadway."

Walter Sheridan beamed from his studio picture, apparently the epitome of charm, good humor, and lightheartedness. He played the judge. "Life's a bowl of cherries."

Jonathan Ravin's face was young and vulnerable. His chin didn't look as if it had quite taken shape. He played the hired man who excites the husband's jealousy. "All I need is a chance."

Laurel did suffer a few pangs of envy as the weekend detectives began their investigation into the murder of a rich playboy at a Riviera château. (The roles played during the day investigation differed, of course, from the roles in that evening's play.) Laurel found the thrill of the chase hard to ignore. But a greater duty called. She consoled herself with thoughts of that great company of fictional sleuths who, like the company of all faithful people, surely were at her shoulder at this very moment (figuratively speaking): Mary Roberts Rinehart's Miss Pinkerton, Patricia Wentworth's Miss Silver (though why one should be dowdy with age mystified Laurel), Heron Carvic's Miss Seeton, Gwen Moffat's Miss Pink, Josephine Tey's Miss Pym, and, of course, Leslie Ford's Grace Latham. (Good for Grace. She, at least, made time in her life for men.)

But Laurel's plan of necessity required that she not be at the forefront of the mystery weekend investigations. In fact, she lagged, and only approached one of the young people playing the mystery roles when the investigators bayed through the inn in search of further elucidation.

She approached by herself, bearing goodies. Did anyone ever outgrow cookies and milk, even if, at later ages, these translated to gin and tonic?

Kelly Winston, who played a countess in the investigations, occupied one alcove in the library. As Laurel approached, the actress made a conscious effort to erase a tight frown and look aggrieved, in keeping with her role of the countess whose diamond tiara had been stolen.

Laurel proffered an inviting Bloody Mary with a sprig of mint. "Hard work, isn't it?" she said cheerfully. "I do so admire you young people. And the life of an actress! So much to be envied, but often such difficult demands, especially when emotions run high. It's so hard with men, isn't it, Kelly?"

Kelly looked at Laurel in surprise, but the drink was welcome. "Aren't you doing the mystery weekend?"

A light trill of laughter. "In a way, my dear. But I'm a writer too. Fiction, let me hasten to add. And I dearly enjoy getting to know my fellow human beings on a personal level. And I can tell that you are *so* unhappy."

The dam burst. Laurel made gentle, cooing noises, such an effective response, and presented an ingenuous face and limpid blue eyes. Kelly admitted that it was too, too awful, the way Walter was glooming around. After all, they'd only dated for a couple of months. Of course, he had helped her get the mystery troupe job, but that didn't mean he owned her, did it? More empathetic coos. And Bill was just the cutest guy she'd ever met!

Laurel found her next quarry, Bill Morgan, with an elbow on the bar. He accepted his drink with alacrity. He was a strapping young man, six foot four at least, with curly brown hair, light blue eyes, and a manly chin. Laurel's glance lingered. She did so admire manly chins. "I do think Kelly is such a dear girl! I hope Walter isn't making things too difficult for you both."

Bill, who was clearly accustomed to female attention from ages six to sixty, expressed no surprise at Laurel's personal interest. He drank half his Bloody Mary in a gulp. "Oh, Kelly's just being dramatic. Actually, it's Carl who gets on my nerves. I didn't even know she'd been involved with him until he got drunk the other night and told me I was a dumb sh—'' He glanced at Laurel, cleared his throat. ". . . jerk to get involved with her. He said she went through men like a gambler through chips.'' He downed the rest of the drink, then looked past Laurel at the main hall and began to wave. "Hi, Jenny. Hey, how about later?''

A tiny, dark-haired girl with an elfin grace paused long enough to blow him a kiss. "Terrific. See you at the pool.''

Laurel waited until Bill realized she was still there, not a usual situation for her. Of course, he was crassly young. When he smiled at her dreamily, obviously still thinking of Jenny, she said bluntly, "Do you think Walter is jealous?''

Bill looked at her blankly. "Jealous?''

"Of you and Kelly,'' she said patiently.

"So who cares?'' he asked lightly.

"And Carl?'' Laurel prodded.

"Oh, he's just a drunk.'' Then he frowned. "But kind of a nasty one.''

Carl looked like he could be a nasty drunk, with his dark, thin face, prominent cheekbones, and small, tight mouth. As Laurel approached, he smoothed back patent-slick hair (he played a French police inspector in the mystery skit). He stared at the Bloody Mary suspiciously.

"So what's in it?'' he snapped. "Ipecac? Valium?''

It was Laurel's turn to be surprised. "Why should I?''

"This isn't my first mystery weekend. People are crazy. They'll do anything.''

Laurel lifted the glass to her lips, took a sip. "One hundred percent pure tomato juice, vodka, and whatever,'' she promised, and smiled winningly.

Carl gave a grudging smile in return. "You aren't one of the nuts?''

"Do I look like a nut?'' she asked softly.

He took the Bloody Mary.

"Actually,'' Laurel confided, "I'm a writer and I'm doing an article on how women mistreat men. Don't you think that's a novel idea? So often, it's the other way around, don't you think?''

Although he looked a little confused, he nodded vehemently. "Damn right. Women mistreat men all the time. Wish they'd get some of their own back."

"Your last girlfriend?" she prompted.

His face hardened. "Should have known better. She two-timed me and made a play for Walter. My best friend. But he's finding out. She isn't any damned good. She'll dump Bill, too, one of these days."

"Isn't it hard, having to act with her?"

Carl looked at her sharply. "Hey, what the hell? How'd you know it was Kelly? Hey, lady, what's going on here?"

"That's what I'm finding out," she caroled. Laurel gave him a sprightly wave and wafted toward the hall. She ignored his calls. A determined sleuth is never deflected.

The abandoned Walter, a French chef in the daytime skit, was short, plump, and genial. His spaniel eyes drooped at the mention of Kelly. "Gee, I wish I'd never gotten involved with her. She just seems to irritate everybody. It hasn't been the same since she came aboard."

"Were you deeply in love with her?" Laurel asked gently.

A whoop of laughter. "Lady, love is a merry-go-round. You hop on and you hop off. No hard feelings."

She found the fifth member of the troupe, Jonathan Ravin, beneath an umbrella at poolside. He played Oscar, a Polish expatriate. Long blond hair curled on his neck. He had unhappy brown eyes and bony shoulders.

He shook away the Bloody Mary. "I never adulterate my tomato juice."

"Oh, I certainly understand that," Laurel said sympathetically. "So dreadful what is done to food today. I cook only organically grown vegetables."

After a lengthy discussion of the merits of oat over wheat bran, Laurel segued nearer her objective. "Do your friends eat as you do?"

"My friends?"

"The other actors, Kelly and Bill and Carl and Walter."

"They aren't my friends," he burst out bitterly. "I thought Bill was. But when Kelly came along, he didn't even have time to play checkers anymore. Why did Walter have to bring her in? We had a wonderful time before she came.''

Mystery teams sat together at dinner, passing notes, engaging in intense conversations with occasional loud outbursts of disagreement. But when the solutions were turned in at eight P.M., there was a general air of relaxation.

Laurel had not even sat with her team. Admittedly a dereliction of duty on her part, but more serious matters dominated. Instead, she settled early at the table closest to the stage, her police chief friend beside her. Their chairs were only a few feet from the downstage-left stairs. As the houselights dimmed, she sat forward, chin in hand, to observe.

As the play unfolded, she was impressed with the skill of the young acting troupe. Kelly was superb as the abused wife on trial for the murder of her husband, the handsome, strapping Bill. Slender, blond Jonathan was an effective hired man, who served as the object of the husband's jealousy. The play began in the courtroom where the widow was on trial for her life for the murder of her husband. She claimed self-defense. Plump Walter, as the judge, looked unaccustomedly stern in his black robe. The prosecutor, played by the dark-visaged Carl, was determined to see her executed for the crime. As Carl badgered her upon the witness stand, she broke down in tears, screaming, ''You can't know what it was like that night!'' The stage went dark. An instant passed and the spots focused downstage on the partial set containing the old bed and the nightstand. Kelly raised up in the bed. She was dressed in the cotton gown she had worn the night of the shooting.

Laurel slipped to her feet and moved toward the downstage-left steps. The police chief, with footsteps as light as a cat's, followed close behind.

Onstage, the door to the bedroom burst open. The husband, played so well by that handsome young man, Bill Morgan, lunged toward the bed. His face aflame with jealousy and anger, he accused her of infidelity. Denying it, Kelly rolled off the bed, trying to escape, but her husband bounded forward. Grabbing Kelly, Bill flung her toward the bed and began to pull his belt from its loops. With a desperate cry, she turned toward the nightstand and yanked at the drawer. Pulling out the gun, she whirled toward Bill—and Laurel was there.

Firmly, Laurel wrested the gun from Kelly's hand. She stepped back.

"Lights." (It had only taken a moment that afternoon to convince Buddy, a charming young hotel man, that a new wrinkle had been added to the evening's entertainment. So many people, it was sad to say, were so credulous. Really, it was no wonder criminals found such easy pickings.)

The stage was bathed in sharp white light.

"What the hell's going on?" Bill demanded.

Laurel held the gun with an extremely competent air. (After all, she had been second highest overall for women at the National Skeet Shooting Association World Championships in San Antonio in 1978.)

"So boring," Laurel trilled, "when everything always goes on schedule. Let's be innovative, listen to the inner promptings of our psyches. What would happen at this moment if this gun were turned upon another? Let us see." She smiled kindly at Bill Morgan, the handsome young man so accustomed to female adoration. "Not you, my dear. You've had your close call for now. But what about Carl? Does he hate you for taking Kelly away?" She swung the pistol toward the dark-visaged actor.

He squinted at her beneath the bright lights. "Lady, you *are* a nut." He folded his arms across his chest and shook his head in disgust.

The barrel poked toward him for a moment.

"No," Laurel said crisply, "not Carl."

The barrel swiveled up to aim at the black-clad judge. "Walter."

"Jesus, lady, get the hell offstage!"

But he made no move to duck or move away. Laurel smiled benignly. "It is important to be open to life. You passed a romantic moment with Kelly, did you not? But you see all liaisons as impermanent. So I think I shan't shoot at you."

She sighed and turned the gun toward the slender young man. Jonathan brushed back a wisp of blond hair. "This isn't funny, even if you think it is," he said pettishly. "What if we don't get paid for tonight?"

"Ah, the Inn will not be unhappy. Mystery lovers prefer excitement in the raw. They wish to experience life upon the edge. And we are now so close to true drama."

She swung around and leveled the pistol, aiming directly at Kelly's heart.

"I believe you will be the victim tonight, my dear. One, two . . ."

Kelly lifted her hands, stumbled backward, turned and began to run. "Stop her, somebody. Stop her before she kills me!"

As Kelly fled down the steps into the hall, Laurel called after her. "My dear, how interesting that you should be afraid. Because all the players know this gun is loaded with blanks."

The police chief, nodding approval at Laurel, hurried after the escaping actress.

Bill's eyes widened like a man who sees an unimaginable horror. "The gun. Blanks. You mean . . ."

Laurel nodded. "I'm afraid so, my dear. She put in real bullets. She would have killed you, of course—and claimed it was an accident, that some malicious person must have made the substitution. It would have been so difficult to prove otherwise. But, fortunately, I was abroad in the still of the night. And the dear police chief and I, such a co-operative man, removed the bullets, just in case, you know, that I didn't move swiftly enough tonight. Though everyone who knows me knows that I am always swift. We have the bullets she put in place of the blanks. They are Exhibits A, B, and C, I believe. The police are *so* efficient."

"Real bullets?" Bill repeated thinly. "My God, why?"

"Oh, my dear young man. You are so young. It would be well to understand that a woman who goes from man to man must do so at her own volition. A woman such as Kelly could never bear to be cast aside." She beamed at the handsome young man. "There is much to be said for constancy, you know." (She forbore to mention her own marital record of five husbands and—but that would be another story entirely.) "In any event, you should be quite safe now. Such a *public* demonstration of evil intent."

Jeanne Hart says that she finds great pleasure in both writing and reading mysteries because ". . . in the chaos of our world, mysteries are ultimately tidy and resolved." Her novel Fetish, *nominated for a Macavity award, chronicles the adventures of three single, middle-aged women whose lives are changed after they run an ad in a local newspaper seeking a shared escort. Lieutenant Carl Pedersen of the California coastal town of Bay Cove (read: Santa Cruz), his wife Freda, and his partner Ronald Tate return in* Some Die Young.*

In "Missing Person," a mother fills her newly empty nest with concern for a young woman who seems to have disappeared.*

MISSING PERSON

by Jeanne Hart

THE AMERICAN LIT paper was due Monday. Due on entrance into class. Ferguson was a no-nonsense professor. It was said of him that he gave one *A* a quarter just to demonstrate that he wasn't as impossible as the student evaluations claimed him to be. The opinion of his students, however, was that he gave the *A* because professors who never gave an *A* were in trouble with the administration.

The young woman huddled cross-legged in the big armchair and pushed her spine against its lumpy back. She yawned, turned a page, and laid the book in her lap. Looking over her shoulder to be sure she was alone, she pried a dog-eared slip of paper from the pocket of her jeans and studied it; then, as her housemate came into the room, she slipped it under her in a protective reflex.

"Not writing your mother *again*?" Her housemate. "Oh, God, Gretchen, I thought you'd finished *Moby Dick*."

Gretchen picked up the book from her lap. "Almost. I'm not reading it because I want to, you know—I have to."

"Babe, you study too much. Life isn't only about hitting the books. Do you realize you've been in school"—she paused—"my God, do you realize that you haven't really taken a break for *two* years and *three* summers? That's crazy. Why doesn't Rog get your head straight on that?"

Gretchen's face tightened. "I have a scholarship to maintain. My mother works hard—"

Her housemate nodded. "I know, Gretch. Don't mind me. But it would be nice if you could come by later. Everybody's going to be there."

"Roger told me. If I can, I will." She sighed deeply. "This is just the first paper for Ferguson's course. Do you think I might like Melville if I didn't have to read him?"

Her housemate laughed. She opened the door. "See you later . . . okay, *maybe*."

The door swung shut after her. As the lock clicked firmly into place, Gretchen put down the book. At times she wished someone would come along, scoop her up and *force* her to stop studying. But Roger was too gentle; he'd never do that.

She sighed and reached beneath her for the folded slip of paper.

The story hit the papers nine days after the disappearance. Tessa read it to her husband at the breakfast table. He was not really listening but studying the classified ads, an habitual activity Tessa found strange in a man who not since his twenties had been unemployed. "Isn't it funny, Tim?" she said. "Why do you suppose they'd wait for over a week to say a girl is missing?"

Her husband looked up. "Who is *they*? And what girl is missing?"

"Some girl on campus. Listen. 'COLLEGE JUNIOR VANISHES. AUTHORITIES BAFFLED. A nineteen-year-old junior . . .' That's just a year younger than Polly." She looked up. "Oh, never mind, read your ads."

He put down his section of the newspaper. "I'm listening. Is she anybody we know? Not one of Polly's friends?"

"No. That's not the point; the thing is, she's disappeared. Vanished."

"What do you mean, vanished? Nobody *vanishes*. You mean she was kidnapped or went off with some guy or ran away."

"It doesn't sound that way. Her housemate last saw her in their living room reading *Moby Dick*. Then when the house-mate came home that night, she was gone. She hadn't taken her bag or money or clothes or anything. Not even a key. And there were no signs of violence."

"How about *Moby Dick*? She take that?"

"Be serious. It really is odd, isn't it?"

"She'll show up. Someone must think she's just gone off or the newspapers would have made more of it." He reached across. "Let me see the news. I want to finish up here and get started on that raking."

Tessa handed him the paper. "No," she said, "I don't think she'll just show up." But he was no longer paying attention.

The girl came to Tessa's mind several times that morning. While she was on sabbatical from teaching, Tessa was doing her own housework, and she found the physical effort—the mindless pushing and hauling of the vacuum along the floor, the scrubbing with an old toothbrush at the corners of the cloudy bathroom fixtures, the cautious sliding of wax onto the kitchen linoleum—a soothing, lulling activity. In teaching, all problems were cerebral. Housework was cerebral only in that it gave you time to think.

The news story had included a photograph, small and fuzzy and perhaps dating back to high school. The young woman—Gretchen Willey was her name—was small and square-jawed and blond. She had been grinning at the photographer, her eyes crinkled almost shut. Her short, streaked hair was tumbled as though she had just climbed from a motorbike or paused during a brisk walk in the wind. It was a likable face and an endearing photograph that somehow suggested Polly; it stayed with her through the morning.

Tim could never understand her intense interest in stories about people of whom she had never before heard—those two young women imprisoned in Turkey, the boy in Mexico. He felt sympathy; it wasn't that he didn't. It was terrible, he agreed, but then he would add, "Why do you dwell on those things? Anyone who can do anything about them is doing it." Tessa was never sure.

She thought about the missing girl as she dusted Polly's room, left empty when she had gone off to school in the East just a little over a year ago. Tessa had *wanted* Polly to be accepted at the college; had she not been, she would have continued on at home and attended the university where Tim taught, and it had become clear Polly did not want that.

That first year had been strange, being a couple again rather than a family. But working and looking forward to summer, to long talks during which Polly would re-create for her all that had happened, the absence of their only child had begun to seem less desolating. It was when Tessa had received Polly's letter saying she would stay on in the East, had in fact accepted a position in New York for the summer, that her absence had finally become a fact, heavy as lead, of Tessa's life. With her sabbatical already scheduled, she faced five more months of days alone in the house that contained the empty bedroom.

It gave her time to think, too much sometimes. Take this Gretchen. The newspapers hadn't even alerted the public till now. No one was watching for her, or hadn't been till today. The abductor, if there was one, could be long gone, Gretchen with him. Or she could have amnesia, and who would know that the girl with the tossed blond hair and the vague smile was not sure of her identity or was filled with fear at this vast gap where memory had been? Maybe she had simply run away—but if she had, wouldn't she have taken things? Her handbag, or money, or clothes? Unless, of course, she didn't want it to appear she had run away. And maybe she had taken money—who could know what she had stashed away?

For that matter, who knew what might have been in Gretchen's mind. She would have sworn she knew Polly's mind, but time had repeatedly proved that she did not. She shook her dust mop at the kitchen door, put it away, poured herself a cup of coffee and carried it into Polly's room. She had taken to sitting in there; it was the sunniest room in the house. She set the mug on Polly's desk alongside the battered copy of *Charlotte's Web* and the worn *Little Prince* that had been inscribed at birth by Tessa's best friend.

No. If Gretchen was wandering around town in a amnesiac fog, surely someone would say, "Hi, Gretchen," and stir her to recall. *If* she was in town; didn't amnesiacs immediately head for buses to some other city?

No, it seemed to come back to abduction, although how anyone could be abducted from her living room without signs of violence or even departure, Tessa could only guess. As Tessa sipped her coffee, she created a little scene.

He would have appeared at the door, the fresh-faced college student with a hidden twist to his personality, a smiling villain, maybe with an endearing scruffy beard, grinning down at her, legs slightly spraddled. "Oh, come on, a walk in the park'll do you good."

"Well . . . one hour. No more, right? Will I need a jacket?"

And he would say, "It's warm, come as you are. Be spontaneous."

"Spontaneous with Steve." She would have laughed and been gone.

But it made no sense, fantasizing about someone she had never met, trying to imagine moments in the life of a person about whom she knew nothing. In a few days it would probably all be explained. She picked up the cup from Polly's old desk and put the whole matter out of her mind.

Later in the day, though, Tessa's exasperation with the laxity of the police and the inadequacies of newspapers returned. Could it be that this was *not* the first reference to Gretchen's disappearance? Could the story have slipped by her? Sometimes she barely skimmed the morning paper.

The old newspapers were stacked and stored in the garage next to the woodpile, ready for recyling. Wrapped in a sweater against the chill of the unheated room, Tessa began to search methodically.

The last week's newspapers yielded up a quarter column. Buried in the third section of Wednesday's paper, Tessa found a terse little statement. The disappearance "remains a mystery"—so the police *had* been informed—"and continues to baffle authorities," said one local detective, who added solemnly, "It's a real case for Sherlock Holmes." The distraught mother, a divorcée interviewed in Florida, stated that the disappearance could not be voluntary. "She wouldn't have done that to me. We've always been very close. She's absolutely faithful about writing every week. She's the most considerate of daughters."

The mother's testimonial seemed not to have moved the police; they had heard before of considerate children. The story included a description of Gretchen and a telephone number so that anyone knowing Gretchen's whereabouts could "come forward."

Tessa carefully tore the story from the newspaper and slipped it into her skirt pocket. How close could they have been, with the mother still in Florida so many days after her daughter's disappearance? If it were she, she would drop everything, rush to the place where her daughter was, search the city herself, street by street if need be, to find Polly.

And what sort of relationship did they have that the girl had to write weekly? Polly, and she was an only child, would have been appalled at such an idea. Of course Polly had never been a letter writer, and with her busy schedule wrote less and less often these days. And why hadn't the father been interviewed? Certainly he had some responsibility for the girl. Had he deserted them?

Sunday morning Tessa woke to a sense of unease. For a moment she could not place what was troubling her—Tim? Polly? Then her anxiety took form: Gretchen, that was it. She slipped from their bed.

Tessa had always been the first one up on Sunday. Until the past year, it had been Polly who had wandered down next, sleepy and hungry, to chat cozily with her mother over croissants and chocolate until her father awoke. Tim regarded Sunday as his day to burrow in, sleep till all hours. Now that Polly was gone, Tessa found herself increasingly impatient with that particular indulgence of Tim's.

The morning air was cool against her skin as she picked up the newspaper from the doorstep. The maple tree at the edge of the lawn was rosy; the birds and squirrels in the ravine were beginning to create a racket; the curtains of the house across the street were still and drawn: the twin boys Polly had played with were also off to college.

The newspaper tucked under one arm, she carried a newly made cup of coffee to Polly's room. She had left a window open; the air had the freshness she associated with clothes dried out-of-doors. Brushing some crumbs from one of the director's chairs, she settled into it. The sunlight crept by degrees across the floorboards as she read.

The story was featured on the front page today, accompanied by a photograph of two police officers (one, Detective Fulton, identified as in charge of the case) standing with several young people outside a frame house. Gretchen's friends, when they were interviewed, told of knowing of only one romantic attachment; despite his eagerness to have her found, the boy had been unable to help. The housemate, her friend from high school, testified to the fact that Gretchen would have gone with no one unless she knew the person. She would never have frightened her mother; they were close and she wrote often, sometimes twice a week. Gretchen was friendly and outgoing but properly wary. And all were agreed that Gretchen was a conscientious student and had declared her intention of devoting the entire October weekend to completing a required paper for one of her courses.

The police were optimistic but had no "leads." Plans were under way to search the woods—an extensive tract, often a lovers' rendezvous and with a few sensitive incidents in its history—first by helicopter and then by foot. Detective Fulton was quoted: "Information from friends confirm that this is a girl who backpacked in Colorado one summer and who has always enjoyed camping out."

Camping out. Tessa gave a small grunt. Fulton's implication was that Gretchen's absence might be voluntary. She read on. He added that the case was "just plain eerie—now you see her, now you don't." Idiot. He repeated that a search team would be sent into the woods on the day after the air search.

The romantic attachment's name had not been given. (Steve?) How did police determine whether or not such a person was involved? If Gretchen had only one such friend, would she have been likely to have gone with any other man? A woman would not have abducted her—women didn't do things like that. Detective Fulton was obviously so intrigued by the Poe-like aspects of the case that he could not see what was right under his nose. The boy needed looking into.

Tessa laid the paper on the little table beside her chair. The mother was strange, not even coming north to help with the investigation. Probably in Florida hunting a rich old husband. Why else would a comparatively young woman go to Florida? And with a daughter close to twenty, she would be young, probably not much older than Tessa. She may not have had her daughter as early as Tessa had, and perhaps Gretchen wasn't an only child, like Polly, but still . . .

But she must be an only child. There had been no mention of sisters and brothers. An only child—and suddenly, no child. She couldn't help feeling sympathy for the woman. What if it were Polly? And if the mother were she, waiting nervously in some airport (for *she* would fly immediately to her daughter's campus). How unreal it would be, standing alone (if the situation were parallel, she and Tim would no longer be married), filled with a hollow chill, a sick sense of horror, unable to imagine what had happened, yet unable to stop imagining. Visualizing the worst. Murder. Rape. No, not that, torture—Polly being kept alive somewhere, hidden, being hurt or terrorized like that girl in *The Collector*.

With a sudden feeling of nausea, Tessa pushed the newspaper aside. This was sick; she must stop. On impulse, she picked up the receiver; the telephone extension still remained in Polly's room.

It was obvious she had awakened Polly. "Mother? Is something wrong?"

"No. That is—no. Everything's fine here. What about you, sweetie? Are you all right?"

"Of course." Polly still sounded puzzled. "You're sure everything's okay?"

"Yes. I was just thinking about you, worrying a little about you. You know us mothers. It's Sunday morning and I felt lonesome for you. Remember how we used to have breakfast while your father slept late?"

"Yes. I miss you, too, Mom. I'm loving being in New York, though. And the job is fantastic."

"You're careful? New York is a dangerous place." For that matter, Tessa reflected, even a Midwestern college town is a dangerous place. "You *are* careful? Polly?"

"Oh, Mother, you sound so anxious." Polly laughed. "Don't *fuss*. I know my way around. I know what's okay to do and what isn't." She paused. "Was there anything special? I just noticed the time. I should be out of here. I'm having brunch with David."

"David? Have I heard of him?"

"He's just a boy I met. I'll write you about him. Mom, I really have to—"

Tessa hung up heavily. David? She was not reassured.

Later, driving to the bakery to pick up fresh croissants and the *Times,* which the bakery obligingly stocked, she swerved off her route.

Without being aware of doing so, she had noted the address in the news story: 259 Wood Street. The house was smarter-looking than the photograph indicated, with the remains of a small front garden that reminded her of some she had seen in Surrey during their English trip with Polly. She slowed. The windows of the downstairs apartment, Gretchen's, were uncurtained. In one hung a vigorous-looking spider plant; through the other Tessa could see books on shelves and a large round paper lamp. Probably there were posters on the walls, maybe a London Transit System poster such as she and Tim had bought Polly or some old Galerie Maeghts like those Polly had carried off with her to college.

Seeing the house made it all more real. Pathetic. Something touching just about being young, full of plans and at the same time filled with the sure, exciting sense that anything might happen, life might be full of unpredictable encounters. Maybe *pathetic* wasn't exactly the word. The unpredictable encounter seemed to have happened to Gretchen, all right. Not quite the sort she might have fantasied, but unpredictable. Yet Gretchen had always seemed like such a sensible, down-to-earth girl.

What nonsense! Tessa swung her car around the next corner and headed for the bakery. What did she know of how sensible and down-to-earth Gretchen was? And why on earth had it crossed her mind to think Gretchen had *always* been that way? She simply must stop thinking about this.

But it refused to be shelved. In the bakery, idly eavesdropping on a conversation ahead of her, she heard Gretchen's name.

". . . hitchhiking probably. They hitchhike and then they're surprised at what happens. Then thousands of our taxpayer dollars get spent trying to locate their bodies."

"But this girl wasn't hitchhiking," the woman just ahead of her demurred. "She was studying when she disappeared."

"Oh, they're deceitful, all right. They can make you think they're studying . . ."

Tessa stepped back and turned away, hoping the woman had noted her rebuff. Someone farther along the line murmured, "Harridan. Poor kid—God knows what's happened to her."

Gretchen awoke to a sense of confusion. She was stretched out on the back seat of a car—a small van, it appeared to be. She was unbound, but with no awareness of where she was or who the couple in the front seat was. She stirred slightly, began to rise on her elbows, then thought better of it and lay still, trying to get her bearings. She could not recall how she had come here but, oddly, she felt no fear.

Gingerly, she touched her head. It was not sore; apparently she had not been struck. Silently, she examined the backs of the people in the front seat. The scruffy-looking man and the blond woman were strangers to her. They were talking in low tones; although she strained, she could not quite hear their conversation.

She gave another thought to confronting them and then, in a strange, weary acquiescence, she lay back and closed her eyes again.

Taxpayers' money, Tessa thought. She was writing a letter to the editor of the *News*. She finished: ". . . and surely, in a town of our resources, a thorough and unremitting investigation can be continued. This is one of our children. We taxpaying citizens are in complete support of the police in this effort." A little heavy, perhaps. She rechecked for typing errors, signed the letter and addressed the envelope. So much for the woman in the bakery. How many days now—eleven? God knows what had happened to her.

Tuesday morning's newspaper reported no findings in the search of the woods and offered a few more comments from Detective Fulton. He was given to clichés: *vanished into thin air; all possibilities will be exhausted; no signs of foul play.* University friends of the girl were planning a door-to-door canvass of the neighborhood, and they had arranged that her photograph be displayed in public places—the supermarket, the dry cleaner's. Tessa, passing it often, was baffled by the elusive resemblance to Polly.

It was after the two-week mark had been reached that the idea of phoning Mrs. Willey took form for Tessa. The idea occurred to her the day she read that "the distraught mother" had been unable to remain in town because of her work. The discovery that she had come, after all, and that she worked, cast a different light on her. She was probably a hostess in one of the big waterfront hotel restaurants, or a waitress. One of the stories had mentioned Miami. Divorced, with a husband no doubt unwilling to provide even for Gretchen's school costs, she worked, perhaps even as a chambermaid, tugging at heavy mattresses, vacuuming carpets dirtied by conventioneers' parties, dodging passes from drunken Legionnaires. Tessa found her former disgust for the uncaring mother transformed into sympathy.

Poor woman, during all of this, despite lying sleepless at night, tearing at her fingernails with her teeth, weeping at images passing through her mind, she must keep at it, working, suffering indignities.

The phone call seemed no more than Mrs. Willey's due. If she knew other mothers like Tessa were thinking of her, worrying about Gretchen, too, wouldn't that compensate, help a little to comfort her? Especially after the thoughts Tessa had had of her—unjust, intolerant thoughts. She owed Mrs. Willey that call. Tessa could see her swollen face, the tension in her thin body, a woman still young and still attractive at other times.

Tessa would need her phone number. One could hardly call information and ask for Mrs. Willey of Miami, if it was Miami. And what if she no longer used her married name? The thing to do was to reach Detective Fulton. She could offer help with the canvassing, if it was still being done, could help offset effects of obstructionists like the bakery woman. Sunday's story had carried the police number to call with information on Gretchen. She supposed she would reach a tape recorder.

She reached Detective Fulton, a man interested in who she was.

"Tessa Lassiter. I'm just a mother. A taxpayer," she explained. "I have a college-age daughter and I'm concerned. I'd like to do something—canvass or whatever, and I thought it might help if I called Gretchen's—that is, the missing girl's—mother to let her know there are other mothers thinking of her."

"You know the girl, Mrs. Lassiter?" Detective Fulton asked.

"No, I've just read about her. I'm concerned."

"You refer to her as Gretchen."

"That's because I've read her name so often." She felt it necessary to defend her interest. "Not everyone is sympathetic. Some people feel you're wasting the taxpayers' money."

"You feel the search is a waste?"

"No, no, you don't understand. *I* want to help."

There was a brief silence.

In a smaller voice, Tessa added, "Can't I help?" *Lord* she thought, *I sound like a child.*

"Perhaps, Mrs. Lassiter," Detective Fulton said, "we could come by to see you." He sounded as though he had turned his head from the phone.

Fear touched Tessa. Did he think she was lying to him? Or knew something? *God,* she thought, *what am I doing? I really have gotten carried away.*

Forcing a firmness into her tone—after all, she was one of those taxpayers responsible for Detective Fulton's livelihood—she said, "Look. I'm just what I say I am: a housewife, a schoolteacher, the wife of a professor at the university, a person who is worried about a girl like my own daughter. I thought I'd help if I could. I thought I'd try to get Mrs. Willey's full name and telephone number to tell her some of us care what's happening to her. You can have your detective come to see me, but he won't learn anything but that. Probably I shouldn't have called."

"It's all right." Detective Fulton's voice had changed. "I'll see that one of my men stops by. We understand that people are concerned."

Setting the receiver back, Tess thought, *He thinks I'm a crank of some sort.* With surprise, she wondered if indeed she was. Wasn't this the way cranks behaved?

The detective was small; he must barely have passed the height requirement for police officers. He was meticulously polite as he submitted to sitting on the edge of a chair. Evidently he had established that she was what she claimed to be—Tessa noted his quick glance at Polly's photograph on the bookshelf—and when he left, he consulted a notepad. "Beatrice Willey, that's her name. She's a supervisor with the phone company in Miami. But she's listed. You can get her phone number from the operator."

Had they phoned Mrs. Willey, forewarning her, giving her instructions for dealing with Tessa? Perhaps Tim's link with the university had cleared away their suspicions. Professors and their wives were viewed with less than warmth by the townspeople, but they were a force in the community and must be reckoned with.

Thursday night was Tim's poker game; he had been invited by a group of graduate students to play and considered it a night off in every respect. Tessa didn't want to think about what Tim, with his extra years and extra wisdom, would say if he knew what she was doing. Someone had to do something and Tim never would, that was certain. The police search had turned up no new leads, and Tessa had noted that the news story had shrunk and moved again to the third section, as though the reporters' interest had lagged. On the campus ice-cream parlor's bulletin board, Tessa had noticed that a dance recital announcement covered part of Gretchen's face. It was only after Tim had departed that Tessa settled herself at Polly's desk beside the telephone extension.

The phone rang in Miami. Before the first ring was complete, the receiver at the other end was lifted. "Yes?" a voice said breathlessly. "Bea Willey—who is it?"

Tessa was suddenly ashamed. This was cruel. This woman was waiting for *the* call, a call from her daughter, from her daughter's abductor, from someone, anyone, who knew something. And she, Tessa Lassiter, was stirring hope in her.

"I'm so sorry," she said. "Mrs. Willey, this is just a mother in the town where your daughter is . . . was. Where she disappeared. I wanted you to know how concerned all of us are. I shouldn't have called."

The silence at the other end was as bleak as though the connection had been broken. Then the voice spoke heavily, devoid of all but exhaustion. "I'm glad people care. It's just so . . ." Tessa could hear her swallowing. "Maybe she just ran away." The statement was almost a question.

Tessa felt called on to respond. "I have a daughter the same age. Kids do strange things." But not Polly. Polly would never run away. *She would never do that to me.*

"Yes," said Mrs. Willey, without hope. "Only Gretchen has never done anything like that and . . ." Her voice trailed off.

"I do think," Tessa consoled, "that the police and everybody here are doing all they can. You know about the searches and the canvassing? And the posters?"

"Yes. But they don't find anything," Mrs. Willey said dully.

"It doesn't mean they won't. Don't Gretchen's friends have any ideas?"

"No. They don't think . . . If you only knew the things I've imagined."

"I can guess," Tessa broke in, not wanting to hear. "But probably none of them happened. Really. Is there anything I—we mothers, that is—can do?"

"No." The low voice sounded as though Bea Willey were tired beyond further speech. "I'm going to try a radio appeal. TV too. But it won't help. Gretchen would know . . . I don't have to tell her . . ."

"What about her father?" Tessa asked, remembering the deserter.

"I haven't seen him in years. He left us when Gretchen was a little girl. He probably doesn't even know she's gone."

"Her boyfriend, what about him?"

"Roger. I don't think he's very bright. Or else he can't have known her very well. He's no help. I've wondered if maybe there was someone else none of us knows about." Her voice became bitter. "But no one knows. No one helps. . . . I have to hang up now, I don't like to tie up the phone."

"Remember," Tessa cried, "if there's anything."

"Thank you." She was gone.

Nothing. She could do nothing, nothing, nothing. Just accept. She had not even had the presence of mind to give Mrs. Willey her phone number. She leaned over and snapped off the desk lamp. She was more tired than she had been in weeks.

The empty room was dark. Without light, she found her way to the rocker Polly had in her last year of junior high painted red and outfitted with black-and-white Marimekko cushions. She remembered Polly's giggle as she looked at the finished product. "Doesn't look like the nursery now, does it?" she had said.

Heavily, Tessa sat down in the rocker, still serviceable after twenty years. For no reason she could properly explain, her eyes filled with tears and a sob caught at her throat. Sitting alone in the dark, empty room, she wept. After a while she thought, *I'm crying. I'm crying for that poor woman who lost her daughter.*

The man was handsome—wide-shouldered, tall, his features strong. He was deeply tanned.

The sun lit his dark face as they walked across the sand to the sea. The young woman beside him was golden-skinned in the light.

"Well," he said, seating himself beside her on the sand. "Think you can stand another day at the beach?"

She smiled up at him. "I haven't been on the beach like this since . . . for a long time." She frowned.

"Don't worry about it, sweetie. Just don't worry. Enjoy." He grinned down at her. "You're not very big, are you?" he said affectionately.

"No, I never was. I was the smallest girl in my class in first grade. Probably ever since." She threw an anxious glance at him. "I remember such funny things."

He looked at her thoughtfully.

After a moment she said, "What I can't figure out is how I dared to hitchhike. Hitching is pretty risky, isn't it?"

"Yep. You were lucky." He smiled. "*We* were."

"But—doing it when I was so—sort of lost. And with only that twenty-dollar bill in my pocket. Though, you know, even if I couldn't remember how I got on the highway—or anything, really—I felt so peaceful. I don't think anything bad could have happened to me, even if I did hitchhike. Nobody could have broken through that feeling."

He sat watching her.

"And that one couple that brought me almost all the way to California and let me sleep in their van, that was lucky. I think they thought I was crazy out there by myself. I suppose I was, in a way."

"Not crazy. What happened to you isn't craziness."

"I wasn't coming here. I don't *think* I was. But I showed them that slip of paper I had with your address . . . even if you had to tell me who you were when I got here." She giggled. "I told them my name was Isabel Archer. I don't think they do much reading. Funny how I remembered that book.'' After a minute she said, ''Did I already tell you I said I was Isabel Archer?''

''You did.'' He smiled.

''I keep telling you things over again, don't I? I think it's because I think it'll make me remember. Anyway, I did come. I had that slip of paper.'' She turned to him, her face puzzled. ''Where do you think I got that?''

''I have no idea. Maybe you'd had it for a long time.''

''You know, funny little pieces come back. A room someplace. I was reading. . . .'' Her forehead wrinkled. ''I think I was tired. Very tired.'' She was quiet for a while. ''Do you suppose someday I'll remember everything? Will I know all about myself?''

He looked out over the sea. ''I'm sure you will. Of course there'll be distortions—''

''Distortions?''

''You'll remember some things the way you wish they were.''

She said nothing for a minute. ''Does that happen with what I have? Amnesia?''

He smiled down at her. ''Quite often. But I'll straighten you out. I won't let you go on believing something that isn't true.''

''You *want* me to find out, don't you?''

''Of course I want you to.''

''You know everything about me.'' It was a statement.

''Not everything.'' He sighed. ''We've been over this, honey. Things should come back naturally. That doctor I spoke to said it would be meaningless if they don't.''

''I know. The only thing . . .'' Her gaze was on the water. ''The only thing that really bothers me is not being able to remember my mother. It seems to me I ought to be able to remember my own mother.''

Slowly Gretchen's father turned his eyes toward her. He studied her face for a long moment, calculating. Finally, he spoke. ''You didn't remember me,'' he said. ''But then,'' he added mildly, ''your mother died when you were so young.''

Joan Hess, nominated for a 1986 Anthony for Strangled Prose, *offers delighted readers three series. Claire Malloy of* Prose *is featured in four books, including* A Really Cute Corpse; Malice in Maggody *and* Mischief in Maggody *recount the hijinks in a small southern town; and* The Night-Blooming Cereus *and* The Deadly Ackee, *written as Joan Hadley, feature Theo Bloomer. Fans would argue that the sprightly and slightly wicked Hess wit is really the highlight of her books.*

In "Too Much to Bare," motivations are stripped to essentials, giving new meaning to the notion of girls' night out.

TOO MUCH TO BARE

by Joan Hess

"MY HUSBAND IS going to kill me," Marjorie announced. It was not the first time she'd suggested the possibility. Anne had lost count.

"Oh, honey," Sylvia said soothingly, "it's not as if we're taking the merchandise home, or even having a chance to do more than study it from a respectable distance. Not that I wouldn't object, should the opportunity arise—if you know what I mean!"

The three other women at the table obligingly giggled at Sylvia's comment. Marjorie, already damp with perspiration in her rumpled polyester pantsuit, flapped a pudgy hand as if to dispel any lingering aura of naughtiness. "You are such a joker," she said. "I don't know how you think of these things."

"I would imagine it comes from hanging around outside the locker room," Bitsy said. Her eyes, heavily accented with mascara and undulating ribbons of blue and gray shadow, closed for a moment as a curtain of black hair fell across her

149

face. She took a sip of beer, wrinkled her nose, and pushed aside her cup. A Christian in the Colosseum could not have looked less delighted.

"Better than hanging around inside," Sylvia said, "unless we're discussing some little jock's strap."

Anne busied herself replenishing their plastic cups with beer from the pitcher, keeping her face lowered in order to hide her expression. Sylvia's jokes were always crude. Most of the teachers at the school avoided the lounge whenever Sylvia sailed in for coffee and conversation; Anne had discovered she preferred to stay in the library rather than listen to the barrage of gossip and off-color humor. A thermos of coffee sufficed. But tonight she found herself taking a certain pleasure in Sylvia's company. A certain pleasure, yes.

The Happy Hour Saloon was swelling with a large and raucous crowd. The music blared from omnipresent speakers, too loud and senseless for Anne's taste, forcing voices to compete in shrieks. The throbbing, repetitive beat seemed to stir the two hundred or so women, however, with promises of erotica, of good times to come. Lights flashed in a dizzying pattern that lacked discernible organization, changing faces from red to green to blue as if they were hapless chameleons. The tables were littered with cups, pitchers, ashtrays heaped with cigarette butts, and spreading wet circles that glittered like kisses as the lights swept across them.

"Isn't this a hoot?" Sylvia demanded of the table. "I went to one of these last year, and it was beyond my wildest imagination." She flung her blond hair over her shoulder and studied the barnlike room with a complacent smile. "This crowd looks a lot worse. We are in for quite a time this evening, ladies. Quite a time."

Marjorie drained her cup and pushed herself to her feet. "If Hank's going to kill me, I might as well die happily. I'm going for another pitcher, after a trip to the can to powder my nose. Anyone else interested?"

Bitsy picked up her purse and tucked it under her arm. "I'm tempted to stay in the ladies' room until the show is over," she said acidly. "I cannot believe I'm actually here. I don't know why we let Sylvia coerce us into this low-class display of vulgarity, although I can understand why it might appeal to her.''

Waggling a finger at her, Sylvia said, ''It's time you saw something more exciting than a kindergarten classroom, my dear. You're beginning to look like one of your five-year-olds.''

Bitsy pursed her lips into a pout. ''This whole thing is nauseating. I should have stayed at my apartment and washed my hair. Let's go, Marjorie. The ladies' room is probably filthy, but I'm not accustomed to beer. Scotch is less fattening, and so much more civilized than this swill.''

Once Marjorie and Bitsy found a path through the crowd of women and vanished around the far corner of the bar, Anne gazed across the table. ''I can't believe I'm here either. It's a good thing Paul's out at the cabin this weekend. Maybe by Sunday night I'll have worked up enough courage to tell him about it.'' Or perhaps she might whisper it in his ear, while he lay in a coffin at the funeral home. Even tell him she'd changed her mind about the divorce—he could file it in hell or wherever he ended up. She bit her lip to hide a quick smile. The irony was delicious.

''What's he doing at the lake?'' Sylvia asked. She lit a cigarette and inhaled deeply.

''He said he had a lot of work to do and wanted to put fifty miles between himself and a telephone. He's been under such stress lately; I hope he has a chance to relax.''

''You still don't have a telephone out there? God, Anne, it's halfway to the end of the world.''

''That's why Paul bought it. I don't really enjoy staying there, but he seems to find ways to amuse himself. I haven't been there in months.'' She crossed her fingers in her lap. She'd been there two days ago, when she'd called in sick and then taken a little field trip, although hardly in a fat yellow school bus. ''He asked if I would drive up this weekend. I told him I absolutely had to finish the semester inventory at the library, but that's only partly true. In all honesty, he's been in a rotten mood for several months, and I have no desire to be cooped up with him in the middle of the woods.''

''Maybe he's in mid-life crisis. My ex went crazy when he

hit forty. His shrink said he'd get over it, but I divorced the bastard on general principle. When men got to that age, they don't seem to know what they want—unless it's a combination of cuddle and sizzle.''

"He's not having an affair," Anne replied firmly. "Paul is much too straitlaced to do anything to threaten his stuffy law practice. I do wish he didn't have to work so hard; we haven't had a proper dinner in three months." He had, though. She'd opened the bill from the credit card company. Lots of restaurants, but she hadn't been invited for any cozy little dinners with elegant wine. She'd been at home, putting gourmet meals down the garbage disposal.

"The old working-late-at-the-office bit?" Sylvia raised two penciled eyebrows. "Well, if you're not going to worry about it, then neither am I, but I think you'd better keep an eye on him. Paul's an attractive man, and he knows it. Did you hear what happened this morning in the teachers' lounge when the toilet backed up?"

Anne forced a smile as Sylvia began to relate a bit of gossip that would, without a doubt, end on a crude bark of laughter. The music drowned out a major part of the story, but she didn't care. Sylvia didn't require more than a superficially attentive audience. The bitch. So she was surprised there was no telephone at the cabin. As if she didn't know. Of course what she and Paul did at the cabin didn't require a telephone—only a mattress. Or any flat surface, for that matter. Her smile wavered, but she tightened her jaw and willed it into obedience.

"Hank is going to kill me," Marjorie said as she set the pitcher on the table and sat down beside Anne. "So when do we see the boys?"

Sylvia consulted her watch. "In about ten minutes, I would guess. The management wants to give all of us time to drink ourselves into a cheerful mood."

Bitsy slipped in next to Sylvia and glared at the rowdier elements of the crowd. "*Cheerful* is hardly the adjective, Sylvia. Nasty and foulmouthed might be closer to the truth. Where do all these women come from? I've never seen so many women about to burst out of their jeans or pop buttons off their blouses.'' She shifted her eyes to Sylvia's ample chest, which was distorting a field of silk flowers.

''This isn't a Sunday prayer meeting,'' Sylvia said, grinning. ''Now you and Marjorie could sneak in the back door of the church if you wanted to, but Anne and I came to have fun. Isn't that right, Anne?''

''Oh, yes,'' Anne murmured. Oh, no, she added to herself as she once again held in a smile. She had come to put the plan in motion. Sylvia needed to know where Paul was, and how lonely he might be for his cooperative slut. She decided to reiterate the information once again, just in case Sylvia had missed it. ''You should have convinced Hank to go fishing with Paul, Marjorie. The poor baby's out at the cabin all by himself for the entire weekend, with no one to entertain him. And he's been acting very odd these last three or four months; I'm worried he might be on the edge of a nervous breakdown.''

''So worried that you felt obliged to come to this horrid show instead of bothering to be with him?'' Bitsy said coolly.

Anne winced as she struggled to hide a flicker of irritation. It was, she lectured herself, an opening to produce her alibi, even if it had been provided in a self-righteous tone of voice. ''He told me he preferred to be alone, Bitsy, and I can't go to the cabin this weekend, in any case. I'm going to spend the next two days locked in the library with Bev to do the semester inventory. We agreed we'd work until midnight Saturday and Sunday if we had to, and send out for sandwiches. Paul will enjoy a chance for relaxation and total solitude.''

''Total solitude?'' Sylvia echoed, laughing. ''Maybe he's having an affair with some nubile specimen of wildlife.''

''That's not a very nice thing to say,'' Bitsy said. ''Just because your husband chased every skirt in town doesn't mean that—''

''Paul's banging a raccoon? My ex would have; he banged everything that breathed.'' Sylvia laughed again, then finished her beer and lit another cigarette from the smoldering butt in her hand. Next to her, Bitsy coughed in complaint and pointedly fanned the air with her hand. Anne covertly studied Sylvia's face, searching for some sign that the blonde's thoughts were centered on the poor lonely husband in the conveniently remote cabin.

Marjorie had managed to mention her impending demise three more times before the music abruptly stopped. A middle-aged man in a pale blue tuxedo bounded onto the stage, a microphone in one hand. The crowd quieted in expectation, as did the four women at the table next to the stage.

"Are you ready?" the man demanded.

"Yes!" the women squealed.

"Are you ready?" he again demanded, leering into what must have resembled a murky aquarium of multicolored faces.

The crowd responded with increased enthusiasm. The ritual continued for several minutes as the emcee warmed up the audience. Anne could not bring herself to join the frenzied promises that she was indeed ready, even though, at a more essential level, the decision had been reached and the plan already set in motion. This man seemed too manipulative to merit response, too crassly chauvinistic—too much like Paul. Sylvia had no such reservations, of course. Marjorie was mouthing the sentiments of the crowd and clapping; Bitsy stared at the tabletop as if she were judging kindergarten finger paintings for potential van Goghs.

"Do you want to meet the men?" the emcee howled. The crowd howled that they most definitely did. The emcee mopped his forehead, assured them that they would in one teeny minute, but first they were going to have the opportunity to order one more round of drinks. Waving good-bye, he bounded off the stage and the music rose to fill the void.

Sylvia began to dig through her purse. "Damn it, I just had that prescription refilled last week," she said as she piled the contents on the table. "Tranquilizers aren't cheap."

But the gaunt blond divorcée was, Anne thought. Too bad she couldn't find her pills, but they had been removed earlier in the week, when Sylvia had negligently left her purse in the lounge. They were a part of the plan, a major part of the plan that would end with a wonderfully melodramatic climax. The other climaxes would occur earlier—in the bed, under the kitchen table, wherever the two opted to indulge their carnal drives.

She really didn't care anymore. Her marriage was a farce, as silly and shallow as the night's entertainment. It would be over by Sunday, and she would be free from Paul's overbearing hypocrisy and Sylvia's treacherous avowals of friendship. A colleague had told her about seeing the two of them at a restaurant. Although the news had initially paralyzed her, she had begun within a matter of days to devise the plan. It had taken several weeks to perfect it; the invitation from Sylvia to the male revue had seemed such a lovely, ironic time for the countdown to begin.

"You really shouldn't mix barbiturates with alcohol. The combination can be lethal," she said, hoping she sounded properly concerned. The advice was based on many hours of research, after all, done while sipping coffee from her thermos. An elementary school library held so many fascinating books and magazines. From both sides of the table, Bitsy and Marjorie nodded their agreement.

Sylvia shrugged and began to cram things back in her purse. "It'd take a handful of the things to do any damage. I must have left them in the bathroom at home, or in another purse. Damnation, I feel a really ghastly tension headache coming on; I'll have to drown it in beer."

Just wait, Anne added under her breath. By Sunday night, Sylvia and Paul were going to be far past the point of feeling anything. The bottle was in the liquor cabinet at the cabin, a brand she knew Paul always kept well stocked. The drifting sediment at the bottom would not prevent the contents from being savored, and the effects would take several hours to be felt. By then, it would be much too late.

Sunday night, or perhaps Monday morning, she would telephone the sheriff's department and in a worried, wifely voice ask them to check the cabin. The suicide note she had typed on Paul's typewriter would be found in her bedside drawer, his illegible signature scrawled across the bottom. It was really quite nicely written, with pained admissions that he could no longer bear a life without Sylvia, that he had taken her pills earlier in the week so they could gently pass away in each other's arms. A bittersweet postscript to his wife, begging her forgiveness. She suspected she would shed a few tears when the police showed it to her. Her friends would all assure her that he had had a nervous breakdown, that he hadn't known what he was writing. They would be right, but she wouldn't tell them that.

"Oh, my lord," whispered Marjorie. "Hank really is going to kill me if I have to call him for bail."

Anne yanked her thoughts to the present moment and turned to the stage. A young man had appeared, dressed in a police uniform. His face was stern as he slapped a billy club across his palm. She felt as if it were slamming against her abdomen. Had Paul found the note and realized what she had arranged for the lovebirds?

"I should arrest all of you," he said, scowling as his eyes flitted around the room. "Run you in, book you, and take you to a cold, dark cell. Fling you across the cot and interrogate you until you beg for mercy. Is that what you want me to do?"

"No," screamed a voice from the crowd. "Take it off!"

His mouth softened; dimples appeared in his cheeks. "Is that what you want me to do?" he demanded of the crowd.

"Take it off!"

Like a prairie dog, the emcee popped up on the platform at the back of the stage. "Do you want Policeman Dick to take it off? You'll have to tell him what you want!"

"Take—it—off!" the crowd howled in unified frenzy.

The music began to pulsate as the young man toyed with the top button of his shirt, his hips synchronized with the beat. The crowd roared their approval. Sylvia leaned forward and said, "You turned absolutely white, Anne. Did you think he was a real cop?"

Anne kept her eyes on the man in the middle of the stage. "Don't be absurd, Sylvia. I don't have a guilty conscience," she said distractedly. The first button was undone, and the graceful fingers had moved down one tantalizing inch. A few curly chest hairs were visible now; she felt a sudden urge to dash onto the stage and brush her hand across them. "Is he going to take it all off?"

"I can't believe you said that," Bitsy sniffed. "I think this is disgusting."

Anne had expected to feel the same way, but now, with the darling young blond man who looked so wholesome, so boyish and innocent and pleased with the response from the crowd—it wasn't disgusting. It was very, very interesting.

Marjorie put her cup down, her eyes wide and her mouth slightly agape. "I don't think it's disgusting," she said in a hollow voice.

Bitsy leaned back in the chair and crossed her arms. "The three of you are slobbering like dogs."

Anne barely heard the condemnation from across the table. Policeman Dick was easing out of his shirt, letting each sleeve slide down his arm so slowly she could feel the ripple of his biceps, the hard turn of his elbows, the soft skin of his forearm, the mounded base of his hand, the long, delicate fingers. She heard herself exhale as the khaki shirt fell to the floor.

His hips still moving with the music, the man flexed his arms and turned slowly so the women could appreciate his flat stomach and broad shoulders. He swaggered across the stage to Anne's table and curled his hands behind Sylvia's neck.

"Unbuckle my belt or I'll run you in," he said, smiling to take the menace from his facetious threat. He noticed Anne's stunned expression and winked at her, sharing the joke in an oddly private message.

"You can run me in anytime you want!" Sylvia smirked as she fumbled with the buckle of his belt. Beside her, Bitsy was almost invisible below the table. Her face was stony, and her mouth a pinched ring of scandalized disapproval.

When the buckle was freed, the man backed away to tease the crowd with his jutting pelvis and bare chest. His trousers began to slide down his hips. Again Anne could feel his skin, now so taut with smooth, muscular slopes. It's been such a long time, she thought, panicked by the intensity of her reaction. If only Paul hadn't lost interest when he began the affair with Sylvia. . . . It was his fault she was responding like a silly, breathless, hormone-driven adolescent.

The uniform was off now; only a small triangle of khaki fabric acknowledged the limits of legality. The young man—Policeman Dick, she amended with a faint smile—began to dance with increased insistence, turning often so that all the women could have an equal opportunity to admire that which deserved admiration. The colored lights flashed across his body in silken hues, shadows to be stroked to find their depth.

As he moved toward the table, Sylvia creased a dollar bill and waved it over Anne's head. "Over here!" she called.

Perplexed, Anne frowned across the table. When Sylvia grinned and pointed, she turned back to see the young man dancing directly in front of her. Blue eyes crinkled in amusement. The dimples back again. And the wondrously unclad body, close enough that she could see the faint sheen of sweat. Feathery blond hair. Muscles that swooped like snow-covered hills. Hard thighs. The mysterious khaki bulge.

Despite the sudden grip of numbness, a wave of Novocain that flooded her chest and froze her lungs, she felt the dollar bill in her hand. The man slowly pulled her to her feet. All around them, women were bellowing in approval, their hands banging the tabletops and their feet pounding the floor. The music seemed to grow louder, a primitive command from a wild and unknown place. The young man curled a finger for Anne to move closer to him. Then, before she could consider her actions, she found herself sliding the bill under the narrow strap that supported his only item of clothing. Her fingers brushed his skin. A baby's skin.

He leaned down and caught her head in his hands. His deliberate kiss caught her by surprise, stunned her into acquiescence, and then, as his lips lingered, into unintentional cooperation. When she felt as if she were losing herself in a tunnel of heat, he eased away and met her eyes. After another disturbing wink, he danced away to collect the dollar bills that now waved like pennants all over the room.

"Sit down!" Bitsy snapped. "Everyone's staring at you. I want you to know that I am simply disgusted with you, Anne. And both of you too," she added to Sylvia and Marjorie. "I've had more of this than I can bear. I'm going home."

Anne wiggled her hand in farewell, but she could not unlock her eyes from the young blond dancer. Coals had been lit deep within her; they flamed and glowed, painfully. Her body ached for him. And he seemed to remain aware of her even as he accepted dollars and gave kisses to the screaming women crowding the edge of the stage.

Then, with a dimpled smile and a wink she felt was hers, he left the stage. The emcee introduced a dark-haired young man in a sequined cape, who began to produce gyrations with his hips as he paraded around the stage.

Anne looked at the dressing-room door in one corner of the room. "Will he be back?" she asked Sylvia.

"Probably. I could see you liked what you saw, Anne. You'd better not tell Paul too much about this when he gets home Sunday. He may not approve of his wife kissing a male stripper."

Marjorie sighed. "What was it like, Anne?"

"Just a kiss." But such a kiss. Soft lips and a faint hint of after-shave. A kiss more innocent than a high-school sweetheart's, but promising more than any boy could offer. A cherub without a robe. Every mother's son, every woman's lover. The ache increased until she felt as if she might slip into a fantasy of such erotic delight that she would never willingly return.

"Looks like our Annie is in love," Sylvia said. She pulled out another dollar bill and waved it over Marjorie's head. "Let's see if we can share the good fortune."

While Marjorie laughingly protested and tried to hide, Anne forced herself to watch the man on stage, who was nearing the same state of undress his predecessor had achieved. It did nothing to distract her from the memory of the kiss. She was startled when a waiter tapped her on the shoulder and handed her a folded note. He nodded in the direction of the dressing-room door and left.

Would she wait for "D" after the show?

There was a bit more, but she could hardly see the written letters. Would she? Did she dare? Anne Carter, wife of a lawyer, respected librarian at the neighborhood elementary school, gracious hostess for countless cocktail parties and elegant buffets designed to charm Paul's clients, was hardly the sort to hang around stage doors for male . . . dancers, dimples or not. She had never . . . done such a thing. It was . . . unthinkable. She simply . . . couldn't.

Men continued to dance on the stage. Dollars were waved; women were kissed and convinced not to pull too strenuously on the elastic straps that kept the show marginally legal. Anne watched it all, sipping beer that had no taste, clapping to music that had no beat, hearing catcalls that had no meaning. Could she be in the blond man's arms while her husband and his mistress unwittingly poisoned themselves with the bottle she had left at the cabin?

Dick appeared during the second half of the show, this time dressed in tight pants and a shirt with flowing sleeves. As he danced at the table next to hers, Anne caught his questioning smile. She nodded. There really was no choice.

She survived the rest of the show, counting the minutes until the room would clear and he would emerge from the dressing room. At last, after a finale of flesh, the emcee thanked the crowd and told them when his show would return to the Happy Hour Saloon. Once the stage was empty, most of the women started for the exits, babbling excitedly about the relative merits of each performer.

"Hank's going to kill me," Marjorie said happily, then pulled herself out of her chair and left.

Anne glanced at Sylvia. "Don't you have a date?" she asked. At a cabin, with a bottle of Scotch and a husband who had strayed too far to ever merit forgiveness. She wanted it to be done.

"I do, and here he comes," Sylvia said, putting her cigarette case in her purse. "But what about you? This is hardly the place for librarians to sit alone and drink beer."

"He's here?" He couldn't be here—he was at the cabin.

Sylvia waved to a man waiting near the door. "My accountant, actually. I've been after him since April, because he saved me an absolute fortune on my taxes this year. If he can get me a refund next year, I may break down and marry him."

"Your accountant?"

"Somebody has to do my taxes. What's wrong with you?"

"I thought—I thought you and Paul—" Anne gasped through a suddenly constricted throat.

"Not me, Annie. Your husband's attractive, but he's more

interested in the younger set. Or those who teach them.'' Sylvia looked at the chair beside her, where Bitsy had sat until she had made the indignant exit. ''You'd better ask Paul about his late nights at the office. I didn't want to say anything, but Bitsy's been awfully concerned the last few months about your schedule.''

''Bitsy?'' All she could manage was a croak. It couldn't be; the suicide note named Sylvia—not Bitsy. Her literary masterpiece would fool no one, not with the wrong name. The police would realize Paul hadn't written it. They would show it to her, ask her if she had been to the cabin lately, demand to know if she had taken barbiturates from Sylvia's purse and left the empty vial under the note in the night-table drawer. She hadn't worried about fingerprints, or mud on her tires, or any such trivial details. The investigation wouldn't have gone that far. The plan was too good.

She searched wildly for a way to prove Sylvia wrong, to catch her in some horridly devious lie. ''But you had dinner with him!''

''He wanted to ask me how I thought you'd react to a divorce,'' Sylvia said gently. ''He made me swear not to mention it to you. It's been Bitsy all along.''

''No, it can't be. It can't be Bitsy.'' She rubbed her face, unable to believe it. ''You're lying.''

''Sorry to be the one to tell you,'' Sylvia said as she stood up. ''I have to run; my gentleman friend's waiting to hear about the strippers. Don't stay here too long.''

As Sylvia left, Anne felt her stomach grow cold with fear. Bitsy had left more than an hour ago, no doubt on her way to the rendezvous Anne herself had suggested. There was no way to telephone Paul, to tell him that the Scotch was filled with barbiturates, that she would no longer contest a divorce if he would quietly pour the bottle down the drain and tear up the damning suicide note.

Perhaps she could drive up there in time to stop them from consuming too much of the Scotch. The two wouldn't start on the bottle immediately. Surely they'd spend a few minutes greeting each other, and Bitsy would relish telling Paul all the details of the vulgarity to which she'd been exposed. Tell him how his wife had actually kissed a stripper. Offer righteous comments about the cheapness of the bar and the ill-bred behavior of the spectators.

Yes, she had time to rush to the cabin and prevent the Scotch from carrying out its lethal assignment. If she left at once. She grabbed her purse and shoved back her chair. She had enough gas in her car; the route to the cabin was still fresh in her mind. She'd have to confront the two and admit what she'd done, but maybe—

"I'm glad you waited for me," a voice murmured in her ear. A hand touched her elbow and pulled her back down to her chair. "You're the sexiest woman I've ever seen, with your lovely dark hair and little-girl eyes."

"I—I have to leave. Now."

His hand tightened around her elbow, sending a flow of electricity up her arm. As disappointment crossed his face, she said, "An errand has come up, something I really and truly have to do. I'm sorry. I'd like to stay for a drink, but I have to go. Right now. There isn't much time. I'm sorry."

"We leave in the morning and won't be through here for at least six months," he said with a sigh, his blue eyes lowered. "I was very excited about getting to know you, if only for one night. I couldn't believe you'd actually waited for me, but I suppose you've changed your mind." He looked up with a wistful smile. "I wanted to make you happy this one night."

Anne took a deep breath as she studied the sweep of his eyelashes, the faint frown that managed to provoke his dimples, the haze of moisture on his neck from a hurried shower. She knew what his shirt and jeans covered, and she could envision what the khaki triangle had hidden. This—or a frantic drive down a dark, rutted road to the cabin to save two treacherous people from a fate they well deserved?

As the lights swept across the room, her face changed from red to blue to green. "The errand's not all that important," she said in a soft, slow voice.

Winner of a 1988 Edgar for Best First Novel, Deidre Laiken's Death Among Strangers *is an elegant story of misguided love as well as a compelling mystery. Her second mystery,* Killing Time in Buffalo, *followed. In addition to writing award-winning fiction, Deidre has won a nomination by the American Library Association for excellence in young adult nonfiction for her book* Listen to Me, I'm Angry. *Deidre's shorter nonfiction has appeared in* New Woman, Glamour, Mademoiselle, *and* McCall's *magazines.*

In "An Act of Loving Kindness," detective Roberta Singer's grandfather, long dead, helps her solve the mystery of an anonymous corpse.

AN ACT OF LOVING KINDNESS

by Deidre Laiken

THE COUPLE WERE seated beside the lake in the full lotus position, legs crossed, palms open toward the setting sun when the corpse surfaced. The woman was the first to see it. The body washed silently to the shore, naked except for a pair of black socks and a string of white fabric around the waist.

The woman screamed.

Her voice shattered the stillness, slicing through the thick summer air, sending ripples of terror along the smooth surface of Swan Lake.

The Hasidic women walked side by side down the dirt road, long skirts brushing noiselessly against their ankles. The scarves covering their heads were tied securely behind their necks. They talked quietly to one another, stopping only to point out a flutter of wings or the sight of a purple wildflower poking up in the late summer grasses. Up ahead,

163

the men were a cluster of black against the golden landscape.

It was *Shabbos*—the Sabbath—and all work was forbidden.
And so they walked, talked, and prayed. The line of Hasidic
Jews moving serenely through the woods was a familiar sight
on Saturday in the Catskill Mountains. No one could have
known that the two women lingering behind the others, the
two women whose heads were bent toward each other like
eager, pecking birds, were different from all the rest. One
was an *agunah*—a woman alone, a ghostly presence suspended in time. The other had a .38 revolver strapped to her
ankle.

The sun was a white burn in the morning sky. Aliza Kleinman turned her head toward the heat. Years ago, before she
had met Natan, she had been able to read the sky. The stars
in certain positions had meant good fortune; in others they
warned of doom. She had believed in astrology and in the I
Ching and in everything but what she now knew was true.
Yet there was still something about fate. *Beshert* was the word
in Yiddish. It was *beshert* that she would have met Natan, a
man old enough to be her father, a man who knew the world
in a way she could only imagine. A man who had seen hell
and who had escaped.

Rivkah moved along beside her, awkward in her long skirt.
Something made her walk unevenly, heavy on one side. This
woman had come to see her several weeks ago. She had worn
pants then, and a uniform with a badge. She called herself
Detective Singer and she had seemed hard and mean. Aliza
now knew that all that had been a front, a protection. Sometimes she even suspected that Detective Singer was frightened. Very little frightened Aliza anymore. Since it happened
it was as if nothing else bad could touch her.

No one had seen Natan leave. There had been no trace. It
was not known if he was dead or alive. After twelve months,
she understood the true meaning of the Hebrew word *agunah*,
which translated as "loner." Not officially a widow, she was

prohibited from remarrying, which she had never once, for a moment, considered.

Her husband had not been an ordinary man. He had taught her everything she knew about faith. He had taken her from a place of confusion and given her something strong and real. Her return to Judaism had been gradual and hesitant. Natan had never faltered. He had been so sure about her. As sure as he had been that day over forty years ago when the train had stopped abruptly at a place his parents had told him was the ''Treblinka Iron Works.'' A labor camp, they had said. But Natan, barely a teenager, could tell from the barbed wire and the smoke that they had been misled. And he suspected when he drove the cart, filled with debris that camouflaged rifles, revolvers, and hand grenades, that he would be one of the few to survive.

She remembered the story as well as she remembered the events of her own life. Natan had been selected, because of his youth and his enormous strength, to be part of the conspiracy. He had helped to smuggle the weapons from the Nazi arsenal and at 3:45 A.M., he had responded to the gunshot that signaled the beginning of an uprising. Natan, along with two hundred others, had escaped. And he had kept running, through the forests of Poland, over borders and into countries where he quickly learned new languages and new ways to survive. He had lived in potato cellars and monasteries. He spoke Polish, Yiddish, Hebrew, German, French, Spanish, Portuguese, and English. He had been a professor in the Netherlands, a journalist in France, and finally a gold engraver in Manhattan. She had met him by chance, in a jewelry shop in the diamond district. Behind the dark beard and the black coat, he had seemed, even then, almost magical. It hadn't mattered to him that she wasn't religious, that she was half his age. He talked to her about art and politics and only once about faith. She had asked him, after Treblinka, after the Holocaust, how he could believe in God. And he had answered with a question. His accent was barely audible. How, he asked after the Holocaust, could he believe in Man?

Within two years she became his wife and a *Baal Tshuva*,

a returnee to the ways of her ancestors. By the time she gave birth to their third child, Aliza forgot that she had ever lived any other way.

And then Natan disappeared.

A black coat flapped in the breeze. Detective Singer watched Aliza's face. The woman was hard to figure. There was something she wasn't saying. Something she knew.

Roberta Singer had come this far. She wouldn't let go until she put all the pieces together. She had been pulled slowly, methodically, into the investigation. It had begun months ago, when a nameless floater had surfaced in Swan Lake. The call had come on Saturday. She was the only one on duty. A couple from the meditation ashram had discovered it, and at first she hadn't believed them. But the body had been real. Badly decomposed, it had washed on shore naked, belly up, on the soft brown sand. She remembered kneeling beside it, noting only that the facial characteristics had been erased by months, possibly years, beneath the water. There were no fingerprints. The hands were skeletal.

After the coroner took the body away, she remembered staring at the imprint the corpse had left in the sand.

Roberta had been the one to read the autopsy report and find the clue that everyone had overlooked. It had come in a flash of insight—like a tiny silver key, she began to work it into a lock that resisted opening.

It was the ragged underwear band that had clung to the body. She hadn't noticed it then, but the coroner reported that the word *Seabridge* and the number 2332 had been stamped in faded black ink on the white elastic.

The image wouldn't go away. Roberta Singer had never seen a floater before. She was a small-town cop used to small-town crime. But this was more than curiosity. She felt driven, compelled. Nights when the sun set in an amber sky and the summer tourists stood in line for frozen custard and chili dogs, Detective Singer checked missing-persons reports. She went back more than five years. But no missing adult male Caucasian matched the description of the floater. The name and the number on the underwear band were all she had to go on.

She made the calls, endless inquiries, until her research yielded results. The number 2332 was a federal registry number registered to a manufacturing firm in Brooklyn listed as Goldbest.

Her hands had trembled as she dialed the number. She asked for the owner, a Mr. Blum. His voice had seemed strangely familiar. She realized it was the accent. Mr. Blum, a Polish Jew, was brief and to the point. His firm manufactured underwear worn exclusively by male Hasidim.

In that moment, Roberta saw it all: the black coats, the fur hats, the language that refused to yield to Americanized English. Detective Singer knew the basics; the Hasidim were a sect of pious Jews who lived in tightly knit communities in Brooklyn. During the summer they moved, with their enormous families, to the ramshackle bungalows that lined the dirt roads around Swan Lake. The Hasidim were not of this century. The men wore the same style clothing they'd worn in the 1600s in Poland. The woman adhered to the strictest rules of modesty, covering their hair with scarves or wigs and making sure their arms and legs were never bare. The Hasids were mystics, faithful followers of a great rabbi who had lived and died in a tiny Polish town over two hundred years ago.

It was unthinkable that a Hasidic man could be the corpse that had risen to the surface of Swan Lake. It was impossible that a member of this religious community could have died violently, only to disappear without being reported. But Roberta Singer knew that the unthinkable and the impossible did not apply here. She understood that the Hasidim were shrouded in mystery and secrecy. She knew they followed the ancient laws obediently and without exception.

She knew because she could have been one of them.

It had all come to her in a dream. Her best ideas always came that way. The word *agunah* had simply reappeared to her. It was an ancient word, one she had heard her grandfather speak through his long beard. And it had stayed in her memory, stored there in some dark corner until she needed

it. When all their leads had dried up, when she and Captain
Mahoney had had their last futile conversation with the Hasidic men who had come to the station house at their request,
she remembered about the *agunah*. Roberta knew it would
be easier to look for the woman than it would be to speculate
on the body whose flesh had been slowly eaten away by time
and water.

She began by visiting all the bungalow colonies asking
about an *agunah*. People seemed surprised, as if they didn't
expect that a woman detective could know about something
like that. Captain Mahoney thought she was on a wild-goose
chase. One afternoon, when they were driving together in the
patrol car, he'd slipped and called the Hasidic men "buffalo
hunters." Roberta felt herself stiffen. It was an expression
the locals used, a derisive term that referred to the fur-
trimmed hats certain Hasidic sects wore on *Shabbos*. After
that, she kept her ideas to herself.

It was as if the faceless corpse had singled her out, made
her feel estranged from her own world as he drew her deeper
into his.

Alvaro Lapa slipped the metal file beneath the wooden
crate. A cabbage leaf fell to the forest floor. He put it in his
mouth, swallowing quickly so as not to leave the slightest bit
of evidence. He watched the procession of black-coats weave
their way through the forest. They were back again. The
beards, the pale faces swaying back and forth in prayer. He
wanted to look away, but he couldn't. There was something
about these people. Jose had told him many stories, bad stories about the black-coats. In their village in Brazil they had
once met a Jew, but these Jews were different. They weren't
like the Jewish people who came to the hotel, who wore
shorts, played tennis, and who laughed at the jokes the co-
median told in the nightclub. These people were not like the
Americans he knew, not like the ones who helped him come
here, the ones who took him and Jose in the bus and gave
them jobs in the kitchen. They had made so many promises.
Money. A house. And finally the green card.

A woodchuck scrambled through the brush, and Alvaro

stiffened with fear. He was frightened all the time now. The crates had been coming in faster and in greater numbers than ever before. Jose made him work alone with the file; that way they could unpack the vegetables behind the hotel kitchen. Alvaro hated being left alone in the woods, especially now that the black-coats were back. Always, they came so close. Too close.

He stood behind a tree, straining to see. But all the faces looked the same. The men bent their heads toward one another. They gestured and spoke in a language Alvaro could never understand. Jose said it was their own language. Like the Gypsies, they spoke words only their own people could recognize. And they had their own books, their special ways. Alvaro wanted to know more. But he was aware how dangerous that could be. He remembered last summer. Jose told him it had never happened, to forget it. Thinking about it meant they would never get the money, the house, the green card.

Alvaro looked away. Everything was finished now. His job was done. He sat down in a pile of soft leaves and watched the black-coats. And waited.

The handle of the revolver felt cool against Roberta's ankle. She needed the reminder. She was a cop and this was an investigation.

One of the women in the group laughed and Roberta watched as Aliza's lips parted in a half smile. Her period of mourning would go on for a year, but the first few weeks, the hardest times, were over. She wondered how Aliza must feel. Her husband, who had been missing for almost twelve months, had washed ashore, an unidentified corpse, in a place no one had ever thought to look.

When Roberta had finally located Aliza, she had tried to remain curt and formal, a professional detective. But once the body had been positively identified, and buried according to Jewish law, Roberta felt even more compelled to find answers.

During the earliest phase of the investigation, Aliza explained how Natan took the bus from Brooklyn to Swan Lake every Friday afternoon, always arriving promptly before sundown. When he didn't appear as expected, she waited for *Shabbos* to end and had driven back to New York. Natan Kleinman was reported missing to the police in the city. He was just one of the 14,000 faceless people who disappeared every year without a trace. She had never considered that Natan would have taken the bus to the Catskill Mountains a day or two earlier, that he would have done so without telling her seemed impossible; that he might have been murdered because of it was a mystery that defied explanation.

Some of the women were speaking Yiddish. Roberta strained to hear. Phrases, words, returned to her. All of this: the long skirts, the men dressed in black, the peace of a *Shabbos* stroll, were not unfamiliar to her. Even the name Rivkah recalled another time. Her grandparents had been immigrants. They had clung to the old ways. Refusing to become fully American, they spoke their own language and followed the time-honored customs. This was the life Roberta's parents had tried so desperately to escape. And they had succeeded. They had become modern, educated Americans. Their children had broken all ties with the past.

But some fragile string, some connection, still remained. It was a force that was building slowly, pulling Roberta back into a past that before had existed only in shadowy reminiscence.

Roberta was aware that Natan and Aliza Kleinman were different from her grandparents. They had once lived in the America where women wore jeans and men played football on *Shabbos*. Like his wife, Natan had not always been pious. That came after Treblinka, after the glowing promises of the secular world dimmed into a muddle of darkness. Natan and Aliza had freely, knowingly chosen to return to the old ways. It was a puzzle Roberta could not easily understand. Yet, she felt sure it was their faith, their beliefs, that were somehow responsible for Natan's death.

This was the second *Shabbos* Roberta spent with the Kleinman family. That first time she remembered standing silently as Aliza lit the candles, covered her eyes, and chanted the

Hebrew prayer Roberta still knew from childhood. When Aliza's son, Aaron, had cut the bread, Roberta found herself quietly mouthing the prayer he sang. Aliza's eyes had met hers then, and suddenly something changed between the two women. An unspoken promise.

And so Roberta returned. She walked with the women along the same path Natan had walked. She tried to look for clues: a road that led deeper into the woods, an abandoned trailer, a hunting cabin that might have been occupied by Natan's murderers. But the road they walked was peaceful and isolated, surrounded by forests on one side and the lake on the other.

She knew not to pry. The mystery of Natan's death would not be solved in the conventional way. First, there would have to be trust; a silent, fragile bond between Aliza and herself. Roberta knew there was more. Something Aliza had not told her, something she had not told anyone.

When the sun set on the second *Shabbos* in August, Roberta watched the sky, a blaze of purple melting into the darkness of the mountains. She was in the Kleinman bungalow, a small cabin filled with books and heady with the smells of *havdalah*, the burning twisted candle and the tiny silver box filled with aromatic spices that mark the end of *Shabbos* observance.

"There's something I'd like you to see." Aliza's voice was gentle, but determined.

This was what Roberta had been waiting for. The opening. But it wasn't like she'd imagined it. These people, their lives, there was something peaceful, good, almost sacred about them. She didn't want to see the ugliness, the dark side.

Aliza led her to a closet in Natan's room. She pushed several hangers aside and pulled out a small brown paper bag.

"I found this after Natan disappeared."

The bag felt soft, light, as though what it contained could hardly be important. Maybe Aliza had made a mistake; maybe the clue was really nothing at all.

The bag contained clothing: a pair of jeans, a flowered

shirt, and a plain blue cap. They still smelled of sweat and earth.

"I believe," Aliza said, "these belonged to my husband."

At first the significance of this discovery meant nothing to Roberta. Then she understood. Natan was a black-coat, a Hasid. He would never wear this clothing.

"I know what you must be thinking, what any cop would think. That's why I never showed these before. We dress as we do to stay separate, to retain our differentness from the world around us. These clothes, I've thought about them for a long time. If Natan wore them, there was a reason. Something he didn't want me to know. Something that might harm me or the children."

The thoughts came quickly, linking up to one another too easily. Natan had tried to escape. He yearned for another way of life. He had become desperate, and somehow in that desperation he had wandered into something that was dangerous. Something deadly.

"You're thinking that Natan betrayed us." Aliza's voice was steady and sure. "That's why I waited. I wanted you to know us, to know Natan through us."

Roberta nodded. The trust was no longer unspoken. She fought against her police sense, against all the evidence that showed Natan Kleinman had deceived his family and returned to the world he had once denounced. That would be the easy, obvious solution. But something powerful, something stronger than her police sense told Roberta it was not correct.

She held the shirt in her hands, trying to conjure up images of the faceless corpse she had found on the beach. She rubbed her fingers along the fabric of the jeans; they were not well worn, not threadbare in the knees. The pockets were empty and clean. Then she held the cap. A man running from his past, abandoning his beliefs, would throw everything away. Perhaps the cap meant that Natan, disguised, still refused to go bareheaded. Roberta knew it was a long shot. After all, half the farmers in the county wore caps, even indoors. It was a straw, but Roberta was desperate, and she grasped it.

Aliza spoke carefully, measuring every word, watching

Roberta's face, waiting for the transformation, for Rivkah to become Detective Singer.

"My husband was a man of many talents. He lived in more worlds, saw more of life than either one of us can imagine. The weeks before he disappeared, he was distracted. There was something on his mind. He never shared it with me, but it was something I could sense. Then, after he was gone, when I was going through his things and I found this package, I also found this."

She handed Roberta a worn copy of the Hebrew Bible.

"Here," she said, pointing to a passage that had been underlined in ink. "The last time I saw my husband, he was reading these words. He drew that line beneath them."

Roberta took the book. The words were from Leviticus 26:37: "And a man shall stumble upon his brother."

It was all there, a crazy quilt of clues that Roberta was unable to unravel.

"Tell me what this means," she said, still holding the leather-bound Bible.

"I'm not a scholar," Aliza said, "but this particular passage has been interpreted to mean that we must try to prevent others from transgressing. If we should, even accidentally, discover someone doing something wrong and we fail to act, we are held liable for the offense."

Roberta looked around the room. It had once belonged to Natan. She tried to imagine him, dressed in his black coat, wearing his skullcap, studying the words in Leviticus, underlining them, making them mean something in his life.

"Can you write this passage down for me?" Roberta asked.

Aliza nodded and wrote the eight words on a piece of paper.

"Before you leave, I want to say one more thing. There's a word we use. *Chesed*. It means compassion, an act of loving kindness. I'm not a detective, but I believe the things I've shown you indicate that my husband was involved in something very important. I believe he was trying to perform an act of *chesed* when he died."

* * *

The night sky had blackened until only the barest outlines of the mountains were visible. Roberta walked into the darkness. She wanted to hear music, to smoke a cigarette, to feel the sensations of her life returning. Everything she knew about herself and about her work told her to doubt Aliza, to laugh her off as a fanatic, a mystic, a wife desperate to justify her husband's betrayal.

The warm summer air brushed against her ankles, twisting sensuously beneath her skirt. She needed to walk, to breathe the fresh air, to listen to the night sounds, to piece together the fragments of a mystery.

There was a place in the woods, not far from the Kleinman's bungalow, where the darkness was dispersed, intersected by shards of yellow light. And there were sounds: slow grating sounds. Metal rubbing against stone. Roberta followed the light with her eyes, listened to the sound. Then there were voices, hushed and nasal, speaking a language she could not understand. She thought about stopping, about following the yellow glints until she found their source, but it was probably only campers, tourists, kids, setting up tents in the dark.

She drove home slowly, thinking about Natan's clothes, about the eight words from Leviticus, about the way Aliza had looked when she said the word *chesed*.

Somewhere in her dream it came to her. Floating in the luminescence of her unconscious, she saw Natan dressed in the jeans and the flowered shirt. She saw him sway back and forth, wearing the cap, holding the scrap of paper upon which Aliza had written the words. She saw him as a young man standing behind the barbed wire of a concentration camp, and she saw him as a skeleton suspended in grayness, surfacing in a bubble of blood. When his face came into focus, it was the face of her father, the face of her grandfather. He reached out of the darkness, his hand a quivering splash of flesh and bone. The letters swirled around his head; Hebrew letters like the ones she had seen in the books in his room. Natan opened his mouth. Out from the emptiness floated a sound. It was a word Roberta had heard in her waking life. It rippled through the darkness, disappearing into a rasp and finally a whisper.

It was 3:45 A.M. when Detective Singer, still wearing her long skirt, strapped the service revolver to her ankle and drove back toward the place in the woods. Daybreak was just beginning to seep over the tips of the mountains. She could find her way without a flashlight.

She walked noiselessly, listening for the sounds. She heard the stones first. The quiet grating. There were no voices. Just the rhythmic hum, something metallic.

Roberta stopped right before the clearing. It was as if someone had cut a slice from the forest. Two men sat side by side. They rubbed metal files against objects she could barely see.

It was then that she felt the fear, smelled the danger, thick and foreboding. Alone in the semidarkness, she realized she was standing where Natan must have stood. She was watching something he, too, had watched. But she had a gun strapped to her ankle. What weapons had Natan Kleinman had? Why had he watched, listened, when he could have simply turned silently and disappeared into the night?

It was the young man who saw her first, the one the other called Alvaro. His eyes were startled, brimming with terror. Like a deer suddenly frozen by the lights of a car, he was temporarily paralyzed. Then he ran. She followed him into the darkness. In an instant the other grabbed her, throwing her down against the hard ground.

In the first pale moments of daylight, Detective Singer understood what she had discovered. The files rested against wooden vegetable crates. False bottoms had been removed, and the weapons, hundreds of them—rifles, carbines, machine guns—lay scattered in the clearing.

She moved slowly, aware the men were still off-balance. The larger one, swarthy with long black hair, flashed her a nicotine grin. He laughed and said something to the younger one. It was that language. Not Spanish, but something she had heard before. Portuguese. Instantly, Roberta knew who these men were. The kitchen help at the hotel near the Kleinman's bungalow colony. Brazilians. Part of a contingent of foreign workers brought over to work during the summer season. Probably illegals.

The younger one, obviously frightened, pleaded with his friend. She knew he was begging for her life.

When he bent over her, Roberta could smell his breath, stale from cigarettes and whiskey. She mentally measured the space between them. He was still too close. He flashed a knife, pushing it against the skin of her throat. She pretended to faint and fell backward, away from him.

It was at this moment that the two men began to argue. She heard the younger one call her attacker Jose. She knew they thought she was like Natan, a Hasid, someone who had stumbled upon them accidentally. Perhaps Natan understood what they were doing. It was only now becoming clear to her. Illegal aliens, they were part of a gunrunning scheme that shipped weapons domestically and overseas. The files removed registration numbers. Jose and Alvaro were small fish, held captive by threats of deportation. They didn't know it, but by summer's end, whoever had hired them would let them go, promising to turn them over to the authorities if they talked.

Roberta felt the revolver, hard and cool against her ankle. She moved her hand slowly beneath her long skirt.

In an instant it was over. She shouted at them not to move, that she was a police officer. Unbelieving, Jose laughed. Roberta held the revolver with both hands. She saw the fear flash in his olive-tinted eyes. Then he charged, running toward her, his knife slashing wildly.

There was only one shot. It rang out clearly, shattering the orange dawn. Jose held the spot just below his knee where the bullet lodged between bone and flesh.

Alvaro stood unmoving. His mouth twisted into a lurid grin. Then the grin dissolved. He began to shriek, tearing at his shirt. He fell to his knees. He was speaking English, the words exploding into one another.

"You were sent by them. The black-coats. I told Jose they would come. They would find us. I knew he would return."

Roberta stood silently in the clearing while Alvaro told her how Natan had died. Like her, he had come upon them. And he had returned, dressed not in his black coat but in jeans and a flowered shirt. He spoke to them in Portuguese. He asked them questions, sat with them, told them he could help get them green cards. He wanted to know about the guns, where they came from, where they were going. Jose, the older man, distrusted the stranger. But Alvaro believed there was a kindness in his eyes.

"He came always the same time. On a Thursday," Alvaro explained. "And he stayed here until we fell asleep. By morning he was gone. We never saw him leave. We never knew where he came from."

Then one morning Jose, awakened by the sound of a deer foraging for food, saw the stranger in the flowered shirt walk toward the road. He followed him and watched as he changed into his black coat. He waited while the stranger swayed back and forth, whispering words in the language he knew was not English.

When Alvaro found them, it had already been done. Natan was dead. His throat had been slashed as he prayed for another day of life.

Roberta tried not to think of that now as she cuffed Jose and walked Alvaro to the squad car. She closed her eyes against the image of Natan, his throat a red gash, his body thrown desperately into the lake.

She radioed Captain Mahoney and waited with Alvaro. Now she could see that he was barely out of his teens.

She wondered if he had been the one to heave Natan's body into the lake, if he had watched as it disappeared beneath the water.

Roberta turned her face toward the pale sky. Natan hadn't vanished. He had been murdered. The man who had survived Treblinka, who had traveled halfway around the world, had spent his final moments here, praying in the same misty light that now seeped from between the trees.

Detective Singer pulled the scrap of paper from her pocket: "And a man shall stumble upon his brother." It had happened exactly like that. Natan had accidentally discovered

Alvaro and Jose. He had lived the words written thousands of years ago.

There was no official way to explain it, no way to make anyone understand why Natan had risked his life for the strangers who had killed him.

As she saw the bubble of light flashing red on the roof of Captain Mahoney's car, saw the dust flying off the unpaved road, Roberta Singer suddenly realized what the *agunah* had known all along. She understood that somehow she and Natan and Aliza were inexplicably linked, their lives intertwined with something ancient, something eternal, something that had led her to this place—this moment.

So when Captain Mahoney, his face smelling of soap, his uniform crisply ironed, and his hands steady as he led the suspects into the patrol car, asked her what had happened, Detective Singer gave the only answer she knew: the answer Natan had tried to tell her in a dream.

Natan Kleinman had died, not for money or passion, not for vengeance or greed, but for a word, an idea. *Chesed.*

T. J. MacGregor's Dark Fields *(nominated for a 1986 Shamus),* Kill Flash, Death Sweet, *and* On Ice *all feature Mike McCleary and Quin St. James, the south Florida husband-and-wife private investigators whose cases often involve high stakes and high passions. Born in Caracas, Venezuela, and widely published as a travel writer, T. J. also writes mysteries as Trish Janeshutz* (In Shadow, Hidden Lake) *and Alison Drake* (Tango Key, Fevered, Black Moon), *keeping her readers happily supplied with exciting stories.*

In "The Works," the manager of a Miami Beach hotel offers a wide range of comforts to the guests.

THE WORKS

by T. J. MacGregor

I KNOW HOW it is down here on the beach for the old ones now, what with rising prices and traffic and crime. They're afraid to go out at night. Their Social Security checks barely cover a month of meals at Wolfie's. They feel like Miami Beach's postscript.

The Art Deco craze did it, you know. Ever since folks decided Deco was in again, those little hotels over on Ocean Drive are booming with business, charging prices like I can't believe, and yeah, people pay them. I mean, seventy bucks for a room no larger than a closet, five dollars for a hard-boiled egg and a slice of bread that's hardly toasted, two bucks for coffee. The old ones can remember when coffee in these places cost a dime.

There's a haughty look to the hotels that really gets me too. They stand so prim and proper at the edge of the sea, all spiffed up in pastels, windows so clean they gleam like jewels. The old ones feel like they can't afford to even walk there, and when they do, shuffling in their tired bones, under the weight of eighty or ninety years of memories, they're nearly trampled by the youthful crowds rushing to this hotel or that bar.

So I keep my prices low and do what I can. When an old one is troubled or sad, sick or too drunk to stand, I take him or her in. Word has gotten around that Millie's Place is where you go when it's gotten bad.

Like tonight, for instance.

Toby wandered in off Washington Avenue a few minutes ago, out of the thick night heat, looking about as bad as a man can look and still be alive. He's ninety-four years old, with a spine so bent he can hardly lift his head, glasses thicker than his arm, a heart that just won't quit.

He's counting one-dollar bills from a tattered envelope with SOCIAL SECURITY ADMINISTRATION in bold black letters across the top. If I remember correctly, he worked nearly half a century for an auto-parts plant that merged with another plant and most of his pension got lost in the transition. His Social Security check amounts to about three hundred dollars a month and we all know what that buys you in Miami Beach.

"The room's only six bucks, Toby," I tell him when he keeps counting out the bills.

"Want a meal too," he mumbles, moving his dentures around in his mouth because they hurt his gums.

"Eight bucks, then."

"And the Works. I think I want the Works, Millie."

"You'd better be sure. It's a bit more expensive."

His head bobs slowly. It reminds me of a beach ball, rising, falling, riding a wave, and I want to stroke it, embrace it, kiss this old, beautiful head. It's as hairless as a chihuahua, with a mass of wrinkles that seems to quiver and dance to the back of the skull. Not so long ago, on a rainy afternoon down at the Ace Club, some of the old ones and I gathered around Toby's head to see if we could read our fortunes in the wrinkles, like they were creases in a palm.

"I'm sure," he says softly, depositing an old canvas bag on the counter, straining to look up. "How much?"

His eyes behind those thick glasses are alarmingly small, almost transparent. I feel like they might disappear at any second. "Twenty-five. I guess you know what all the fee includes."

His smile creases his mouth and, like a widening ripple in a pond, touches all the other wrinkles in his face. For a moment or two, his features shift and slide, rearranging themselves. "Sure. I came with Mink, remember?"

Mink: right. She was close to a hundred, small as a toy doll with white hair that had fallen out in spots, exposing soft pink patches of skull. She had cancer and the radiation or the chemo or whatever it was they'd used on her had rotted her from the inside out, but her heart ticked on. She took baby steps, I remember, like a toddler learning to walk, and drooled a little when she talked.

It's true that decades stretch between infancy and old age, but children and old ones aren't all that different. Both are afraid. Both have special needs. Both require love. I understand that and they know it.

"There. Twenty-five." He taps the stack of bills against the counter, straightening them, then slides the pile toward me.

"Sure?"

"Positive."

"Okay, let's go take a look at the menu."

I ring for Sammy to man the desk and he shuffles in, big as a truck and all muscle. He's not an old one, but he was living on the streets until I took him in and now I don't know how I'd run this place without him. I've never heard him speak. I don't know if it's because he can't or just that he chooses not to.

I come out from behind the counter and Toby hooks his old, tired arm in mine. The kitchen is in the back and while it's not as grand as the ones in the fancy hotels on Ocean Drive, it feels like home to me. The fridge is always filled with everyone's favorites—home-baked pies, drumsticks, potato salad, coleslaw, cookies by the dozens, turkeys.

When I was doing private-duty nursing a long time ago, I made a point of cooking for my patients. They appreciated it. A lot of them were old ones, too, and I learned to prepare the food to accommodate dentures, taste buds that had gone smooth and dull as river stones, noses that no longer worked right. It taught me the importance of spices, sauces, garnishes that dressed the food good enough to make your mouth water.

Toby's mouth is watering now, as we peer into the fridge together. I can tell. He points at what he wants. One of those, one of these, this, that. His finger is curved into a permanent claw from arthritis; just looking at it hurts me. That's how it is with me and them. That's how it always is when someone I care for is in pain. It becomes my pain.

"And cookies," he finishes. "Chocolate-chip cookies."

"They've got nuts in them."

"Soft nuts?"

"Not really."

"Aw, so what. Nuts are fine."

Together, we remove the items from the fridge and set them out on the counter. Before I begin preparing the meal, though, I show him to the best room in the house. It's on the top floor, in back. There's a skylight over the huge bed, a color TV and VCR, forty or fifty videocassettes for him to choose from, and an adjoining bath with a sunken tub that swirls like a Jacuzzi, where fluffy towels, a silk robe, and matching pajamas are laid out. He sighs as his feet sink into the thick carpeting on the floor and sighs again as he eases his tired bones onto the bed and peers up, up into a sky strewn with stars.

"You'll tell me when dinner's ready?" he asks, frowning as though he doesn't quite trust me now.

"I'll bring it up here. Feathers is going to smell that chicken. You mind if she comes up too?"

"No, no, of course not," he says, hooking his hands under his head, lost in the stars. He doesn't hear me leave, but Feathers hears me enter the kitchen.

She's a white Persian who has a definite fondness for chicken and old ones. She likes to curl up on their chests and knead their soft bones with her gentle paws. I toss her tidbits as I prepare the meal and explain the situation to her. She blinks those sweet amber eyes as if to say she understands perfectly, and follows me upstairs when I take Toby his meal.

He's perched on the wicker couch in the black silk pajamas and robe, squinting at the TV, watching *Cocoon*. It's a favorite with all the old ones. I set his tray down on the table and pull up the other chair.

Feathers flops over Toby's feet, covering them like a rug, and he looks down at her and laughs. I can't remember the last time I heard him laugh and I've known Toby for ten or twelve years, since he moved down here after his wife died. I don't know if he has kids. He's never spoken of them if he does. But that's how it is with a lot of the old ones. When they get too old for their kids to deal with them, when there's talk of nursing homes, of confinement, they get scared and run away. Who can blame them?

"Watch this, Millie," he says excitedly, stabbing a gnarled finger at the screen. "This is where they swim in the rejuvenation pool."

I divide my attention between the screen and the turkey, which I cut up into small, manageable bites for him. I pass him a napkin, which he tucks under his throat like a bib, and pass him his plate. He sets it on his lap, impales a chunk of meat, and dips it in a scoop of dressing. His hand trembles as it rises toward his mouth. A dab of dressing rests on his chin, but he doesn't seem to notice it. He chews slowly, thoughtfully, eyes glued to the screen.

"Will it hurt?" he asks, not looking at me.

"Of course not."

"Are you sure?"

"You were here with Mink," I remind him. "Did she look like she hurt?"

Mouth puckering around a cranberry: "She always hurt. From the cancer. Or the radiation. From something."

Physical pain or psychic pain; the difference isn't that great. Shift your focus and one becomes the other. Mink knew that. "She's okay now, though."

"You talked to her?"

"Sure. I talk to her pretty often."

"And she's okay?"

"A lot better."

"How come she doesn't come around anymore?"

"She's finished with the beach, Toby."

He mulls this over, nods, dips his fork into the steaming squash. "Can you do me a favor, Millie?"

"Sure. Anything."

He reaches into the pocket of the robe and pulls out a sheet of notebook paper. The words on it are printed, almost illegible. I can see Toby hunched over the bar at the Ace Club, where some of the old ones hang out, moving a pen up and down against the paper, putting his thoughts in order. I get the point. "Okay," I tell him, and slip the sheet inside the old canvas bag, which slumps on the floor beside the bed like an aged and faithful pet.

"Can I watch another movie after this one?"

"Whatever you want. When you get tired, just pick up the phone and ring the desk. I'll be up to tuck you in."

"Don't go," he says quickly. "Stay here with me, Millie."

I pat his hand. "Let me get some iced tea and your slice of pie and I'll be right back. Was it pumpkin or apple that you wanted, Toby?"

"Both." He grins mischievously, dark spaces in his mouth where there should be teeth. He's removed part of his denture.

"Both it is."

Feathers doesn't move as I get up; she knows the routine.

From the kitchen, I fetch iced tea for myself and two slices of pie for Toby and some Friskies for Feathers. In my bedroom, I bring out the Works, running my hands over the smooth, cool leather, remembering. New York. My old life. The business with the nursing board. Such unpleasantness, really. Like the old ones, I have secrets I would rather forget.

I change into more comfortable clothes, cotton that breathes, that's the color of pearls. Makeup next. A touch of eye shadow, mascara, blush, lipstick. The way I look is part of the Works. Sometimes the old ones ask me to hold them, stroke them, caress them, make love to them. Other times they want to listen to Frank Sinatra and dance or they ask me to walk on the beach with them, in the moonlight. Their requests are as different as they are, and I always comply. But with all of them, there's a need for a special memory, an event that perhaps reminds them of something else. It's as if this memory will accompany them, comfort them somehow, like a friend.

Toby is still watching the movie when I return. His supper plate is clean. His eyes widen when he sees the pieces of pie and he attacks the apple first, devouring it with childlike exuberance, then polishes off the pumpkin as well. We watch the rest of the movie together, Feathers purring between us on the couch. Now and then, his chin drops to his chest as he nods off, but he comes quickly awake, blinking fast as if to make sure he hasn't missed anything.

While the movie rewinds, I fold back the sheets on the bed. They're sea blue, decorated with shells and sea horses, the same ones Mink slept in. "Can we listen to music?" he asks, crouching in front of the stereo on the other side of the room.

"Sure. Whatever you want. Choose an album."

Harry Belafonte.

Toby holds out his arms and I move into them. I'm taller than he is, but it doesn't matter. We sway, his silk robe rustling. I rest my chin on his head and feel all those wrinkles quivering, shifting, warm as sand against my skin. He presses his cheek to my chest, eyes shut. The lemon scent of his skin haunts me a little, reminds me of all the old ones who have come here for the Works. I've loved each of them, and love them still.

When the record ends, Toby and I stretch out in the king-size bed, holding each other, talking softly, the moon smack in the heart of the skylight now. He falls asleep with his head on my shoulder, and for a long time I lay there just listening to him breathe, watching stars against the black dome of sky above us.

The window is partially open, admitting a taste of wind, the scent of stars, the whispering sea. I imagine that death is like this window, opening onto a pastel world where everything is what you will it to be. Yellow skies, if that's what you want. Silver seas. A youthful body. A sound mind. A family that cares. A state of grace.

And that's my gift to the old ones.

I untangle my arms and rise, drawing the covers over Toby. His wrinkled head sinks into the pillow. I bring the syringe from my leather case and fill it. I have trouble finding a vein in his arm. They're lost in the folds of skin, collapsed beneath tissue, and I have to inject the morphine into his neck, just below the ear.

And then I wait.

Always, in the final moment, there's something that seems to escape from the old shell of bones and flesh, an almost visible thing, a puff of air, a kind of fragrance, the soul released. It leaves Toby when he sighs, fluttering from his mouth like a bird, and sweeps through the crack in the window, free at last.

Funny, but the wrinkles on top of his skull don't seem quite as deep now. His spine doesn't look as hunched. If I tried, I know I could straighten out his fingers. But the most I do is kiss him good-bye.

I get rid of the syringe. Sammy will take care of getting Toby's body to the pauper cemetery. There won't be a headstone, of course. I do have to make some concessions. But the burial will be proper, with an old pine box and all.

I unzip his canvas bag for the sheet of paper I slipped in here earlier and read it over. The list of who gets what is simple; all the names are old ones who hang out at the Ace Club. His belongings are in the bag. I sling it over my shoulder and walk downstairs, where Sammy is still at the desk. He looks up and I nod. He reaches under the desk and switches on the VACANCY sign outside. I take his place at the desk and he leaves to attend to Toby.

Most of the old ones will know about Toby before they hear it from me. They'll know because the only time the VACANCY sign goes on is when the Works are finished.

Tomorrow, when I go down to the Ace, I'll also pass out my card to newcomers. After all, I've got to drum up business just like anyone else. MILLIE'S PLACE. CHEAPEST RENT ON THE BEACH. GOOD FOOD. SPACIOUS ROOMS. THE WORKS.

Margaret Maron's Sigrid Harald of the NYPD has been featured in six books, including Baby Doll Games, One Coffee With, *and* Corpus Christmas. *An embodiment of the new breed of (fictional) no-nonsense women in law enforcement, Lieutenant Harald deals not only with crime but also with an uneasy but growing acceptance of her own physical and emotional quirks, a theme explored bravely and with good humor.*

"Out of Whole Cloth" weaves a tale of deceit that forms the fabric of a family celebration.

OUT OF WHOLE CLOTH

by Margaret Maron

CAIT FABRICS' ANNUAL banquet had always been one of Turlton's most glittering galas; but after tonight, the Cait sisters would be officially retired, so this year's celebration was expected to out-glitter all previous banquets. And since Cait Fabrics affected businesses far beyond the city's booming economy, the banquet had even occasioned a few inches in *The Wall Street Journal*:

> Turlton, NC—Control of a small but prosperous company passes tonight to a new generation. Named president of Cait Fabrics is Lucinda Ashley, granddaughter of Sarah Cait Engles and great-niece of Naomi Cait, cofounders of the North Carolina firm.
>
> The Cait sisters inherited a run-down gingham mill in 1930, and expanded it to a leading producer of high-quality industrial textiles by an early recognition of the automotive industry's need for rugged but attractive fabrics.

A graduate of Harvard Business School, Ms. Ashley follows the family tradition of aggressive marketing. Cait recently signed contracts to furnish all fabrics for the new multi-million-dollar convention center in Stuttgart, West Germany.

In her private suite high above the hotel ballroom where other Cait Fabrics personnel were gathering for pre-banquet cocktails, Sarah Cait Engles lifted a crystal goblet with a hand that was wrinkled but steady. "To Stuttgart!" she said.

"To Lucinda!" Naomi Cait smiled fondly.

Gowned in apricot silk, her dark hair braided with gold ribbons, Lu Ashley looked like a fashion model as she accepted their tribute, but her brown eyes held executive wariness when her brother raised his own glass and said, "To the New York Stock Exchange."

"And just what is that supposed to mean?"

"Oh, Lu," their mother said with a sigh. "Nicky didn't mean a thing." Sally Engles Ashley had spent thirty years explaining her firstborn to her mother and aunt. Now it began to look as if she'd spend the next thirty explaining him to her daughter. "What Nicky meant—"

"I know what he meant, Mother, and he can forget it! Cait Fabrics isn't going after the private home market."

"Don't count on it, baby sister," Nicky mocked, sipping his champagne as he lounged on his grandmother's velvet sofa. An unrepentant grasshopper, he had sneered at his sister's antlike devotion to work too often to expect the company presidency; but being passed over rankled, and he did not look forward to tonight's public coronation. "I'm not the only stockholder who thinks dividends would be larger if the company diversified."

Fearing fresh arguments, Sally Ashley peered at her diamond watch in pretended alarm. "Oh, dear! We're late for our own party. Come down with me, Nicky? I promised the senator you and I would have a drink with him before dinner."

Nicky started to argue, then gave a what-the-hell shrug and stood up.

Relieved, Sally adjusted her mink stole. "I'll tell everyone you'll be right down," she told the others, and hurried Nicky out to the private elevator before he could further antagonize them.

As the door closed behind her daughter and grandson, Sarah Cait Engles held out her glass for more champagne. "They can't start dinner without us," she said serenely.

Even with silver hair, the two sisters were still slim of body and straight of spine. Sarah had been nineteen, Naomi twenty, when they were left to run the broken-down mill.

"Nicky's an ass," said Lu, "but he could stir up the stockholders."

"You'll manage," Naomi said. "Cait women have always been a match for Cait men. Remember how we managed dear Uncle Bob, Sarah?" Her voice put quotation marks around *dear Uncle Bob*.

"Your father's brother?" asked Lu, vaguely remembering. "Didn't he try to take over the company back at the beginning?"

"Nicky's very much a Cait man," said Sarah, and Naomi nodded.

"Papa and Uncle Bob inherited the mill from their father but Uncle Bob was so taken with the novelty of airplanes and flying that Papa bought him out with Mama's dowry. When she died, Papa started drinking and would've let the mill go under, only Uncle Bob talked him into flying around the world in his new hydroplane. They both disappeared, the Depression worsened, and we almost lost the mill."

Lu was familiar with their long hard struggle—the skepticism of their customers, the reluctance of bankers to lend dwindling funds to mere girls, the loyalty of their workers. Gradually, however, the red ink had begun to blacken.

"If Sarah hadn't talked Continental Motors into using our fabric in their new runabouts—"

"Your designs sold themselves," Sarah said generously.

Six years after the two men disappeared, the sisters had toasted their first real profits with the last bottle of Grandfather Cait's pre-Prohibition brandy. A week later, their small piece of the sky fell in.

Sarah had looked up from her desk to see a man striding across their office. "Sarah!" he cried. "Naomi! My little girls!"

"Papa?" they'd asked wonderingly.

Edward Cait had left with black hair and mustache. This man was clean-shaven and completely gray. According to him, their plane had floundered off the coast of France. Bob drowned, but Ed had been picked up by a homeward-bound Japanese steamer and it had taken him this long to work his way back from Tokyo.

"Six years?" asked Lu, watching champagne bubbles effervesce in her glass.

"He kept getting sidetracked," said Sarah; and Naomi murmured, "A large Hawaiian woman, a cook in L.A., and wasn't that Kansas woman who kept writing him letters a librarian?"

He had toured the renovated mill and generously praised what the sisters had achieved. "But now that Papa's home, my little girls can be ladies again." He smiled. "You'll go to parties, go to dances . . ."

The sisters exchanged horrified glances. "Who'll run the mill?" they asked.

"It needs a man's firm hand on the stick. Things young ladies can't understand. Making cloth for car seats is just a start. This is 1936! Aeroplanes carry people almost as regularly as trains. Bob was right: The future's in flight and Cait Mills will move with the future!"

The analogy of a man's firm hand on the stick confirmed the sisters' worst fears.

That night, after the fatted calf had been eaten and the prodigal had retired to an early bed, Naomi and Sarah asked one of his guests to remain behind. Judge Sims had considered himself a sort of substitute father to the two young women during his friend's long absence, but his indulgent smile changed to a frown when they said, "He's not Papa."

The judge had spent the evening reminiscing about boyhood days with Ed and Bob Cait, and now Ed's daughters were saying he was an impostor?

"Rubbish," said Sims. "He knew about our Haw River

mud slides and snitching ice chunks from the ice wagon and—"

"He's Uncle Bob," Sarah said. "It must have been Papa who drowned, and now that Uncle Bob's tired of bumming around the world, he wants to come back and take over *our* mill."

"Would our own father abandon us for six whole years?" asked Naomi.

If the judge remembered a streak of irresponsibility in both Cait boys, he suppressed it. "I suppose Bob *could* pass himself off as Ed," he said, rubbing his long chin judiciously, "but proving it might be difficult."

"*Prove?*" roared a voice from the hall. "*Prove?* You know who I am, Sims. Naomi, Sarah—*why*?"

"We're sorry, Uncle Bob, but we cannot let you take our papa's place," they told him firmly.

The story swept through Turlton and within days everyone in town had chosen sides. Pulp thrillers had popularized the infallibility of fingerprints; unfortunately, neither brother's had ever been recorded. Doc Harris recalled cutting out Bob's appendix, but not Ed's. If this was Ed, let him show a smooth belly.

The returnee admitted a scar but claimed it'd been done in Tokyo. Doc Harris said he recognized his own stitch marks, and Cait called him an old fool. Those who saw the scar said it looked fairly new.

Dental records might have helped, but hoping to cover his stock-market losses, Dr. Todd had burned down his office for the insurance money and was now serving time for arson.

Judge Sims remembered that one of his boyhood chums had a webbed little toe, but was that Ed or was it Bob?

"Ed!" cried half of the old swimming-hole gang. "Bob!" shouted the other half.

Turlton might still be divided if Flossie Lanigan hadn't gone to Judge Sims and reminded him of the nights Ed Cait had drowned his sorrows down at Sullivan's speakeasy after his wife died. Flossie was a woman "no better than she ought to be,'' and what she whispered in Judge Sims's ear was soon snickered about all over town.

That was when Cait gave in. He was willing to take off a shoe and sock and he didn't mind lifting his shirt, but he'd be damned if he was going to drop his pants so the whole town could verify what he swore was a dirty lie in the first place.

He took the small allowance Naomi and Sarah offered and left them in undisputed control of Cait Fabrics. It was thought he ended his days in Hawaii, half a world from Turlton's ribald laughter.

"What did that Lanigan woman *say*?" asked Lu, amused.

"We were never quite sure," Sarah said primly. "Nice young ladies didn't know about such things back then."

"Well, I just hope I have your luck when the showdown with Nicky comes," said Lu, gathering up her wrap.

"It wasn't luck, dear," said Naomi as Sarah daintily swallowed the last of her champagne. "We knew Flossie wanted a respectable job at the mill."

"You mean you gave her a good job because she convinced Judge Sims that Uncle Bob wasn't your father?"

"Oh, no, dear." Her grandmother beamed. "We gave her a *very* good job because she convinced Judge Sims that *Papa* was dear Uncle Bob."

Lia Matera, nominated for a 1988 Edgar for A Radical Departure, *is a lawyer. So are Willa Jansson, featured in 1987
Anthony nominee* Where Lawyers Fear to Tread, Departure,
and Hidden Agenda, *and Laura Di Palma, of* The Smart
Money, *and* The Good Fight. *Lia says, "My writer friends
think I'm crazy not to practice law but my lawyer friends
know I'm damned lucky." Lia's loyal readers are the ones
who feel fortunate that she made the choice to write!*

*In "Destroying Angel," a mycologist's troubles keep on
mushrooming on one fateful day.*

DESTROYING ANGEL

by Lia Matera

I WAS SQUATTING a few feet from a live oak tree, poison
oak all around me (an occupational hazard for mycolo-
gists). I brushed wet leaves off a small mound and found
two young mushrooms. I carefully dug around one of them
with my trowel, coaxing it out of the ground.

I held it up and looked at it. It was a perfect woodland
agaricus. The cap was firm, snow white with a hint of yellow.
The gills under the cap were still white; chocolate-colored
spores hadn't yet tinged them. A ring of tissue (an annulus)
circled the stipe like a floppy collar. A few strands of mycelia
(the underground plant of which the mushroom is the fruit)
hung from the base. I pinched the mycelia off and smelled
the gills. The woodland agaricus smells like it tastes, like a
cross between a mushroom, an apple, and a stalk of fennel.

I brushed leaves off the other mushroom and dug it out of
the ground. It resembled the first mushroom. It had a white
cap, white gills, an annulus. But a fleshy volva covered the
bottom third of the stipe like a small paper bag. It was all

193

that remained of a fungal "egg" from which stipe and cap
had burst; characteristic of Amanitas, not Agaricus. The volva
was the reason I'd dug so carefully around the base of the
mushroom. I had to be sure I'd dug the whole thing out. If
I'd left the volva in the ground, the mushroom would have
been virtually indistinguishable from the woodland agaricus.

The mushroom was beautiful, pristine, stately, reputedly
delicious (though you wouldn't live to eat it a second time).
But it was a deadly Amanita, a destroying angel, and I left it
on the carpet of duff.

I filled my basket with woodland agaricus and I littered the
duff with discarded destroying angels. A flock of birds
swooped out of a tree and startled me off my haunches and
onto my back, and I decided to call it a morning.

I walked the three or four miles back to the road, rubber
boots squelching through mud. I watched mist float over
manzanitas, drift along horizontal branches of live oaks, drip
through mosses, mute the evergreen of firs and redwoods.
The air smelled of loam and wet leaves and pine sap. Wood-
peckers tapped, squirrels scrambled, and birds drank from
curled bark. There were mushrooms everywhere, tiny brown
ones no one had bothered to classify, fuchsia-colored Rus-
solas, bits of orange chanterelles peeking out of leaf mounds.
Most people don't see anything but leaves and pine needles
when they look at a forest floor; they don't recognize the
subtle patterns. But then, most people are content to see nature from a car window, to do their hiking in a shopping mall,
to settle for flavorless mass-produced fungi.

Not me.

The museum was ready for the annual Fungus Fair. We'd
carried the stuffed coyotes and pumas and the trays of butter-
flies and beetles down to the basement. We'd wheeled the
waterfowl displays into the gift shop. There was still an occasional otter or egret peeking out from behind a table, but
we'd managed to clear most of the main room.

We'd covered several tables with sand sculpted into gentle
hills (two days' work), and we'd covered the sand with duff
(another whole day). We had a hundred and twenty-seven

species of fungus scattered over this ersatz forest floor, all labeled with Latin and common names and descriptions of their properties. Some were edible, some were medicinal, some glowed in the dark, some bled colored latex, some were used to make dye, some were used to make rocket fuel, some were poisonous; all were fascinating. To me, anyway; but then, I write mushroom field guides. I teach mushroom identification classes.

"Looks good." James Ransome, the museum curator, glowed with satisfaction. James has a square pink face, rimless aviator glasses, and wavy black hair. He's fortyish, with a little potbelly under his inevitable button-down shirt and sweater vest. I like James a lot.

"We should move the knobcone pines," Don Herlihy grumbled. Again.

Don was doing me a favor, helping out with the fair. He helps every year. He's a botanist and an ornithologist; like me, not affiliated with a university. He gets by landscaping, specializing in drought-resistant native plants. He's a friend from a dozen college botany labs, and he throws a little landscaping my way when he's got the extra work and my museum classes aren't paying the rent. I wish Don were more than just a friend, but he always goes for the angora-sweater type. I keep hoping.

"They're going to fry when the sun shifts." Don didn't think we should bring in potted trees at all, but James wanted "atmosphere," and it was James's museum.

I didn't care much about atmosphere, but I cared less about the knobcones. I just wanted peace between my two best friends.

I said, "You know what I found this morning?"

Don continued scowling at the scraggly pines. "They'll get knocked over—if they don't fry first."

"We need them to screen the tidepool tank." James was calm, knowing he'd get his way, as usual. "Last year we found it full of Dixie cups and plastic forks."

"Woodland agaricus," I continued. "I'm going to sauté it this afternoon as part of the tasting."

James blinked at me. "You cooked that for me a few years ago. Told me never to harvest it alone."

"It's easy to mistake for destroying angels." I bent over my basket of agaricus, pulling out a young specimen. "But that's the beauty of it! Very few people have the expertise to harvest it." I glanced at a table set up with hot plates and frying pans for the mushroom tasting. "People coming today probably won't ever to get to taste it again."

James took the agaricus from me, turning it over. He knew enough about mushrooms to spot differences and appreciate similarities—if someone else made the initial identification.

Don walked over to the row of spindly pines, pulling them a few inches farther from the window. He always sweated the small stuff—and looked at me like I should back him up. When I didn't, he scowled. "Even experts make mistakes, Lucy."

James didn't bother moving the trees back. Later, I knew, we'd find them where he wanted them.

Don scratched his thick beard, squinting at me like I'd wimped out on him. "Guy who taught me everything I know about rock climbing fell and broke his neck in the Tetons last summer."

"Thanks for the vote of confidence." I took the agaricus back from James. "In the history of mycology, no expert—I don't mean guys who take a class or two and go out with their field guides—no *professional* has ever died of mushroom poisoning." I could feel myself flush. People are so damn afraid of mushrooms. It's irrational, something you don't see in other cultures, where families routinely go mushroom hunting together. "Look, no one ever worries about their parsley being hemlock or their bay leaves being oleander! People don't get scared that whoever harvested it—"

"Uh-oh," James said grimly. "Lucy's hobbyhorse."

There was a tapping sound from the front of the museum. Someone knocking on the glass doors. Probably several people; the Fungus Fair always attracts a big crowd: amateur naturalists, people with kids, hippie types into natural dyes and psychedelics, mushroom gourmets, people who just like a colorful display.

By the time I finished the yarn-dyeing demonstration and spent some time identifying mushrooms people had found in their lawns, there were maybe fifty people jammed into the main room.

Time to cook some mushrooms.

I started with shaggy parasols, went on to horns of plenty, chanterelles, the prince, coccoli, ceps. So different from each other, with flavors ranging brothy to herby to fruity; and so very different from that Velveeta of fungus, the supermarket mushroom.

It got pretty frantic: people trooping by with little Dixie cups and plastic forks, and always a couple of gourmets to tell you a better way to cook whatever you're cooking (as if you can go wrong sautéing in butter), and then every time James had the tiniest problem, he wanted me to leave everything and come solve it, so I ended up sweating and rushing around replacing maggoty mushrooms from baskets of extras in the basement, and getting more butter, and checking to see if the yarn from the dyeing demonstration was drying okay.

One thing I did make time to do: I bent down and looked through the basket of woodland agaricus. A couple of caps had snapped off their stipes, but that always happens when you transport mushrooms. No volvas on any of the stipes.

By the time I started frying the agaricus, the place was so crowded, you could hardly move. I felt clammy from the buttery steam, tired from days of gathering and planning and getting the museum ready. It sort of hit me all at once, and I remember thinking as I sliced up the agaricus how glad I was I'd gone out to the woods that morning. The woods were a tonic, just to think about.

James's wife came in and interrupted my meditation. Karen Ransome was a voluptuous, big-eyed woman with fluffy yellow hair and a lot of wiggly, giggly mannerisms. I didn't know her very well, even though I hung out with James a lot. Mostly I heard about her from Mary Clardy, who runs the museum gift shop. Mary told me Karen didn't like to hike, and wasn't it too bad because James enjoyed it so much, and you'd think Karen could take the kids to their soccer games once in a while and let James have a free Saturday, and wasn't it awful that Karen expected James to watch the kids on weekends, considering she left them with baby-sitters all week long even though she didn't work for a living, and Karen must realize it didn't help James's career when she got drunk at Museum Committee parties and flirted with the city attorney.

Karen came and stood beside me while I cooked. She chattered about a shopping excursion, but I wasn't really listening to her. Her breath smelled of booze, and she laughed and said, "This isn't one of those mushrooms you can't eat if you've been drinking, is it?"

There's a kind of inky cap that turns your nose and fingers red and makes your heart pound wildly for a few hours if you consume it with alcohol.

I scooped some mushroom into a Dixie cup. "No. Here, be my guinea pig. Woodland agaricus."

James came out of the gift shop, saw Karen eating the agaricus, and turned a little red. He pushed across to us in time to hear Karen repeat "Woodland 'garicus" and giggle.

James looked embarrassed; he usually did in public with his wife. He murmured, "Karen, where are the kids?"

She wrinkled up her nose. "Guess I better go relieve the sitter—boy next door, honey, with all the freckles, you know who I mean. Let me just go to the gift stop—gift *shop*—"

"No!" James looked alarmed. "He can't be ten yet. Go see what the kids—" He put his arm around her, marching her to the door. I heard him ask where had she *been*, anyway.

I thought maybe he should have called her a cab, but he was a better judge than I was.

People were lined up to taste the agaricus. I watched their faces as they tasted it. Many had never tasted wild mushrooms; they looked like they'd gone to heaven.

I decided to fry up a second panful when James came back. "Everyone loves it," I boasted.

James seemed distracted. He helped me wipe off a couple of caps, then worked his way through the crowd toward the gift shop.

A young couple, wrapped in woolly scarves and looking like refugees from Woodstock, stood beside the table, Dixie cups at the ready. The woman, long-haired with a vaguely foolish expression, was flipping through a pamphlet of mine they sell in the gift shop, tilted "Edible Mushrooms and Their Nonedible Look-alikes." The young man, whose smile was irresistible, asked me what I was cooking and I told him.

The woman pointed to a photograph of the woodland agaricus in my pamphlet. "This one? The one it says not to pick unless an expert says it's okay?"

"Well, she's an expert," the man pointed out. "We usually stick to fly agaric." He grinned. "No mistaking that."

The fly agaric is bright red with cottony white "warts" (actually bits of a burst veil). It's psychotropic. Used for thousands of years in places like Siberia where alcohol made a late appearance.

I tried not to look too disapproving, but I hate people who think of mushrooms as just another way to get high.

Mary Clardy materialized beside me, her porcelain cheeks flushed almost as red as her curls.

"I saw Karen leaving. 'A happy drunk.' " Mary's tone was sarcastic. "They always think that about themselves, don't they?" Her chin was thrust forward.

The scarf-wrapped couple was exclaiming about the woodland agaricus, but Mary had interposed herself between me and the compliments.

"It's been ridiculous around here lately," she complained, pulling furry puffs off her sweater. "James having to run out of meetings to pick up those kids. Someone should report Karen for child neglect!"

Don Herlihy joined us; homing in on Mary's pheromones, damn him. He was supposed to be giving a demonstration on how nurseries coat sapling roots with spores. The mushroom mycelia provide a protective sheath for the roots; trees grow twice as tall when they grow with mushrooms.

Mary turned to Don with a slightly smug smile; the angora queen and her courtier. "I hear you're leaving us," she said, putting some sadness into her voice. "Taking a job down south."

I turned off the hot plate, not looking at Don. We'd covered thousands of acres together; looking for mushrooms, looking for night herons, looking for obscure strands of fescue for his botany masters. It was the closest I'd come to romance. He and James and the classes I taught were my entire social life.

Don shuffled a step closer to me, standing stiffly. His clothes smelled of damp grass. "I guess I'm getting old." He sounded guilty, hadn't even told me he was thinking of going. "The knee's bothering me more and more. And with the wet weather this year . . . The money . . ."

I knew he was just squeaking by; that's how it always is with us. But I guess I thought it didn't matter to him; I guess I depended on it not mattering. Because if it mattered to him, maybe it should matter to me. If Don Herlihy put on a suit, maybe I'd have to, too, someday soon.

James wandered back over, looking a little surprised to find the three of us—the help—huddled together, not identifying, demonstrating, or selling anything.

I glanced at Don and found him giving Mary a heart-on-his-sleeve kind of look.

Mary had the same look, but it was aimed at James.

I excused myself and dashed down to the basement. It was cool and dark down there; just me and the stuffed coyotes, the boxes of mushrooms, the mountains of leftover duff. I sat at the fungus-strewn conference table and I could almost see my students emptying their baskets, chattering about what they'd found in the woods, about the "one that got away," that inevitable boletus ("this big") that was riddled with maggots.

I was thirty-one years old and nobody loved me. I was too broke to afford a decent car, even secondhand. I was forever choosing between housemates or a hovel (just now, it was the hovel). I wore my clothes until the flannel turned to powder. But I had my classes, didn't I? I'd generated a lot of enthusiasm for fungus over the years, and I'd knocked down a lot of silly phobias. I was out in the woods most days. That should count for something, shouldn't it?

It should count for something with Don, bad knee or not. *I* should count for something.

The basement door swung open. "What I wish," Don said from the doorway, "is that I had a rich wife, like James. In fact"—a gloomy frown—"I wish I *were* James. I wish I had a silver Audi and a big house. I wish I had a job where people did what I told them."

"James isn't happy," I replied, though I'd never considered the point before.

Don shrugged. "Mary's crazy about him because she can't have him." I knew the feeling. "Even his problems work to his advantage."

"Where are you going?"

"Electronics firm in Encino."

Encino. Endless, unshaded concrete.

Please, God, may I never end up in Encino.

The lab technician at Community Hospital handed me a box of glass slides. This made the third time in eight years I'd done them this service. The third time in eight years they'd suspected mushroom poisoning and summoned the local expert. But it was different this time. I heard the slides rattle as I took the box in hand.

I pulled out a slide and, with a sterile swab, smeared some brown matter over the center. It was from a petri dish labeled "Feces—Peterson, Robin J." I dropped a coverslip into place.

I knew I would find some spores. I knew it because I'd watched Robin Peterson eat mushrooms. I'd watched him taste my woodland agaricus and smile a charming smile and try to tell me how much he loved it (with Mary Clardy in the way).

I told them at the hospital, "I didn't make a mistake—honest! Peterson ate a harmless mushroom. If he's sick, it's some kind of one-in-a-million allergy. That's all."

But they said he was showing signs of liver damage. They worried about kidney failure. The kind of symptoms produced by amanita toxins. By the destroying angel.

I maneuvered the slide back and forth until I spotted two quivering spores in the miasma. One was brown and oval; the woodland agaricus has brown oval spores. The other was white and round. I sat back. It was an Amanita (not an Agaricus) spore.

All Amanitas have round, white spores, but not all Amanitas are poisonous. There were three, maybe four edible species fruiting in nearby woods and fields. I closed my eyes and envisioned them, trying to influence the spores on the slide. Maybe Peterson had gotten hold of one of the edibles. Maybe this wasn't a death sentence.

I reached for the tiny stoppered bottle I'd brought with me. It was full of Melzer's reagent, an oily, yellow-red iodine solution. It stains certain spores—"amyloid" spores—gray. The deadly Amanitas have amyloid spores. The edible Amanitas don't.

I put a drop of Melzer's at the edge of the coverslip and watched it seep into the broth, tinging the whole mess grenadine. I breathed deeply, hoped deeply, and looked into the microscope.

The spore had turned light gray. It was amyloid.

Robin Peterson was lying there with a bunch of tubes coming out of him and a computer monitor blipping beside his bed. His mouth was hanging open and his skin was a dull apricot color with bruises all over it. I was too shaken to ask him if he'd gone collecting on his own, if he'd found himself some Amanitas and made a meal of them.

The poor man began retching. A nurse peeled the sheet off his abdomen and legs, and I could see that he lay in a pool of bloody excrement. It was the awfulest sight I'd ever seen. I backed out of Intensive Care. I backed into James.

James was talking to a doctor and the doctor was saying, "Judging by the extent of liver and kidney damage—I believe it's been sixteen hours since he ingested the fungus?"

"Usually it takes longer," I said mechanically. "As long as three days for symptoms to show up."

The doctor shook his head angrily. "And a small amount can be fatal?"

"Two cubic centimeters." My voice seemed disembodied, like something out of the PA system. "That's the smallest known fatal dose."

"One mushroom, in other words."

"Yes, but—"

"But nothing!" The doctor rubbed liver-spotted knuckles over Peterson's chart, as if trying to erase it. "Your mushroom's going to kill this man if we don't find him a new liver pretty damn soon!''

''I gave him a harmless Agaricus, a relative of the super-market mushroom. I know my mushrooms. Honestly! I wouldn't have—I *didn't*—make a mistake.''

James put his arm around me, wincing. ''Of course not, Lucy. Of course he didn't get the mushroom from you. As soon as he can be asked, he'll tell them.''

The doctor looked like it cost him a lot not to slap us. He pushed between us and went back into Intensive Care.

James pulled me onto a padded bench. There was a sheen to his pale skin. ''Don't let this get to you, Lucy. You know this isn't your fault.'' He searched my eyes. ''You *know* that.'' But it sounded like a question.

''What about the other people?''

He touched my cheek. ''What other people?''

''Who had mushrooms at the Fair. They'll get scared when they hear.''

He sighed, looking away. ''The Museum Association and the city attorney have insisted we broadcast an appeal, telling everyone who had mushrooms at the Fair to come to the hospital.'' He looked at me again. ''But it's just to satisfy the lawyers. Don't take it as a vote of no confidence. People who know you aren't going to bother.''

''We'll never be able to serve mushrooms again, will we?'' Whatever happened to Robin Peterson, the Fungus Fair was dead. Such a good little fair too. And no one would want to take my classes anymore.

I felt selfish thinking about it, with Peterson in there pass-ing blood.

A woman drifted out of the elevator toward us. Peterson's companion of the day before, with her lank, center-parted hair and layers of sixties clothes.

She stopped when she saw me. She bent close, close enough for me to smell patchouli and damp wool.

It was easier to focus on her scarf than her face, under the circumstances. ''Jack-o-lantern mushrooms,'' I murmured.

She fingered the scarf. ''Uh-huh. We boiled them and put in chrome and iron and alum to get these colors.''

"You know about mushrooms."

She nodded.

"Did Peterson go collecting? Before the fair? Or after?"

"No." She startled me by stroking my hair. "But it's not your fault. It's Robin's karma. I'm not sick. You're not sick. It must be Robin's karma. He's a fisher. A tuna fisher."

"Are you sure he didn't go collecting?"

"We didn't go out. We had Soma at home, dried. We ate that." Her face crinkled, as if the memory disturbed her. "We saw dolphins, ones that drowned in Robin's nets."

Soma. The subject of a six-thousand-year-old treatise in the *Rg Vedas*, the oldest specimen of written language. Soma the ingestible god. Also known as *Amanita muscaria,* the fly agaric, psychotropic but "poisonous" only in the way alcohol and recreational drugs are poisonous. Its spores are not amyloid. It wasn't a fly agaric spore I'd found and stained on that glass slide.

The doctor came out and stood over us. "Peterson's dead!"

James wrapped his arms around me. The young woman dropped to the floor, curling into an upright fetal position. "I can feel his soul," she whispered. Her head snapped back and she stared at me. "He'll speak to you in Soma."

James stayed with me that night, brewing me pots of herb tea that I couldn't drink and talking to me about anything, everything: his kids, his holidays, what we could expect from the wet weather in terms of timing the Wildflower Festival.

I knew that outside our cocoon, Fungus Fair attendees rushed themselves to the hospital; botanists who knew nothing about fungus fueled the public's phobia with misinformation; newspapers published alarmist lies. I'd spent a career trying to change people's attitudes about one of the world's most intriguing (and often health-preserving) life-forms. It was all wiped out now, all my work—seven six-session classes a year for eight years, the expeditions I'd led, two editions of my field guide, the edible mushrooms pamphlet. Now people would remember me as the mycologist who'd killed a man at a mushroom fair.

And I hadn't. How could I have made a mistake? I know mushrooms, really know them.

I felt like jumping off a cliff.

James tried hard to make me feel better, but I could see how upset he was, underneath. I ended up crying all over him.

I fell asleep around dawn, with James yawning and telling me about a cruise to Alaska, a cruise he very much wanted to take, if he could just persuade Karen to travel so far from Macy's.

I woke up a few hours later to find James asleep in my sprung easy chair. I tiptoed out of the house (maybe "shack" is a better word), put on my boots, and drove out to the woods. It's the only place I feel at home.

The mushrooms were beautiful, tomato-red with puffy white "warts." They were in a clearing by themselves, the center of attention, fresh and perfect, without a single bug in their gills, without a trace of decay. Yet I looked at them and felt afraid, afraid of what they might do to me. I reminded myself that people had been eating them for thousands of years. And I'd never heard of any fatalities (except in a British mystery novel).

I was doing it myself—letting phobia overcome what I knew to be true about the mushroom.

I forced myself to kneel in the duff before the great god Soma. At the base of one mushroom, a stunned fly skittered in the wind, attracted and then drugged by the fungus.

I snapped the broad caps off their stipes.

When I got home, James was gone. Just as well.

I sliced the fly agaric and spent an hour trying to copy the method of ingestion described by the Aryans in the *Rg Vedas*. I swallowed the yogurty mess. It tasted like moldy leaves.

For half an hour nothing happened, except that I was scared: scared of the mushroom and scared of Robin Peterson's ghost.

And then I was on the floor, supine and sweating. The ceiling swirled. For years I'd studied mushrooms, hunted them, examined them under microscopes, cooked them, served them, eaten them, arranged them, lectured about them, and photographed them. Now I saw myself as part of a continuum. I saw reindeer butt each other in savage contest for the fungus; I saw Aryan priests drink Soma milk; I saw bearded Siberians leap and stagger and laugh; I saw flower children peel the red skin off the cap and roll it into cigarettes.

And then I saw myself:

A cool, misty morning, me with my raincoat on, my basket on the ground beside me. There were two dozen mushrooms in it already, some very young, with veils covering their white gills, some with broad caps and gills dusted with brown spores.

I looked up. The wet branches of a live oak spread like gnarled arms against the white of the sky. Birds chattered somewhere in the tree, calling *scree scree scree*.

I looked back down. There were several mushrooms on the duff. Destroying angels, their caps so similar to the woodland agaricus that only the sacklike volva at the base of the stipe proclaimed them to be deadly.

I looked at the mushrooms in my basket. I inhaled the cold air. I listened to the *scree* of birds overhead, to the rustling of squirrels and the distant thud of falling pinecones. Life was good.

I dug in the duff. There were two young mushrooms there, caps snow white, round and small with partial veils and strong, crisp stipes. I dug carefully, recognizing the danger.

One was a destroying angel and one was a woodland agaricus. Strands of mycelia hung from the base of one. I pinched them off. The other was covered with a sacklike volva. I tossed that mushroom. Tossed it and then noticed a purple stain on its volva, like a bit of oozy ink.

It wasn't uncommon to find an aberrant mushroom, a mushroom harboring some unusual parasite or staining some uncharacteristic shade. I enjoyed finding the aberrations; they were part of the fun of hunting.

I picked up the destroying angel and sloughed off the stained volva. The ooze had not touched the stipe. Probably something in the ground; nothing to do with the mushroom itself. I tossed it aside again.

From the branches overhead, the *scree scree scree* of birds grew frantic. I looked up in time to see a small cloud of them swooping down. They seemed to be diving for me. I fell out of my squat and onto my back. As the birds pulled up and flew away, I saw a flash of white under their wings. I'd have to ask Don what kind they were.

I stood up, pulling twigs out of my hair and flicking soggy duff off my raincoat.

I bent to pick up my basket. Time to go to the museum.

I reached out to pick up the young woodland agaricus I'd just found.

Robin Peterson's icy hand closed over mine as I picked up the wrong mushroom.

A pounding on my front door dragged me out of a stuporous sleep. Someone was shouting my name.

I sat up. My furniture was all rearranged, pulled to the middle of the room. Why the hell had I done that?

I crawled on hands and knees to the front door, using the knob to pull myself to my feet.

It was Don Herlihy. He looked ashen, ill. He said, "Did you hear about Karen yet? Karen Ransome?"

"Oh, my God." I'd handed James's wife a Dixie cup of what I thought was woodland agaricus. Handed it to her with a boastful word and a proud smile.

"She's dead, Lucy. James was away, I guess, for most of the night. And no one told Karen about going to the hospital to get tested. By the time James got home and found her, she was too far gone."

"James was over here," I heard myself say. "It's my fault Karen didn't get help in time."

Don said, "No, Lucy," but he didn't come in.

There was a receipt sticking out of his shirt pocket; I could see Community Hospital's logo. He'd been to the hospital to get tested. I had no right to feel hurt, but I did.

* * *

"Come in, Lucy," James said kindly. "I've been worrying about you."

I heard children crying somewhere in the upstairs of James's house, and I heard the calm voice of an adult woman. James wore jeans and cashmere. His skin looked like candle wax, he was so pale. His hair stood up in rumpled waves against a backdrop of oak paneling.

I followed him inside. I followed him through the living room, through the formal dining room, through the hall, and back into a kitchen bigger than my whole house. There was a sweater slung across the tile counter: Mary Clardy's. It was her voice I'd heard; her voice consoling the children.

"I'm most comfortable in this room," James said, running a listless hand over the tile. "In fact, it probably seems gruesome, but now that everyone's finally gone, I was going to chop some stuff for stir-fry."

"If it relaxes you." How many times had I watched James slice mushrooms and debone chicken? My friend; how kind of him to let me into his kitchen.

"It's awful, but I'm hungry. I just—" He looked at me with bright eyes. "Have a meal with me, would you, Lucy? Make me feel like I'm not being abnormal?"

I couldn't imagine forcing food down my throat. "If you want me to. If you're really not—" Not mad at me.

He turned and began collecting things: A wok, some ginger, calamari in a plastic bag, oyster mushrooms, supermarket agaricus, bok choy, sesame oil.

I watched him set up the wok, heat the oil, toss in the ginger, then the bok choy. What I saw was my own hand reaching out for that one fatal mushroom, the one on the duff.

Such a small mushroom, such a small destroying angel, to kill two healthy—

It was like a knife in my gut: A small mushroom. A very small mushroom to have killed two healthy people.

The smallest fatal dose on record was two cubic centimeters: the size of a modest cap.

I watched James slice the oyster mushrooms and the supermarket mushrooms. And I remembered him wiping a cap and handing it to me at the Fungus Fair. I'd been slicing woodland agaricus into the skillet, right before serving Robin Peterson. Right *after* serving Karen Ransome.

James looked at me, his head cocked. Sighing, he tossed a handful of sliced mushrooms into the wok.

He could have it all now: Karen's wealth. Mary's love.

From that perspective, it was convenient he'd spent the night supporting and consoling me. Convenient he didn't tell his wife to watch for signs of mushroom poisoning; that he wasn't home to notice her symptoms and rush her to the hospital.

I watched James reach into a cupboard and pull out two dishes and two wineglasses. He handed the glasses to me.

We'd done this many times over the last eight years. I'd set the breakfast-nook table a hundred times. A hundred times we'd discussed museum business over stir-fry or bagels or mulligatawny soup, with Karen passed out drunk upstairs.

I pulled place mats out of a hutch, pulled a bottle of Chardonnay off the wine rack, pulled chopsticks out of the drawer. My back was to James. I was afraid—horrified by the suspicion I suddenly harbored.

He brought two steaming bowls of stir-fry to the table. He set one at my usual place. "No oyster sauce in that one," he said. "I know you hate the stuff."

I know how much destroying angel it takes to kill two people. I know that if I did make a mistake, it involved only one mushroom, the one with the stained volva. I know that if I did make a mistake, only one person would be dead now, not two.

I picked up my chopsticks and glanced down at the bowl. Sesame oil sizzled on a bed of mushrooms, calamari, and vegetables.

I unfolded my linen napkin while James uncorked the wine.

I looked around the room. The wainscoting was golden oak, the walls were papered a rich green, the floor was tiled in glossy terra-cotta. The breakfast nook windows faced a koi pond ringed with willows.

I remembered Don Herlihy saying, "I wish I had a rich wife."

And I was suddenly sure: I did not see the spirit of Robin

Peterson in my psychotropic vision. I did not see the truth. I saw my own fear. My worst nightmare.

I would not have picked up the wrong mushroom. Even if I had, I'd have noticed *something*, something a little odd about the sloughed stipe when I examined the mushrooms later.

It wasn't my mistake. Relief momentarily blurred my vision, like film melting in a projector.

Then I focused on James.

James. He had watched Karen eat the woodland agaricus. She'd been drinking again, neglecting the children. So unlike Mary Clardy.

He would serve Karen destroying angels at home, later. He would be rid of her; he would rescue his children from her incompetent care without depriving them of her big house. And it would look like an accident. An honest mistake. Especially if someone else at the fair got sick too.

After Karen left the museum, James handed me a mushroom cap to slice and serve. A destroying angel from the museum display. He would not have known so small a quantity could kill. Two cubic centimeters—only a mushroom expert would know that.

Now James said, "Eat it while it's hot, Lucy. There's comfort in food." He attacked his stir-fry like he needed comfort badly.

But he was doing better than me. He had a big house and two nice kids and somebody to love him. What did I have?

I used to think I had two friends; maybe not much else, but two best friends.

Don Herlihy, and he was leaving.

And James Ransome. How many canoe trips had we taken together? How many exhibits had we set up?

I thought James cared about me. How could he ruin my reputation—my *life*—just to arrange things so they suited him better?

I poked at the contents of my bowl.

Even if I told people, they wouldn't believe me. They'd consider it a rank excuse, a cheap shot, an attempt to pass the buck. And I couldn't prove anything anyway. Even if I wanted to orphan James's kids, I couldn't prove anything.

Two best friends. I thought of Don Herlihy shuffling on my doorstep, that hospital receipt in his pocket. After years of studying with him, working with him, he didn't trust me. He didn't love me.

And James. I thought he was my friend, staying with me last night. But he'd wrecked my life.

No matter what I did or said now, my career was ruined. No one would believe it wasn't my fault. If I couldn't convince Don Herlihy, how could I convince a bunch of strangers?

I'd never be considered an "expert" again; only someone who, in her hubris, continued denying what everybody else knew: that mushrooms should be feared and shunned, regardless of who serves them.

James was slumped over his meal now, not eating. His eyelids looked painfully puffy and red.

I was surprised I didn't feel more anger. Maybe I was too sad. Maybe I couldn't stand to let go of my last friend.

I tasted a few slivers of mushroom. They were perfectly seasoned. James was a good cook. (Mary was lucky.)

Upstairs somewhere, children's voices were raised with Mary's in a hymn. James covered his eyes with his hands.

No, it wouldn't do me any good to accuse James. Proof required confidence in my expertise. No one would believe me; and no one would trust me, ever again. I'd never earn a living as a mycologist, ever again. I would have to put on a suit. Work in some concrete purgatory.

I couldn't live with it. It was as simple as that: I couldn't live with it.

Today I had experimented with Soma, something I never thought that I would do. Tonight I would experiment again. I would go home and eat the destroying angel. I would see if it really was delicious.

Sharyn McCrumb, winner of a 1988 Edgar for Bimbos of the Death Sun, *says that* ". . . *culture has become optional these days—there are so many to choose from: yuppies, Trekkies, moral majority, etc.*" *Such a perspective is well suited to her trained-in-sociology sleuth Elizabeth Mac-Pherson* (Paying the Piper, Highland Laddie Gone) *and to engineer/author Jay Omega of* Bimbos. If I Ever Return, Pretty Peggy-O *features Spencer Arrowood, a Tennessee sheriff compelled to confront the decades-old ghost of the Vietnam War and its social consequences.*

In "The Luncheon," *we are treated to a sample of Sharyn's keen sense of the delicious—in ironic as well as culinary terms.*

THE LUNCHEON

by Sharyn McCrumb

S HE MUST BE careful not to let her anxiety show. Even if something were said during the lunch hour, she must take it calmly, or even better, pretend not to understand at all. Above all she must seem just as usual, no more or less quiet, attentive to the eddies in their lives.

Usually this was not difficult. Kathryn and Jayne required no more than token contributions from her, since it was tacitly understood that her life was less interesting than theirs. Occasionally Thursday lunch turned into an inquisition, when she let something negative slip—such as a quarrel with Andrew that morning. Jayne had pounced, demanding that her problem be "shared," and they had dissected it over chicken breast in wine sauce. By the time the dessert crepes had arrived, Andrew's forgetting to put mustard instead of mayonnaise on her sandwich had become an act of chauvinism.

Miriam had said that she would rather handle matters with Andrew in her own way, but they had laughed and asked her if she were trying to be *The Total Woman*. Kathryn told her that if Andrew refused to respect her personhood, she should take a lover; but Jayne contended that self-awareness was a healthier approach. She insisted that Miriam attend self-assertiveness training class with her, so Miriam went twice, because she didn't want to say no. Usually when other people insisted on a thing, and Miriam didn't care much either way, she let them have their own way. She had noticed, though, that some people nearly always cared a great deal about everything—such as where they had lunch and when they went—so that Miriam seldom got the default of getting to choose. But each thing was too trivial in Miriam's view to be assertive about. Somehow, though, they added up.

The jeweler's clock said 12:20, and she only had another block to go. Miriam slowed her walk to a trudge, but she still arrived for 12:30 lunch at 12:23. She decided, against her own inclinations, to go into the Post and Lentils and wait. It had been Kathryn's choice today, so lunch would be one of the Post's thirty-seven salad combinations, with commentary from Kathryn on the nutrition value of each ingredient. Miriam wished she'd bought a newspaper. She hated waiting with nothing to do. Jayne would not come for another fifteen minutes—to show that as an executive, she was not tied to the clock hands. She had nearly memorized the menu by the time Kathryn arrived.

"Well, hello, there, Miriam. How are *you*?"

Miriam wondered why Kathryn always seemed surprised to see her when they met for lunch every week. In fact, the Vietcong streak in Miriam's mind bristled at the inevitable greeting, but the meek and courteous part which was usually in control of her actions mumbled: "Fine. And you?"

She let Meek and Courteous continue the conversation on automatic pilot while the rest of her considered the question of why Kathryn made her uncomfortable. She was friendly, even effusive—but—but it was that *gushing* kindness—the way the Homecoming Queen treats the fat girl, as if to say: "You know you're not worth it, and I know you're not worth it, but I'll be kind to you to show everyone what a swell person I am." Miriam thought that putting up with Kathryn might be good practice for when she was eighty and was treated that way by everybody.

"Am I late?" cooed Kathryn. "I hope you didn't mind waiting."

Miriam said no, she never minded waiting. Sometimes, of course, she did mind, and she made great violent scenes in her head, scenes that were always scrapped when the other person arrived. Usually, though, she enjoyed a short wait. It was like a little breather offstage while you waited for your next scene. She would study the trees and the sky, and perhaps run over a bit of forthcoming dialogue, making sure to stay in character, and by then whoever she was waiting for turned up, and her self-awareness dissolved in a flurry of civilities.

"God, I'm tired," Kathryn was saying. "It can't be my blood sugar. I just had it checked." She pulled a bottle of pills from her purse and studied it thoughtfully. "More iron? Maybe I should have kelp today."

Miriam didn't smile. She was studying the abstract painting hanging above the booth and wondering how anybody could pay to have such ugliness about them, regardless of its technical merit. She had wanted to be an artist herself once, until it was impressed upon her that being able to draw well had nothing to do with it. She still liked to look at paintings, but she wondered why no one ever did pleasant or harmonious things. *Suppose I had to hang that in my bedroom for a year,* she would say to herself. She once ventured this opinion to Kathryn and Jayne, and they had smiled at her together and gently explained that paintings were not supposed to be pretty; they were supposed to reflect life. Miriam had wanted to answer that an artist of all people ought to be able to see the beauty in life, but the conversation had gone on by then to other topics.

"Having lunch with the Gorgons today?" Andrew had asked her. It was his oft-stated opinion that the ys in Kathryn and Jayne's names were their compensation for a missing, but coveted, male chromosome. He said he got along perfectly well with Jayne when he needed library material put on reserve, and since Kathryn was a secretary for the department next door to Geology, he often said hello to her in the halls, but their friendship with his wife did not extend to him. Perhaps, in fact, it excluded him automatically. (But she didn't want to think about Andrew.)

Miriam sometimes wondered why she kept up the lunch dates. The staff computer class where she had met them was long since over, but their habit of a weekly luncheon persisted. Still, you had to eat *somewhere,* and Miriam could not face the paper-bag lunch five days a week. It made it too easy to spend your hour running errands instead of eating, and then you were more tired than when you started. She supposed that she had nothing better to do: many, if not most, university friendships amounted to no more than that.

"I can't eat too much today," Kathryn was saying. "I'm playing racquetball this afternoon with Kit. I didn't get to see him last weekend because his daughter was down visiting. I think we have our relationship more clearly defined now. . . ."

Miriam wondered what she was going to think about until Kathryn finished her monologue. She always thought of it as the *Cosmo* Speech. Whenever you go out to lunch with an unattached woman over thirty, her conversation always comes around to a speech that sounds like a feature article from the magazine: His Career/My Career; His Kids/My Kids; or, most often, He Says He Loves Me, But He'll Screw Anything That Moves.

Miriam had heard variations on all these themes enough to know that it was never wise to offer any advice, particularly common sense, which almost always amounted to *Dump the Creep.* So she tried to look earnest while they talked, and behind the glazed look in her eyes she thought about her other regular outing "with the girls," as Andrew facetiously put it, although surely everybody in the Chataqua County Garden Club was over fifty. Except herself, of course. They were meeting tonight. Since refreshments were served at the meeting, she had told Andrew that she would be leaving him a salad to eat with the leftover lasagna.

She had expected Kathryn and Jayne to approve of the Chataqua County Garden Club (a "sisterhood," of sorts), but oddly enough they hadn't. They had not come right out and said so, but their attitude implied: *Of course it is chic for professors (and their wives) to move out into the country, but not so far out as Miriam and Andrew moved . . . and not to socialize with the . . . locals.* Once Miriam had made the mistake of mentioning that one of their neighbors had offered them some deer meat. Jayne had been unable to eat another forkful of lentil loaf, and for the rest of the lunch hour they had said dark things about the "carnivores" who were native to the North Carolina hills.

Miriam understood that the proper country place for university people to live was south of the campus town, in Williamson County, a lovely, unspoiled rural haven, with an herb shop; a "free press" (the word *Nicaragua* was always contained on page one, while the back pages were vegetarian recipes and ads for goat milk and meditation classes); and evening yoga classes at the Alternative Children's Academy. If Miriam and Andrew should wish to pursue rural living, according to Kathryn and Jayne, they should do so in Williamson County with the civilized people. Miriam had mentioned this to Andrew, and he'd laughed about it, and said that he didn't see why all those Earth Shoe People didn't just move to California, but that maybe they wouldn't have to. Maybe, he said, California would just suck them right across the country like a giant vacuum cleaner. After that, Miriam told people that she didn't want to live in Williamson County because of a fear of tornadoes.

Andrew had only agreed to move there because it was so much cheaper than closer places, but Miriam liked Chataqua County. Conversations with the neighboring farmers made a nice change from all the university talk that she got during the rest of the week. (Most of the farmers had been to college, too, but they weren't Academic, which is not the same thing as being educated.) Sometimes Barbara down the road would tell her about an auction at the old schoolhouse in Sinking Creek, and they'd go for the evening, packed tighter than baled hay in the little auditorium, eating hot dogs from the 4-H concession stand and watching somebody else's life pass before them as a string of possessions. Sometimes they'd bid on an applewood rocking chair or a collection of old kitchen utensils, but never on the really nice pieces of furniture or the silverware. Dealers always jacked the price up on those. Or the university people. "You got to watch out for the skinny women with no makeup, wearing jeans and an *old* cashmere sweater," Barbara warned her. "They got all kinds of money."

Chataqua County was lambs in the spring, and Ruritan apple butter, and the garden club. One Tuesday a month in the Sunday-school room of the Mt. Olive Baptist Church, two dozen ladies would meet to compare flower arrangements, discuss civic projects (like taking baked goods to the senior-citizen home), and catch up on all the news. It had taken Miriam a good while to follow it all, being the only one "not from around here," but she was beginning to get it sorted out now.

Miriam's favorite part of the garden club meetings, though, was the plant lore. The older women, especially, were full of tales about healing plants, and herbal teas, and old traditions. "You know why they's a mountain ash planted beside most every door in Scotch Creek?" they'd ask her. "Why, because the mountain ash is the American kin of the rowan tree back in Scotland. My grandmother used to say that in the old days, folk thought a rowan would protect you from the evil spirits, so them Scots that came over here went on a-planting 'em by the doorway."

Miriam was always afraid that someone from Sociology with a tape recorder, or one of the Earth Shoe People, would find out about the garden club and horn in, but so far they hadn't. Last November, when Kathryn was dating the latest divorce-casualty in Appalachian Studies, she had suggested that they drive out for the meeting, but Miriam had put her off by reminding her that it was hunting season, and perhaps not entirely safe. The matter had rested there.

"Sorry I'm late," said Jayne, not sounding sorry in the least. "Some guy needed a reference, and I could *not* get him off the phone." Jayne was the humanities reference librarian, which she described as "having to suffer fools gladly." She was in her not-to-be-mistaken-for-a-secretary outfit: navy-blue straight skirt and blazer, blue tailored blouse, red foulard tie. Sleek, short haircut; no mascara. Sometimes, Southern-born professors over sixty absentmindedly called her "dear," but everyone else got the message.

She sat down and looked meaningfully at Kathryn before picking up the menu. Uh-oh, thought Miriam.

"So," said Jayne, glancing through the salad list. "What have you been talking about?"

"Nothing much," said Kathryn. She meant, *I haven't said anything yet*.

Miriam said, "I think we'd better order. I need to get back."

Kathryn glanced at her watch. "It *is* getting late."

The waitress appeared then, and the next few minutes were occupied with detailed instructions—"Iced tea. Very light ice." "Is that low sodium?"—and so on. Miriam toyed with a pink packet of saccharin while these proceedings were taking place. She was trying to think about something else.

"How is Andrew?" asked Jayne, trying to make it sound perfunctory.

"He's fine," said Miriam. *He doesn't know that I know. I wondered if he suspected that you did.* Andrew had forgotten that she had taken the university computer course for staff. As a professor, he had an electronic mailbox, and one day (just for fun?) she had accessed his "mail" on her terminal. The password was easy to figure out. True to his specialization, Andrew alternated between *aquifer* and *mineral*. Miriam did not know what she had expected to find on the university computer system. Love letters, perhaps, since Andrew had been preoccupied lately. She supposed, after all, that electronic mail was just as private as the other kind. Or just as un-private.

So she had found out about Andrew's project weeks ago, and now that it was nearly to the press-release stage, Kathryn must have learned about it from gossip in the department of . . . Andrew's coconspirator. He had not discussed it with her, of course. He was going to present her with a fait accompli. He would make a lot of money from the sale, and as the letters from the other professor had stated, "There weren't many people to be considered.'' Chataqua County was not populous. She knew that sooner or later the weekly luncheon would be devoted to a discussion of Andrew and his project, but Miriam did not want to ''articulate her feelings'' with Kathryn and Jayne. They'd be on the same side for once, but she preferred to handle matters in her own way.

She had already talked the matter over with the garden club. A couple of the older ones had to have things like ''toxic chemicals'' and ''groundwater'' explained to them, but finally they understood why she was so upset about Andrew's offer to sell the farm to the university for a landfill. She told them about some of the chemicals that certain departments couldn't dump down the sink anymore, and what had happened to the pond on campus when they used it for dumping.

After that there had been complete silence for a good three minutes. And then the talk returned to gardening. At first Miriam thought that the issue had been too complex for them to understand. She wondered if she ought to explain about cancer and crop contamination, and all the other dangers. Listening to their calm discussion of plants, she thought that they had just given up considering the problem altogether, but looking back on it later, she understood.

''Cohosh sure does look nice in a flower arrangement, doesn't it?'' said Mrs. Calloway. ''Nice big purple berries that look like a cross between blueberries and grapes. There's some up the hill behind our place.''

''You wouldn't want to use them in a salad, though,'' said Mrs. Dehart thoughtfully. ''Bein' poison and all. 'Course, they might not kill you.''

''We lost a cow to eating chokecherry leaves once,'' said Mrs. Fletcher. ''It almost always kills a cow if you let one in a field with chokecherry. I never heard tell of a human getting hold of any, though. We got some growing in our woods, but it's outside the fence.''

''That ain't nothin' to hemlock,'' sniffed Serena Walkenshaw. ''Looks just like parsley, if you don't know any better. They're kin, of course. Wild carrot family, same as Queen Anne's Lace. But that hemlock beats all you ever seen for being . . . *toxic*?''

Miriam nodded. "I don't suppose you find it much around here."

Serena Walkenshaw shrugged. "I believe I saw some in the marsh near that little creek on your place. 'Course, it might have been parsley. . . ."

Miriam felt a tug on her sleeve and looked up to see Kathryn peering at her intently. "Are you all right, Miriam? You're just staring at your salad."

Miriam smiled. "I was just thinking that I had to fix a salad for Andrew tonight, before I go off to the garden club."

Jayne laughed. "The *garden club*! What can you possibly get out of that?"

"Recipes," said Miriam softly.

Marcia Muller says that ". . . what interests me most in the mystery novel is character and how plot evolves from it." Her seventeen novels, including There's Something in a Sunday, The Shape of Dread, Eye of the Storm, The Cavalier in White, *and* Dark Star, *bear witness to her success in creating multidimensional characters coping with complex situations. Marcia is co-editor with Bill Pronzini of nine mystery anthologies and a major critical work,* 1001 Midnights, *nominated for an Edgar in 1986.*

In "The Place That Time Forgot," private investigator Sharon McCone tunes in to her memory to help her solve a case.

THE PLACE THAT TIME FORGOT

by Marcia Muller

IN SAN FRANCISCO'S Glen Park district there is a small building with the words GREENGLASS 5 & 10¢ STORE painted in faded red letters on its wooden facade. Broadleaf ivy grows in planter boxes below its windows and partially covers their dusty panes. Inside is a counter with jars of candy and bubble gum on top and cigars, cigarettes, and pipe tobacco down below. An old-fashioned jukebox—the kind with colored glass tubes—hulks against the opposite wall. The rest of the room is taken up by counters laden with merchandise that has been purchased at fire sales and manufacturers' liquidations. In a single shopping spree, it is possible for a customer to buy socks, playing cards, off-brand cosmetics, school supplies, kitchen utensils, sports equipment, toys, and light bulbs—all at prices of at least ten years ago.

It is a place forgotten by time, a fragment of yesterday in the midst of today's city.

I have now come to know the curious little store well, but

up until one rainy Wednesday last March, I'd done no more than glance inside while passing. But that morning Hank Zahn, my boss at All Souls Legal Cooperative, had asked me to pay a call on its owner, Jody Greenglass. Greenglass was a client who had asked if Hank knew an investigator who could trace a missing relative for him. It didn't sound like a particularly challenging assignment, but my assistant, who usually handles routine work, was out sick. So at ten o'clock, I put on my raincoat and went over there.

When I pushed open the door I saw there wasn't a customer in sight. The interior was gloomy and damp; a fly buzzed fitfully against one of the windows. I was about to call out, thinking the proprietor must be beyond the curtained doorway at the rear, when I realized a man was sitting on a stool behind the counter. That was all he was doing—just sitting, his eyes fixed on the wall above the jukebox.

He was a big man, elderly, with a belly that bulged out under his yellow shirt and black suspenders. His hair and beard were white and luxuriant, his eyebrows startlingly black by contrast. When I said, "Mr. Greenglass?" he looked at me, and I saw an expression of deep melancholy.

"Yes?" he asked politely.

"I'm Sharon McCone, from All Souls Legal Cooperative."

"Ah, yes. Mr. Zahn said he would send someone."

"I understand you want to locate a missing relative."

"My granddaughter."

"If you'll give me the particulars, I can get on it right away." I looked around for a place to sit, but didn't see any chairs.

Greenglass stood. "I'll get you a stool." He went toward the curtained doorway, moving gingerly, as if his feet hurt him. They were encased in floppy slippers.

While I waited for him, I looked up at the wall behind the counter and saw it was plastered with faded pieces of slick paper that at first I took to be playbills. Upon closer examination I realized they were sheet music, probably of forties and fifties vintage. Their artwork was of that era anyway: formally dressed couples performing intricate dance steps;

showgirls in extravagant costumes; men with patent-leather hair singing their hearts out; perfectly coiffed women showing plenty of even, pearly white teeth. Some of the song titles were vaguely familiar to me: "Dreams of You," "The Heart Never Lies," "Sweet Mystique." Others I had never heard of.

Jody Greenglass came back with a wooden stool and set it on my side of the counter. I thanked him and perched on it, then took a pencil and notebook from my bag. He hoisted himself onto his own stool, sighing heavily.

"I see you were looking at my songs," he said.

"Yes. I haven't really seen any sheet music since my piano teacher gave up on me when I was about twelve. Some of those are pretty old, aren't they?"

"Not nearly as old as I am." He smiled wryly. "I wrote the first in thirty-nine, the last in fifty-three. Thirty-seven of them in all. A number were hits."

"*You* wrote them?"

He nodded and pointed to the credit line on the one closest to him: "Words and Music by Jody Greenglass."

"Well, for heaven's sake," I said. "I've never met a song-writer before. Were these recorded too?"

"Sure. I've got them all on the jukebox. Some good singers performed them—Como, Crosby." His smile faded. "But then, in the fifties, popular music changed. Presley, Holly, those fellows—that's what did it. I couldn't change with it. Luckily, I'd always had the store; music was more of a hobby for me. 'My Little Girl' "—he indicated a sheet with a picture-pretty toddler on it—"was the last song I ever sold. Wrote it for my granddaughter when she was born in fifty-three. It was *not* a big hit."

"This is the granddaughter you want me to locate?"

"Yes. Stephanie Ann Weiss. If she's still alive, she's thirty-seven now."

"Let's talk about her. I take it she's your daughter's daughter."

"My daughter Ruth's. I only had the one child."

"Is your daughter still living?"

"I don't know." His eyes clouded. "There was a . . . an

estrangement. I lost track of both of them a couple of years after Stephanie was born.''

''If it's not too painful, I'd like to hear about that.''

''It's painful, but I can talk about it.'' He paused, thoughtful. ''It's funny. For a long time it didn't hurt, because I had my anger and disappointment to shield myself. But those kinds of emotions can't last without fuel. Now that they're gone, I hurt as much as if it happened yesterday. That's what made me decide to try to make amends to my granddaughter.''

''But not your daughter too?''

He made a hand motion as if to erase the memory of her. ''Our parting was too bitter; there are some things that can't be atoned for, and frankly, I'm afraid to try. But Stephanie— if her mother hasn't completely turned her against me, there might be a chance for us.''

''Tell me about this parting.''

In a halting manner that conveyed exactly how deep his pain went, he related his story.

Jody Greenglass had been widowed when his daughter was only ten and had raised the girl alone. Shortly after Ruth graduated from high school, she married the boy next door. The Weiss family had lived in the house next to Greenglass's Glen Park cottage for close to twenty years, and their son, Eddie, and Ruth were such fast childhood friends that a gate was installed in the fence between their adjoining backyards. Jody, in fact, thought of Eddie as his own son.

After their wedding the couple moved north to the small town of Petaluma, where Eddie had found a good job in the accounting department of one of the big egg hatcheries. In 1953, Stephanie Ann was born. Greenglass didn't know exactly when or why they began having marital problems; perhaps they hadn't been ready for parenthood, or perhaps the move from the city to the country didn't suit them. But by 1955, Ruth had divorced Eddie and taken up with a Mexican national named Victor Rios.

''I like to think I'm not prejudiced,'' Greenglass said to me. ''I've mellowed with the years, I've learned. But you've got to remember that this was the mid-fifties. Divorce wasn't all that common in my circle. And people like us didn't even marry outside our faith, much less form relationships out of wedlock with those of a different race. Rios was an illiterate laborer, not even an American citizen. I was shocked that Ruth was living with this man, exposing her child to such a situation."

"So you tried to stop her."

He nodded wearily. "I tried. But Ruth wasn't listening to me anymore. She'd always been such a good girl. Maybe that was the problem—she'd been *too* good and it was her time to rebel. We quarreled bitterly, more than once. Finally I told her that if she kept on living with Rios, she and her child would be dead to me. She said that was just fine with her. I never saw or heard from her again."

"Never made any effort to contact her?"

"Not until a couple of weeks ago. I nursed my anger and bitterness, nursed them well. But then in the fall I had some health problems—my heart—and realized I'd be leaving this world without once seeing my grown-up granddaughter. So when I was back on my feet again, I went up to Petaluma, checked the phone book, asked around their old neighborhood. Nobody remembered them. That was when I decided I needed a detective."

I was silent, thinking of the thirty-some years that had elapsed. Locating Stephanie Ann Weiss—or whatever name she might now be using—after all that time would be difficult. Difficult, but not impossible, given she was still alive. And certainly more challenging than the job I'd initially envisioned.

Greenglass seemed to interpret my silence as pessimism. He said, "I know it's been a very long time, but isn't there something you can do for me? I'm seventy-eight years old; I want to make amends before I die."

I felt the prickle of excitement that I often experience when faced with an out-of-the-ordinary problem. I said, "I'll try to help you. As I said before, I can get on it right away."

I gathered more information from him—exact spelling of names, dates—then asked for the last address he had for Ruth in Petaluma. He had to go in the back of the store where, he explained, he now lived, to look it up. While he did so, I wandered over to the jukebox and studied the titles of the 78s. There was a basket of metal slugs on top of the machine, and on a whim I fed it one and punched out selection E-3, ''My Little Girl.'' The somewhat treacly lyrics boomed forth in a smarmy baritone; I could understand why the song hadn't gone over in the days when America was gearing up to feverishly embrace the likes of Elvis Presley. Still, I had to admit the melody was pleasing—downright catchy, in fact. By the time Greenglass returned with the address, I was humming along.

Back in my office at All Souls, I set a skiptrace in motion, starting with an inquiry to my friend Tracy at the Department of Motor Vehicles regarding Ruth Greenglass, Ruth Weiss, Ruth Rios, Stephanie Ann Weiss, Stephanie Ann Rios, or any variant thereof. A check with directory assistance revealed that neither woman currently had a phone in Petaluma or the surrounding communities. The Petaluma Library had nothing on them in their reverse street directory. Since I didn't know either woman's occupation, professional affiliations, doctor, or dentist, those avenues were closed to me. Petaluma High School would not divulge information about graduates, but the woman in Records with whom I spoke assured me that no one named Stephanie Weiss or Stephanie Rios had attended during the mid- to late-sixties. The county's voter registration had a similar lack of information. The next line of inquiry to pursue while waiting for a reply from the DMV was vital statistics—primarily marriage licenses and death certificates—but for those I would need to go to the Sonoma County Courthouse in Santa Rosa. I checked my watch, saw it was only a little after one, and decided to drive up there.

Santa Rosa, some fifty miles north of San Francisco, is a former country town that has risen to the challenge of migrations from the crowded communities of the Bay Area and become a full-fledged city with a population nearing a hundred thousand. Testimony to this is the new County Administration Center on its outskirts, where I found the Recorder's Office housed in a building on the aptly named Fiscal Drive.

My hour-and-a-half journey up there proved well worth the time: the clerk I dealt with was extremely helpful, the records easily accessed. Within half an hour, for a nominal fee, I was in possession of a copy of Ruth Greenglass Weiss's death certificate. She had died of cancer at Petaluma General Hospital in June of 1974; her next of kin was shown as Stephanie Ann Weiss, at an address on Bassett Street in Petaluma. It was a different address than the last one Greenglass had had for them.

The melody of "My Little Girl" was still running through my head as I drove back down the freeway to Petaluma, the southernmost community in the county. A picturesque river town with a core of nineteenth-century business buildings, Victorian homes, and a park with a bandstand, it is surrounded by little hills—which is what the Indian word *petaluma* means. The town used to be called the Egg Basket of the World, because of the proliferation of hatcheries such as the one where Eddie Weiss worked, but since the decline of the egg- and chicken-ranching businesses, it has become a trendy retreat for those seeking to avoid the high housing costs of San Francisco and Marin. I had friends there—people who had moved up from the city for just that reason—so I knew the lay of the land fairly well.

Bassett Street was on the older west side of town, far from the bland, treeless tracts that have sprung up to the east. The address I was seeking turned out to be a small white frame bungalow with a row of lilac bushes planted along the property line on either side. Their branches hung heavy with as yet unopened blossoms; in a few weeks the air would be sweet with their perfume.

When I went up on the front porch and rang the bell, I was greeted by a very pregnant young woman. Her name, she said, was Bonita Clark; she and her husband Russ had bought the house two years before from some people named Berry. The Berrys had lived there for at least ten years and had never mentioned anyone named Weiss.

I hadn't really expected to find Stephanie Weiss still in

residence, but I'd hoped the present owner could tell me where she had moved. I said, "Do you know anyone on the street who might have lived here in the early seventies?"

"Well, there's old Mrs. Caubet. The pink house on the corner with all the rosebushes. She's lived here forever."

I thanked her and went down the sidewalk to the house she'd indicated. Its front yard was a thicket of rosebushes whose colors ranged from yellows to reds to a particularly beautiful silvery purple. The rain had stopped before I'd reached town, but not all that long ago; the roses' velvety petals were beaded with droplets.

Mrs. Caubet turned out to be a tall, slender woman with sleek gray hair, vigorous-looking in a blue sweatsuit and athletic shoes. I felt a flicker of amusement when I first saw her, thinking of how Bonita Clark had called her "old," said she'd lived there "forever." Interesting, I thought, how one's perspective shifts. . . .

Yes, Mrs. Caubet said after she'd examined my credentials, she remembered the Weisses well. They'd moved to Bassett Street in 1970. "Ruth was already ill with the cancer that killed her," she added. "Steff was only seventeen, but so grown-up, the way she took care of her mother."

"Did either of them ever mention a man named Victor Rios?"

The woman's expression became guarded. "You say you're working for Ruth's father?"

"Yes."

She looked thoughtful, then motioned at a pair of white wicker chairs on the wraparound porch. "Let's sit down."

We sat. Mrs. Caubet continued to look thoughtful, pleating the ribbing on the cuff of her sleeve between her fingers. I waited.

After a time she said, "I wondered if Ruth's father would ever regret disowning her."

"He's in poor health. It's made him realize he doesn't have much longer to make amends."

"A pity that it took until now. He's missed a great deal because of his stubbornness. I know; I'm a grandparent myself. And I'd like to put him in touch with Steff, but I don't know what happened to her. She left Petaluma six months after Ruth died.''

''Did she say where she planned to go?''

''Just something about getting in touch with relatives. By that I assumed she meant her father's family in the city. She promised to write, but she never did, not even a Christmas card.''

''Will you tell me what you remember about Ruth and Stephanie? It may give me some sort of lead, and besides, I'm sure my client will want to know about their lives after his falling-out with Ruth.''

She shrugged. ''It can't hurt. And to answer your earlier question, I have heard of Victor Rios. He was Ruth's second husband; although the marriage was a fairly long one, it was not a particularly good one. When she was diagnosed as having cancer, Rios couldn't deal with her illness, and he left her. Ruth divorced him, took back her first husband's name. It was either that, she once told me, or Greenglass, and she was even more bitter toward her father than toward Rios.''

''After Victor Rios left, what did Ruth and Stephanie live on? I assume Ruth couldn't work.''

''She had some savings—and, I suppose, alimony.''

''It couldn't have been much. Jody Greenglass told me Rios was an illiterate laborer.''

Mrs. Caubet frowned. ''That's nonsense! He must have manufactured the idea, out of prejudice and anger at Ruth for leaving her first husband. He considered Eddie Weiss a son, you know. It's true that when Ruth met Rios, he didn't have as good a command of the English language as he might, but he did have a good job at Sunset Line and Twine. They weren't rich, but I gather they never lacked for the essentials.''

It made me wonder what else Greenglass had manufactured. ''Did Ruth ever admit to living with Rios before their marriage?''

''No, but it wouldn't have surprised me. She always struck me as a nonconformist. And that, of course, would better explain her father's attitude.''

"One other thing puzzles me," I said. "I checked with the high school, and they have no record of Stephanie attending."

"That's because she went to parochial school. Rios was Catholic, and that's what he wanted. Ruth didn't care either way. As it was, Steff dropped out in her junior year to care for her mother. I offered to arrange home care so she might finish her education—I was once a social worker and knew how to go about it—but Steff said no. The only thing she really missed about school, she claimed, was choir and music class. She had a beautiful singing voice."

So she'd inherited her grandfather's talent, I thought. A talent I was coming to regard as considerable, since I still couldn't shake the lingering melody of "My Little Girl."

"How did Stephanie feel about her grandfather? And Victor Rios?" I asked.

"I think she was fond of Rios, in spite of what he'd done to her mother. Her feelings toward her grandfather I'm less sure of. I do remember that toward the end Steff had become very like her mother; observing that alarmed me somewhat."

"Why?"

"Ruth was a very bitter woman, totally turned in on herself. She had no real friends, and she seemed to want to draw Steff into a little circle from which the two of them could fend off the world together. By the time Steff left Petaluma she'd closed off, too, withdrawn from what few friends she'd been permitted. I'd say such bitterness in so young a woman is cause for alarm, wouldn't you?"

"I certainly would. And I suspect that if I do find her, it's going to be very hard to persuade her to reconcile with her grandfather."

Mrs. Caubet was silent for a moment, then said, "She might surprise you."

"Why do you say that?"

"It's just a feeling I have. There was a song Mr. Greenglass wrote in celebration of Steff's birth. Do you know about it?"

I nodded.

"They had a record of it. Ruth once told me that it was

the only thing he'd ever given them, and she couldn't bear to take that away from Steff. Anyway, she used to play it occasionally. Sometimes I'd go over there, and Steff would be humming the melody while she worked around the house."

That didn't mean much, I thought. After all, I'd been mentally humming it since that morning.

When I arrived back in the city I first checked at All Souls to see if there had been a response to my inquiry from my friend at the DMV. There hadn't. Then I headed for Glen Park to break the news about his daughter's death to Jody Greenglass, as well as to get some additional information.

This time there were a few customers in the store: a young couple poking around in Housewares; an older woman selecting some knitting yarn. Greenglass sat at his customary position behind the counter. When I gave him the copy of Ruth's death certificate, he read it slowly, then folded it carefully and placed it in his shirt pocket. His lips trembled inside his nest of fluffy white beard, but otherwise he betrayed no emotion. He said, "I take it you didn't find Stephanie Ann at that address."

"She left Petaluma about six months after Ruth died. A neighbor thought she might have planned to go to relatives. Would that be the Weisses, do you suppose?"

He shook his head. "Norma and Al died within months of each other in the mid-sixties. They had a daughter, name of Sandra, but she married and moved away before Eddie and Ruth did. To Los Angeles, I think. I've no idea what her husband's name might be."

"What about Eddie Weiss—what happened to him?"

"I didn't tell you?"

"No."

"He died a few months after Ruth divorced him. Auto accident. He'd been drinking. Damned near killed his parents, following so close on the divorce. That was when Norma and Al stopped talking to me; I guess they blamed Ruth. Things got so uncomfortable there on the old street that I decided to come to live here at the store."

The customer who had been looking at yarn came up, her arms piled high with heather-blue skeins. I stepped aside so Greenglass could ring up the sale, glanced over my shoulder at the jukebox, then went up to it and played "My Little Girl" again. As the mellow notes poured from the machine, I realized that what had been running through my head all day was not quite the same. Close, very close, but there were subtle differences.

And come to think of it, why should the song have made such an impression, when I'd only heard it once? It was catchy, but there was no reason for it to haunt me as it did.

Unless I'd heard something like it. Heard it more than once. And recently . . .

I went around the counter and asked Greenglass if I could use his phone. Dialed the familiar number of radio KSUN, the Light of the Bay. My former lover, Don Del Boccio, had just come into the studio for his six-to-midnight stint as disc jockey, heartthrob, and hero to half a million teenagers who have to be either hearing-impaired or brain-damaged, and probably both. Don said he'd be glad to provide expert assistance, but not until he got off work. Why didn't I meet him at his loft around twelve-thirty?

I said I would and hung up, thanking the Lord that I somehow manage to remain on mostly good terms with the men from whom I've parted.

Don said, "Hum it again."

"You know I'm tone-deaf."

"You have no vocal capabilities. You can distinguish tone, though. And I can interpret your warbling. Hum it."

We were seated in his big loft in the industrial district off Third Street, surrounded by his baby grand piano, drums, sound equipment, books, and—a recent acquisition—a huge aquarium of tropical fish. I'd taken a nap after going home from Greenglass's and felt reasonably fresh. Don—a big, easygoing man who enjoys his minor celebrity status and also keeps up his serious musical interests—was reasonably wired. We were drinking red wine and picking at a plate of antipasto he'd casually thrown together.

"Hum it," he said again.

I hummed, badly, my face growing hot as I listened to myself.

He imitated me—on key. "It's definitely not rock, not with that tempo. Soft rock? Possibly. There's something about it . . . that sextolet—"

"That what?"

"An irregular rhythmic grouping. One of the things that makes it stick in your mind. Folk? Maybe country. You say you think you've been hearing it recently?"

"That's the only explanation I can come up with for it sticking in my mind the way it has."

"Hmm. There's been some new stuff coming along recently, out of L.A. rather than Nashville, that might . . . You listen to a country station?"

"KNEW, when I'm driving sometimes."

"Disloyal thing."

"I never listened to KSUN much, even when we . . ."

Our eyes met and held. We were both remembering, but I doubted if the mental images were the same. Don and I are too different; that was what ultimately broke us up.

After a moment he grinned and said, "Well, no one over the mental age of twelve does. Listen, what I guess is that you've been hearing a song that's a variation on the melody of the original one. Which is odd, because it's an uncommon one to begin with."

"Unless the person who wrote the new song knew the old one."

"Which you tell me isn't likely, since it wasn't very popular. What is it you're investigating—a plagiarism case?"

I shook my head. If Jody Greenglass's last song had been plagiarized, I doubted it was intentional—at least not on the conscious level. I said, "Is it possible to track down the song, do you suppose?"

"Sure. Care to run over to the studio? I can do a scan on our library, see what we've got."

"But KSUN doesn't play anything except hard rock."

"No, but we get all sorts of promos, new releases. Let's give it a try."

* * *

"There you are," Don said. " 'It Never Stops Hurting.' Steff Rivers. Atlas Records. Released last November."

I remembered it now, half heard as I'd driven the city streets with my old MG's radio tuned low. Understandable that for her professional name she'd Anglicized that of the only father figure she'd ever known.

"Play it again," I said.

Don pressed the button on the console and the song flooded the sound booth, the woman's voice soaring and clean. The lyrics were about grieving for a lost lover, but I thought I knew other experiences that had gone into creating the naked emotion behind them: the scarcely known father who had died after the mother left him; the grandfather who had rejected both mother and child; the stepfather who had been unable to cope with fatal illness and had run away.

When the song ended and silence filled the little booth, I said to Don, "How would I go about locating her?"

He grinned. "One of the Atlas reps just happens to be a good friend of mine. I'll give her a call in the morning, see what I can do."

The rain started again early the next morning. It made the coastal road that wound north on the high cliffs above the Pacific dangerously slick. By the time I arrived at the village of Gualala, just over the Mendocino County line, it was close to three and the cloud cover was beginning to break up.

The town, I found, was just a strip of homes and businesses between the densely forested hills and the sea. A few small shopping centers, some unpretentious eateries, the ubiquitous realty offices, a new motel, and a hotel built during the logging boom of the late 1800s—that was about it. It would be an ideal place, I thought, for retirees or starving artists, as well as a young woman seeking frequent escape from the pressures of a career in the entertainment industry.

Don's record-company friend had checked with someone she knew in Steff Rivers's producer's office to find out her present whereabouts, had sworn me to secrecy about where I'd received the information and given me an address. I'd pinpointed the turnoff from the main highway on a county map. It was a small lane that curved off toward the sea about a half mile north of town; the house at its end was actually a pair of A frames, weathered gray shingle, connected by a glassed-in walkway. Hydrangeas and geraniums bloomed in tubs on either side of the front door; a stained-glass oval depicting a sea gull in flight hung in the window. I left the MG next to a gold Toyota sports car parked in the drive.

There was no answer to my knock. After a minute I skirted the house and went around back. The lawn there was weedy and uneven; it sloped down toward a low grapestake fence that guarded the edge of the ice-plant-covered bluff. On a bench in front of it sat a small figure wearing a red rain slicker, the hood turned up against the fine mist. The person was motionless, staring out at the flat, gray ocean.

When I started across the lawn, the figure turned. I recognized Steff Rivers from the publicity photo Don had dug out of KSUN's files the night before. Her hair was black and cut very short, molded to her head like a bathing cap; her eyes were large, long-lashed, and darkly luminous. In her strong features I saw traces of Jody Greenglass's.

She called out, "Be careful there. Some damn rodent has dug the yard up."

I walked cautiously the rest of the way to the bench.

"I don't know what's wrong with it," she said, gesturing at a hot tub on a deck opening off the glassed-in walkway of the house. "All I can figure is something's plugging the drain."

"I'm sorry?"

"Aren't you the plumber?"

"No."

"Oh. I knew she was a woman, and I thought . . . Who are you, then?"

I took out my identification and showed it to her. Told her why I was there.

Steff Rivers seemed to shrink inside her loose slicker. She drew her knees up and hugged them with her arms.

"He needs to see you," I concluded. "He wants to make amends."

She shook her head. "It's too late for that."

"Maybe. But he *is* sincere."

"Too bad." She was silent for a moment, turning her gaze back toward the sea. "How did you find me? Atlas and my agent know better than to give out this address."

"Once I knew Stephanie Weiss was Steff Rivers, it was easy."

"And how did you find *that* out?"

"The first clue I had was 'It Never Stops Hurting.' You adapted the melody of 'My Little Girl' for it."

"I what?" She turned her head toward me, features frozen in surprise. Then she was very still, seeming to listen to the song inside her head. "I guess I did. My God . . . I *did*!"

"You didn't do it consciously?"

"No. I haven't thought of that song in years. I . . . I broke the only copy of the record that I had the day my mother died." After a moment she added, "I suppose the son of a bitch will want to sue me."

"You know that's not so." I sat down beside her on the wet bench, turned my collar up against the mist. "The lyrics of that song say a lot about you, you know."

"Yeah—that everybody's left me or fucked me over as long as I've lived."

"Your grandfather wants to change that pattern. He wants to come back to you."

"Well, he can't. I don't want him."

A good deal of her toughness was probably real—would have to be, in order for her to survive in her business—but I sensed some of it was armor that she could don quickly whenever anything threatened the vulnerable core of her persona. I remained silent for a few minutes, wondering how to get through to her, watching the waves ebb and flow on the beach at the foot of the cliff. Eroding the land, giving some of it back again. Take and give, take and give . . .

Finally I asked, "Why were you sitting out here in the rain?"

"They said it would clear around three. I was just waiting. Waiting for something good to happen."

"A lot of good things must happen to you. Your career's going well. This is a lovely house, a great place to escape to."

"Yeah, I've done all right. 'It Never Stops Hurting' wasn't my first hit, you know."

"Do you remember a neighbor of yours in Petaluma—a Mrs. Caubet?"

"God! I haven't thought of her in years either. How is she?"

"She's fine. I talked with her yesterday. She mentioned your talent."

"Mrs. Caubet. Petaluma. That all seems so long ago."

"Where did you go after you left there?"

"To my Aunt Sandra, in L.A. She was married to a record-company flack. It made breaking in a little easier."

"And then?"

"Sandra died of a drug overdose. She found out that the bastard she was married to had someone else."

"What did you do then?"

"What do you think? Kept on singing and writing songs. Got married."

"And?"

"What the hell is this and-and-and? Why am I even talking to you?"

I didn't reply.

"All right. Maybe I need to talk to somebody. That didn't work out—the marriage, I mean—and neither did the next one. Or about a dozen other relationships. But things just kept clicking along with my career. The money kept coming in. One weekend a few years ago I was up here visiting friends at Sea Ranch. I saw this place while we were just driving around, and . . . now I live here when I don't have to be in L.A. Alone. Secure. Happy."

"Happy, Steff?"

"Enough." She paused, arms tightening around her drawn-up knees. "Actually, I don't think much about being happy anymore."

"You're a lot like your grandfather."

She rolled her eyes. "Here we go again!"

"I mean it. You know how he lives? Alone in the back of his store. He doesn't think much about being happy either."

"He still has that store?"

"Yes." I described it, concluding, "It's a place that's just been forgotten by time. *He's* been forgotten. When he dies there won't be anybody to care—unless you do something to change that."

"Well, it's too bad about him, but in a way he had it coming."

"You're pretty bitter toward someone you don't even know."

"Oh, I know enough about him. Mama saw to that. You think *I'm* bitter? You should have known her. She'd been thrown out by her own father, had two rotten marriages, and then she got cancer. Mama was a very bitter, angry woman."

I didn't say anything, just looked out at the faint sheen of sunlight that had appeared on the gray water.

Steff seemed to be listening to what she'd just said. "I'm turning out exactly like my mother, aren't I?"

"It's a danger."

"I don't seem to be able to help it. I mean, it's all there in that song. It never *does* stop hurting."

"No, but some things can ease the pain."

"The store—it's in the Glen Park district, isn't it?"

"Yes. Why?"

"I get down to the city occasionally."

"How soon can you be packed?"

She looked over her shoulder at the house, where she had been secure in her loneliness. "I'm not ready for that yet."

"You'll never be ready. I'll drive you, go to the store with you. If it doesn't work out, I'll bring you right back here."

"Why are you doing this? I'm a total stranger. Why didn't you just turn my address over to my grandfather, let him take it from there?"

"Because you have a right to refuse comfort and happiness. We all have that."

Steff Rivers tried to glare at me but couldn't quite manage

it. Finally—as a patch of blue sky appeared offshore and the sea began to glimmer in the sun's rays—she unwrapped her arms from her knees and stood.

"I'll go get my stuff," she said.

Nancy Pickard is the creator of the popular Jenny Cain mystery series and a past president of the organization Sisters in Crime. For her novels, Generous Death, Say No to Murder, No Body, Marriage Is Murder, and Dead Crazy, she has been a four-time nominee and once a winner of the Anthony award, winner of a Macavity, and nominee for an Agatha. Her latest novel, Bum Steer, is set mainly in her native Kansas.

In "Storm Warnings," a whirlwind of deception rips through the lives of some Midwesterners, leaving devastation in its path.

STORM WARNINGS

by Nancy Pickard

WHEN A BAD storm approached on the prairie, it came roiling in from the west like a furious posse on huge black horses. All her life, Elizabeth Randolph had loved those storms. They made her heart pound and her stomach clench and her skin prickle. In the electric moments before it arrived, a storm made her feel like her lover was coming and she hardly had time to wash up. It made her feel like she was twenty instead of fifty and that there was plenty of time for her time to come. At the first lick of wind, Elizabeth would run to the porch to stare toward the west, imagining those towering black clouds were coming to carry her away from the farm, like Dorothy in *The Wizard of Oz*. When the storm passed, she always felt limp, sad, and a little privately disappointed that it hadn't swept her off her feet and slammed her against the barn and damn near killed her.

In the days before she met Ed Cuddy face-to-face for the first time, Elizabeth felt as if just such a storm was blowing into her life. She hoped she wouldn't be disappointed. She hoped this quiet man would be the whirlwind that swept her out of Kansas forever.

"What do you look like, Elizabeth?" he said to her over the phone the day before they were going to meet for the first time.

"Like you think a tall woman looks."

He laughed. "Tall, you mean?"

"No, like the picture in your mind." She almost wished they never had to meet, that they could just carry on by phone forever. "Angular. Elbows. Neck. Wrists. You know."

He chuckled again, but she heard a pause that told her how he'd imagined her.

"Well, I guess I'll know you when I see you, Elizabeth," he said in a gently teasing tone. "I'll just look for the woman with the elbows and neck and wrists."

"You'll recognize me, Ed." And then she boldly added, "We'd know each other anywhere."

He had been a wrong number and they'd started talking.

"Oh, I'm afraid I've dialed wrong," he said apologetically. So many people aren't apologetic, Elizabeth knew from experience. When such people get a wrong number and you tell them so, they just hang up on you. Or they demand to know what *your* number is, as if it's any business of theirs. So she noticed when the unfamiliar male voice said, "I hope I haven't bothered you. I'm awfully sorry."

"What number do you want?"

"555-4575."

"This is 4577."

"Ah, well, I dialed a seven instead of a five."

"I've done that. It's an easy thing to do."

"I am sorry, though." He sounded quite nice and sincere. "I hope I didn't disturb your evening."

"Not at all, that's all right."

"Thanks very much. Good-bye."

Neither of them had seemed to want to hang up.

He called again the next night and then every night after that. She had a nice voice, he said. He also said right away that he was married and lived in town. He hoped he wasn't bothering her.

"I don't imagine it will do any harm," she said.

By the fifth call, she knew his name was Edwin P. Cuddy. Her name was Elizabeth Randolph and she lived alone on the farm now, she told him.

"Mother died three years ago," Elizabeth explained. "With her and Dad both gone, it's been hard."

"I *am* sorry," he said. She appreciated the respectful pause of a couple of seconds before he spoke again. "You run the place by yourself, do you, Elizabeth?"

"Well, I don't suppose you'd say I *run* this place," she told him in a rueful tone. "I keep a garden, of course, but the rest of it I lease out to a fellow for his cattle."

What she didn't say was that she had told the "fellow"— Richard Jackson—about her caller and that she and Jackson discussed him every evening when Jackson stopped by for coffee after hard days of selling his cattle to early spring buyers.

Jackson took to asking, "How's your gentleman caller?" It always made her smile. Jackson, who'd known Elizabeth's father, advised her strongly to consider what her father would have thought of the situation.

"This Cuddy sounds all right to me," Jackson finally observed one day, much to Elizabeth's pleasure. "If your dad were here, I think he'd approve."

"Mother wouldn't, though," she said.

"Well, no, of course not."

As the calls continued every night, Elizabeth began to eat her supper early, so she'd have the kitchen all cleaned up by the time Ed phoned from the store at six o'clock. She began to take her baths in the afternoons, instead of just before she went to bed at night. She'd pour in bubble bath and lie back, dreaming, until the bubbles disappeared and the water cooled. At about four forty-five, she'd climb out of the old porcelain claw-foot tub and towel herself dry. Then she'd pat on dusting powder, drawing the puff under her arms and beneath her breasts and between them, and then patting it between her legs and on the bottoms of her feet. When she was dressed again in a clean blouse and slacks, she'd sit at the vanity table in her bedroom and fool with her long black hair, even though it always ended up pulled into a chignon at the back of her head. She wondered if she should dye the gray out of it. In honor of spring and hope, Elizabeth took to poking sprigs of wildflowers into her hair.

Elizabeth even told the banty hens about Ed.

"His name is Ed," she informed them as she sprinkled feed on the ground for them. "He's sixty-three years old. And he doesn't have a happy marriage. And he works in a farm-implement store in Duncan." Once she said to the hens, "I don't know if he can take a joke." She pronounced it *yoke*. "I'll have to ask him!" That amused her so much that she had to sit down on a rock wall and laugh while the chickens scrabbled around her feet and gabbled as if they enjoyed the pun.

On a Thursday, after two weeks of "wrong numbers," there were tornado warnings for both of their counties. Edwin called early that evening, just to be sure she knew. He called again after the storm, when the air seemed to her to be as clear and clean as freshly washed glass. It was then that he suggested they meet.

"I only have a half hour for lunch most days," he said. She smiled to herself at the gentlemanly tone of apology with which he expressed regret that it was she who would have to drive in to meet him. She didn't mind, she said truthfully, she was happy to do it.

On Friday, she walked nervously out of the sunshine and into the cool of the café where they'd agreed to meet. It was, she was relieved to see, clean, respectable, and out of the way, a place where a man who happened to be married could meet a friend who happened to be female without giving rise to gossip. Surely, no one would even remember having seen them there together. Anyway, none of the "help" or the customers would recognize her, since she neither lived nor shopped in Duncan. Elizabeth looked around for a man sitting alone. She located him in a green vinyl-covered booth against a wall.

"Edwin?" she nearly whispered it.

"Elizabeth?" He stood up so fast, he spilled a little of his coffee. She grabbed napkins to help him wipe it up, and soon they were laughing and settling back into opposite sides of the booth.

She tried not to stare at him.

"I guess you thought I'd look different," he said with a self-deprecating smile. It was true that his hair was thinner than she'd imagined, and not combed very neatly. But then the wind was blowing hard outside, as it always did in May in Kansas. He was wearing a yellow-and-blue-striped polyester short-sleeved shirt and a yellow tie; his blue trousers were the type that didn't require a belt but seemed to be held in place merely by the force of his paunch against his waistband.

His eyes, however, were blue and sincere.

After only a moment or so, Elizabeth relaxed, feeling sure that he was the man of character that she and Richard Jackson had agreed he must be. Just the sort of man of whom her father would have approved.

Over lunch—he ordered the roast beef special, after which she did, too—Ed told her he needed her advice.

"I feel I can trust your opinion," he said.

An investment opportunity had come his way, he said, involving natural-gas wells.

"Well," Elizabeth said, "my father always said a man had to be careful when he drilled for oil or gas, because he might only come up with hot air." She was glad to see him smile at that. "My father, I should tell you, was a fool about money."

"That's exactly what I don't want to be, Elizabeth."

And yet, he confided, it did seem such an attractive investment, with a really astonishing rate of return. He'd even heard that several of the wealthiest people in the county had put their money into it. But, he said, he didn't know how he could manage it, since a fellow needed to be able to put down $25,000 in cash right away.

"Oh, my," she breathed.

He admitted—and she saw that it pained him, for he was a proud man—that he did not have $25,000 to invest. "I might be able to scrape $15,000 together. I do have that much put away toward retirement."

"Ed," she said, feeling wonderful and light, "I have $10,000 my parents left me. I want you to take all of it and add it to your funds and make the investment for *us*."

"No," he protested, "I couldn't!"

"Yes, really, I insist."

"But, my dear—" He looked so startled at his own use of the intimate words that she smiled at him. "I mean, oh, my dear Elizabeth, I'm overwhelmed by your trust and by the generosity of your heart."

Ed called the farm-implement store where he worked to tell them he'd be late coming back from lunch. Then he let Elizabeth drive him to her bank in the town of Bennett and he waited in her car while she drew out the money. She made a charming little ceremony out of handing over to him the $10,000 in cash.

Ed sat for a moment with the money in his lap. When he looked up at Elizabeth, she could have sworn there were tears in his blue eyes. He lifted his brown vinyl briefcase from the floor and carefully tucked the money inside it.

"Elizabeth," he said in a husky voice. "Dear Elizabeth, my dear wrong number, would it be all right if I kissed you?"

At her shy nod, he kissed her on her left cheek.

"Good-bye, dear Elizabeth," he said when he got out of her car back at the café. His eyes were so bright, she had to look away from him. "I'll call you right after I meet with the gas man to give him the money." He got out of her car, the briefcase clasped firmly in his right hand.

That afternoon there were tornado warnings again. The electric excitement of the impending storm sparked Elizabeth's own inner eagerness until she could barely stand to wait for Ed's call. She didn't even try to enjoy a bath, but took a quick shower instead. The time for dreaming was done; now was the time for her dreams to come true. When the phone finally rang at six-thirty P.M., she nearly dropped it in her rush to answer.

"Elizabeth?"

He didn't begin by saying playfully, as he had every other evening, "Do I have the wrong number?" His voice sounded heavy and strange.

"Ed? What's wrong?"

"Oh, my God, Elizabeth." She had never before heard him swear. Then suddenly, horribly, he was weeping. She imagined his face all screwed up, his shoulders sagging, his free hand flung to his forehead in a melodramatic gesture of despair.

"I don't know how to tell you," he said.

But he found a way, through his tears. He hated to tell her, he hated himself. It was all his fault, he'd never forgive himself. They had lost all their money, all $15,000 of his retirement savings and all of the $10,000 her parents had left her. Yes, he'd met with the gas man, and yes, they'd exchanged cash for papers. But the papers were worthless! There wasn't any gas well! The scoundrel had lied, had suckered him and skipped town with their money.

"How do you know?"

"Because he's gone, Elizabeth. Oh, my God in heaven. I tried to call him at his motel to ask him a question and they had never heard of him. Whoever he was, he's gone now. I don't know how to find him again, Elizabeth. I'd better go to the sheriff."

"Sure." Her voice sounded as bright and hard as the real world is after a sweet dream. "And you tell him how you called me up every night for weeks and how you got to know all about me. And how you got me to trust you and give you my money. And you tell him about this famous gas man that nobody but you has ever seen on the face of this gas earth. And how this fellow just disappears into thin air. You just go ahead and tell him that, Ed, or whatever your name is!"

"Elizabeth!"

"Don't you bother about the sheriff." She began to weep

along with him, in sobs so loud and harsh, they hardly sounded human or even real. "*I'll* see the sheriff. You'd better believe I'll see the sheriff!"

"No!" Now he sounded frightened. He had no proof of his innocent intent, he said. He begged her to believe he never meant to hurt her. He begged her not to drag his family into scandal.

And in the end, in a dead and defeated-sounding voice, Elizabeth told him she would not go to the police—that she knew she had no proof of his guilt—but that he must never tell a living soul what a fool she'd been. He must never call her or speak of her again. After having practically seduced her and taken every cent she had in the world, she said, that was surely the least she could ask of him. She loathed him when he continued to weep and to call out her name until she hung up on him.

When she turned from the phone, she heard the radio announcer warning all residents of the county to take cover immediately.

Elizabeth ran to the window to look out, and then she ran out of the house, onto the side porch, and stared up at the oily, greenish-black fist of a sky, from which a single thick finger dipped low in the distance. She watched the fat black finger curl and straighten, curl and straighten, seeming to beckon to her.

"*Come on and get me!*"

The wind slapped the porch swing back and forth wildly against the house. Elizabeth ran down the porch steps. The wind flipped her skirts about her and whipped the flowers out of her hair and flung them in her face. She ran toward the weaning pasture behind the cattle pens. The rain began to pour. Breathless, soaked, she raced for the cabin in the pasture.

"*Richard!*"

The tornado was coming, roaring like a locomotive now, and her scream seemed to disappear under the tracks.

She barged into the one-room shack and stood dripping on the threshold. Here was where Jackson lived during the months he worked the cattle on the land he had leased from her father and then from her.

"Jackson?"

His clothes and shaving kit were gone from the pine shelves in the corner. The potbellied stove was there, and the cot. But it was stripped bare. His clothes were gone.

In the face of the stripped and abandoned cabin, Elizabeth got the picture. If there was a sucker born every minute, she was this minute's fool.

Jackson was gone.

Jackson, who'd been selling off his cattle earlier than usual, was gone. With his big promises and plans. With Ed Cuddy's money and with her money, which was only supposed to have been used as bait. With his talk of how even her father would have approved of the scam.

Now Jackson's words reverberated in her head: "Your dad always said to find somebody who's old and lonely. Make him trust you and want you, then take the sucker for all he's worth."

How many nights had she lain awake fantasizing of them, of Richard Jackson and her, running away together with the money, running somewhere, away from all these miles of nothing, nothing . . .

Elizabeth stumbled out of the barren cabin into a suddenly dead, still world. In the eerie, malevolent moment before the twister struck, Elizabeth's wild and triumphant glee shattered into panic.

"Jackson!" she screamed. "You bastard!"

She started running again, with the twister roaring behind her, both of them aiming for the dead cottonwood tree that stood on the highest point of the pasture.

Elizabeth reached it first and turned around, pinning her back against the dead tree to watch the tornado come and get her. As it roared closer, she began to laugh. Weakly at first, then wildly, hysterically. *Jackson found himself somebody who was feeling old and lonely, Dad, just like you said, and he got her to trust him and want him, and then he took the sucker for all she was worth.* The world was flying into a million pieces and soon she would be one of them. . . .

But the tornado, like Jackson, failed her.

It passed behind the cabin, sucked an abandoned outhouse into its obscene, churning bowels, and veered off away from the cottonwood tree on a crazy skitter to the northeast. Elizabeth stood with her back to the tree for a long time, until the rain stopped and the storm disappeared behind her.

Julie Smith has a knack for investing deadly situations with comic possibilities and conveying it all in her unique tone of ironic understatement. Julie, a former reporter for the San Francisco Chronicle, *has added three intriguing sleuths to the annals of mystery fiction: lawyer Rebecca Schwartz, featured in* Death Turns a Trick, The Sourdough Wars, *and* Tourist Trap; *mystery writer Paul McDonald, of* True-Life Adventure *and* Huckleberry Fiend; *and Officer Skip Langdon of the New Orleans Police Department, introduced in her latest novel,* New Orleans Mourning.

In "Cul-de-Sac," Rebecca helps an acquaintance understand that some of life's journeys may lead to a dead end.

CUL-DE-SAC

by Julie Smith

"I DON'T BELIEVE it. Listen to this one." Belief had no effect on Coralie's enthusiasm. She circled the ad, starred it three times, and read it aloud. " 'Reduced rent for the right person. Beautiful old Victorian in quiet cul-de-sac. Four bedrooms, three baths, all the charm of yesteryear. Mature gentleman will share and reduce rent for caring prof. lady, can be household manager. View of vineyards, landscaped beyond belief. Cost negot.' "

"You've got to watch that word *charm*," I said, "especially in the same phrase with *yesteryear*."

"It sounds too good to be true, huh?"

"When he says 'right person,' he probably means strapping female carpenter. Suitable for renovating old homes by day, rejuvenating 'mature' bones by night."

"Well, it can't hurt to call."

I handed her the phone, trying not to be too cross about it. My cherished next-door neighbor, Tony the Bartender, had left six months before to try his luck in Alaska, and Coralie McKinnon had moved in.

Coralie had straight black hair that blew in the wind most of the time. She wore purple and black, with deep red lipstick and she must have weighed something in the neighborhood of a hundred and sixty but she was five-eight and she could almost carry it. She was pushing fifty, I guess, because she'd moved to the city for purposes of dumping her husband of twenty-five years.

The quarter century of domesticity had taken its toll. She always had something bubbling on the stove—chili or gumbo or goulash or split-pea soup or cassoulet. She was made for North Beach—and she was a next-door neighbor from heaven.

Quite possibly she was the only human in the world who could get away with calling me "matzo ball." This was meant neither as a slur on my ethnicity nor as an insult to my slightly rounded person. Coralie felt I was a little on the unleavened side. Though *I* feel I'm the most casual of lawyers, Coralie thought I got too involved in my cases and too bent out of shape when my so called beau, Rob Burns, got too involved in *his* work.

So Coralie had decided to lighten me up. She recruited me for fabulous nature walks, and she took me to every comedy club and every half-baked neighborhood theater in the city and she introduced me to all her kooky actor friends. In a word, Coralie was a kick.

Some city people would give anything to live in the wine country, but Coralie had brought up two kids there (a third had died of bone cancer), all the while longing for the Bohemian life of North Beach. I guess nobody'd told her the rents had gone up and the beatniks had moved on shortly before she got married (except for the random washed-up poet still popping into Specs now and then for a picon punch).

The latter fact disappointed her not at all—North Beach is still a neighborhood with enough zip and dash for just about anybody—but the former was a problem, and so was the commute. Coralie taught drama part-time at Sonoma State, and try as she might, she couldn't make city life work out for her.

She'd gotten a lump sum from her ex and her funds were dwindling. So she was moving back to Sonoma. She'd told me about it with Piaf on the stereo, belting out *"Je ne regrette rien . . ."* (A flair for drama went with the territory.)

"It's been the best six months of my life," she'd said, "but I want to travel sometime. I have to think about investing. . . ."

I felt awful. I wished I'd been her divorce lawyer and knew if I had been, she'd have done a lot better in court. I felt awful for myself too. By now she wasn't just a neighbor, she was a good friend.

Coralie handed back the phone and I hung it on the wall. "Call me Ms. Right," she said. "He lost his mom a while ago. I think he's looking for another, and I'm auditioning tomorrow. What do you think? Am I the mom from Central Casting?"

"How old is he—ten?"

"In his fifties, I'd say."

"Sounds harmless enough."

"Rebecca, you don't know the half of it. The guy's an interior designer."

I helped her move in two weeks later. I won't say I found Murray Dodds weird, exactly, but he was certainly on the taciturn side and a little gloomy as well. Stereotypes notwithstanding, I didn't get the impression he was gay. Though I'd never suggest you can tell sexual preference by appearance (except in cases of extreme and purposeful limp-wristedness), I maintain there are nonverbal clues. I refer to what I call ambient testosterone.

No doubt science would disagree with me, but no matter, the truth is this: All interested men exude testosterone clouds in which they envelop the women to whom they're attracted. This is true of married men, guys who come to fix the washing machine, and rival lawyers, as well as horny guys in bars, your own boyfriend, and teenagers (who spray the stuff willy-nilly all over everything). If a man is interested in several women in a room, each will receive her own discrete cloud. The clouds cannot be seen by anyone other than the women on whom they land, and cannot be missed by their targets. Their denseness depends on the man's degree of interest. If the guy's in love, these things can obscure the visibility of both parties like tule fog.

Murray's ambient testosterone didn't exactly amount to a pea-souper, but if he was gay, he was a closet straight. He was about six feet tall and slender, with hair more colorless than gray and shoulders beginning to stoop. There was something lackluster about his skin—and about his demeanor. He was a worrier, I thought, and I hoped he wasn't obsessive about the family homestead. However, if he'd been Count Dracula it still might have been worth it to take a chance on him. The Victorian in the cul-de-sac was smashing.

It was in the Valley of the Moon, just outside of Glen Ellen, and it was beautifully kept up and freshly painted. It was landscaped, as the ad had bragged, beyond belief, its roses and rhododendrons truly displaying all the charm of yesteryear. Plus it had a nice garage to park the Volvo in, with a freezer in it that looked as if it could hold enough provisions for a hard winter—if ever Sonoma County had one, which was about as likely as palm trees in Moscow.

For the special, negotiated reduced rent on which these star-crossed housemates had agreed, Coralie was to share the kitchen, living room, dining room, TV room, garage, and basement storage space —all the rooms except Murray's bedroom and guest bedroom, and she was to have two bedrooms for herself, one of which she was also free to use as a guest room.

In return for the rent break, all she had to do was shop for groceries, supervise a housecleaner, and keep what Murray called "the household books," which meant paying his bills and balancing his checkbook. It wasn't part of the agreement, but I knew—and I was sure Murray knew—that she was going to cook for him as well. Cooking was part of her software.

Murray'd made a shrewd deal, but unless he turned out to be some kind of mild-mannered Norman Bates, it looked as if none of my dire (and probably self-serving) predictions had come true.

I picked up a box of books—probably cookbooks—decided I could handle another, piled it on, and headed up the stairs. "Second door on your left," Coralie called.

The boxes were heavier than I'd anticipated and my attention was on holding on to them; I paid her directions little heed. Then, too, puffing under the weight of my load, I simply *wanted* Coralie's room to be the first doorway, so that was the one through which I staggered, eyes on my precarious load, which I promptly dropped, scattering dust.

The impact of the fall knocked over a picture on the dresser, which, it was now clear, wasn't Coralie's. I'd wandered into Murray's room. Glancing quickly around, I assured myself he wasn't lurking half dressed and thoroughly embarrassed in the shadows, and then had a closer look. It was a nice room, especially for that of a single man—one into which someone had put a lot of thought. The walls were a kind of Wedgwood blue—a flat color with a lot of gray in it, very masculine and a little melancholy. The bed was an old mahogany four-poster, covered with a quilt in bright colors, a still-new quilt that hadn't been washed much, also very masculine. At the foot of the bed was an antique wooden trunk painted a slightly darker blue than the walls and draped with a soft dark-blue blanket.

I picked up the picture and straightened it. It was a photo of a woman about Coralie's age, with dark hair and the same joie de vivre; you could see it in her smile. There was something about the lift of her eyebrows . . . did she look like Coralie?

"My mother," said Murray, from behind me. "She died last year."

I whirled. "Murray, I'm so sorry—I wandered in by mistake."

He gave me a benign look that was almost a smile, but not quite. "It's okay. I like to have pretty ladies in my bedroom."

"It's a beautiful room. A lot of work obviously went into it. Did your mother make the quilt?"

He nodded briefly, as if his friendly mood had come suddenly to an end. I wasn't done, though. I wanted to know who this odd man was that Coralie intended to live with. "Did your mother live with you?"

Again the little nod. Nothing else.

"I guess it's painful to talk about it."

He shifted his eyes, avoiding mine, and I was sorry I'd upset him. But there was no denying the fact I was also sorry I couldn't civilly ask him any more questions. Like whether he'd ever been married or had any children.

Luckily for me, he and his housemate had already told each other all. Coralie filled me in while I helped her unpack and arrange her room.

Murray had never married and he had no children, though he seemed to regret it.

"Ah," I interjected. "Never too late."

She thought that one over. "Nah. Too wimpy for me. Though maybe you—"

"Forget it. Maybe one of us has a nice domineering friend who'd love a sweet guy to boss."

"I'll give it some thought."

"So back to his story."

"There isn't that much more." She shrugged. "I know he likes kids—he nearly cried when I told him about Mikey dying. But anyway, he didn't have them—he got caught up in the family business. By the way, he's not really an interior designer. His mother was one. His father, who was much older, ran Dodds Designs, an upholstery business here in town, and his mother worked there. She married her boss, who died while Murray was in his teens, and young Murray started helping her run the business. He stayed on and I guess he stayed on in the family home as well."

"No wonder he needs a mother."

Murray spoke behind us, as he had before in his own room: "Mother?"

"Murray, you're so quiet in those tennies," said Coralie. "We didn't hear you come in."

"Oh, Coralie. Sorry." And he walked out, looking baffled.

Coralie stared after him. "Bet *she* was a piece of work."

"Who?"

"Mom."

"You're not kidding. Lived with her all his life—never married. Ow."

She shrugged. "He's making a recovery, though. He threw out everything in the house and got the new decorator at Dodds to do the place over for him. That's saying good-bye, wouldn't you say?"

"Either that or he was trying to make it nice for a room-mate. I'd also say she did a terrific job. I'll bet she designed his room around that great quilt his mother made."

Coralie stared at me, bewildered. "His mother didn't make that quilt. My friend Maggie Ruth did—she has the quilt store in Sonoma. Murray came in with the decorator and picked it out—after I recognized it, I went over and asked Maggie Ruth all about him."

"What'd she say?"

Coralie looked at her lap, which was full of small things she was dusting. "Well, she did say the decorator thought he was a little weird."

"So did you go ask the decorator?"

"I tried, but she quit a month ago and left town."

Three days later I gave Coralie a call to see how things were going. Things were going fine, she said, except for that one time Murray walked in on her while she was taking a shower. But no problem, she assured me, she'd gotten locks on her bathroom door and her bedroom door as well. She'd call back in a couple of days.

But she didn't. I phoned a week later, left a message with Murray, and didn't hear from her. I left more messages. Murray always told me he'd given her all the previous ones. Still she didn't call.

Then one day, before I got home from work, she left this on my machine: "Things are getting weird here. But don't bother to call—I have to wait for a good time to talk. I'll call back, okay?"

Uh-uh. Not okay. Not even a little bit okay. I canceled my

appointments—fortunately I didn't have to be in court—and drove up the next day.

Coralie's car was nowhere in sight and Murray was in the front yard, digging. He was digging a hole about six feet long and he was digging it too deep for roses.

"Hi, Murray. New flower bed?"

He stared as if he'd never seen me before in his life.

"Don't you know me? From moving day? I'm Coralie's friend, Rebecca Schwartz."

He smiled as if I'd made his day, and clasped my outstretched hand with both of his. "Rebecca. How nice to see you."

"Nice to see you too." (Except for the goose bumps.) "Is Coralie here?"

He removed the baseball cap he was wearing and scratched his temple. "I don't think so. Hasn't been around much lately." He looked sad.

"You don't know where she is, do you?"

He put his cap back on and stared determinedly at the horizon. "Yeah." He paused. "Yeah. I'm pretty sure she went to the store."

"The grocery store?"

"Uh-huh."

"Do you know where she shops?

"No. That's *her* job."

"You never went with her?"

"No. Guess I never will now."

"What?" (Had I heard right?)

Murray didn't answer, just went back to digging. Palms sweaty, I maneuvered my car back down the lane to the main road, where I stopped and sat for a while, wishing so many unfamiliar muscle groups would stop shaking. What was I supposed to think? What was there to think? I looked at my watch—I'd been here half an hour. Surely no one could take more than an hour to shop, and I wasn't sure I could drive yet. I waited another thirty minutes, my fantasies getting more and more out of hand. Coralie didn't return.

Should I call the police? I didn't think my not being able to find her in an hour's time would make her a missing person in their eyes, but maybe it would. It might if other women had moved into Murray's house and disappeared. Or even if he had a reputation for being eccentric and scary. Or maybe a criminal record.

My scalp prickled as I tried to fight off the most provocative "if" of all: If his mother had died in suspicious circumstances.

I didn't succeed, or come close to succeeding. I was reminded of that stock admonition of gurus to their pupils, "Don't think of an elephant." How, once the idea was planted, could I think of anything else?

I headed for the local library and looked at obituary columns in the neighborhood of a year ago. I started with February, since that was exactly a year ago, then moved on to March, April, and May; after that, back to January, December, and November; and finally, puzzled, all the way to September, since anything under a year and a half might be loosely considered a year. There was no record in any of the local papers of the death of a Mrs. Dodds. I wondered if she'd married again.

The librarian looked friendly and, better still, old enough to know and care about the local lore. "Do you know the Dodds family?" I asked. "Of Dodds Designs?"

She had aquamarine eyes magnified to quarter-size behind a pair of glasses that had been stylish when I was getting my first *C* in algebra. "Murray Dodds? Sure. Had him reupholster my sofa just last year, and two chairs done, oh, seven or eight years ago. They do a nice job there. He's selling the business, though."

"I didn't know that."

"Umm-hmm. Retiring, I hear. At the ripe old age of fifty-two." She shook her head. "Must be nice."

"You know him well?"

"Only that way now—in business. We used to visit a lot more whenever he'd come in. Used to be more of a reader than he is now." She sighed. "Guess a lot of people did. These VCRs—"

I cut her off. "I met him a few weeks ago. Seemed like a nice man."

She beamed. "Oh, he is! A lovely man. I remember how it tore him up when his mother died. He kept her at home, you know—up till she finally had to go into a home. There's not many would do that."

"A nursing home? Did she die there?"

The friendly eyes went blank, but I wasn't sure why. Had it been an odd question? "I don't know. I guess so."

"Can you remember when she died?"

She stared to raise her shoulders in a mammoth shrug, but the phone interrupted the gesture. Relief flooded her face as she answered the call. I waited a few minutes, hoping to get her attention again, but she was engrossed in a matter involving the late Jack London. I must have been too pushy.

Murray, still digging in the front yard, didn't seem unhappy to see me again, but he didn't seem thrilled about it either. Did I dare push my luck? Yes; it was what I'd come for.

"Coralie's not back yet?"

"Nope. Must have been held up."

"I should have let her know I was coming up. May I go in and leave a note for her?"

He nodded and kept on digging.

I moved fast, first to the kitchen to find myself a weapon, just in case. Coralie kept her cleaver sharp as a razor blade and hanging on a magnet on the wall. I slipped it into my purse, handle sticking out just enough to get a good grip.

Heart thumping, I opened the connecting door to the garage and saw a rolled-up rug. Thumping heart now in throat, I examined it and found no body. I threw open the freezer—empty, thank God. I cased the lower floor next—all was okay—and then the basement. The bulb was burned out. Heart-in-throat now on overload, soaking with sweat, I searched the crannies with my pocket flash. No Coralie, dead or held captive, and no mummified corpse of Murray's mom, but I was going to have to take a stress-management course if *I* lived.

Brushing off cobwebs, I shut the basement door noiselessly

and checked out the window for Murray. He was still digging. Okay, the upstairs. The door to the guest bathroom was closed, which seemed a little odd until I opened it. It was a wreck, as if someone was systematically taking it apart, sorting out Coralie's things, perhaps to throw them out.

Barely remembering to close the door, I rushed to Coralie's room. Another wreck—all the neatly unpacked stuff half packed again.

Panicky, I thought of Murray's antique trunk and headed for his room. Brushing aside the blue blanket, I raised the lid, nervous as Tom Sawyer in the haunted house. But my tense shoulders dropped as I felt the blood rush back to my face—no Coralie, no Mom Dodds. I started breathing normally again. There wasn't much in the trunk—just a couple of blankets and a plastic box full of old papers and letters and photos.

On the top of the pile was a clipping of a news story—the news story I'd just spend an hour searching for. Mrs. Dodd's obituary said she had died at a convalescent home after a long illness—in September of 1967. Nearly twenty-three years before.

I heard the front door click shut. Quickly, I closed the trunk, rearranged the blanket, and stepped into the hall. "Coralie?"

Murray trudged up the stairs. "Oh, is Coralie home?"

Why didn't he know she wasn't home? Had he gone somewhere? I didn't know. I just knew I was terrified to be alone in the house with him. "Uh-huh," I said casually. "She's in the bathroom."

"Oh. I was going to go myself."

He was blocking my way.

"Aren't there other bathrooms?"

"I need something in this one."

I had to get past him, but what to do? I gripped the handle of the cleaver, trying to plot strategy. He stared at the floor. "I'm really going to miss Coralie."

"Miss her?"

"I wanted to take her on a trip around the world." Impatient, he banged on the bathroom door. "Coralie, hurry, will you?"

I got hold of myself. Clearly, if he thought Coralie was in the bathroom, then Coralie was still alive. Testing, I stepped slowly past him; he made no move to stop me. "I guess I'd better be going."

"Bye."

When I'd reached the first landing and felt I had a good head start, I said, "By the way, Murray, what's that you're working on out in the yard?"

"My ass," he said mildly, and then I saw the corners of his mouth turn up. I realized I'd never seen him smile.

"Excuse me?"

Murray laughed long and hard and hysterically. "I don't know my ass from a hole in the ground."

I got out of there.

I still didn't see how I could go to the police, and yet I couldn't go home, haunted as I was by the memory of Murray digging a grave in the front yard. Not without making absolutely sure Coralie was safe. I drove into Sonoma to have coffee and think things over.

If Murray was in his early fifties, his mother had died young. And yet, apparently of natural causes.

Why had he said she died last year?

The librarian had said he hadn't been the same since her death.

He hadn't married.

And Coralie looked like the mother.

It really did sound like Norman Bates revisited, however you added it up. The hot coffee couldn't prevent a little frisson when I thought of the way he'd tried to isolate Coralie, conveniently forgetting to tell her I'd phoned.

The creepy memory of that hysterical laugh of his popped into my head: *I don't know my ass from a hole in the ground.* Truly the maundering of a crazy person. At some level, Murray knew he wasn't playing with a full deck. Had he had warnings? Did insanity run in the Dodds family?

His mother!

I got it. It had taken me nearly all day, but I finally got it.

I need something in this *bathroom.*
I hoped I wouldn't be too late.

Murray was lying in the grave he'd dug for himself, showered and nicely dressed, eyes closed, arms crossed over his chest. I shook him. Surely he couldn't be dead—I'd been gone less than an hour and he'd had to finish the grave and get dressed.

"Coralie?" he said, and opened his eyes. He moaned and closed them again when he saw it was only me. "She took care of her little boy," he said. "I thought she'd take care of me."

I shook him hard this time. "Murray. Murray, what did you take?"

"Pills. Handful of pills."

I went in to call an ambulance, came back out, and pulled him to a sitting position. "Murray, you're going to be okay. Just talk to me." I wanted to stimulate him, get him walking if I could.

"I'm sleepy." He closed his eyes.

I rubbed his hands. "I found out about your mother—that she died more than twenty years ago."

His eyes popped open. "You did?" I could have sworn he looked relieved.

"She had Alzheimer's, didn't she?"

"Nobody called it that until ten or fifteen years ago. In those days they called it 'premature senility.' She was only fifty-four when she died. I didn't want Coralie to know. I lied to her. She might think I . . . I mean, she'd know."

"I know. It runs in families. The chances of passing it on are about pretty good, aren't they?"

"I forget the percentage. Can't remember anything anymore."

Even Coralie's phone messages. And where his quilt came from (though he knew perfectly well his mother couldn't have made it—the short-term memory does go first). No wonder Coralie had said things were getting weird, had started packing to move out.

"Try to get up, okay? Maybe I can help you walk till the ambulance gets here."

He lay back down. "Don't want to walk. Want to die."

Leaving a note for Coralie, I rode to the hospital with him. She arrived shortly after we did, having been nowhere more sinister than a rehearsal of *Grease*.

She'd seen Murray's "grave," of course, and while the doctors pumped out the pills, I filled her in on the rest. I'd thought she'd go all soft and teary, but after murmuring "that poor man" in a soft, sad voice, she went straight from distress to analysis and planning, maternal instincts in high gear.

"He didn't really want to die, Rebecca. Staging a spectacle like that has to be what the shrinks call 'a cry for help.' He just didn't want me to move out, that's all. So I won't. But why didn't he tell me what was wrong? I thought I'd moved in with a crazy man. He kept changing his stories and getting mad when I told him that wasn't what he'd said before. How was I to know he couldn't remember?"

"He must have been incredibly frustrated—he wanted you to take care of him, but he didn't have the nerve to admit he really had Alzheimer's. Even though he couldn't run his business or even balance his own checkbook anymore."

"Did he really say he wanted to go around the world with me?"

"Uh-huh."

"I'm going to take him."

"I don't know—I think he's too far gone to travel."

But a few weeks later she dropped by my office after a visit to the passport office: "You wouldn't *believe* how much better he is. You know what? That suicide attempt was partly for real—at his stage of Alzheimer's, depression is really common. And it makes the dementia symptoms a lot worse. So when they control the depression, the patient not only cheers up, but gets better."

"That's great."

"He'll need a professional care-giver at some point, but

for right now all he needs is a pushy housemate. The doctors say he should be fine for a short trip.''

''You won't be able to make it around the world, I guess.''

''Murray says he can live with that. He said he heard Europe has all the charm of yesteryear. And he smiled when he said it.''

I admired his courage. I thought most people, in a similar cul-de-sac, wouldn't be nearly so cheerful.

Deborah Valentine's Unorthodox Methods *and* A Collector of Photographs *feature Kevin Bryce, a former Placer County, California, sheriff's detective who is drawn into unofficial investigations of art-world crime through his relationship with sculptor Katharine Craig. The novels emphasize ". . . motivations rather than detailing the mechanics of the crime or the investigation. Put the right people together and something is going to happen."*

In "Kindness," what happens may make the reader wonder whether the right people ever really do get together.

KINDNESS

by Deborah Valentine

THAT HE SHOULDN'T have died was the consensus of the doctor, the nurse, his favorite orderly. True, he was seventy-one—but in reasonably good health, still active. He should have gone home minus a piece or two, a little less gastric, in the long run more comfortable. Well, old people are unpredictable and county hospitals are not given to extensive introspection. It requires too much time, and theirs is spent, every minute, with the practical, the functional; rendered safe from psychology by a distance composed of clinical details.

Rodriguez, Gabriel. Cause of death: heart failure.

The family was unquestioning. They were hardworking people, one generation from migrant farm workers. They knew the soil, had the hands-on familiarity with the progression of animal from supple youth into infirmity; of vegetable from ripeness to decay. It was simply Gabriel's time to feed the land.

The funeral was held in an old chapel kept scrupulously

clean and whitewashed though a network of cracks spread over the walls like broken capillaries. A fly hopscotched from one black vein to another, using the same small nervous jumps Gabriel had often used in life. (This stay in the coffin was the first rest he had known in over fifty years. His widow had made sure of that.) Candles sputtered light. Mourners rocked in a slow jerky rhythm. Sweat threaded through the hair at their temples, mixed with the tears on their cheeks. October, held fast in the grip of Indian summer, was too warm to be dressed in black and grief-stricken. The pungent scent of the living rose to the ceiling while the priest droned on.

The widow, a thick stump on the front pew, did not sweat nor did she cry.

The four sons were inconsolable. Each would begin a simple eulogy only to choke; and the next would start, doomed to end the same way, picked off one by one like tin soldiers in a child's game. Their grandsons sat in the third row. Short brown legs in short black pants dangled toward the floor while beautiful brown eyes gazed at the adults around them, perhaps a little bored.

After the service the mourners met at the modest stucco house of the only daughter. Everyone brought their favorite casserole and the air was full of the fragrance of tamales, chicken, sweet bread, menudo. The children played soccer on the backyard grass. The adults mourned with a full stomach and were so much the better for it. They talked, they remembered, they gossiped.

The widow sat in one corner, immovable as Gibraltar, inclining her head only slightly to acknowledge the condolences of those who skittered past her. Once in a while someone would take her hand, kiss her hard cheek, but say nothing.

When the table held but a few remnants of the potluck, when all but two sons who stood in the kitchen talking low had left, the daughter stood by the window and tucked a stray coil of hair into a hairpin. She was far younger than her brothers, the accident of a middle-aged woman who felt secure that her life-giving years were over. The daughter was thirty, and her thin face, though showing the tiredness of a long day, was tranquil. Her husband—tall, athletic, blond—came behind her and gently ran his finger along her cheek. Circling her waist with a muscular arm, he kissed her as she relaxed against him.

The widow struggled to her feet. Taking some plates from the table, she went to the kitchen, the serving pieces clattering violently in her hands. It was almost night. She gathered her purse and made to leave.

"Mama, I'll take you home—"

But she drew herself up as straight as her bent back and enormous bosoms would allow. There was no further discussion.

She waddled slowly up the street. A black handbag nearly the size of a suitcase balanced her heavily to one side. Her shoes were stout, orthopedic, though they had not the power to heal her. The homes they carried her past were old, compact, solid, very much alike in design. Many were in good condition: stucco painted, yards planted and weeded. Others showed the strain of neglect: parched yards, plaster falling, boards in windows. She took no notice of the neighborhood. Took no notice of the ground she walked on either, for she caught one thick heel on the lip of the sidewalk and tripped forward. Grasping the top of a short block fence, she kept herself from falling, but in steadying herself she scraped her calf against the cement. A line of blood like small blisters raised through the rip in her heavy stocking and she stared because it hurt, and it made her remember.

Her blood had been redder fifty years before. Or could it be that her ability to appreciate color had been sharper then? Everything seemed to have dulled except her ability to hate, which was firm and strong from years of exercise, as tough as the calluses on her misused hands. Had she ever been pretty? Not exactly. But she had been straight-backed; her cheekbones high, her skin good. Her hair had been thick and black and long enough to sit on. And when she danced . . . ah, when she danced, everyone had looked and laughed and clapped their hands. There had been joy. And there had been the confidence, not only of youth, but of a woman who had a man in reserve. Gabriel, always Gabriel. Since she was five there had been Gabriel, worshipful as a puppy. In childhood games, if she should hit him he would accept the punch, happy as if she had kissed him. When they grew older she teased him cruelly and he was flattered. If he had been handsome she hadn't noticed. Just as his devotion provided her with an early confidence, this long unsolicited devotion also produced in her boredom. Gabriel had been too easy.

She'd met Louis her last year at school. He had been a big, blond boy; the son of immigrant parents, educated people. He was not Catholic. To her family he did not seem particularly hardworking. He spent his days at the marina—"pissing his time away," her father said. Louis laughed a lot, often at things she did not find funny. He was affectionate and helpful in a way that was nice but perhaps, as her brother had been quick to point out, not quite manly. He talked a lot about things that weren't true . . . yet. His high hopes had both excited and frightened her. He had a curiosity that was not practical—what good was his interest in boats? In books? He loved to watch her dance, loved to listen to her speak Spanish, soon surprised her by speaking it himself. He was more quick-witted than she and could be very sharp, and in a strange way, this made her afraid of him. Maybe their romance had been as much inspired by their differences as it had been motivated by love. These distinctions were no longer clear but were blurred by fifty years of daydreams, of uncertain futures turning into solid acts of history, of looking back through the distorted mirror of resentment.

They had made plans to run away together. In a fit of pique she hadn't met him as she promised she would. He'd been impatient with her their last meeting, accused her of not really wanting to go. She had decided she would teach him a lesson, wanted the security a little begging on his part would bring. She had unpacked her bag that night with a light heart, the unknown put off for another day. She thought he would not leave without her. She had been wrong.

Eventually she had married Gabriel, as her father wished. Dependable, sensible, providing an unchanging line of life like the blood on her leg, becoming dull and hard before her eyes.

The old woman straightened and walked on, turning the corner. A man closing his grocery store greeted her in Spanish, offering condolences. She responded without breaking stride just as the streetlights switched on.

Sometimes, in the early years of her marriage, when she was at the sink or diapering a baby, she would whisper Louis's name, just to hear it. His name sounded so good, felt nice on the tongue. She would go to the library to check out books or read the papers because somehow she thought it would be something that would please him, made her feel closer to the sense of challenge being with him had given her as a girl. She took her children faithfully every Wednesday to return books from the week before and get new ones. On one Wednesday afternoon—her youngest child's twelfth birthday—she saw Louis's picture in the newspaper. On her way home she bought her own copy, and when Gabriel and the children were in bed she stayed up to read the article carefully. Louis was doing well. A traveler. An important man. A man whose life was never the same.

She read it several times before she shredded the paper with the kitchen scissors.

She would still say Louis's name suddenly. Had repeated it so often over the years that it ceased to be his name and became simply her word for lost opportunity, for despair. Some days she would say it until she choked with tears.

Gabriel would make her choke too. The way he chewed, slow and deliberate, suspicious of all but the blandest food— plain meat and flan, tortillas with butter and sugar. The way his pants slipped halfway down his ass. The way he would laugh at shows on the television, reaching a falsetto. The dumb contentment on his face as he fell asleep in his chair, TV blaring. He possessed no fault, no crude gesture, engaged in no small negligence that was not cataloged to him by her with the precision of an ingredients label. As the years progressed, so did the pitch of her voice. It became as high and incisive as a pig's squeal.

She turned the last corner, now a half a block from home.

It was funny the way Gabriel himself had provided her with the one opportunity in life she would not miss. He had become ill and had gone to the hospital. Gallstones, the doctor said. The operation was not overly serious but would be difficult for a man of his advanced age. She had seen him, drained of color against the sheets, wet from fear of the knife and of pain, and felt suddenly that she would no longer punish him for his stupidity, for the cruel boredom of her life. She would forgive. They were both old and soon to be dead; perhaps it would be good to die at peace with each other. It would be her first step toward wisdom, the acceptance of fate.

She countered bitterness with enthusiasm. She made him soup, fresh chicken soup with a deep yellow broth and wide noodles and finely chopped meat. Cooking it carefully, spicing it just right, she fed it to him with a spoon. The hospital staff was impressed with such care, clucked sweet sentiments to each other when they observed this stout, elderly woman sitting next to the bed holding her husband's hand in the dark. One day she brought him a stuffed monkey and set it in the bedpan, arranging its arm so it appeared to wave gaily at him. It was the kind of vulgar joke she thought he might appreciate.

Gabriel lost weight, his skin became pasty. His eyes, now overly bright, would dart from one corner of the room to the other as if he expected something evil to emerge from out of the shadows. The more she tried to calm him, the more agitated he became. When touched, he would jerk like a horse twitching a fly away. Gabriel, usually so mild, became a grump, a sniper. She took on the countenance of a saint.

It was her daughter who finally approached her. She did so in her own home, inviting her mother for coffee. In the harsh morning sun they sat at the kitchen table. It was made of wood and modern in design, not expensive but very well made, and as the conversation progressed, the old woman kept running her hand over its satin finish.

"Mama," the daughter had said, using the same combination of directness and diplomacy that had been her technique as a child. "You have always pushed us to do better, to educate ourselves. Manners, books—these were things you constantly brought to our attention as children, and to Papa's attention at every opportunity. As I look back I cannot say I always agreed with the way you did it, but as an adult I recognize that my brothers and I are the only children out of the family to have finished school. Manuel and Javier even went to college, and for this I give you credit. You pushed hard. Perhaps you felt you had to. We all recognize that you wanted something better than a field for us. Perhaps no one more than Papa. If it hadn't been for your . . . guidance . . . he might never have gotten a job in a trade union, did as well as he did. He appreciated that about you. Perhaps you were not always pleasant but you were effective. It was your way and he was used to it.

"But now," she went on carefully, "you have changed. In some ways it is very nice—the favors, the sweet talk. But Papa always loved you the way you were—he understood that kind of rough affection. This, especially coming now"—the daughter groped uncomfortably for words—"makes him think he's dying."

Affection? *Rough* affection? The old woman sat quietly for some time; flushing red and white, hot and cold.

She couldn't help it. She redoubled her kindness. She tripled it. Gabriel's room filled with flowers and small silly presents. She even arranged for the priest to visit. To cheer him up, she told her children later. Gabriel had taken one look at him coming through the door and fainted.

The gate creaked as she opened it. She stopped to pluck a ripe tomato from her vegetable garden.

Her daughter, this time with her oldest son—himself a gray-haired man—tried again to talk to her. But she just patted them on the knee, telling them what silly children they were, that soon she would have to face God and she must do so knowing she had done all she could to Gabriel.

She was fluffing a pillow for him when he died.

She pulled herself up the steps and through the back door into her spotless kitchen. She deposited her hat and purse and tomato on the table. She put some milk on the stove for

Ibarra. In the living room she placed her broad rear in the old man's favorite chair, a brown vinyl Lay-Z-Boy. With difficulty she bent to remove the shoes from her swollen feet and contemplated the ankles that were no longer discernible from the rest of her leg. Heaving a sigh, she sat back in the chair and smiled.

Carolyn Wheat's Dead Man's Thoughts, *nominated for a 1983 Edgar, introduced Cass Jameson, a Brooklyn criminal lawyer who was also featured in* Where Nobody Dies. *Drawing on her own experiences as a lawyer for the New York Legal Aid Society and for the Legal Bureau of the NYPD, Carolyn paints richly colored and compelling portraits of New Yorkers enmeshed in that city's criminal-justice system.*

In "Cousin Cora," Carolyn journeys far from contemporary mean streets to a rural Ohio community in a story that chronicles the loss of innocence in an apparently simpler time.

COUSIN CORA

by Carolyn Wheat

"Now the left hand," I ordered in my official Scotland Yard voice. The most dangerous criminal in London (portrayed by my six-year-old brother Lionel) placed his pudgy little paw in mine. I rolled the fingers one by one onto the satisfying squish of ink pad, then pressed them onto a sheet of Mama's best cream notepaper. The result: a perfect fingerprint record, as guaranteed by the Hawkshaw Junior Detective Kit Company of Racine, Wisconsin.

I gave Lionel back his hand. "Mind you don't wipe them on your knickerbockers," I warned, "or we'll both catch Hail Columbia." Lionel nodded, his round blue eyes lending the scene all the solemnity any detective could have wished.

We were in the barn, temporarily renamed 221-B Baker Street. I was the great Sherlock; Lionel had taken the parts, as required, of Dr. Watson, Mycroft Holmes, several Baker Street irregulars, Mrs. Hudson, and Toby the hound. At the moment, he was basking in the notoriety of Professor Mor-

iarty, the effect only slightly spoiled by the smudge of fingerprinting ink on his button nose.

It was the summer the very trees seemed to sway to the
Merry Widow Waltz. It was the summer my feet (which were
growing at a rate that alarmed even me) began to leave the
barefoot path of boyhood. It was the summer I sucked dry
the bitter fruit of the knowledge of good and evil. It was the
summer of Cousin Cora.

"Sa-am," a voice called in the distance. Lionel and I
locked eyes, one thought in both our minds. What was the
most dangerous criminal in London compared to our big sister Lucy, the most dangerous tattletale in Springfield Town-
ship?

"Sa-am, where a-aare you?" her voice was getting closer.
She'd be in the barn any minute, and then she'd see Lionel's
inky fingers, and then she'd spy the Hawkshaw Junior Detective Kit, and then—

It was a well-known fact that women were incapable of
appreciating the Art and Science of Detection.

"Quick," I told Lionel, "scoot out the back and put your
hands under the pump." He scooted. Even at six, my brother
had a sound grasp of life's essentials.

I gathered up the fingerprint record of Professor Lionel
Moriarty, closed the ink-pad tin, and put both into the cardboard box containing the Detective Kit. Then I shoved the
whole shebang into the corncrib, making sure a layer of cobs
lay on top, so Lucy wouldn't see the scowling face of Hawkshaw the Detective on the cover.

I whipped my mouth organ out of my pocket and com-
menced to play—probably the Merry Widow, which I'd been
trying to learn all summer just to get Lucy's goat. It was her
favorite tune, but I didn't think she really cared for it on the
harmonica.

"Sam, what on earth are you doing in this musty old barn
on such a beautiful day?" My sister stood in the doorway in
the stance favored by women throughout history for criticiz-
ing men: feet planted solidly apart, hands on hips, arms
akimbo. Looking for all the world like an indignant milk jug.

I muttered something in which the term *beeswax* figured largely.

"What do you mean it's none of my— Why, Mama sent me to fetch you, so there."

"What for?"

"Mama's Cousin Coramae's come for a visit, and Mama wants you to wash up and wear your Sunday collar to supper."

"Cousin Coramae?" My detective instincts leapt to the fore. True, Mama was Southern and therefore considered persons of the remotest connection her cousins, but why had I never heard tell of a Coramae? "And why didn't Mama say anything at breakfast?"

It was scarcely my intention to ask the question aloud, particularly of Lucy. Ever since turning seventeen and putting her hair up, she'd been impossible to live with. Putting on airs and looking down her nose at a fellow just because he was three years younger and didn't pomade his hair like the boys who went to Webley's Corners High School.

"I suppose you think Mama ought to consult you before asking her own kin for a visit," Lucy said, with a superior toss of her head. For a moment I thought her honey-blond pompadour would shake loose from its moorings and tumble down her back, but no such luck. "And besides, how could she tell us when she didn't know herself? Cousin Coramae just turned up on the doorstep not twenty minutes ago. All alone." Lucy's eyes grew as round as Lionel's; her voice dropped into a conspiratorial tone. For a moment it was as if the bossy older sister had vanished, replaced by the pigtailed equal of former days.

"She didn't come in the hack." This momentous pronouncement was followed by another, equally startling. "And she brought no more luggage than a moth-eaten carpetbag and a hatbox."

This was news indeed. Mama's relations sent letters to announce their coming, telegrams to say they were en route, and invariably arrived in the depot hack with an army of bandboxes, steamer trunks, cowhide valises, and lesser impedimenta.

Cousin Coramae was a Mystery.

I hastened to the parlor, spitting into my hand and slicking down my hair as I raced past the kitchen garden toward the back door.

The house was dark and cool, sunlight kept at bay by heavy damask curtains pulled tight so the Turkey carpet wouldn't fade. I stood a moment outside the parlor door, conducting surveillance. Mama's voice was high and fluting, the way it sounded when she was making small talk with someone she didn't know well. The voice that answered was dryly precise, with a hard Yankee edge that surprised me. Mama's kin had Southern drawls, putting a lazy, questioning emphasis on the wrong words. Not like Papa's Midwestern yawp, which came down as hard on consonants as a Baptist preacher on sin. Cousin Coramae's accent was different, as though she was related to no one but herself.

I was on the verge of stepping into the parlor to pay my respects when my mother's words fixed me in place like a chloroformed moth.

". . . my husband. What shall I tell him?" Mama's voice sounded like the high end of the piano. "I'd rather die than have him learn the truth."

"Tell him nothing," the Yankee voice replied. "I have come for a brief visit. That is all anyone need know."

"Brief?" Mama seized upon the word as though it meant sure salvation. "How brief, Tommy?"

I no sooner had time to absorb the unexpected nickname than the visitor replied, "Until I get the money."

Silence followed, thick as barn dust. I crept forward, hidden by the half-closed door.

The mysterious cousin was a tiny woman. Frail, too, with bird bones and parchment skin stretched too tight over a pinched schoolmarm face. You'd have said she looked worn-out, though she was about my mother's age, but there was an inner something that told me she was tough as twine.

Her hair was mud-colored and looked in need of a wash. Her skirt was travel-stained, and her high-button shoes were worn at the heels. At her throat she wore a lace jabot that looked the way my school collars did on Saturday night. My

father would have said she'd been rode hard and put away
wet.

She sat in the second-best chair.

The first-best chair—the green velvet plush with mahogany
arms—was reserved for Grandfather Parsloe and other household gods. The third-best chairs (which had no arms) were
reserved for whichever children were privileged to enter the
parlor, and for Uncle Samuel, whose frequent indulgence in
strong spirits no longer entitled him to chairs with mahogany
arms. How did Cousin Coramae, with her pauper's luggage
and her bedraggled appearance, rate the second-best chair?

I leaned in closer. Mama perched on the edge of the rose-
colored chair as though afraid to lean back into its plush
depths. A stranger would have thought Cousin Coramae the
self-assured hostess and Mama the nervous guest.

"The money." My mother's tone was flat as an iron, hollow as an owl tree. "And just where do you think I can put
my hands on such a sum?"

"Come, Lia, you married women always have little stores
put by, amounts your husbands don't know about. Am I
right?"

Lia. A name I'd never heard in my life. Mama was Lillian,
Lily to her sisters, Lil to Papa in a joshing mood. Never Lia.

Mama's answering sigh was a surrender. "There's the
butter-and-egg money, I suppose. But I had hoped to buy
Lucy a dress for graduation."

"I *need* the money, Lia."

"You don't understand, Tommy. It *isn't* money, not really." Mama's words tumbled over one another like shelled
peas rollings into a bowl. "Mr. Benbow at the general store
keeps an account of what he owes me, and then gives me
credit when I need something special, like the silk for Lucy's
dress."

"Couldn't you ask him for cash instead?"

"He'd be mighty suspicious if I did—and he'd tell Harry
for sure. Men stick together."

"I see." Cousin Coramae sat still as a barn owl, her pred-
ator's eyes fixed on Mama. "Then we must concoct a story

your husband will accept. An unpaid debt? Or perhaps I stand in need of a life-saving operation."

I stood behind the door, knowing how wrong it was to eavesdrop but unable to move. If Cousin Coramae was an owl, it was I, not Mama, who was the mouse. Sweat poured down my back; I wiped my forehead with a hand still gray with fingerprinting ink. I had plenty of chores to do before supper, including scrubbing all evidence of ink off my fingers with Papa's lye soap. Yet nothing could have moved me from my vantage point.

"Why me, Tommy?" Mama asked. "Why not one of the others?"

The mysterious visitor shrugged. "You were the closest to the college. The train station was watched, I'm sure of it, so I didn't dare travel by rail."

This was better than the dime novel I had hidden under my mattress. A mysterious woman, arriving unexpectedly, unable to travel by train. The college, I was sure, meant Springfield State Teachers College, where Mama went before she married.

"Are you so certain they suspect—"

"They suspect a great deal more than they can prove. But the family is both influential and persistent, and I decided discretion was the better part of valor. Still, Lia, I am sorry it had to be you."

"I know, Tommy," Mama said, her voice like the soothing syrup she gave me when I was sick. "I know. And I'll get the money on Saturday, I promise. That's when Harry takes me to Mr. Benbow's store to shop for the week."

The parlor looked as it always did: Great-grandmother Hartley's silver tea service resting on the mahogany butler's table alongside the bone-china cups and saucers. I'd watched Mama pour tea into those cups countless times.

Today was different. Today blackmail hung in the air, heavy as honeysuckle.

There was plenty to occupy my mind as I sat on the back porch, shucking corn for supper. I pulled each ear free of husk with a tearing sound that satisfied my soul and watched mounds of corn silk billow to my feet. It looked as though every doll in the house had been scalped.

My first real case. No more playing Sherlock in the barn—I had a true-life female Professor Moriarty staying under my own roof. Deep secrets lay between these two strangers, one called Tommy and the other Lia. Secrets my father wasn't to know.

What could I do? Tell Papa? I stripped the last ear of corn, running my hand along the pearly golden kernels, then setting it on the pile with the others.

No—telling Papa was betraying Mama, and that I would not do under any circumstances.

Confront Cousin Coramae—If she was even Mama's cousin, which I doubted—and tell her I knew everything, like a hero in a melodrama? She had only to threaten to tell Papa the terrible secret, and I'd be back where I started.

As I carried my load of corn into the kitchen for Maisie the hired girl to put on the boil, I reflected that there was nothing in the Hawkshaw Junior Detective Kit to cover this situation. I was on my own.

It was one of Papa's town days. Although we lived on the farm his father and grandfather worked before him, Papa's real business was the Feed and Grain. He spent three or four days a week in Webley's Corners. Which meant that he was dressed for company when he walked through the front door.

We were all at the dining-room table, empty soup plates resting on two layers of china before each plate. My Sunday collar chafed my neck; Lionel squirmed like a tadpole. Lucy, in her new sprigged waist, sat next to me, still as a tree stump, showing how grown-up she was by her refusal to fidget.

Mama, at the foot of the table, seemed taut as a barbed-wire fence. Every time there was a noise at the door, she started. She lifted her glass of ice water to her lips every few minutes, but seemed not to drink it, for the level remained the same. Her slender fingers played with the heavy silverware.

She looked everywhere except at Cousin Coramae.

As soon as Papa's tread was heard on the porch, she jumped from her seat, jiggling the table and spilling some of her water. "Harry," she called in the high, fluting voice I associated with nerves, "you'll never guess who's come for a visit."

They talked in the vestibule, among the umbrellas and canes. I could only hear a few words: ". . . my second cousin twice-removed . . . I haven't seen her in so many years . . . it seems the letter she sent was lost in the mail, isn't that something?"

Papa's baritone was easier to hear, though he was trying his best to mute it. ". . . can't say I do remember, Lil, but then you have so many cousins. . . . Certainly she's welcome, letter or no letter. Now, let's have supper. I'm hungry as a bear."

Papa entered the room like a bear, his big masculine presence filling space out of proportion to the actual size of his body. He wasn't a tall man, but broad-shouldered, with thick brown hair and a mustache I envied with all my heart. Would I someday outgrow my weedy slenderness and thin, sandy hair, becoming a real man like my father?

"Harry, I'd like you to meet my cousin, Miss Coramae Jones." Jones was not a name I'd ever heard in my mother's family. And since Mama had said, "Miss," it wasn't her married name. Whoever our visitor was, I was willing to bet every marble I owned, plus my slingshot, that her last name wasn't Jones.

Supper began as soon as Papa took his place at the head of the table. Maisie brought out the soup, ladling it into the shallow bowls one by one. It was cherry soup, which I loved because it was cold and sweet and nobody else I knew had it for supper in their house.

"Cherry soup," Cousin Coramae said, her green-apple voice ripening just a bit. "This does take me back, Lillian."

Not Lia. Just as Mama said, "Remember, Coramae? We both learned to make it from that Scandinavian girl . . . what was her name?"

"Inga. Inga Gustavsen. A brain like a feather pillow, but cooked like an angel."

"I didn't know angels could cook," Lionel said. "What do they make, angel food cake?"

Papa's laugh boomed out. Mama and Lucy smiled. But Cousin Coramae exploded with laughter, as though something bottled up was being released. She pulled a dingy lace handkerchief from her sleeve and held it to pursed lips, but still the laughter came. Her eyes teared, as though the very act of laughing touched her in some deep way. Her laughter hurt, as though she'd all but forgotten there were things in the world to laugh about.

She dabbed at her eyes with her handkerchief, the tip of her nose red. She gave herself a good shake and said, "There, now. I shall subside. I must apologize . . . difficult railroad journey." All at the table nodded, the notorious strain of travel upon the female sex too obvious to warrant remark. Only I knew that however Cousin Coramae had reached our farm, it hadn't been by train.

The thing about cherry soup was: Maisie had never learned to pit the cherries first. Each spoonful was a potential social disaster. Mama and Lucy ate with delicacy, gently removing each pit into their spoons and sliding it discreetly under the bowl.

I tried to do the same. Honestly, I did. But one pit got past me and slid down my throat, causing a coughing fit that sprayed red juice over my portion of the damask tablecloth. Lucy shot me a withering glance and said, "Cousin Coramae, I must apologize for my brother. He isn't really housebroken."

My face burned as though stung with nettles. I wished Lucy at the bottom of Hale Pond, which everyone knew was bottomless.

Coramae Jones fixed Lucy with a stare only an owl could have duplicated. "In my day," she began, her tone as tart as a pippin, "it was considered the height of bad manners to call attention to someone else's faux pas."

Lucy hung her head. Now her face looked as though it had had the nettle treatment.

Another piece of the puzzle fell into place: This woman had been a Teacher.

* * *

Stars fat as bumblebees hung low in the summer sky. I was outside, walking with Cousin Coramae. I was both afraid and curious, walking in the dark with a suspected blackmailer. There was excitement, too, in knowing that I was conducting my very first interrogation as a detective.

"Will you look at that moon!" The visitor pointed at a low point of sky, her finger twig-thin. We had passed the hitching block and were well on our way toward the dirt road into town.

I looked; the moon was a crescent, but it lay on its side, points curving upward. "It looks like a boat," I said.

"Exactly," my companion agreed. "Like the gondolas I saw in Venice." In the pale moonlight, her weathered face took on a look of rapture.

"Have you really been to Italy?"

"Didn't your mother tell you?"

"My mother?"

"She was there too. We were a party of young ladies," she explained. "We toured Rome, Florence, and Venice. It was a very special trip for all of us."

Lia. An Italian pet name from an Italian trip. A trip no one in the family had ever heard about.

I tried to keep my voice casual. "Did you ever visit Mama at the Teachers College?"

"Why, yes, I suppose I must have. Once or twice." There was dismissal in the flat tone. We walked in silence for a minute or two, our shoes scuffling the summer dust. I could hear birds in the woods on the other side of the road; our side was rich-smelling alfalfa and a little spring wheat.

My companion broke the silence. "The Hunter stalks tonight," she said.

"What?" It was not a polite reply, but I was too startled to remember my manners.

"Up in the sky." The twig-finger pointed again. "There's Orion, the Hunter. See . . . the one that looks like an H with a crooked bar."

I found Orion without much difficulty. He was big, dominating his part of the sky the way my father dominated our dining room.

"Artemis, whom the Romans called Diana, killed him and placed him among the stars. She was a huntress, the Virgin Goddess."

"You sound like a teacher." It was part calculated, part blurted out, but I had to know.

"You are a very observant young man." She stated a fact, without judgment. "You notice things. You have eyes that catalogue, like an accountant. Or perhaps," she went on, the tart-apple taste coming back into her voice, "like a spy."

It was as though the fugitive could see right into the barn, through the corncrib, under the dry cobs, to where the Hawkshaw Junior Detective Kit lay.

We passed the hollow tree where I'd seen a hoot owl the week before. The crick I fished in burbled in the distance. Up ahead was the water tower, looming over the horizon the way the Methodist Church steeple overshadowed the town.

I had to smile as I looked at the tower. There were some initials at the top I had reason to be mighty proud of.

"It takes considerable nerve to climb a tower that high," my companion remarked.

"What—what makes you think I climbed it, Cousin Coramae?"

"Please, call me Cora. I have always loathed my full given name, a fact I have some difficulty impressing upon your mother."

"Well, then, Cousin Cora"—I had been brought up never to use an adult's name without some sort of title in front of it, so Cousin Cora she became—"the truth is that one night Red Beaudine, Spider Crowley, and I climbed clear to the top of that tower and painted our initials on the back. In red paint."

"Bully for you," Cousin Cora said. "That's one peck of wild oats sown."

Even Papa, who always wanted me to be manly, wouldn't have said that. My heart warmed toward the strange visitor, and I told her things that night I'd never told another soul.

How I hated farm life. How I wanted more than anything in the world to set off for the city, maybe even California.

I didn't say a word about Hawkshaw Junior Detective Kits or the conversation I'd overheard in the parlor. I kept a few secrets. But as to the rest, Cousin Cora made no criticism. Everything I said seemed reasonable to her. Every dream I expressed she agreed could be reality if I wanted it badly enough.

As we walked toward home, our way lit by a ghostly crescent moon, I decided I'd been reading too many dime novels. This skinny spinster lady who smelled of violet water was no blackmailer.

The next morning I was out with Papa, mending fences by the dirt road. We were stringing new barbed wire and pounding the fence posts in tighter, so they'd withstand the summer rains. It was hot, dry work and we'd been at it since sunup. My arms hurt and my shirt was soaked with sweat; Papa looked the worse for wear, but I knew he could go till sunset without a pause or a meal if he had to.

When he lifted the heavy hammer over his head, his huge arm muscles knotted and tensed as the hammer rose high into blue sky, then struck the fence post with a force that shook the very ground. Bit by bit, blow by blow, the wood drove deeper into the caked soil.

I held the fence posts, my hardest job being not to flinch as the hammer swung down, all of Papa's strength behind it. I wondered if the day would ever come when I could swing the hammer while Lionel held the post. Right now, it was all I could do to lift the hammer, let alone hoist it with Papa's ease.

Hoofbeats caught my attention. Sheriff Caleb Anson trotted by on Midnight, his black mare. "What say, Cal?" Papa called out. He put down the hammer and gave the sheriff a straight-armed wave.

Sheriff Cal pulled his horse up short. "Say, Harry," he said, "didn't your wife go to the Teachers College in Springfield?"

"You know she did, Cal."

"Well, I'd surely hate to upset Lillian, but there's been a little trouble up that way." Sheriff Cal gentled his mare, patting her coal-black neck. Still the animal fretted and stamped, eager to trot. "I'd appreciate your letting me have a word with Lillian. Seems the woman who's involved was one of her classmates. She stayed on to teach at the college after they graduated."

At the word *teach,* my ears pricked like a jackrabbit's. Hadn't I already deduced that Cousin Cora had taught school? I stood beside the fence, hoping to be taken for a fence post and ignored.

"Involved in what, Cal?" Papa asked. He pushed back his hat, wiping his forehead with his hand.

"Not before the boy," the sheriff said. Papa edged toward Midnight; the sheriff leaned down to speak as privately as possible.

I could only overhear snatches: ". . . family very upset . . . girl died of laudanum poisoning . . ."

Papa's voice was easier to hear. "Over a lover, I suppose. That's what all these young girls get up to." I was reminded how angry he got when Eddie Ruckleshaus came to take Lucy to the church social. You'd have thought Eddie was about to start my sister on the road to ruin instead of treating her to peach ice cream at Christian Endeavor.

". . . know how it is, Harry. All-female seminary . . . women cooped up together. These things happen."

"Disgusting!" Papa gave up any effort to keep his voice low. "If you dare bring filthy talk like that into my house, Caleb Anson, I'll—"

"Could be murder, Harry." Sheriff Anson's calm tone cut through Papa's anger like a wire cutter. "Leastwise, the Pargeters, the family of the dead girl, think so. And they've got a fair amount of influence in Springfield, so—"

"Springfield is Springfield," Papa interrupted, "and Webley's Corners is Webley's Corners."

I knew Papa in this mood; now the sheriff would be lucky to get directions to his own house from him. All I could think of were the words I'd overheard in the parlor yesterday, Cousin Cora talking about an influential family, and some reason she couldn't travel by train. Was it possible the woman I'd walked with under the stars the night before was a murderess? I should have felt excited. Instead, I felt sick.

"All the same, Harry, Lillian could—"

"Hellfire, Cal!" Papa shouted. He tore the hat from his head and slapped his thigh with it, raising a cloud of dust. The horse shied back; the sheriff pulled tight on her reins. "It's been nigh on to twenty years since Lil graduated that school. I won't have you upsetting her over something she can't possibly know anything about."

"Harry, I already told you." The sheriff's tone was patient but insistent. "This teacher, Miss Tomlin, was a student with Lillian twenty years ago. Your wife might just remember her, know where her family lives."

Miss Tomlin. Tommy. My ears buzzed, and for a moment I could say nothing. Then I cleared my throat and said, "I never heard Mama mention anyone by that name."

"There now," Papa said. "If Sam here never heard of the woman, then Lily doesn't know her and that's a fact. She's forever going on about that school. She'd have been bound to mention this Miss Tomlin if she'd known her. Right, Sam?"

"Right, Papa." I felt dizzy, as though the sun were frying my brain. Of course Mama knew Miss Tomlin. She called her Tommy and was being blackmailed into helping her escape.

"So there's nothing more to say, is there, Cal? You won't be coming around to bother Lily, and that's that."

The sheriff raised his palm and eased Midnight away from the fence. "Can't say as I blame you, Harry. I guess I'd do the same if it was my wife." He dug his knees into the mare's flanks and Midnight gratefully accepted the hint. Man and horse disappeared in a cloud of dust.

Papa and I finished the fence posts in silence. I wanted him to tell me what the sheriff had said, wanted him to trust me man-to-man, but all he did was swing his hammer and pound wood deeper into hard-packed ground.

As soon as Papa and I finished, I made my way to the sewing room. On the wall, proudly framed in gilt, was Mama's diploma from Springfield State Teachers College. In one corner, next to the workbasket, sat a two-shelf book stand. The top shelf contained what I wanted: the yearbook of Mama's graduating class. I opened it, starting where I always did, with Mama's photograph.

She was Lillian Wanderley then. The face that looked at me was at once familiar as my own hand and as remote as the moon. She was my mother, but she didn't know me. Didn't know I would ever exist. Didn't know she would marry Papa and live in Webley's Corners.

She was president of the Poetry Society. Under her name was the quote: "Shall I compare thee to a summer's day?" Every time I read those words I thought how true they were. It wasn't just my mother's sun-bright hair and sky-blue eyes that made her seem summery—it was her laughter and lightness.

I turned the pages backwards, stopping at a picture of a dark-haired girl with huge black eyes in a thin face. Under the photograph was the name Letitia Coramae Tomlin. Secretary of the Poetry Society.

Papa had told Sheriff Cal the truth. Mama did go on about Springfield College, telling Lucy and me all about her friends, her teachers, the fun she'd had. I'd heard stories of every picnic, every midnight revel after curfew, every funny incident in class.

Why had I never heard of Cora Tomlin—or the trip to Italy?

The next day, I rose at five, did my usual milking, and swept out the barn. As I worked, I thought about Cousin Cora, and what I ought to do. It was wrong to let Cousin Cora take my mama's money, wrong to let her go without telling the sheriff where she was, wrong to let her escape.

On the other hand, there was the terrible secret—whatever it was Mama was so desperate to hide. I remembered what Sheriff Anson and Papa had talked about. What if Cousin Cora really had killed the Pargeter girl? Could I let her go, knowing what I knew?

I needed more evidence. As I passed the corncrib, I took out the Hawkshaw Junior Detective Kit and hid it under the bib of my overalls.

It was just as well I did. On the way out of the barn, I met Lucy, dressed in a gingham skirt with a matching ribbon in her hair. "Going to town with us, Sam?" she asked, tossing her head. Practicing for the Webley's Corners beaux.

"Don't know," I replied. It was Saturday, the day Papa took Mama to Benbow's General Store. The day Cousin Cora would get her butter-and-egg money.

"Your sweetheart will be leaving today," she teased. "Mama says Cousin Coramae's taking the four-fifty to Chicago this afternoon. Don't you want to be there to say good-bye?"

"Not 'specially." I stuck my hands in my pockets and began to whistle, hoping to discourage conversation.

Nothing discouraged Lucy when she was bent on talking. "I don't know what you find so fascinating about Cousin Coramae," she said. "She's just a dried-up old stick, if you ask me." When my continued whistling convinced her she'd get nothing more out of me, Lucy flounced toward the kitchen door.

I thought Lucy wasn't wrong: Cousin Cora was like one of those stick-insects that looked like a twig and then scared the bejesus out of you when it started to move.

The guest room looked as though no one had slept there for years. The bed, with its rose satin coverlet, was neatly made, the bolsters propped against the cherry headboard. The dresser, with its hand-embroidered scarf, was empty of Cousin Cora's personal belongings. The only evidence that she had ever occupied the room was the hatbox and carpetbag sitting beside the door.

Mama's Singer whirred in the sewing room next door. I was glad; no one would hear me with that noise going on. I pulled the Hawkshaw Junior Detective Kit out from under my overalls and opened it. Inside I had fingerprint powder, an insufflator, and special tape to lift latent prints.

There were plenty of surfaces in the room that ought to have given me prints: the top of the dresser, the night table, the washstand. None did. Every time I puffed away the excess powder with my insufflator, there was nothing there. The room had been wiped clean. Either Maisie had suddenly become the perfect housemaid, or Cousin Cora had erased all traces of herself.

I was so busy working, I didn't notice at first that the sewing machine had stopped. I froze. Was Mama about to come into the guest room? What would I tell her if she did?

Then I heard the sobs.

I crept down the hallway toward the sewing room. The door was open, but I didn't go in. Mama sat in the rocking chair, her head in her hands, her shoulders heaving. On her lap was the yearbook.

"Mama?" My heart thudded inside me like Papa's hammer striking the fence posts. I could count on the fingers of one hand the number of times I'd seen my mother cry.

"Sam." Mama raised her tear-streaked face and gave me a watery smile. "I was just looking through my book, and so many memories came back. So many memories." She wiped her cheeks like a child, without benefit of handkerchief.

"Are—are you all right, Mama?"

"Yes, Sam. Please just let me be." She attempted a smile. "I was just reminiscing, that's all. You'll understand when you're older."

"Mama, I know the truth," I began.

"And what truth is that, Sam?"

I stepped over to where she sat and knelt beside the rocker. "I know about the dead girl at the college and about Cousin Cora's not being our cousin but being Miss Tomlin instead. And," I finished boldly, "I know you mean to give her money and let her get away."

Mama turned her gaze toward the window, where the last lilacs drooped on the bush. They were brown-edged now but still filled the sewing room with a fragrance that reminded me of Mama.

"If you know that much, then you know I have to, Sam. I have no choice."

"But, Mama, couldn't we—"

"*No*, Sam." Her voice sharp as sewing scissors, she cut

off my words. "Please, for my sake, don't ask any more questions. Just let it be."

I left her turning the pages of her yearbook. When she thought I was out of the room, she bent her head. A tear fell onto the page, and then another. I crept away quietly, as though from a sickroom.

What would Sherlock Holmes do? Find the truth at all costs. What would Papa do? Protect Mama at all costs. What was I to do?

I went back to the guest room. I didn't know what I wanted: the truth or comfortable lies, or if I wanted to turn back the clock so that Cousin Cora had never entered our lives. I only knew that whatever I wanted, the truth was what I had to have.

I opened the carpetbag. Inside, among the neatly folded clothes smelling faintly of violet, was a small packet of letters tied with a black-velvet ribbon. I drew them out and recognized my mother's elegant penmanship.

Love letters, to someone not my father. Some were four and five pages of thick vellum, others were just notes. On the back of one of Mama's engraved calling cards: "I so loved our picnic by the river, Dear One." On monogrammed pink notepaper: "How do I love thee? Let me count the ways." On a torn-out sheet of school tablet paper: "I dare not ask a kiss, I dare not beg a smile."

I felt like a fence post on the receiving end of Papa's hammer. I was face-to-face with the terrible secret, the hold Cousin Cora had over my mother. Mama had had a lover when she was at the Teachers College, a lover who received letters with poetry in them. Letters signed "Lia."

Someone besides Cora Tomlin had known my mother by that name. Someone she had met in Italy? And how had Cousin Cora come to have the letters?

The last note said only: "Since there's no help, come let us kiss and part."

It was when I put the letters back that I found the vial of laudanum.

I drew it out, turning it in my fingers. Cousin Cora, black-mailer, using Mama's letters to her lost lover as a weapon to extort money. Cousin Cora, murderess, using laudanum to poison a girl at the college. Had Cousin Cora blackmailed the dead girl, too, then killed her to prevent her telling anyone?

There was only one thing I could do. It felt like betrayal, and yet with murder at stake I had no other choice. Besides, Papa would understand. He often joked with Mama about the beaux she could have had back in her Virginia hometown. I took the letters out of the bag and put them in the pocket of my overalls.

Papa was in the bedroom, standing before his shaving glass, straight razor in his hand. His face was lathered, except for the precious mustache. Ordinarily, I loved watching Papa shave, taking mental notes so that I could handle the razor with ease when I had enough whiskers to worry about.

I came straight to the point. "Papa, there's something I have to tell you."

It was as though an anarchist's bomb went off in our little farmhouse. Papa exploded out of the room, lather still on his face. He made straight for the guest room, picked up Cousin Cora's bags, and tossed them out the front door. He ordered Maisie to tell Cousin Cora, who was out strolling in the woods, to hightail it off his property at once.

Then he marched to the sewing room. I hid behind the stairwell, feeling as though I was weathering a tornado. Papa's angry shouts filled the air, followed by Mama's tearful replies.

". . . phony cousin. Wanted by the police, of all things."

". . . don't understand, Harry . . . not murder. The poor child took her own . . . wasn't Tommy's fault."

"Tommy! Is that what you call the creature?"

Lucy came down from upstairs, her face anxious. When she saw me behind the stairwell, she whispered, "What's wrong?"

"Not sure," I lied. But I couldn't look at her. Whatever was happening behind that closed door was my doing.

I felt even worse when Lionel came out of the kitchen, one

half of a gingerbread boy still in his hand. He looked as scared as he had the day he nearly fell into the well.

"How could you, Lily?" Papa asked. It was a plea, a prayer.

"I was so lonely," Mama answered. "Away from home for the first time . . . Tommy was good to me. I didn't understand at first, and then—I was in love."

"Love! You call that love?" Papa's voice sounded wrenched from him. "It's a sin, Lily, a sin against nature." His words ended with a sob.

The air felt heavy, the way it had when the baby died. Mama had been betrayed, but not by Cousin Cora. I'd wanted to protect her, but it was me she'd needed protection from.

The last I saw of Cousin Cora, she was walking up the dirt road, back straight, carrying her carpetbag and hatbox in either hand.

Nothing was ever the same again. We never had cherry soup. Mama's sunshine nature faded like the lilacs. Papa worked later and later in town, sometimes staying over at Mrs. Hepwhite's boardinghouse. He never again called Mama Lil.

As for me, my detecting days were done. I swapped my magnifying glass to Red Beaudine for a peashooter and three immies I didn't really want. The rest of Hawkshaw Junior Detective Kit I burned behind the woodshed. As the flames curled around the scowling face of Hawkshaw the Detective on the cardboard cover of the box, I decided hell was the right place for anyone who caused that much pain.